OUTSTANDING PRAISE FOR
LINDA BARNES AND HER MYSTERIES

HEART OF THE WORLD

"The breakout book of the series . . . that will shock and surprise the reader. Essential reading."   —*Library Journal*

"With every novel, Linda Barnes reminds us of two key facts—she was one of the first and she remains one of the best. *Heart of the World* has everything that Carlotta Carlyle fans have come to expect from this seminal series. Barnes has never been better, and that's saying a lot."

—Laura Lippman, author of *To the Power of Three*

"Linda Barnes has long been one of the most skilled and artful writers of the crime novel. With *Heart of the World* she proves it and takes it up to a new level. This is her best."

—Michael Connelly, author of *The Lincoln Lawyer*

"*Heart of the World* illuminates the power of our deepest regrets and the fleeting chances we sometimes get to fill the emptiness in our souls. Writing with sensitivity and grace, Linda Barnes once more demonstrates why ex-cop Carlotta Carlyle has become a treasured mainstay in the field of crime fiction."

—Robert Crais, author of *The Forgotten Man*

DEEP POCKETS

"[There's] plenty to keep a reader chasing after the delightful Carlyle while she chases after the bad guys."   —*Entertainment Weekly*

"Barnes weaves an intricate web with a pleasingly poisonous spider at its center . . . Barnes makes superb use of the town-grown tensions . . . the twists and turns in this nail-biter are at once startling without ever becoming absurd."   —*Publishers Weekly*

MORE . . .

"With *Deep Pockets*, Barnes locks in her position as one of the foremost practitioners of middle-of-the-road, character-based mystery . . . I suppose I could have put it down. But I didn't want to."

—Orson Scott Card

THE BIG DIG

"Pure pleasure."   —*Kirkus Reviews*

"A true page-turner . . . nobody knows Boston like Linda Barnes's red-haired private investigator Carlotta Carlyle . . . Barnes's knack for crisp, snappy dialogue, and devising a mystery that has both timeless and contemporary appeal is a winner."   —*Boston Herald*

"Barnes grabs the detective genre by the throat but rarely lets style overtake substance. The plot is thick and original and sure to surprise."

—*Washington Times*

"Carlotta Carlyle combines the sensitivity of Robert Parker's Spenser with the stubbornness of Paretsky's V.I. Warshawski, and she's rapidly carving out a place of her own."   —*Chicago Tribune*

"A shrewd piece of writing, well researched and smartly told."

—Marilyn Stasio, *The New York Times Book Review*

"Carlotta is an engaging narrator with a brisk, easygoing style . . . a worthy competitor in the private eye business."

—*The Washington Post*

COLD CASE

"[A] vivid puzzler and a walloping good read . . . lay in the supply of midnight oil before you pick up this book."

—*Albuquerque Journal*

"A satisfyingly complex tale!"   —*Entertainment Weekly*

"A must for every mystery fan. Barnes is a master storyteller, and her latest—in a series that just keeps getting better—is a riveting read that is at once poignant, funny, sad, suspenseful, and hopeful."

—*Booklist*

"Barnes continues to write some of the best female detective mysteries on the market today. Readers will dive into the action from start to finish. Carlotta is a great female sleuth and the supporting cast adds dichotomous local color to the tale."

—Harriet Klausner, *Painted Rock Reviews*

"Engrossing. . . . The pages keep turning."   —*Publishers Weekly*

"Compelling."   —*Kirkus Reviews*

"Absorbing . . . Barnes keeps readers flipping pages. . . . The quickly paced tale neatly balances thought and action, past events and present consequences."   —*Orlando Sentinel*

"*Cold Case* is as good as it gets! Linda Barnes is one of today's best authors, mystery or not. Each new book gives us the best in writing, plot and character development."   —Kate's Mystery Books

HARDWARE

"Ms. Barnes makes a fist and puts some muscle in this strong plot about an extortionist scheme to corner the market in the taxi medallions."   —*The New York Times Book Review*

"Warning, this is a difficult book to put down!"   —*Kansas Ledger*

"More than Grafton and far more than Paretsky—Barnes manages to overcome the too tough tendencies of her detective with salvos of self-deprecating wit . . . "   —*Booklist*

SNAPSHOT

"Barnes' best work yet . . . some of the best detective fiction you'll read."   —*Detroit Free Press*

"A stunner!"   —*Denver Post*

"Irresistible!"   —*Chicago Sun-Times*

"Barnes scored a direct hit with *Steel Guitar*, and her P.I. is in top form here."   —*Chicago Tribune*

"*Snapshot* is destined to secure Barnes' position in the hotshot ranks of detective fiction."
—*Arizona Republic*

STEEL GUITAR

"Carlotta—tall, vivacious, sensitive—unravels all the knots with breathtaking verve, leaving the reader gasping for more. Super."
—*Library Journal*

"A gripping tale, packed with taut, energy-charged images."
—*Publishers Weekly*

"Another of Barnes's superb mixes of warmth, enthusiasm, clever plotting, vivid characters, and overall brio."
—*Kirkus Reviews*

COYOTE

"Like the best of the new detectives . . . [Carlotta Carlyle] is a woman of wit and gravity, compassion and toughness, a heroine worth spending time with. . . . [Those of us] who yearn for whodunits with character as well wrought as plot, can only thank Linda Barnes."
—*The New York Times Book Review*

"Linda Barnes is once again brilliant. *Coyote* is damned good."
—Robert B. Parker

"Carlotta Carlyle is better than ever and *Coyote* is the perfect vehicle."
—Sue Grafton

"Linda Barnes has another winner in *Coyote* . . . a great, only-in-Boston climax."
—Jeremiah Healy

"The most refreshing, creative female character to hit mystery fiction since Sue Grafton's Kinsey Millhone . . . the other first ladies of crime better watch their backs."
—*People*

"Her first person prose is well-honed, and her touch is sure enough to float her fast-paced narrative while still allowing for sharp development of an intriguing cast of characters . . . best of all, Barnes can turn a phrase well enough to make even Paretsky and Grafton jealous."
—*Houston Chronicle*

ALSO BY LINDA BARNES

HEART
OF THE
WORLD

LINDA
BARNES

St. Martin's Paperbacks

This is a work of fiction. All of the characters, organizations and events portrayed in this novel are either products of the author's imagination or are used fictitiously.

HEART OF THE WORLD

Copyright © 2006 by Linda Appelblatt Barnes.

Cover photo of woman © John Halpern. Cover photo of background courtesy Corbis Royalty Free.

Library of Congress Catalog Card Number: 2006041708

ISBN: 0-312-36273-0
EAN: 9780312-36273-7

Printed in the United States of America

St. Martin's Press hardcover edition / May 2006
St. Martin's Paperbacks edition / June 2007

St. Martin's Paperbacks are published by St. Martin's Press, 175 Fifth Avenue, New York, NY 10010.

10 9 8 7 6 5 4 3 2 1

For Monica

Aquí, no pasa nada.
Nothing happens here.

GABRIEL GARCIA MARQUEZ,
A Hundred Years of Solitude

Everything was complicated; nothing was clear.
It was Colombia.

MARIA DUZAN,
Death Beat

Cuchacique, the Tairona chieftain who had led the uprising in 1599, was condemned "to be tied to and dragged by the tails of two wild colts, then quartered, the parts to be set on the pathways and the head placed in a cage, from whence none shall remove it, or be sentenced to death penalty . . . "

GERARDO REICHEL DOLMATOFF,
Arqueologia de Colombia: Un Texto Introductorio

ACKNOWLEDGMENTS

I am indebted to Alan Ereira's excellent book, *The Elder Brothers*, for information concerning the Kogi people and for the Kogi chant used in the prologue. Thanks also to Richard, Sam, my South American family, Sarah Smith, Kelley Ragland, and Gina Maccoby.

SIERRA NEVADA DE SANTA MARTA

THE SMALL MAN wore white from the tip of his pointed hat to the rolled-up cuffs of his baggy trousers. His shapeless tunic hung to his narrow hips. His feet were bare, and his *mochila,* the handwoven bag slung over his shoulder, was broadly striped in brown and white, with a touch of bright yellow, like an unexpected flower. He was less than five feet tall, and young, but his brown skin was lined, so he didn't look like a young man. His pace was slow, which added to the impression of age, but that was because his outer vision was poor. His inner vision was keen and he progressed with a steady gait, his feet firm on the rocky ground. He knew how to walk; he knew the right way to walk, the old way, the way the Mother had taught the first people. He knew how to dress, in white like the snow, with a hat like the peak of the snowy mountain. As he walked, he chanted in the old tongue, in the simple language of the Elder Brother, now known by only a few.

It did not make him sad that so few Elder Brothers remained in the great world. Everything was how it should be. He had brought the sacred offerings, the white potatoes, the white grubs, the special things that nourished the spirits of the Mothers of the Lost City. He had brought food for the Mother of the Jaguars and the Mother of the Water Spirit and the Mother of the Green Plants, and he spoke the proper words of offering as he walked the proper way.

"*There are all things in Aluna; in Aluna there are all things.*"

The repetitive chanting brought him to his center and gave him peace, but the words of Mama Parello still rang in his ears. He had little outer vision, but the other *mamas* saw like great hunting hawks, and they said the snow on the highest mountain peak was not as it should be, the small tundra trees dead or dying, the grasses of the *páramo* turning yellow and dry. That was very bad. If the snow was not deep, as it should be, then the icy water in the streams would not be as it should be. If the water was not good, the maize, the plantains, and the potatoes would not be good. If the plants were not good, the Kogi could not thrive. All these things were connected as all things were connected on the great earth. "*In Aluna there are all things.*"

He used his *poporo* then, as a man does, taking the coca leaves from his *mochila* and placing them in his mouth the right way, the way the Mother taught since time began, using his stick to add the ground lime from the gourd. As he chewed, mixing the lime with saliva and leaf, he thought about the Mother and why she had allowed the Younger Brother to come back from his exile across the Great Sea.

Once, he knew, the Elder Brother and the Younger Brother lived in harmony here in the heart of the world. Much was known then, of spirit and sky; all the ceremonies were new and fresh. The people traded their crops up and down the mountain, fish and salt from the sea, monkey and alligator meat from the jungle, sugarcane from the wooded savannah. The *mamas* taught the right ways and the people prospered. The spirit was strong then, and the *mamas* danced—how they danced!—with the holy gold.

But the Younger Brother took the wrong turning. He fell in love with his machines and forgot the old ways. He hurt the Mother's body with his machines, and for his carelessness, and for the protection of the Older Brother, he was banished to the far side of the world.

Peaceful were the years of his banishment, but he had returned. He had come back to the pain of the Elder Brother, to the diminishment of the true people. He had brought grief then. And now, now, what had he done? Had the Younger Brother, in his folly, made trouble even with the snow on the holy mountaintop?

The coca leaves were fresh and the lime strong. As he chewed, the tiredness passed from his body like a wave passes through the sea, and he walked the earth refreshed and smelled the good smells of the spicy grasses and the crisp thin air. He chanted to keep his thoughts on the right things to do when approaching the Great City of the Mother. *"There are all things in Aluna; yes, in Aluna there are all things."*

Aluna was the place of creation, where all things began, where time was stilled and everything that was or that would be existed in the garden of the Mother's great and eternal mind. He tried not to worry about the melting snow, but it was a thing to bring trouble. Still, if he nourished and cared for the good Mothers of the City as he always did, as the Elder Brothers had always done, then it would go well. There was much lost, yes, much lost, but much remembered of the Old Ways. The Elder Brothers knew how to keep the good in the world, how to keep the snow deep, how to make the rain fall, how to make the plants grow. The Elder Brothers would not falter. *"There are all things in Aluna."*

When he crested the high ridge, he heard the low hum, the pesky sound of the great moth, a troubling angry buzz. *There are all things in Aluna,* so even the ugly iron moth of the foolish Younger Brother was there, an idea before it had a form, an idea in the mind of the Great Mother. This moth was hard to see, fuzzy and far away, but it grew closer and bigger and louder, a great black moth hovering near the City of the Mother, an ugly iron moth that came singing out of the sky, out of the pure white blanket of the clouds. The moth was black like night and gray like ash. The Younger Brother made the moth, but he did not build it from sticks or weave it on a loom. He did not create it with the proper spirit in the proper way, with humility and prayer and guidance.

The small man's feet hurried on the stones and he had to

remind himself to do the thing right, to approach the city in the correct frame of mind, in the right way, so that his holy offerings would be good. Things had to be done right, or they were no good. There was a way to do things. This was what the Younger Brother had never learned. As the buzzing faded away, the small man slowed his pace and spoke the words carefully, remembering to say them the way Mama Parello said them, remembering the right melody and the right rhythm, remembering the way that was the one right way.

Another steep path led to a flight of stone steps. The steps, edged in emerald moss, were not slippery to bare feet. The small man thought they looked like the petals of a great flower. He knew how to walk them. He took deep breaths as he climbed, and he thought how short the long journey had been, how many good things he had smelled along the way, how many strong steps he had taken.

What was that noise, that rhythmic pat-pat-pat? It wasn't the echo of his own climbing steps; no, his feet traveled as silently on stone as they did on sand and earth. The sound was one he knew, a melody of planting time, the steady thud of the iron spade digging the earth, but there were no people in the City and no crops to till. He tried to keep the right thoughts in his head, the right words on his tongue. He quickened his pace, and when he'd climbed every step, when he stood on the flat holy ground, his eyes did not have to see well to see that this was wrong.

The ancient words dried on his tongue. What were the words for this new and terrible thing? Unbidden, they came to him, the words the *mamas* of the Sierra Nevada sang long ago when the Younger Brother first returned from across the sea, words he had known in darkness and in light. He chanted them with all his breath, with grave concentration, as though they could make this wrong thing right:

When Columbus came, they took the things that were ours.
They took our golden things, all our sacred gold.
They set dogs on us and we had to flee.

We ran in fear from the sea to the jungle,
  from the jungle to the mountain.
We ran in fear, and as we ran we left everything behind us.
They took our soul. They took everything.
Before then, everyone knew how to dance,
All the Indians, all of them, all of them,
Every Indian knew how to dance.

He knew the next words, the next lines, but the words would not come. On the rise of a ridge, strangers worked the holy ground. Men in uniform raised iron tools and cut into the thin soil. They were laughing, drinking, even using the black picture boxes of the Younger Brother to create unholy images of the desecration. This was evil beyond carelessness, evil beyond thought. They were digging the very bones of the Mother. They were tearing out her lungs. They were tearing out her liver and her heart. Here in the Holy City, they were digging up the last good Mothers, stealing them from the great earth.

The snow would fail; yes, it would fail. The life-bringing rain would fail. The cooling river would fail. The root crops and the cotton and the maize would fail. The Elder Brother could not protect them from their folly now. If the Younger Brother stole all the Mothers from the earth, everything would die. Everyone would die. The earth would die.

The small man stood still as the iguana stands, stunned by the heat of the sun. He watched as though his eyes were the eyes of a swooping condor instead of the weak eyes of a half-blind man. He felt the violation of the Mother in his stomach, in his liver, and in his heart.

Never before had they come to the sacred mountain. He did not know what to say. He did not know the right thing to do.

PAOLINA

SHE MOVED DOWN the hallway in a gaggle of other teens, but she traveled in a lane of her own. She wasn't with the three blonde girls a step ahead, and she wasn't with the two Goth kids who lagged behind. The boy nerd beside her was beside her for only a second, and that instantaneous brush was due to the two arrogant jocks who gave him a shove in her direction as they passed.

She moved with grace, with a rhythm all her own, like she was dancing to a syncopated beat no one else could hear. Oh, she wasn't as slim as she wanted to be, but who was? The way she put it, she had a butt like a Latina, and who'd want to have one of those flat-ass Anglo butts anyway? She wasn't very tall either, just five-two, and that was a disappointment, but a lot of the boys liked short girls better and it gave her more options in the boyfriend department, because the short boys didn't want beanpole girlfriends. Not even the harshest critic could find fault with the shiny dark hair that brushed her shoulders in the front and hung two inches longer in the back. When she flipped it away from her face, the way she did while bent in concentration over the drums, her dark brown eyes sparkled.

Paolina Fuentes. Paolina *Roldán* Fuentes. She didn't use the name "Roldán," not ever, but she had started thinking of herself as Paolina Roldán Fuentes, using "R" for a middle initial instead of leaving the line blank. Paolina Roldán, that had a rhythm. Her mother hadn't given her a middle name, and Paolina thought it was because coming up with two names for an unwanted child would have been twice the chore. Children who were wanted had middle names, beautiful, lyrical names like Melissa or Guinevere, names you could sing. She didn't like the name Paolina, didn't like its harsh choppy syllables. None of the teachers even pronounced it right, and Fuentes, well; she wasn't a Fuentes at all. She didn't have anything to do with Jimmy Fuentes. He was the father of her brothers, not her own father at all.

Roldán was her true name, and that's why she'd decided to take it as her middle name. In Colombia, she would have three names: her own name, Paolina, followed by her father's name, Roldán, and then her mother's maiden name, Silva. Three names, but her father's would be the most important. He had three names, too: Carlos Roldán Gonzales, but most people simply called him Roldán. Everyone in Colombia knew who you meant when you said Roldán. She smiled as she came to her locker. It was like a magic word. He was like a movie star, a man who needed only one name.

She knew what they said he'd done, but she didn't believe it, and anyway, she didn't care. He was handsome; she knew that. He was good-looking and probably kind, too. He was a legend; he was important, somebody like the men they read about in world history. She wondered if he was thinking about her, thinking about his daughter the same way that she was thinking about him, wondering what she was really like the same way she wondered about him. When she imagined him thinking about her, it made her feel as warm as one of the baby chicks that waddled under the heat lamps of the biology lab. He must think about her a lot, because he sent her presents.

She glanced quickly right and left, considered reaching toward the back of the high shelf where she kept her latest treasure hidden. She wanted to feel its smooth surface, to touch it and wonder where it came from, but there wasn't time to do the thing justice, to appreciate the magic of the gift. Somebody might stop and ask questions. *Where'd you get that? You steal it? Lemme see it.* She didn't want anybody else touching it, smearing her father's fingerprints with greasy cafeteria hands.

After swapping her biology text for her history book, she banged her locker shut, spun the dial on the lock, and hurried through the second-floor hallway of Cambridge Rindge and Latin, the buzz of fellow students echoing in her wake. She didn't hear it really, because she didn't care what Karlene whispered about Jimmy B. or what Gigi shrieked about the goddamn test in biology. She didn't even care what Gigi said about Diego, and what anybody said about Diego used to be vital. Now, with so much going on in her head, so many possibilities circling each other like caged animals, she couldn't be bothered about Diego. He was such a child, really, always thinking about who to hang out with, and who he could con into buying him a beer, like it was important.

She touched the pocket of her low-slung jeans, tracing the outline of the letter, and felt a secret shudder of anticipation. She could ask Diego what he thought about it, but why should she? It wasn't like he was going to make any decisions for her. She absolutely hated that, the way everybody thought they could boss her around. At home, her mom, and here, any guy you called boyfriend thought he could tell you what to do like you were some kind of slave. Maybe the Anglo boys weren't like that, but the Latino boys, man, they took pride in it: If I tell my girl to jump off the roof, she better jump off quick, she knows what's good for her.

Now she wished she'd taken the time to touch the secret talisman in her locker. It would keep her safe; she knew it would. Following the letter's instructions wasn't a bad thing. It wasn't like these people were strangers. It wasn't like she was doing something she'd promised she wouldn't, like drinking Diego's stupid beer or smoking pot or taking one of Andrea's hyper pills. And, besides, in every adventure there was some level of risk. You don't work up the nerve to audition for the band, you never make it. No pain, no gain. It wasn't like she couldn't walk away.

Probably it was just another letter or another present, a new and different method of delivery. She'd say thank you to whoever brought it, and maybe she'd have time to write a thank-you note. That's what she told herself walking down the hall, but there was another hope inside her, that her father would be there in the flesh, that he'd come and fetch her, that he'd carry her away to some new existence she couldn't even imagine, some fairy-tale-princess world where she'd be in charge. She remembered the dark, high-ceilinged rooms in Bogotá, the elegant home of the man who was her grandfather, a house with carved mantels over blazing fireplaces, with more rooms than she could count, with hushed, cool hallways, and a garden fragrant with pink roses. Captivated by memory, she must have slowed her pace.

The thin voice sounded right in her ear. "Hurry up now, you'll be late."

Jesus. Everybody thought they could boss her around. Even the dried-up prune of a gym teacher, thin as a stick, no breasts at all, with a stupid whistle hung around a neck as scrawny as a chicken's. Even she could boss Paolina Fuentes around.

Paolina Roldán.

She gave the gym teacher her sweetest, most submissive smile and raced down the hallway to her last class of the day.

CHAPTER 1

COLD.

It was as bitter a January morning as New England could spew. Gray clouds blocked the weak sun like heavy curtains and I smelled snow that had yet to fall, an unseen edge of white in the icy sky. Numb gloved fingers tugged my scarf so high it touched the tip of my nose. Breath fogged the air. *Cold.* But the exterior iciness was nothing compared to the chill I felt inside.

The apartment building at 47 Orchard Court Road was wedged tightly between two taller buildings. A dingy street, Orchard Court Road. No orchard, no courtyard, the pretentious name all that remained of some past glory, or more likely, a come-on for the unwary buyer or desperate renter.

I checked my watch, then shoved my hands deep into the pockets of my parka. Six thirty and barely a glimmer of pale sunlight. Sunshine would have been a relief, cutting the edge of the cold. Snow would have been a relief. Anything but the endless gray and the bitter cold, cement parking lots staring at stunted trees, everything shaded in grays and browns, as though all the color had seeped out of the city along with the warmth.

Mission Hill isn't Boston's finest neighborhood. Split by Huntington Avenue with its battered green trolley cars, stretching south to Jamaica Plain and east to Roxbury, it's at best working-class poor, at worst subsistence housing. It's hard to park in Mission Hill. Too many abandoned wrecks, some immobilized by the infamous Denver boot. After circling the area for twenty minutes, I'd found an iffy slot for my battered Rent-A-Wreck across the street from the housing project and trudged uphill. Whether the car would still be there when I returned was a question best to ignore.

I blew out a breath, raising another cloud of steam, and considered when it might have been, that elusive last time I'd been warm. Two nights ago, in bed, when problems had seemed contained and controllable, the usual work dilemmas, a due diligence for a small insurance firm, a store clerk who might or might not have a hand in the till. I'd been debating what kind of car I could buy with considerable urgency and limited means. And arguing with Sam Gianelli, who's been a source of joy and consternation in my life for years.

I'd been in bed, blissfully warm but not asleep, when he'd entered the room with hardly a squeak of the floorboards. He'd removed his shoes at the front door, a thoughtful act, perhaps. Isn't it odd how you can read any motive into any act when there's hostility as well as attraction? Given the hour, I'd read deceit: Sam didn't want me to realize how late he was coming to bed, didn't want me to wake. If he'd been deliberately noisy, I'm pretty sure I'd have found an unkind reason for that as well.

Face it, the past month or so the only place Sam and I have been comfortable with each other has been in bed. That's always been our strong suit, the meshing of bodies, the pulsing rhythm of stimulation and release. Chemistry. Who knows what sparks that thing between men and women that brings them together in the night?

The phone call had interrupted a long-standing yet oddly silent argument. At least it was a silent argument on my part; maybe Sam never thought about it at all. I mean, how can you tell? It bothered me all the time what he did for a living, if you can call working for the Mob a living. Once he'd talked to me openly about getting out. Once, he'd tried to make a clean break. But when his father got sick, he knuckled under and went back to being Daddy's bright-eyed boy.

Maybe that's what he would always be, never my companion, always his father's son, and I didn't think I could live with that. And I wasn't sure I wanted to live without it. So, really what could I say?

If he were a teenager, I'd have said, "Where've you been?"

If he were a teenager, he'd have said, "Out."

Lawyer friends always tell me not to ask the question if I don't want to hear the answer. I guess that's why instead of arguing about the big thing, the great white whale of our on-again, off-again relationship, we wind up arguing so viciously about the small things, and maybe that's what we'd keep doing until the small things drove us apart. Again.

Monday night, the phone interrupted us and I was momentarily grateful for it, despite the lateness of the hour.

I recognized the voice straight off, but it spoke such rapid-fire angry Spanish that I had to tell Marta to slow down twice before I could follow the flow. It's not that she doesn't speak English, it's that she won't. Not to me.

"Lemme talk to her, right now." Her voice was slurred and rough and I thought she'd been drinking again. Sam raised his eyebrows and muttered something under his breath.

"*¿Sabes qué hora es, Marta?*"

"I don't need you telling me anything, not what time it is, and certainly not how to take care of a daughter." She muttered something under her breath, too, and of course I heard it, and it was distinctly unflattering, something about the red-headed bitch, which is what she often calls me.

"Why don't you call back when you sober up?" My hand was moving the receiver away from my ear when I heard an increase in volume along with a change of tone.

"*Por favor,* I *must* talk with her. I need her to— She promised me."

"Marta, Paolina isn't here. It's Monday night. Look in her room."

The woman's called me before when she's forgotten where her daughter is. Once she'd scared the hell out of me when Paolina was sleeping over at a girlfriend's and Marta'd forgotten all about it.

"She's not here."

"Did she leave a note on the refrigerator?"

"What you think? I'm too drunk to know where my daughter is? Always, *always,* she says she'll be with you when she isn't here."

The conversation slid downhill from there, down a steep and ugly slope.

I'd slept that night convinced that Paolina was visiting Aurelia or Heather or Vanessa or any one of a number of girls I'd heard about or met, a classmate at the local high school, certain I'd have been informed as usual if my "little sister" had skipped school. Tuesday morning, before seven, I'd made fruitless calls to the girlfriends. Then I'd gone to the high school and found that the man charged with tracking down AWOL students was himself AWOL, and Paolina hadn't turned up for classes Monday at all.

Now it was Wednesday, *Wednesday,* for chrissake, and I was jumping every time my cell phone rang, nervous as a cat. All my paying jobs had been put on hold, my argument with Sam was simmering, and I was out in the cold at 6:30 A.M., determined to strike before my elusive target could leave for work.

Josefina Parte was the name I was looking for, and I found it, a battered tag, J. Parte, under a mailbox that read 4C and showed the scars of a recent crowbar assault. I rang the bell and waited in a pocket-sized vestibule maybe ten degrees warmer than the frigid outdoors. No response. I rang again.

Through the pebbled half-glass of the interior door, the stairway was narrow and steep. I could see it if I shaded my eyes and slanted my glance sideways. A direct stare brought only my own reflection, a pale oval of a face, wide-apart hazel-green eyes, slightly crooked nose. It was the eyes, I thought, that showed it most, the effect of two sleepless nights. The glass grayed my face, leaching the color from my skin and hair, and I had a sudden vision of myself grown old.

If I lived on Orchard Court Road and someone rang my bell, I might not answer it either. Not if I wasn't expecting a friend or relative to drop by. Good news probably didn't climb to the fourth floor often, and Josefina Parte might have long since stopped expecting it.

Josefina was the aunt or possibly the great-aunt of one Diego Martinez, and it had taken me a while to trace him, because juveniles who aren't registered in the system, who live with people who have different last names than their own, who go to a high school in an area they have no business going to, can be hard to find. I wasn't planning to bust Diego for lying to the Cambridge school system. He wasn't a crook or a bail jumper. I wasn't going to get paid for finding him. He was the current boyfriend of my little sister, Paolina, and she'd been gone for three days, possibly five. Two nights and a day had passed since Marta had needed the girl to babysit for her younger brothers and so noticed that she was inconveniently missing.

I swallowed the bitter taste in my mouth. I was running out of places to look for my sister. I didn't know what I'd do, where I'd go if Diego wasn't there, if she wasn't there with him.

The inner door of the Orchard Court building had a lock that wouldn't have taken more than a minute to pick, but I punched other doorbells first, to see whether some foolish tenant would buzz me in sight unseen. There's usually somebody, a kid home alone, an elderly woman eager for conversation. The vestibule didn't have the usual intercom, so no one could inquire who was there. No one bothered to look, but the buzzer sounded. I pushed my way inside. The door was heavy.

The stairwell—you couldn't call it a lobby—smelled of grease and disinfectant and rotting rubber mats. The wallpaper was peeling at the joins and defaced with gang graffiti.

A door opened above and a low voice yelled, "Somebody there?"

"Forgot my key," I answered. "Thanks a lot."

The door slammed shut in response to my reassuringly female voice and I began climbing the steep stairs. I started hearing voices at the second floor. They grew louder at the third and crescendoed outside 4C. Someone was very much at home or else the TV had been turned up to entertain the houseplants and keep away the burglars. I raised my hand, about to knock.

Either they were listening to Spanish language TV or they were arguing. I let my hand drop to my side and made no bones about eavesdropping.

It takes a moment for Spanish to land in my head as distinct words and sentences. At first I hear it as a rush of sound, but then something clicks and I'm back in Mexico City where I spent childhood days with my mother's cousins, time stolen from Detroit winters, coinciding not with school vacations but with periods my mother and father didn't get along. I forgot my Spanish when I returned to the States, then relearned it as a cop, specializing in what we called "perp Spanish." Paolina helped me regain some fluency and I needed it. These people weren't speaking slowly. I could distinguish two arguing voices, one male, one female. "Diego," I heard, several times, and swearing, too. I'm fluent in that.

I knocked firmly.

Sometimes I miss the days when I could follow up that authoritative knock with the word "police." "Police" opened doors. It gave people a reason to answer when I asked questions.

I knocked again. A silence had started with the first knock so I knew they'd heard me.

"Señora Parte," I said clearly, "please open the door. I just want to talk." I spoke in Spanish. Why not?

The door opened slowly and a young woman peered out through a narrow crack. She had dark hair pulled back into a tight knot and an anxious expression on a sweet earnest face. I got the toe of my boot past the sill but didn't force my way in.

"What do you want?" she said. "I'm busy here."

I took a business card from my wallet. It said CARLOTTA CARLYLE, PRIVATE INVESTIGATIONS. She studied it for a long moment with her tongue fixed firmly between her small teeth and then passed it behind her.

"*¿Policía?*" It was the man's deep voice. "So sorry if we bother any of the old bitches in the apartment downstairs."

"Señor," I said, raising my voice, "there are no complaints about you."

The door opened to display both of them. He was a thin wiry man with badly pocked skin.

He said, "Then what you want? Collect for the church? They can find their own money, sell their gold candlesticks for all I care."

"Señora, your nephew, Diego, I need to speak to him."

The man glanced automatically down the hallway to his right. "What about?"

"He's in no trouble from me. But he hasn't been in school the past three days."

"You're from the school?"

"No."

"What you care then? The boy's sick. When he's better, he go to the school. Nosy goddamn busybodies. Time I'm his age, I work full time."

"I need to talk to him about a girl in his class."

"Hah, he do something to a girl?"

"Señora," I said to the silent woman. "Let me talk to him." She looked stricken, like a deer in the headlights, her mouth half open.

"He's not here." The man gave the door a push, but my foot held it ajar and I wedged myself through.

"A girl in his class is missing and he may know where she is. His room's down here?"

The single front room was sparsely furnished, ashtrays overflowing on the stained coffee table. A narrow archway led to a corridor.

"Diego? You here?" I moved quickly.

"I already told you—" The man moved quickly, too, edging between me and the hallway.

"Look," I said, "if he's not here, it's because he's run off with my sister, Paolina Fuentes. You know that name? If he's not here, I'm going to get in your business big time, so it's better for you if you let me see him." I raised my voice, hoping Diego would hear.

Behind the wiry man, in the corridor, I heard a door creak.

"Hey." The voice was low and sullen.

"Don't you come out of that room!" the man thundered.

Josefina finally moved, putting a restraining hand on the man's shoulder. I walked past him to the half-open door on the right-hand side of the hallway.

"Hey," the kid said. "What's the deal?"

I shoved the door, my eyes flicking from the unmade bed to the narrow chest of drawers. No one else inside the small room. No closet. No place to hide.

"Where is she, Diego?" I addressed the back of his lanky frame, his dirty white T-shirt and long dark hair. "Diego?"

He turned to face me, an eruption of acne on his left cheek, but that wasn't what I noticed first. His nose was pushed to one side of his face and his left eye was puffy and swollen. Dried blood decorated the front of his shirt.

"Jesus, Diego, was she with you when it happened? Where is she?"

"What is this shit?"

"You were at a party Friday night, with Paolina Fuentes."

"Paolina? For a while, yeah. Then she left." He sounded angry and puzzled. The way he stood in the doorway was stiff and unnatural, like he had bruises under his thin T-shirt, maybe broken ribs.

"She left alone?"

"That's what I'm saying."

"You two break up?"

"What if we did?"

"Did she go with a new guy? Is he the one who hit you?"

He shook his head. Maybe it hurt to move his mouth. His lips were swollen.

"He fell down the stairs," the man said loudly. "That's all."

Josefina Parte made a noise.

"Boy's clumsy like an ox," the man said.

I studied Diego's eye. The injury was recent, more recent than Friday night. The man's reluctance to let me near the boy suddenly made sense. My right hand clenched, but I kept my eyes focused on Diego. "She say anything about running away?"

He shook his head again, more slowly. "That's dumb, man, running away."

"Was she happy, sad, excited? Different?"

"Yeah, man, she was different, okay. She was hard, ya know? She was like way into herself, and I don't put up with that kinda shit, ya know? Not from a girl."

"That's right." The man's voice again, grating like metal on glass. "You don't take no shit from girls. You don't answer no more questions either."

Frustration simmered behind my eyebrows. All the time I'd wasted tracking him, for nothing. All the certainty that Paolina's disappearance was linked to his, unfounded. The boy shifted his weight in an attempt to get more comfortable. I could smell the sweat on his body. I looked at the silent scared woman, the wiry lying man, telltale damage on his knuckles, and anger kindled like a flame.

"You want to leave here, Diego?" I said softly. "You want to see a doctor about that nose?"

I could sense the man behind me stiffen, feel the tension rise.

"If you want to leave, I'll take you out." I wasn't carrying, but it was no idle boast. I was furious. I wanted to hit somebody, I had the height advantage, and I'd learned to fight dirty at an early age.

"I'll stay with my aunt," Diego said.

"You get outta here now, bitch." The wiry man's brown eyes had an edge of yellow. He looked defiant, almost proud of himself for what he'd done to the boy, and I considered a shot to the nose or a punch in the gut.

"*Please, just go.*" Josefina stepped between us.

"Walk me out, Señora," I said. She must have thought I wanted safe passage past the wiry man, so she did what I asked and accompanied me through the hallway. Behind me, I heard the sharp crack of Diego's swiftly closing door, and I thought, good for you, boy, keep it shut. Josefina opened the apartment door to dismiss me, but I urged her through it, and spoke in a low voice.

"What are you going to do?" I said.

She looked at me, her frightened eyes so wide that white showed all around the pupils.

"Are you married to that man?"

"Por favor," she said, shaking her head, "understand. I love him. I love them both."

"Your nephew needs a doctor. Otherwise his nose will stay crooked. They'll need to break it again to reset it."

"Please. They'll put him in jail."

Where he belongs, I thought. "Diego needs to go to school," I said.

"He'll go, he'll go. Tomorrow, next week, soon. You go now."

"You make a choice, understand, Señora? You have to make a choice."

"What do you mean? I got no choice."

"Take your nephew to the hospital. I'll stay until you go. I won't let him hurt you."

"I can't."

"You can."

I waited for her response in the dingy hallway. The next-door neighbors' alarm clock buzzed, their cat yowled, and Josefina Parte stared at the worn linoleum like she was waiting for the channel to change.

"If you choose to do nothing, Señora," I said, "that's also a choice."

"Leave. Go away. You make only trouble."

The apartment door opened a crack. The wiry man didn't come outside, but both of us could hear him breathing. He wanted Josefina to know he was listening.

"I'll help you," I said.

"Just go away."

"It's your choice," I said.

She turned and reentered the flat without meeting my eyes.

I waited, but I didn't hear raised voices much less the sound of physical blows. The wiry man didn't venture into the hall-way, so I didn't get to hit him. Instead, on the way downstairs, I made the choice for Señora Parte, using my cell to phone the cops. I told them to send a unit to check out a minor in need of protective services. I told them to use extreme caution because the perp was on the premises. Then I jammed my hands back in my pockets and trudged downhill to my car, thinking I'd hit a dead end, another dead end, the last dead end. Thinking that now I didn't know where the hell else to look for Paolina.

I barely felt the cold.

CHAPTER 2

IN A HOMICIDE investigation the first twenty-four hours are crucial. A missing persons case takes as long as it takes; there's no cut-and-dried rule, no drop-dead critical time frame. Small children stumble home unharmed after two days and nights in a snowy forest. A teenage boy moves into the garage and his parents don't realize he's living there until he starts a fire in the charcoal grill. Middle-aged adults discover their grown siblings living down the block after a bitter separation of twenty-seven years and wonder why they ever stopped speaking in the first place.

Delay didn't mean defeat, I told myself, but the knowledge didn't lessen my growing panic. There are plenty of other tales, grim tales, brutal tales: a sixteen-year-old lifeguard never returns from a sunny morning at the beach; a three-year-old wanders from a campsite and is never anything more than memories and smudgy photographs.

I leaned against the rusty fender of the rental, suddenly exhausted, deflated as a leaky tire. The search for Diego, the conviction that finding him would yield Paolina, had sustained me thus far. Now I felt hungry, hollow, scared. I fumbled for the car keys in the pocket of my coat and wished Josefina Parte had found the courage to call the police herself.

Back in the car, I tried for some heat. A few gulps of chilly air coughed through the vents as I veered off Route 9 onto Harvard Street. Rush-hour-heavy traffic headed mainly in the other direction, so I counted my blessings: Traffic was moving; the child-beater hadn't pulled a gun.

Why didn't all my previous experience with missing persons cases help me now? Why were there so many questions and so few answers? Was Paolina involved with some new boy? Would Diego have known if she were? Why didn't I know? Why couldn't I read her mind after all these years? Why did she remain so stubbornly other, so difficult to understand?

Sometimes I thought all my questions about Paolina boiled down to one: Had I made her life better or worse? I'd taken her on as a Little Sister when she was seven, hoping to improve her life, but the fact was she'd improved mine. The trips to Franklin Park Zoo would have been empty without her game of naming all the animals. The sunlight on New Hampshire ponds was brighter shared with a kid full of wonder at the fish and frogs. Maybe I'd pushed her too hard, maneuvering to keep her playing in the band, trying to give her a dream better than the dream her mother pushed so constantly: marriage and motherhood, marriage and motherhood. Nothing wrong with that dream, I'd told her. It was all the things Marta's vision didn't include that made me see red, like success in school and a good job, like stretching yourself and using your talent. And all the things it did include, like the marriage and money trade-off: Paolina's youth and beauty for some older man's bank account.

Marry, I'd told her, as though I had any right to preach. Raise great kids. But first be a person, a complete package, so that when you find a guy it's not a matter of molding yourself into the person he wants you to be, but a blending of souls. Don't be the one who compromises all the time. I'd thought she was doing fine, growing, learning, starting to emerge on the other side of a sullen adolescence, beginning to accept herself for who she was, strengths and weaknesses included.

At the Cambridge Street traffic light, I wriggled my toes inside my boots. They moved reassuringly; no frostbite. A green Pontiac, lights flashing, blocked the right lane, engine dead from the cold. I'd been so sure I'd find her this morning, retrieve her, entrust her to a social worker at the high school, go home to deal with the due diligence and the suspect clerk. Instead I took a right, then a left, and turned into the driveway of Marvin's Magnificent Cabs, also known as Black & Blue due to the unfortunate color of the cabs, pulling the nasty rental right into the cab garage, thinking maybe Leroy could take a peek at the heater, tell me what the hell I had to do to get some heat.

"Buy something decent," he said.

That was another problem. I'd put off buying a replacement car, first waiting for the slow-as-molasses insurance settlement on my old Toyota, then relying on a great used-car deal that fell through at the last minute. Now I was debating between a Crown Vic ex-cop car I could afford and a brand new Mazda from a dealership recommended by Sam. The guy at the dealership had offered me the car at way below invoice, and I wasn't sure I wanted to get involved with a business that was undoubtedly a Mob front.

Gloria, my friend, as well as the chief dispatcher and owner of the cab company, was busy at her console, but she picked up the sound of my slushy footsteps and lifted her head. Her face grew somber when she saw the expression on mine.

"Nothing?"

I shut the door quickly to conserve the heat. The new office is a hundred percent better than the old one, but the cold spell was a challenge to any heater.

Gloria wore a dress, a robe more like it, of bright printed cotton, like an African tribal gown. Over that, a sweatshirt and a shawl, and the whole thing looked right on her somehow, as right as a dress can look on a 250-pound wheelchair-bound woman with a round pretty face and bright inquisitive eyes.

"Worse than nothing." I peeled off my gloves and scarf. "Wrong trail."

"You found the boyfriend?"

I unzipped my parka. "Dammit, Gloria, it seemed reason-

able. She disappears; he disappears. I thought they'd be together. It seemed logical, goddammit."

"Don't get mad, Carlotta, for what I'm gonna say, but do
you think this is some kind of challenge? I mean, lost kids
are something you do. You think she got tired of waiting for
you to look for her?"

"What do you mean?"

"How much time you spent with her lately?"

I started to reply, hotly, then shut my mouth. Why get
mad at Gloria for telling me the same stuff I'd been telling
myself?

"She's a smart girl," Gloria said, eyes narrowing. "Maybe
she went somewhere she knows you'll find her."

"Gloria, this isn't a scavenger hunt."

"Maybe she told you about it, sometime when you
weren't listening. Maybe she said she had a favorite place or
a secret dream or a hideaway."

"I *did* listen to her occasionally."

"How was she with Sam?"

"She adores Sam. You know that. What are you saying,
that she's jealous of him?"

Gloria shrugged her massive shoulders. "She knows you
always have time for work. Maybe she's making herself
your work." Hit by a car when she was a teenager, Gloria
moves fine from the waist up.

I sat on a rickety stool in the corner. "I hear what you're
saying, Gloria. I know I haven't been perfect here, but if
Paolina's playing some game with me, I don't know the
rules."

"Sorry."

The phone rang and she took a minute to send cabs
buzzing around the city. Then she said, "Roz is checking out
more of her classmates over at Rindge."

"Yeah, I'm going to meet her there later."

Roz, my tenant and assistant, a punk twenty-something,
doesn't look like a grown-up, so I'd decided she'd be the one
to investigate Paolina's classmates, a nonthreatening inter-
rogator. She'd ferreted out the news that Diego had gone

missing at the same time as Paolina. I'd fastened on that too quickly, leaped to the wrong conclusion.

Gloria said, "None of my cabbies picked her up."

"What about other companies?"

"I put the word out and sweetened it with a C-note. For a C-note, most cabbies will turn in their mothers, their sweethearts, and their best boyhood pals."

In other words, she hadn't heard anything.

"You eat breakfast?"

I shook my head impatiently.

"You gotta eat. Want a bite?"

I considered the assortment of bags and jars on Gloria's desk. "What are these?"

"Those? Sheer heaven. They're like potato chips made outta chocolate. You know, I been complaining about a lack of imagination in the junk food industry for years, but now I take it all back." She took a wavy dark shape from a can and used it to scoop up a gob of Marshmallow Fluff. "Strong enough for peanut butter," she said admiringly.

"Did you check the hospitals again?" I asked.

She chewed, swallowed, and nodded.

"Nothing from the cops?" I was spinning my wheels; if Gloria had found any leads, she'd have gotten in touch. We both knew the drill. I hadn't even tried to tell the Missing Persons detail in Cambridge that this was different, because up till now, I hadn't felt it was different.

Paolina hadn't run off with Diego. A chasm had opened under my feet, and it seemed as though I couldn't stop myself from falling, careening down a rabbit-hole Wonderland that wasn't wonderful at all, that was scary and dark as a mine shaft.

"You got a last sighting yet?" Gloria's voice brought me back.

"Aurelia Gutierrez saw her Friday night at the Macys' party, around eleven o'clock. Nobody saw her leave with anybody."

"But she left."

"She's not still there, Gloria, that's all I can say."

It was hurting Gloria, too. She'd never have left the last row of Fig Newtons in the bag if Paolina hadn't been gone. I reached over and took one. It tasted like straw and I quickly swallowed some water from the cooler to wash it down.

Steps out into the frigid night and disappears. It was like I could see the words in print, a huge black headline in a giant newspaper.

My little sister is a street-smart girl. Central Square, where the Macy twins had held their party, is an urban center jammed with people. The party had broken up by one in the morning, and no one recalled seeing Paolina after 11:15. Eleven fifteen isn't 3:00 A.M. Central Square is still active at midnight. The porch lights are on; the houses and apartments are close together and close to the street. If someone had attacked her on the street she'd have screamed and kicked up one hell of a fuss. She doesn't get in cars with strangers. She doesn't walk alone at night. She carries a whistle.

God, I went over and over it in my head. You don't just step out into the frigid night and disappear.

She'd tried to run away before.

Gloria said, "I read in one of my newspapers about all these Mexican girls got kidnapped as sex slaves."

She reads grocery-store tabloids, alternates them with romance magazines.

"Who's on the airport?" I asked, hoping to avoid the sex-slave stories, aware that I'd known who went out to Logan at one time, but forgotten, what with all the people I'd mobilized in the last two days.

"Paolina didn't cab there," Gloria said. "That was one of the first things I checked. And Lemon went airline to airline, showing her photo."

Lemon is one of Roz's many, many boyfriends. I used my cell again.

"Did you question the screeners?" I asked him. "The Homeland Security guys?"

"Tried to, but I got in trouble, interfering with their duties and shit. Thought I'd wind up in the can. I mean, isn't it their job to help?"

I hung up without answering. I'd have to do it myself. I'd have to split myself in tiny pieces and go over everything myself.

Gloria said, "Carlotta, calm down, okay. He's trying. We're all trying."

"I know."

"What are you gonna do now?"

"It's time to check her room. Nobody saw her with a suitcase, but it's the next step."

She raised her eyebrows. "Marta give the okay?"

"No." I should have forced the issue, demanded entry, but I'd been convinced my litle sister was joyriding with Diego.

"Good luck." Gloria pressed her lips together.

"What?" I said. "Spit it out."

"If you find her, don't smack her."

"Gloria, I would never—"

"You look like you want to hit somebody."

I felt like punching my fist through the wall. I felt like grabbing the next stranger I saw and throttling him. I felt like running a red light.

I used to have this neighbor, as proper an elderly Brahmin lady as ever you'd want to meet. One evening, well-lubricated by gin, she'd confessed her cure for frustration. When she wanted to maim and throttle her kin, she crept into her backyard in the wee hours and hurled ice cubes over the fence, punctuating each throw with a curse.

"Drive carefully," Gloria said as I zipped my parka and left.

CHAPTER 3

BEFORE HEADING TO Marta's, I drove to my place, listening attentively to the kind of all-news AM sludge I never bother to tune to, an "If it bleeds, it leads" nightmare station, aware that in some recess of my brain I was waiting with dread for the tale of the unidentified corpse of a teenage girl found in an alley. Instead I got a fatal fire, Big Dig leaks, and political corruption hearings. At my Cambridge home, a quick shower in a steamy tub took the place of a night's sleep. I changed automatically into clean clothes—navy slacks, white turtleneck, navy zip-front sweater—forced down a breakfast more ample than the single Fig Newton, got back in the car, and sped down Mt. Auburn Street while the radio brayed. Mega-mergers: GSC swallows BrackenCorp; will Mark Bracken be forced to retire? Celebrity weddings: Will this superstar's nuptials trump that one's in cost, security, and elaborate paparazzi avoidance? When did this drivel become news? I switched channels: Iraqi war casualties, corporate scandals, a crop-spraying plane downed by gunfire in Colombia. While judging whether or not to speed through a yellow traffic light, I glanced in my rearview mirror and braked abruptly, transfixed by the desperation in my eyes, the same look I'd seen in the eyes of clients, parents or guardians of runaways.

My beautiful girl, *gone*. Seven-year-old Paolina, with her red knit hat tied under her chin; nine-year-old Paolina, huddling under a blanket on the living room sofa, solemnly counting the seconds after each lightning strike, scared of sudden thunder. Anyone seeing her now, on a bus, on a street corner, in her form-fitting clothes, with her world-weary pose, would see only the hardening shell of the teenager, nothing of the past that had shaped her. No wonder my clients had trouble describing their kids to me. Kids are layered, filled with hidden aspects, with mood-swinging smiles that change their entire faces. A self-contained banker once wept when I asked the color of his son's eyes.

The light changed and I hit the gas. Pity didn't help a damn thing; sympathy didn't help. Fear didn't help. I had skills and I needed to use them, dispassionately, coolly.

For all intents and purposes I presented a professional appearance when I rang the bell of Marta Fuentes's small white house in Watertown. No one could hear the refrain humming through my mind: *Should have come at once, should have come earlier.* I tamped down the admonition. How could I have known that two whole days after Marta's phone call I'd be back at the starting gate, searching for a trail, sniffing the frigid air? I'd done it by the book, tracked down the leads one at a time. What else could I have done? What else could I do?

The house looked sad and weathered, a tiny single-family in a two-family neighborhood, the servants' dwelling for a grand Victorian that had burned years ago. Not a great location, but miles better than the old apartment in the East Cambridge projects. Even Marta admitted it was better for the kids, a pocket yard, a basketball hoop with a real net instead of hanging chain, a swing set that wasn't routinely vandalized.

I rang the bell. I knocked. I waited. I was contemplating a little breaking and entering by the time Marta finally opened the door, her dark hair tousled and her eyes swollen. She wore tight gray sweatpants and a matching tank top. She didn't say a word, just stared at me and crossed her arms protectively over her chest.

"Marta, sorry if I woke you."

"You don' wake me," she said. "But I don' got no time."

"Marta, I need to look at her room."

"I'm goin' out, soon as I fix my face." She was a small,

curvy woman, still attractive, I supposed, still sexy, provided you liked your women predatory. I could count on the fingers of one hand the number of times I'd seen her without heavy-duty makeup. "You know as well as I know, she goes with some boy," she went on. "Always the same thing, some boy. She don' care about me, about her family. She don' care about you, neither. We can die from worry, she don' care."

It didn't look like Marta was going to die from worry any time soon.

"I'll just take a look." I pushed the screen door open a little harder than I needed to and stepped inside. "You go ahead with whatever you have to do." I didn't want her company, didn't want her hovering over me, detailing Paolina's failures as a daughter. If she insisted, I'd be tempted to detail her failings as a mother and then I'd get kicked out of the house.

She stared up at me, taking a moment to decide that this was a fight she couldn't win. "Go on, then. Go ahead," she muttered.

I didn't need directions. I'd been there often enough, picking up Paolina for Saturday volleyball followed by our continuing search for the perfect ice cream cone, a quest that took us out to Kendall's in Littleton in summer, to Toscanini's in Cambridge, and Herrell's in Brighton. The hunt was less fervent in winter, but we soldiered on, my little sister in search of the ideal strawberry; me, mocha, sometimes mocha chip.

The house was small and Paolina's room tiny. The family who lived there previously had used it as a laundry room, and the washer-dryer hookup remained, enclosed now by a pair of slatted wooden blinds that hung from the ceiling. My sister's bed was a couch, and Marta referred to the place as the den, declaring she did so only so the boys wouldn't be jealous that Paolina had a room of her own.

Room of her own, Paolina scoffed. Sure, and every time she wanted to be alone her mother decided to do the laundry.

The blinds were up, the washer and dryer covered with dirty clothes that hadn't made it into any laundry hamper.

How does a teenager organize life in a laundry room? When I found myself checking my cell phone to make sure

the battery was charged, I realized how much I was hoping
for a call, a message, a reprieve. *I've got her,* Roz or Gloria
would say; *she just showed up*—and then I wouldn't need to
paw through the debris.

I sucked in a deep breath and told myself I was goddamn
lucky. If Marta had rigorously cleaned every surface, tossed
every scrap, I'd have nowhere to turn. The woman's dislike
of organization, not to mention mops, sponges, and dusters,
was in my favor.

The laundry room didn't boast a closet. Instead there was
one of those steel tubing coat racks, the kind you see at the
door when somebody throws a big party. I went through
Paolina's hanging items quickly, marveling at the lack of
pockets in modern girls' attire. I can't say the majority of
clothing in the room was hung on the rack. Much of it was
scattered on the floor. I folded items haphazardly, more to
distinguish them from the stuff I hadn't yet fingered than to
make things neater. I searched shirts and sweaters, summer
tees, dungarees, cutoffs, read penciled notes to girlfriends,
homework reminders, a history quiz graded C+.

What did Paolina do with stuff she didn't want her mother
to see? I'd expected a hidden stash of secret items at my house,
but I'd already been through the bedroom she uses two nights a
week and found it disappointingly bare, although pretty
enough on the surface, with bright posters of Colombia on the
rose-colored walls.

Colombia . . . where guerrilla troops shot down coca-
spraying crop-dusters. When Paolina ran off before, it was a
single half-assed effort, a kid's fairy-tale journey to meet her
long-lost dad, to find the father she'd never met. She'd made
it as far as the airport. I'd found her there, crying in a toilet
stall. Was Colombia still her dream, her father a martyred
hero despite his unsavory reputation?

I had a photo of the man, Carlos Roldán Gonzales, cut
from an aged copy of *Newsweek,* folded in a bureau drawer.
It was a group shot, five men, high mountains in the background. The caption listed five names, all leaders of drug
cartels. They'd been photographed brandishing automatic

weapons, young and defiant. At least three of the five were
dead now.

The small four-drawer pine dresser was packed to overflowing, the top drawer devoted to old birthday cards, post-
cards, bits of wrapping paper and ribbon. I fumbled inside
and came out with a hard Plexiglas cube. A music box. I
twisted the silver key and listened to the raggedy metallic
melody—"Teddy Bears' Picnic," a tune I always associate
with the gruff, bluesy vocals of Dave Van Ronk. I remembered Paolina winding the key and stomping her feet to the
rhythm till the people in the downstairs apartment started
smacking the ceiling with a broom handle. I swallowed and
inhaled the scent of stale cologne.

Second drawer: underwear and scarves. Third drawer: socks
and tights jammed in with smelly sweaters. Bottom drawer:
stuff. Old gift boxes and school notebooks from the fourth
grade. Class photos. A pair of holey socks. A beaded bracelet
with half the beads fallen off. Going through the bottom drawer
felt like excavating an old cache. This wasn't where she stored
her current treasures, and there was no sign of her backpack. I
couldn't tell from the disorganized drawers whether underwear
was missing or not. I didn't see her favorite sweater, but she
could have left it at a friend's house or in her locker.

A flickering shadow on the drapes told me someone was
watching. I turned and found Marta standing in the doorway.
She'd changed into a short cranberry-colored skirt, a tight
print blouse with a low-cut V. Her face was carefully made
up; eyeliner dark around shadowed eyes.

"You done yet?"

"Marta, let me make you a cup of coffee."

"I have to go."

I raised an eyebrow. Her job doesn't start till late afternoon and she knows I know it.

"I have a hair appointment," she said.

"What time?"

"I thought if I get there early, maybe they can do my
nails." The excuse sounded lame even as she gave it. "I
guess I— You want coffee, I'll make it."

I followed her into the kitchen, thinking that I couldn't possibly choke down more caffeine, thinking that maybe if I sat in a chair with a coffee cup in front of me, she wouldn't be so quick to toss me out the door, thinking I needed to ask questions she wasn't going to want to answer. I watched while she flicked on the burner under the kettle, quickly rinsed two ceramic mugs in the sink, and plunked teaspoons of instant coffee into them.

"It's all I have, this powdered stuff. You'd probably rather have tea," she said.

"Instant's fine."

She gave me a look. I suppose she feels constantly criticized by me in the same way I feel constantly criticized by her; we'd made choices about our lives as different as our preference in clothing, as different as our hair and makeup. I tried small talk, commenting on the nasty weather, anything I could find to set her at ease, reminding myself that at bottom we were both women who loved the same child.

"Maybe she's better off on her own," Marta said as she sat, unable to find sugar or milk, angry with me for the shambles of her kitchen.

"She's fifteen."

"When I'm her age, I'm on my own. I'm working all the time, living away from home, making money."

And in no time, pregnant. The way I'd heard the story, she'd been a servant in Paolina's father's house, a uniformed housemaid. Whether it had been a teen love affair or rape, I didn't know. There had been no marriage.

Marta took a quick sip of coffee and placed the cup back on the table with emphasis. "She's like a baby, playing hide-and-seek, that's what I think. And she wants *you* to find her, not me. When she's a real baby, when she's sick on the floor, I'm the one cleans up after her, I'm the one stays home with her, can't find a good job or a new man. And now, now you gonna find her. You gonna step up, be some kind of hero, find her and save her. But I'm the one has to take care of her when nobody else will. I'm the one has to wipe her nose when it runs."

The coffee was lukewarm and grainy, but I didn't care.

She said, "What do you want?"

I want my little girl back. I want this headache to stop. I want to go home and pull the covers over my head. "Just the answers to a few more questions."

No, she didn't know her daughter had broken up with Diego. As far as she knew, or as far as she would admit, there were no new boys, no new friends, no school troubles. I wondered whether mother and daughter ever spoke.

I drank bad coffee.

"Is that all?"

"Marta, are you in touch with her father?"

"With Jimmy, you mean?"

"With Roldán. Have you asked his family for money, done anything that might bring Paolina to their attention?"

"What are you getting at?"

Custodial kidnapping was what I was getting at. Until she was ten years old, my little sister believed her father was the man who'd lived in her house till she was six, the father of her younger brothers, a Puerto Rican drunk named Jimmy Fuentes. Why not believe it? She had his name. And then, at ten, her mother had flown with her to Bogotá, driven to a big house with servants, and presented her to a man she was told to call "Grandpa."

"The Roldán family," I said. "They know about her. Is it possible they took her?"

"The old man's dead." She stared into her cup and I wondered if she was deliberately avoiding my eyes.

"And his son?"

"Dead, too. Even if he's alive, what would he want with a daughter, a man like that, who lives in the hills and hides from the law? He never even saw her. He never tried to get in touch with her."

I didn't contradict her, but I knew her statement wasn't true. Years ago, on five separate occasions, Roldán had sent Paolina money, through me. The Watertown house had been paid for with Roldán's money.

"You haven't tried to get in touch with him?" I repeated.

"I told you. He's dead, as far as I'm concerned."

"Has Paolina said anything about Colombia?"

"We don't talk about it here. She's the boys' sister here."
She stood and walked to the sink, emptying her cup, watching the murky liquid disappear down the drain.

"And you said you still have her passport."

"I said it's here, somewhere." She glanced around the tiny kitchen as if the cupboards and closets had magically appeared out of nowhere, as if she had no knowledge of their contents.

"Marta, have you *seen* her passport since she disappeared?"

"It's here, okay. I'm just not sure where I put it."

"Let's look for it. Now. It's important."

"Don' tell me what's important. What's important is I need to leave here in two minutes." She looked at me with a challenge in her eyes.

I took it. "You have a new man in your life? Somebody you're getting your hair fixed for?"

"What if I do?" she said, stung. "What's wrong with that? I got a right to a life, I think."

"You meet him at work?"

Marta's a part-time hostess at a bar/restaurant called McKinley's, a pickup joint in Waltham.

"So I meet somebody at work, so what? You know it's a good job for that. Nice men, businessmen. Most of them married, but some divorced. This guy's real nice. He's got no ring, and I think maybe it's gonna work out."

"What's his name?"

"Why you wanna know?"

"Have you been seeing him long?"

"A month, maybe. I don't hide him. The boys like him."

"And Paolina?" She hadn't mentioned a new man to me.

Marta's not dim. She makes lightning leaps sometimes and she made one now. Her eyes narrowed. "Wait a minute. You trying to say my boyfriend is doing something with my daughter?"

"Marta, she's gone. Somebody knows something."

"*Not him.* Not me. You can leave anytime. Matter of fact, you can leave now."

"What's the guy's name, Marta?"

"You gonna turn him in to the cops, right? That's gonna make it real nice for me."

"I'm going to make sure he doesn't have a record, Marta. That's all. Better you should know now than later."

I insisted on the name, and desperate to leave, she finally gave me one: Gregor Maltic, but the way she said it I wasn't sure whether that was really the guy she was dating or some waiter at the restaurant she wanted to get in trouble.

"Where's he from?"

"Someplace in Russia, what you think?"

"U.S. citizen?"

That's the sort of thing Marta would always know about a guy she's going out with, what's his citizenship status, how much money he makes, is he married. She wet her lips and said she didn't know.

"Look, I'm gonna be late. They'll take somebody else."

"You go. I'm staying till I find Paolina's passport."

"I don't want you going through my things."

"Then go through them yourself. I'm in no hurry."

"But I don't remember where I put it."

"I'll look in the likely places. I know what I'm doing."

She shot a glance at her bedroom door. "It would be in the kitchen," she said. "Maybe in the living room."

I could almost see her thoughts: Was I planning to search the place for drugs, for evidence that she was an unfit mother? I could see her waver, decide that I was probably more concerned with finding Paolina than with seeing her serve time.

"You're going to be late," I said.

"I want you to leave."

She's stubborn, but so am I. She had something else to do and I didn't, so I won the round. I promised to lock the front door and drop the spare key through the mail chute.

After she left, I took the place apart. I know how many eggs she kept in the fridge, how many pairs of earrings in her jewelry box, how much dust under the beds. I found nothing remarkable till I came across three crisp one-hundred-dollar bills tucked into a cracked sugar bowl on top of the refrigerator. Where had it come from? The new boyfriend? What was it for? Mad money? An emergency stash? If Paolina had planned to run away, if she'd known about the bills, wouldn't she have taken them?

I bit my lip. I could ask Marta, but she certainly wouldn't believe I'd been searching for a passport in her sugar bowl. I wished I knew, say, whether there'd been other large bills, whether a few were missing. But I probably didn't need to ask; Marta would have complained long and loud if Paolina had taken money.

I found two passports in a stack of yellowing travel folders on the third shelf of a linen closet used as a catchall cupboard. Marta's photo smiled and flirted from under a fringe of dark lashes. I checked her birth date and discovered she was barely thirty. She'd given birth to Paolina at fifteen.

Paolina's passport, useless for current identification, expired in two months. She'd been a wide-eyed child when the photo was snapped, a tiny heart-shaped locket around her neck.

I stared at her picture till the image blurred, then replaced it where I'd found it. I left the money in the sugar bowl, returned to the bedroom/laundry room, and removed the little music box from the drawer. I wrapped it in a tiny tank top that smelled of Paolina's favorite cologne, shoved it in my backpack, and took it with me into the frosty afternoon.

I stole it.

CHAPTER 4

GREGOR MALTIC. I ran the name over my tongue as though nationality were some pungent spice I could identify by taste. Could be Russian, like Marta said; New England has a growing Russian immigrant community. Could be Serbian or Bosnian, could be all-American-anything, and what had the man actually done besides have the balls to date Marta? Driving down Huntington Avenue, careening between potholes and icy raised trolley tracks on the way to Boston Police Headquarters, I decided to ask for a background check on Maltic. Why not, when I was planning to call in all my favors at once?

I found the perfect parking place. Legal, on the street, time on the meter; no need to hang a left into a lot where the public parked erratically at best, people heading to the police station not being generally in the mood to fit their vehicle neatly between the white lines. I try to avoid the lot if I can.

I edged the car into the space and cut the engine. And then I sat, staring out the windshield, hoping I hadn't used up any much-needed luck on the parking space, watching slush drip off bare branches and plop onto frozen stands of leafless bushes. A mother and a small child balanced on the swings in the tiny handkerchief park on the corner of Ruggles and Tremont. The kid, dressed in a bright red parka and deep blue gloves, looked like he was having a grand time. The mother's smile looked frozen and determined.

I gave a preparatory shiver and opened the car door. Not so bad, I told myself, lying shamelessly. The sleet came down like a silver curtain and I skidded over the slippery sidewalk to the glass front doors.

The BPD building at One Schroeder Plaza dates from 1997. It cost a cool seventy million, and for the big bucks the architects not only planned a modern glass, granite, and steel facility, they tried to transfer some departmental tradition from the Back Bay to the new Crosstown site. Etched in the stone walls are seventy names of officers killed in the line of duty since 1854. The Roll of Honor includes the Schroeder brothers for whom the site is named.

I'd already visited the Cambridge cops and the Watertown cops. There was no urgent need to declare Paolina missing in yet another city, so I wasn't planning to brace Boston's Missing Persons officer. I was going to visit my old friend, Detective Captain Joseph Mooney. Because Mooney knew Paolina, and Mooney was my former boss. Not only did I owe it to him to let him know, he might be in a position to help.

That was the pep talk I gave myself to push my reluctant body through the door, but I hated the idea of telling him. I'd put it off, hoping I wouldn't need to, hoping I'd find her. Then I'd convinced myself he deserved a visit, not a phone call. Then I'd been busy, and the simple truth was I should have told him right off the bat. He's known Paolina for years; he cares about her.

Another reason my steps were slow: Mooney and I had argued, a doozy of a shouting match not three weeks ago. Not over work; we haven't worked together in years, and when we did we never bickered, not over procedure or respective responsibility or results. We'd argued about my reigniting the flame with Sam Gianelli, about what Mooney refers to as my "continuing involvement" with a mobster. Mooney has long maintained that any man I look at twice is a probable felon, and there's too much truth in the statement for me to find it amusing. The damned argument wasn't funny at all, and we hadn't spoken since.

What the hell gave him the right to pass judgment on my

private life? Just because we'd worked on the same team, shared an occasional drink, because I'd confided in him, treated him like a friend—I shoved the double doors and stepped into the overheated foyer, unzipping my parka and stripping off my gloves.

The first floor lobby looked more like a bank than a cop house. It had customer windows like a bank, with signs directing visitors to Child Care or Public Service. There was a restaurant and a media room. The desk sergeant wouldn't let me go up without phoning first. Used to be, I could just slip up the back stairs. New police commissioner, new building, new procedures. A gate that opened only on command. Elevators that could be stopped and locked down.

It wasn't just that I was reluctant to ask Mooney for help after he'd barged uninvited into my love life. I didn't want to say the damn words out loud: Paolina's disappearance was no longer a matter of her running off with Diego to New York City. Without Diego as accomplice and companion, Paolina's disappearance made no sense, and acknowledging that fact opened my mind to a tabloid fear that swam beneath the surface like a hungry shark. Grainy news photos lurk at the back of every mother's mind, a litany of half-remembered names, skeletons, horrors. There are girls who vanish and never come back, girls whose clean white bones are dug up years later in vacant lots and distant forests.

I jammed the lid on the specters as the elevator doors opened. Second floor. Forensics to the right, Major Cases and Homicide to the left. I turned left and made my way down cool blue-gray carpeting to Mooney's office. He's Head of Homicide, has been for years. Every now and again, the brass threaten to elevate him to Bureau Chief of Investigative Services, but he promptly reminds them how badly he plays the game of interdepartmental politics, and they leave him in peace.

His door was open as usual. He was on the phone, nodding and muttering. Often when I think of him, the image comes with a receiver planted in his ear, a toothpick jutting from the corner of his mouth. Used to be a cigarette, but he keeps trying to reform, and lately it's been a peppermint-flavored toothpick grabbed from one of many eateries scattered around town. I kid him that he chooses his restaurants based on the availability of flavored toothpicks.

His blue broadcloth shirt was tucked into gray pants. The matching jacket hung over the back of the chair in the corner. Made me wonder whether he had a trial date, but no tie, so maybe not, maybe just an afternoon meeting with a bigwig. Mooney doesn't pay attention to clothes; he buys shirts on sale by the half-dozen, and they all look the same. *Not like Sam.*

Why do I always compare the two, even though Moon and I have never been an item? Why do I still think we might be, someday? He's tall, with a linebacker build, a round Irish face, and sad brown eyes. He's not graceful or elegant or drop-dead sexy like Gianelli, but when we worked together, I had to steel myself against him. Lock the door and toss away the key; no way was I going to sleep with the boss. Maybe what's left is simply curiosity, wondering what I missed.

I don't kid myself. One of the reasons I can walk into Moon's office is that the powers that be assume we sleep together. They wink at it, never thinking that Moon might be giving a PI info she shouldn't have. Don't think I don't use the few advantages a woman has in this system. Unfortunately, most of them involve sex or being seriously underrated. I always think the guys will learn, but they don't.

Mooney never had to be taught. Not by me. I never got along with his mother, but she did something right with her boy. Mooney and I can work together.

Could work together. Used to work together. I sucked in a breath. He needed to know what was going on, but I was reluctant to offer up yet another aspect of my life for criticism.

His office was as impersonal as ever. If you went by Moon's decor, you'd think there was an injunction from on high: no posters, no photos, no plants. You'd think he had no bossy mom, no self-involved long-distance sisters, no ex-wife. He swiveled his chair abruptly, as though sensing my scrutiny.

"What? No food?" he said, replacing the receiver. No hello, no smile, still annoyed about Sam. "What do you think you're gonna worm out of me, you don't even bring me a doughnut as a peace offering?"

Add a stop at a Dunkin' Donuts to the twenty other things I should have done and didn't. I sank into his spindly guest chair and closed my eyes for an instant, hoping that when I opened them again they'd focus clearly.

Mooney's voice broke through the fog. "What's wrong?"

Just blurt it out, I ordered myself. "Paolina. She's gone, and I don't know where else to—"

"Whoa, whoa— Gone? Her and Marta? The whole family?"

"Just her. Went to school Friday, went to a party Friday night, and nobody's seen her since." There. The words were out; harsh, bald, and ugly. *Nobody's seen her.*

He put his pen down carefully on the desk, as gently as if both desk and pen were made of glass. "Carlotta, it's Wednesday." Which meant: Why didn't you tell me sooner?

"I'm sorry, Moon. I didn't find out till Monday night. Marta assumed Paolina was with me; I don't know why. I wasn't supposed to see her last weekend. Then I thought—I *assumed* she was with Diego, her boyfriend. Took me till this morning to track him down. He doesn't know where she is." It cost me, using "assumed" to describe what I'd done; assuming anything is a cardinal sin in an investigation.

"Is he telling the truth?"

Not, "Do you think he's telling the truth?" Moon still trusted my judgment in matters unrelated to romance. I pictured the kid's lumpy broken nose, the hurt in his eyes.

"He didn't know she was gone." I wondered briefly whether *I* still trusted my judgment. "They broke up Friday night."

"Give me his name."

I spelled it out, gave his aunt's name and address as well, told Moon everything that had gone down at Josefina Parte's apartment. He made notes.

"So the kid might already be in the system," he said. "Name of the guy who hit him?"

"I didn't get it."

"You didn't think he was a player."

I shook my head. "A two-bit bully."

He said, "Okay, what lines are you following?"

"I've done a Missing Persons in Cambridge and Watertown. Gloria's got the cabbie-network looking. Roz is interviewing high-school kids. Kinko's is running off copies of a photo. I've called at least fifty shelters. I'm planning to visit the locals this afternoon, but—"

"What are you trying to say, Carlotta?"

"Her favorite jeans are in the closet at my place. Her best boots. Her toothbrush is in the bathroom."

"A toothbrush is easy to replace."

"Yeah, but Mooney—all those things, what do they add up to? If I hadn't known about Diego, fastened on Diego—"

His eyes flickered. "You're thinking she didn't run. That she was taken?"

I nodded, grateful he hadn't made me say the words.

"Okay, Carlotta, let's get this straight. You're saying that if this were a client, if Marta came to you with this, and you didn't know Marta, that's what you'd think?"

"Shit, Mooney, I *do* know Marta. Matter of fact, that's something you can do. Marta's got a new man, a guy named Gregor Maltic. Can you run the name, see if he's got a record?" I was avoiding his question. I knew it; he knew it, but he just passed me a sheet of paper and asked me to print the name.

I didn't know the answer to the question because it was Paolina, because it was Marta, because I wasn't objective about any of this. I was flat-out scared.

He said, "Okay, how else can I help? Let's do a full-court press on this. You check the buses, the trains, the airlines?"

The word "help" shifted the knot in my throat and suddenly I could talk more freely. "I did buses, Roz did trains, Lemon hit the ticket counters with a photo. Gloria phoned the airlines. Lemon handled Logan, too. Paolina wasn't holding a reservation."

"I'll get somebody to check passenger lists."

She was smart enough to use an alias. Mooney knew that as well as I did. I knew without asking that he'd extend the search to similar names, to Paula Fords and Patsy Fines.

He pressed his lips together and stared at the phone. "School locker?"

"I'm on my way to check it now."

"She have a credit card? Cash?"

"No card. I don't have any idea how much cash, but she can't get into our joint account without me, and Marta's not missing any money."

"You tracing calls?"

I nodded. "Number ID on my phone and Marta's."

"Good, that's good."

"But if she calls my cell . . ."

"Yeah," he said, "damn cells. She calls you there you gotta find a way to talk her in."

"Moon, there haven't even been hang-ups. I'm doing everything I can think of—"

"Now we'll do everything the both of us can think of."

"Thanks."

He looked away, rubbing his jawline like he was checking to see whether he'd remembered to shave. He used to use the gesture in interrogations, right before springing a tough question on a suspected perp.

"Carlotta," he said quietly, "did the two of you fight?"

"Jeez, Mooney, I'd have told you if—"

"What about Gianelli?"

"What *about* him?" I snapped the question off, jaw tight. Mooney didn't reply right away, just stared at me, waiting.

"Mooney, Sam and Paolina get along fine."

"Yeah, Carlotta, that's exactly what I'm saying. You ever think that somebody who wants his own back with Gianelli—and that list's gonna run to a couple hundred creeps—might take it out on you or the kid?"

I was shaking my head before he finished the sentence. "Sam's not—"

"Please, Carlotta, don't tell me what he is. You asked me to check out this Gregor Maltic, right? Just because he's seeing Marta? Find out what kinda stuff he's into? Well, I don't have to run any check on Gianelli to know he's big trouble. I hear things that keep me up nights."

"Mooney—" I held up a hand to stop him, but I guess he'd been hanging on to what he wanted to say so long he couldn't control the flow once the dam broke.

"This old-school North End Boston Mafia crap is over, Carlotta. This isn't some *Godfather* movie with family loyalty and old men kissing each others' rings. It's big fish chomping little ones, and the Boston Mob is small-time, always has been. New York's coming to town, and Miami, too. Believe me, Gianelli couldn't get a life insurance policy from Lloyd's of London. And you want me to check on *Maltic,* see if *he's* trouble?"

I sucked in a deep breath and stood. My head was pounding again and I had to make an effort to keep my voice level. "Look, I just came to let you know what's going on, to say I appreciate anything you can do."

"Ask Gianelli what he knows about contract killers from Miami. Ask *him* where Paolina is."

Contract killers from Miami? I tried to swallow, but the lump was back in my throat. "He doesn't know where she is."

"How come you think he's telling you the truth, Carlotta? You tell him from me, if he knows anything about this he's not telling—"

"That's enough, Moon. I'm sorry I—"

"Oh? You think that's enough?"

More than enough, I thought. *Stop,* I thought.

"Then you didn't come here to ask if I'd found any Jane Doe teens these past few days?"

I stared at the same blue-gray carpet that ran down the hallway. There were scuff marks near the corner of his desk. A phone rang several offices away, once, twice, three times.

"I'm sorry, Carlotta. That was out of line, and I'm sorry." His hand was on my shoulder before I realized he'd moved from behind his desk. "Look, give me her picture so I can fax it around. You must have something more recent than this."

His top desk drawer was open; he must have removed the

photo from the drawer. He'd not only kept, but framed Paolina's school shot from two years ago. Why keep a framed photo in a drawer? I thought as I handed him a wallet-sized update.

"I'll messenger a bigger one once we get the copies."

I could have saved my breath. I don't think he heard me. He was staring at the photo, taking in the changes, eyeing the sleek hair, the curve of a breast in the V of the low-cut blouse, the kohl-rimmed eyes.

"God," he said, "nobody's gonna buy her being underage."

"She's fifteen, Mooney."

"How the hell did that happen?" he said, shaking his head from side to side, as though denial could stop time in its tracks.

As though anything could.

CHAPTER 5

I MADE IT to my car as quickly as the icy sidewalk would allow, beating out a meter reader by a good ten seconds, shoving the keys at the ignition while trying to simultaneously slam the door and eyeball my watch. Didn't work; the keys flew out of my hand and came to rest on the floor at my feet, and then I was leaning my forehead on the steering wheel, blinking to hold back tears, praying the meter maid wouldn't notice and haul me out of the car for a Breathalyzer test.

Damn Mooney anyway. He hadn't quizzed me about any crazed felons I'd nailed when I was a cop, any goon recently freed from prison and hungering for revenge. No, he'd gone straight for the jugular, straight for Sam Gianelli. And damn Sam for not saying a word about any work-related troubles. But how could I damn him for not telling me what I'd expressly said I didn't want to hear?

I fumbled on the floor mat till my hand found the keys. Studied my watch in disbelief. There are times when the clock moves slowly and times when it speeds; it had sprinted for the finish line while I was closeted with Mooney. I'd be hard-pressed to meet Roz at the high school. I ran a hand through my hair and promised myself time for a full-blown breakdown at a later date. The meter maid was watching, her face carefully blank. I gave her a smile that must have looked more like a grimace and gunned the engine.

Cutting behind the Museum School, speeding down Fenway to Park Drive, I tried to outrace what Mooney had said about Sam. And failed. I'd need to talk to him, mention the unmentionable. I couldn't avoid the consequences of my actions any more than Josefina Parte could—or Marta Fuentes, for that matter. Across the BU Bridge, traffic crawled on Putnam Street. The question wasn't whether anyone was crazy enough to take their hatred for Sam out on Paolina; people are loony enough to hijack airplanes and shoot up their local elementary schools. A line of cars waited to cross Mass. Ave. at Putnam Circle, delayed by semi-frozen pedestrians darting suicidally across the street against the light.

Cambridge Rindge and Latin, a huge concrete bunker located next to the public library, has been remodeled and restructured and redesigned so many times I never know what to expect when I walk past the metal detectors. Those, I expect. And the smell of chalk dust, unwashed bodies, wet sneakers; the smell manages to stay the same.

Quarter to three. I sucked in a deep breath. Where had the long hours gone? The bell had chimed to end the day; the kids had fled, loosed into the community. One had left a backpack and a torn blue sweater at the curb, lying in a heap like a forlorn abandoned pet. They weren't Paolina's; her backpack is worn and red. Someone else, or maybe the same careless teen, had left a battered French horn case on the front stoop.

Roz was in the lobby, sipping from a steaming Styrofoam cup, sitting on a bench with her knees drawn up, staring at nothing while two loitering teenage boys watched her out of the corners of their eyes, trying to look up her skirt. She wore ripped black tights, high-heeled boots, a short red wool skirt, and a low-cut plum-colored top that clung to her breasts like paint. Her hair was silvery white, her lipstick deep purple. A silver stud pierced her left nostril. When she saw me, she lowered her legs, and the boys averted their gaze. Slowly she got to her feet and wandered in my direction. I kept walking. We strolled past the principal's office, turned a corner, and stopped near a deserted stairwell.

"I dunno." She shook her head slowly, frowning. "These kids, man, like to them, I'm *old*. I'm not sure they're dealing straight up with me."

"The dudes in the lobby thought you were hot," I said to comfort her, and the thought cheered her enough to give me what little she had. Aurelia Gutierrez, Paolina's best friend, insisted that Paolina hadn't said word one about running away. The truant officer, recently returned to duty, was clueless, an old townie more eager to reminisce about other missing kids who'd eventually turned up than reveal anything about current cases. Paolina's homeroom teacher had treated Roz to a lecture on school overcrowding, Proposition 2½, and local property taxes, his way of saying he had too many kids to grade, much less monitor for quality of life.

"Get back to Aurelia; go for gossip. Any point in me talking to the homeroom guy?" I was thinking maybe he hadn't responded positively to Roz's outfit.

"You need a lecture, go right ahead." She glanced at the back of her hand where numerals were scrawled in bright blue ink. "I got her locker number: 2336. The bastard wouldn't open it, so I pled my case with the janitor. Read me the riot act on First Amendment rights."

Where else but Cambridge can you find a janitor in touch with the First Amendment? "When does he go home?" I asked.

She shrugged. "You know the kind of guy, looks like he lives here. Oh, yeah, I got the flyers. Guy at Kinko's said it was his third missing-kid sheet this week."

It was going to come to that, sticking her picture up on street signs and telephone poles, on community bulletin boards in Shaw's and Whole Foods, like a lost dog. I tried not to think about all those kids with their faces on the backs of milk cartons.

I said, "Where's the janitor now?"

"I told you, he's not gonna—"

"Find him and stay with him, come on to him, whatever. I'm gonna do her locker and I don't want interruptions."

"Bust the lock?" she said eagerly.

"Keep him occupied."

Locker 2336 was on the second floor down a long hallway of locker-lined walls broken by classroom doorways. The linoleum gleamed underfoot, and the low hum of a polisher buzzed along an intersecting corridor. The tubby janitor had his back toward me as he shoved the machine, heading away from my destination with a long path yet to shine. If he was the same janitor who'd given Roz the legal two-step, I hoped she'd have the brains to let him work.

I'd transferred a pry bar from the car trunk to my backpack, just in case, and I was tempted to use it simply because it would have felt good, the exertion, the satisfaction of twisting metal. I hadn't played volleyball or gone swimming at the Y, hadn't gotten any of the physical exercise I normally get, and I could feel tension knotting my neck and shoulders. I regretted the pry bar as I manipulated the lock, but there was no need for it. You're a PI and you can't bust a school locker without a bar, it's time to find a new racket.

My cell rang, and I grabbed it, willing Paolina's voice, hoping the janitor hadn't heard the sound.

"Dinner?" Sam's baritone. "We could try the Harvest."

Not Paolina. I tried not to let either disappointment or accusation seep into my response. "I don't think I'll have time."

"You haven't found her?"

"No. Sam—"

"You gotta eat—"

I might have to stuff fuel down my throat, but there was no way I could see myself sitting at a white-tablecloth restaurant poring over a menu. "This isn't a great time to talk." I'd follow up on Mooney's idea later; I had the locker to crack now.

"You think I oughta talk to Marta? She might—"

"Sam, no. I appreciate it, but . . ." He believes women confide in him. What they do—what Marta does, anyway— is flirt with him. She'd shoot the breeze all night, tell him anything he wanted to hear.

"Let me do *something*," he said.

I closed my eyes and listened to the faint hum of the polishing machine. Should I ask whether some organized crime hit man might have snatched my little sister? Instead I said, "Marta's got a new guy named Gregor Maltic." I spelled it. "You might—"

"I'll see if anybody knows him. And you gotta sleep, right, so I'll come by later."

He hung up before I had time to reply. Plenty of time to ask about Mob-related complications tonight, I figured, so I stowed the phone and opened the locker as noiselessly as possible, imagining my little sister's hand, warm on the same metal, less than a week ago.

The first thing that hit me was the smell, a combination of scents, floral, citrusy, musky, overwhelming. Lined on the top shelf, a row of tiny bottles and flasks glittered: perfume, cologne, and toilet water. My little sister started collecting cosmetic-counter giveaways at the age of eight. Probably a line of girls at her locker each morning, begging to borrow the latest fragrance.

A pink sweatshirt on a hook, a brief tie-dyed tee beneath it, stuff she'd have worn in early fall when it was still warm. A plastic bag held gym clothes, navy shorts and a white shirt, wrinkled and smelly.

The hall lighting was dim. I got a flashlight from my backpack, took every item out of the lower part of the locker and placed it on the floor for further inspection, fighting against the rising conviction that there was nothing to find, that I was wasting my time, that she'd been snatched randomly off the street. I unrolled a pair of socks and shook them out. I unfolded pages of lined three-hole paper to discover rough drafts of homework assignments, reassembled a sheet that had been ripped to pieces to find a "D" on a quiz for act 2, scene 2 of *Julius Caesar*. Used spiral notebooks, broken pens. Where was her backpack? If she was using it as a suitcase, I'd have expected to find her textbooks abandoned somewhere. They weren't at my house. They weren't at the Watertown house. They weren't here.

I aimed the flashlight beam into the back corner of the locker floor, then the rear of the high shelf behind the row of perfume vials. Something was jammed in the back corner, an envelope, maybe. I didn't want to knock over all the scent bottles, so I took each container out, one by one, placing them on the floor in a rickety row. A few more scraps of paper, scrunched exams, discarded attempts at essays. I reached into the corner recess, touched cloth, and withdrew a small drawstring bag made of rough brown felt.

It was maybe three inches by four, with a thin brown cord gathered tightly at the top, and pinked edges. The bottom of the pouch felt lumpy. I tugged at the top edges to spread the cord, held the sack in my right hand, and spilled the contents into my left. Something tumbled out, wrapped tightly in white tissue paper.

Pills, I thought, powder, but the shape was stiff and unyielding. I put my back to a neighboring locker, bent my knees, and slid to the floor, catching the pouch in my lap while my hands fumbled with the tissue.

Ornamental, some kind of jewelry, a pin, maybe, but no—I turned it over with careful fingertips—there was no clasp on the back of the small gold shape. It was an odd shape, whimsical, unusual.

It was gold, or gold-colored, but not the kind of gold usually seen in jewelry. More of a red-gold, an assertive gold. Not much shine to it, but depth. For its size, it felt heavy. It was the form of a man or, possibly, the more I gazed at it, a bird. The tiny body had two rows of raised ornamental ridges. The outspread arms, or wings, were arched. The head was triangular and a beak-like nose protruded beneath bulbous eyes. The areas that weren't raised were smooth. The figure was symmetrical, but not perfectly so, as though it had been made by hand, possibly hammered. The back side looked less finished than the front, the beak-like nose a hollow void.

Face up, the protruding eyes looked blind. The face belonged to something not quite human and not quite animal. I was still peering at it, running my fingers over the metal when Roz interrupted with news that, with the janitor safely drinking coffee at a nearby store counter, she'd raised Aurelia on the phone: the gossip thing hadn't panned out, what now?

I displayed the little birdman.

"Hey, cool." She whistled softly and held out a scarlet-taloned hand. I was reluctant to part with the figure, but she didn't seem to sense my hesitation, and grabbed it eagerly. Staring at it closely, nose to beak, she traced the ornamental ridges with a fingertip. "Looks pre-Columbian. Not Mayan, though. Definitely not Mayan."

Roz calls herself a post-punk artist, and from the acrylic oddities she paints, you can't really tell she's educated in the arts. Slowly, over the years, the truth has emerged: She's studied at some very classy places, the MFA School and Pratt included. Never hung around long enough to get a degree.

I said, "Colombian." I guess I gave it the Spanish long *o* pronunciation. That's what I was thinking: Colombia, the country, Paolina's birthplace.

"Pre-Columbian," Roz corrected. "That's before Columbus hit America. With the *u*, not the *o*. But they got plenty of pre-Columbian stuff in Colombia, shit that was there before the Europeans invaded. Most pre-Columbian gold is South American."

"This is gold?"

She stroked it with her small fingers. "I think so. Some kind of blend of copper and gold. I knew about it when I made jewelry; it'll come to me."

I stuck my hand out. She ignored it.

"Can I have it back?"

She glared at me frostily. "I wasn't gonna steal it." But her hands seemed as reluctant as mine had been to give it up. "Where'd you get it? Is it Paolina's?"

I bit my lip. I'm not sure how long I sat like that, the little birdman warm in my palm.

"We going to the Pit or what?" Roz was staring at me oddly. "Aren't we supposed to go there next, hand out flyers?"

When they extended the Red Line and redesigned the Harvard Square MBTA station, someone had the bright idea of making the entryway inviting, with a circular plaza surrounded by stone benches. If the powers that be had foreseen the actual use the plaza would be put to, the architect would have been drawn and quartered; I doubt the City Council wanted to attract the homeless, the druggies, the unemployed and unemployable, seeking to get high. Teens converge there, townies mainly, but a sprinkling of college kids, the ones who don't quite fit in or can't afford the freight at the trendy cafés. You can buy just about anything at the Pit. The older men come out late at night, especially when it's cold, because after midnight the barter gets serious, shelter for food and sex. Runaways throng there.

I looked into the birdman's blank eyes and shook my head. "Help me repack the locker. Then you can handle the Pit on your own." She'd do fine solo, distributing the flyers, questioning the misfits.

Normally Roz would have pounced on any change of plans, demanding to know why I'd changed my mind. She's gotten interested in the investigation racket and thinks she might try it on her own someday. Something in my eyes must have stopped her. She quickly gathered perfume vials and dirty clothes and dumped them back in the locker.

I wrapped the gold birdman in the wrinkled tissue and stowed him in his felt pouch, thinking pre-Columbian, South American, Colombian. Thinking goddamn Marta didn't say a word about this. Thinking she'd be at work by the time I got there.

CHAPTER 6

IF A COP had been patrolling Mt. Auburn Street or Trapelo Road, lurking unseen behind a billboard or liquor store, I'd have gotten the chance to lead a cruiser on a high-speed chase. The traffic police were busy elsewhere, so I exceeded the speed limit and charged through amber lights unimpeded.

It may not be true that Waltham bars have gotten busier since Cambridge and Boston caught no-smoking fever, but you couldn't prove it by the early crowd at McKinley's. The place hadn't been open more than forty-five minutes and already the haze of smoke over the L-shaped bar was as thick as a low-hanging cloud. From her station at the hostess stand, Marta glanced at the door, a welcoming smile firmly in place. When she saw me, the smile froze and her hands dropped the square of stiff red cloth she'd been folding. Crumpled, the napkin lay on the scratched wooden floor like a puddle of blood.

"You can't bother me here; I'm working!" Her heels clacked furiously as she approached, and her whisper attracted the attention of drinkers at the tables dotted to the right of the bar. She wore the same short skirt she'd set off in this morning, but she had yanked her top down to expose bare shoulders. Her hair swung like a heavy curtain around her face. The blonde streaks were new.

I don't know. If my daughter were missing, I might skip the blow-dry. If my daughter were missing and the woman looking for her showed up unannounced at my place of business, I might ask after the child's welfare. I tried to get my face to relax, but I don't think I managed a smile.

I was a cop long enough to learn that the surface doesn't reflect the inner core. I've interrogated distraught suspects who turned out to be complete innocents and cool-as-ice liars who were felons from the toenails up. I've been alive long enough to know that appearances lie. When I was sixteen, everybody thought I was doing so well after my mother's death, so damn well, right up until the night I jumped a bus and left town.

"Take a break," I suggested.

We glared at each other for an instant; then she snatched the fallen napkin off the floor and slapped it down on a tabletop. "What? You find something?"

She was worried about what I'd seen at her house. Hastily I reviewed the search. I'd been so focused on finding the passport. What had I missed?

"Let me buy you a drink," I said.

The place was dark the way daytime bars are dark, with the artificial dimness of heavy shades over small windows and minimal overhead light. I watched her eyes to see whether she signaled to any of the waitstaff, any of the customers. It was too early for a bouncer.

She turned abruptly and her heels pocked the floor again. She murmured something to the bartender, a rangy blond who shot me a quick glance. Then she grabbed a tray, two glasses, two bottles of Bud, and ferried them to a corner booth. I followed and slid onto a saggy leather bench.

She sat across from me. I waited, sipping beer without tasting it, rerunning a mental tape of the house search: kitchen, den, bedroom, closet. *Closet.* I reviewed the clothing in Marta's closet, item by item, the stuffed racks, the dangling tags.

Sometimes, you wait long enough, a perp will get so uncomfortable he'll spill his guts; Marta held up well.

"Your hair looks good," I said, deciding she'd sit silently till her blonde streaks faded. "Nice earrings."

"These? These are—".

"They're new. Like a lot of the clothes in your closet."

"So? I buy a few things. I work hard. What're you doing?"

Spreading my napkin on the table like a place mat, I emptied the brown felt pouch and unwrapped the tissue paper. The tiny statue caught the light.

"I never seen it before," she said quickly.

Up till that moment, I hadn't been sure, but she was so immediately defensive it was clear she was lying. As soon as the words left her lips, she realized her mistake; they must have rung as tinnily false to her ears as they did to mine.

I sucked in a deep breath, desperate for a cigarette. After six long years of good behavior, the beer and the smoke had triggered a deep longing in my lungs. Besides, if I had something to hold in my right hand, it might stop clenching.

"A father has a right to send a gift to his daughter, I think," Marta said defiantly.

I took another sip of tasteless beer, the glass icy in my hand. I replaced it on the table, in the exact center of the wet circle it had left on the wooden top. I remembered her downcast eyes when I'd asked her whether she was in touch with Roldán's family. Assuming he was dead, I'd never asked if she'd been in touch with Roldán himself. There it was again, that ugly word: assuming.

With effort, I kept my voice soft and uninflected. "Okay, Marta, when did he get in touch? How? Did he write? Did he call?"

No response.

"He sent you money, right? *Did you sell her, for chrissake?*"

"Hey, you watch what you say!"

"Any trouble?" The bartender barely raised his voice. A couple of men at the bar gave me the evil eye.

"It's okay," she said, tossing him a forced smile. Then she refocused on me, lowering her voice. "Don't go getting me in trouble here. I lose my job, I'll kill you."

"Come on, Marta, talk to me."

"What's the big deal? I don't know nothing about where she is. All I know is he writes me a letter, maybe eight, nine months ago, says how he's sorry for not taking care of me better. Is nice, no? After fifteen years, he remembers he gave me a little something to remember him by." She made a bitter sound, half laugh, half grunt.

"You have the letter?"

"Why would I keep it? I don't still have the money he sent, either."

No? I thought. Not even a little bit, in a sugar bowl? "How much?" I asked.

"You think I'm folding napkins in a bar and I'm a millionaire? He send a couple hundred, a couple hundred when he's got millions stashed away, maybe billions."

There'd been three hundred in the sugar bowl, but the real question was why send Marta a dime? When I'd last spoken to Roldán, he'd said he never wanted to deal with her again. They told different tales concerning their brief time together. Knowing Marta, I'd been willing to take his word for it. Now I reminded myself that just because one side is lying doesn't mean the other is telling the truth.

"Marta, this can come out in dribs and drabs, take all night, and cost you your job. Why not start at the beginning, tell me what you know, and I'll leave you alone?"

She pressed her lips together and considered how to spin the story so she'd come out looking good. A skinny man got up from his barstool and fed fifty cents into the jukebox. Marta, the good hostess, beamed at him to keep in practice, and the speakers blared the opening bars of an oldie named "Sweet Caroline." I'd never heard it sung by anybody but drunken baseball fans at Fenway Park. I preferred it that way.

She leaned back in her chair and regarded me coolly. "I get a letter, like I say, signed Carlito. I used to call him that. There's a couple bills tucked inside, and he asks can he send a few things to his girl. Paolina, he means. After that, the letters are only for her. Personal and private."

I didn't believe for a minute that Marta hadn't read them.

She held the little birdman up to the dim light. "If he sent her this, I never saw it. You know, the mail, it gets to the house so late I'm already on the way to work. Most girls, you know, they get a present, they show it to their mother, but she likes to keep secrets. She's a sly one. Always, she's like that, even when she's a baby."

I knew her before you did. I know her better than you do. Sooner or later every conversation we've ever had comes down to that.

"Do you know what it is?" I held out my hand to reclaim the figure.

"It's pretty," she said, placing it reluctantly in my palm. "Just some little thing. I don't know what you call it."

"So you're telling me you got one letter, a couple hundred bucks, and that's it? You weren't curious. You didn't want more? You didn't write back—"

"You think there's a return address or something?" she said angrily. "There's nothing. Roldán calls the shots, like always."

"There was a postmark."

"Miami. Yeah, big deal."

"You didn't tell anybody you'd heard from him?"

"Who's to tell?"

"How many times did he write to Paolina? How often?"

"You mean she didn't run and tell you all about it?"

I moistened my lips. The bar was too quiet, the jukebox silent now, the clientele too interested in our discussion. I caught the bartender's eye and nodded at the TV screen. He upped the volume on a sports news show and the customers' eyes flickered to the screen.

"Okay, Marta," I said, "this happened months ago, right?"

"Right." Her eyes flickered, just a sideways glance at the surface of the table, just a slight aversion to meeting my eyes.

"But something happened more recently, this week, last week?"

Silence.

"Marta, don't you want to get back to work? Bartender's doing a good job greeting people. They might realize they don't need you."

She glared at me, the mascara so thick on her lashes, I wondered if she could feel the heavy goo. "It's nothing."

"Marta! Just tell me."

"Okay, okay, when the lady calls from Carlito and asks can he have her picture, I go along. What's so wrong with that?"

"What lady? *What picture?*"

"Hey, let go, you're hurting me."

I wasn't sure when I'd caught her arm, but she was right; my fingers were fastened like tentacles to her wrist. The rage that had growled behind my eyes ever since I'd left the crummy apartment on Orchard Court Road pounded at my temples. There was movement behind me, to my right, quick footsteps from soft-soled shoes.

"No cat fights, ladies." The bartender's hand was heavy on my shoulder; maybe he doubled as the bouncer.

When I smiled up at him, it felt more like baring my teeth. I forced my hand to let go of Marta. "It's just business," I said. "I'm working for her, looking for her daughter."

I waited to see whether Marta would deny it. Her lips parted, closed, then parted again, her tongue pale against her dark lipstick. "Is okay, Greg."

"Gregor Maltic?"

"Yeah."

A broad gold wedding band circled the third finger of his left hand. A rich unmarried customer. Right.

"You two go out together?" I asked him.

"So?" Cool blue eyes in a broad Slavic face. Narrow shoulders and hips. He wore a thin white shirt and khaki pants, but I didn't know whether that was a job requirement or a fashion choice.

"None of my business," I said, "unless you happen to know where her daughter is."

"Then it's none of your business. Why don't you get the hell out of here, stop pestering the lady?"

I found myself contemplating assault for the second time in a single day. I could stomp his toe with a booted foot, land a hard one in his gut. Spend the night in jail. Accomplish nothing. With effort, I turned away, leveling my gaze at my little sister's mother. Gregor Maltic locked eyes with Marta, then measured eight long steps toward the bar.

"Okay," I said, "a woman phoned you. What was her name?"

"She didn't say. She was calling for Roldán, like a secretary or something. She didn't say much, just could I leave a photo of Paolina in the mailbox, and she'll come by and pick it up." Her right arm rested on the table. There were angry marks where I'd grabbed her wrist.

"What did she look like?"

"How am I supposed to know? You think I got a phone with pictures?"

"You never saw her?"

"The photo was gone, so she came okay. I'm a busy woman. I work. I don't stay home all the time."

No need to ask whether the unseen woman had paid for Paolina's photo. Three hundred-dollar bills in the sugar bowl.

"And when Paolina disappeared, you never mentioned this?" I said flatly.

"Why would I? A woman calls for a picture, that's all. What's the harm in a woman?"

What's the harm in a stranger demanding a photograph of a teenage girl? I opened my mouth to ask which planet she lived on; I wanted to call her a stupid bitch, smack her across her lipsticked mouth.

"*Paolina ran away,*" she said, like it was written in neon letters ten feet high, obvious and undeniable. "She ran away with some boy she's screwing, some no-account nothing. She's never home when she should be, she don' care about her brothers, she don' even do the dishes right. She's—"

How I made it outside without doing grievous bodily harm to the woman, I don't know, but I didn't linger to hear the end of her tirade. I pushed my way out of the booth, leaving the beer, escaping the cigarette smog, and I was in the frigid parking lot fumbling for my keys before I remembered to put on my coat.

CHAPTER 7

"**SO THE WAY** you figure, the woman who got the photo from Marta grabbed Paolina?" Sam's sleepy murmur was soft in my ear.

"Acting for Roldán. That's what I think." Beside him, wrapped in a cocoon of wrinkled sheets, I was warm at last, but wide awake and way too uneasy to sleep. I'd assumed Paolina was with Diego. *Wrong.* I'd assumed Roldán was dead. *Wrong.*

"Just because this woman used Roldán's name on the phone." The way he said it, he might as well have said: *Don't you think you're snatching at straws?* Maybe I was, I thought. Maybe I am.

"Why would Roldán want her?" Now Sam sounded like he was thinking out loud.

"She's his daughter," I said.

"But why now?"

"Why write Marta? Why send her presents? After all these years?" The long and the short of it was I didn't know. I didn't know why. I didn't know why *now*. I only knew this: If she'd been taken by someone *other* than Roldán, I had nothing; I was nowhere. I'd run out of leads. I'd have to wait for the phone to ring. For a knock at the door.

Sam's breath ruffled my hair. "You told the cops about all this, the woman, the photo, the statue?"

"Yes." I'd gotten Mooney involved first, then the Cambridge PD, goading them till they'd changed the label on Paolina's disappearance from runaway to possible kidnapping. "Possible" was as far as they'd go.

"The feds?" He sounded casual enough, but the muscles in his arm tightened and I remembered Mooney's warning.

"The locals don't like to bring them in unless there's a ransom demand, but Mooney's going to get them to sign on tomorrow, no matter what."

Unless something else turns up, the older of the Cambridge cops had said, nodding his head so his double chin wobbled.

What the hell else could turn up? I'd thought. The chill had penetrated clear to the bone when I'd realized he meant her body. Paolina. Dead.

"The FBI will want to talk to you," Sam said. "Tomorrow."

Hell with them, I thought; I've worked with the feebies before. I had a pretty good idea how skeptical they'd be, how slowly they'd proceed. Two weeks of paperwork and the trail would be as cold as the slush on Orchard Park Court.

"You never know with family," Sam said. "Maybe Roldán's been keeping an eye on her."

It was possible. Roldán once hired a PI to check up on me. Maybe he didn't like the way Marta was raising her. Maybe he didn't like the way I'd been ignoring her.

"It's not your fault," Sam said. "Stop doing this to yourself."

"What?"

"You're yanking your hair out."

It's true; I pull my hair. There's a fancy name for it: trichotillomania; rolls right off the tongue. I do it when I feel rotten about something I've done or haven't done. It's an addictive behavior, a named illness. Now I was indulging the demon because I felt guilty. There was a voice in my head saying: *You should have known Marta was up to something, you should have taken better care of your little sister.* An old familiar tune, guilt, one I knew as well as I knew the plaintive Billie Holiday song on the CD.

Too tense to lie still, I eluded Sam's arm and got out of bed. Walked as far as the window, lifted the corner of the shade. I always think I'll splurge and buy curtains, but I never get around to it.

"What are you doing?"

"Trying to see whether the snow's stopped."

Sam's penthouse at Charles River Park has heavy gold blackout drapes over triple-glazed windows, a king-sized bed, and carpet your toes can get lost in. My drafty old Victorian has chilly hardwood floors and plain white walls. The house has good bones, good space. Potential, a realtor would rave. It belonged to my Aunt Bea, and she left it to me, free and clear, except for property taxes that rise like Iowa corn in July.

"Sounds more like rain," Sam said.

"Sleet." I shivered in the chill, and the CD ended. Instead of sticking another disc in the player, I picked up the Plexiglas music box off the top of the dresser, the one I'd found in Paolina's room, and turned the silver key. Inside the clear plastic, gears meshed and rotated, and the first halting notes of "Teddy Bears' Picnic" emerged.

When Paolina was barely seven years old, when we first met, she was behind in a lot of ways, shy and fearful. Because I was not her mother, not exactly a friend, not a teacher, we had the freedom to regress, to go back and do some of the things she'd never done with her mom, play the baby games, read the baby books. I remembered endless rounds of hide-and-seek to the refrain of "Teddy Bears' Picnic." By the time the music box ran down, one of us had to be safely hidden. Not till the music wavered and died could the other yell, "Ready or not, here I come."

"Sam?"

He grunted sleepily.

"Any chance she could have been snatched because of you? Because of your—what you do?"

He didn't reply for such a long time I thought he might not have heard me. Then he said, "You spent time with your cop pal today. Mooney. The one who wants to get into your pants."

"Hey," I said. "He might have mentioned it first, but I'd

have gotten there on my own, sooner or later. And you know he's my friend, and that's all he is."

"Don't tell me he wouldn't like to be more."

"Sam, stop it. Just answer the damn question."

"The answer's no. Plain and simple. No. Nobody's going to go after Paolina because of me. Nobody in their right mind."

"I'm not worried about people in their right mind. I'm worried about contract killers from Miami."

"Where the hell did that come from? Late-night TV? Listen, I work with businessmen. Get it? I don't operate some low-rent street gang. I don't do Jamaican drug rings and—"

"How about Colombian?" I said sharply. "What exactly do you know about Roldán? What do you hear?"

The room was dark. I could tell by his outline that he'd turned to face me, but I couldn't see his eyes. "I thought we had an agreement, remember? I'm not your window into the Mob. You don't want to know about the business."

"Sam, come on. Am I some little Mafia wifey? Hear no evil? See no evil? I know the Italian thing isn't a gents' club anymore, running policy numbers and strip shows and shit. It's drugs now, Sam. That's where the money is, right? Drugs. And I'm asking because I need to know. This isn't some case; *this is Paolina.*"

"The money's in legitimate businesses," he said.

"Yeah," I said. Right. I clamped my lips together but I couldn't stop. "Sam, don't you see? Every day, you're getting in deeper. Can't you get away from it?"

"My dad," he said softly. That was all. *My dad.*

Anthony "Big Tony" Gianelli, Mob patriarch, Sam's father, was in a nursing home. The first stroke had been mild, but there'd been others, each minor, but with a cumulative effect that required constant care. Or maybe not. Maybe his much-married father was taking advantage of his last surviving son, using his illness to bind Sam closer to the family business. There wasn't much I'd put past Tony or his latest conniving wife.

"What I have to do," Sam said, "it's gonna take a while. I can't back out."

Can't, I thought, or won't? I stared out the window through the skeletal tree to the yellow glow of the street lamp.

"You're going after her, aren't you?" he said.

"Tomorrow." I had a reservation on a flight to Florida first thing in the morning. If the planes could take off in the crappy weather.

"To Colombia?"

"If that's where she is." I waited for him to speak. He didn't, so I said, "If you know anyone in Colombia, anyone who might run in the same circles as Roldán, I could use some help."

Silence.

"I'll see what I can find out." His voice had changed, become edgy and cool where it had been warm.

"Thanks."

More silence.

"Hey, you'll freeze in that thing," he said.

"What thing?" The only item I was wearing was a thin gold chain around my neck.

"Come back to bed. I promise you, I'll try to find out about Roldán. But I haven't heard his name for years. The stuff's coming out of Cali lately, and that's not his territory."

I craned my neck, peering again at the spot where the street lamp shines through the big elm on the pocket-sized lawn. It seemed to me the sleet was falling more lightly than the earlier snow, but that could have been wishful thinking. I padded back to bed, burrowing under the worn sheets and heavy quilt.

"When I find her, Sam," I said, shivering and sliding close to take advantage of his heat, "she's going to live here full time." It would alter our current arrangement, so I thought I owned him an early warning. Times have changed; I'm not a prude, but I didn't want to put myself in a situation where I'd have to constantly explain why it was okay if I slept with my boyfriend and not okay if Paolina slept with hers. Her hypocrisy-meter is fine-tuned.

His chest rose and fell. I could feel his heartbeat, count the pulsing thump. Music box blues, sleet tapping the roof, and Sam's reassuring heartbeat; sweet music.

"She's the family you want?" he said quietly.

"Mmmm."

"All of it? Don't you want to hold little babies in your arms?" Even in the dark, I could tell he was smiling, teasing.

I don't take queries about children lightly. When I was fourteen, younger than Paolina is now, younger than Marta was when she had Paolina, I gave birth to a child. I gave the baby up for adoption. I don't know whether it was a boy or a girl. Sam doesn't know about it. No one does.

I said, "I don't know. . . . To be responsible for someone's whole life—"

"You did it when you were a cop."

I thought, Yeah, and I sure screwed that up.

He replied as though he'd heard the unspoken words. "You're older and wiser."

"Yep," I said, "that's why I ought to be packing right now."

"Don't go. The cops will—"

"Sam, I have to." If there'd been a seat on a Miami-bound flight tonight I'd have been in it, but the planes were snowed in on the runways, the terminals packed with travelers lined up to escape to sunnier climes.

I was trying to decide how many T-shirts I could squeeze into my duffel bag when Sam said, "Will you marry me?"

My first thought was that I hadn't heard him correctly. The words themselves sounded odd, rusty and worn. My mouth went dry.

"Jesus, Sam, you do that just to get my attention?"

"Well, it did." Then he said, "Shove over," so I rolled onto my back. He turned to face me, weight on his right elbow and arm, his features in shadow. "Look, Monday, Wednesday, Friday, I come here. Tuesday, Thursday, Saturday, you come to my place. We're getting in a rut."

The rut wasn't deeply carved; we'd started seeing each other again only a few months ago. The rut would change if Paolina lived with me. I didn't say anything. I wished I could see his eyes more clearly.

"If you have to go up against Marta in court, wouldn't it be better to face off as a married woman?"

"Have you thought this through, Sam?"

I met him when I was nineteen and foolish, a part-time cabbie way too young to manage a torrid affair with the owner of the company. We argued; he left. I married on the rebound, and he did too, so we both have divorces under our belts. Since then, we've dated and fought and slept together. Slept with others.

"It's no good," he said. "Even when I'm with another woman, I think about you."

Would that keep him out of bed with another woman? I wanted to ask: *Would you mean it, the part in the ceremony about forsaking all others?*

Would I mean it?

"Yeah," he said, "I've thought about it. We could buy another place, someplace safer than this, in a good neighborhood. Or we could get a condo in a high-rise, do the gatekeeper thing."

I already live in a good neighborhood. The North End building where Sam's father held court for years had two guards in the lobby. Discreet, heavily armed men shadowed the old man whenever he went out.

"Sam, after I get Paolina back, ask me then, okay?"

"Bad timing."

"I can't deal with this now."

"I'd come with you tomorrow. You know that. But I've got business that won't wait."

There was always that. Business.

"I've got to get to Las Vegas," he said. "Take care of a few things."

Right. And I couldn't ask which things. I couldn't ask if he was headed to Las Vegas to avoid a Miami hit squad.

"You need money?"

"I'm okay." I was planning to use Roldán's money for a while, the cash he'd sent over the years. I've tried to keep it for Paolina's college fund, but if I couldn't bring her back there wouldn't be college.

"Let me know," he said, and I knew he meant about getting married, not about money.

"I will, Sam. I love you."

I knew how he'd respond. He'd say what he always says: "Yeah, babe," or "Me, too, kid." It wasn't a litmus test or anything. Oh, it used to be; I admit it. I used to wonder why he'd never say the words, why they seemed to stick in his throat when they slipped so easily from mine.

"I love you, Carlotta."

There wasn't much light in the bedroom, just the dim glow from the street lamp in front of the next house, but what light there was glinted off the corner of his eye.

"Sam?"

"Yeah?"

"This Las Vegas trip." I traced the outline of his mouth with my index finger.

"Yeah?"

There were too many things I wanted to say, too many questions blocked by too much history.

"You're okay, right?" That's all that came out.

He smiled and kissed my fingertip. "How about I drive you to the airport in the morning?"

PAOLINA

THE DOOR WAS wooden and so warped she had to try twice to secure the rusty latch. Dark wood showed through the white paint, especially at eye level where most of the graffiti were scratched. DORIS LOVES JOEY. DORIS PUTS OUT. Paolina wondered what moms said when they brought little kids into the bathroom and the four-year-olds asked about the swear words on the door. Even as she had the thought, the toilet in the other tiny stall flushed. Jeez, Ana would start calling her name any minute. She wished they would just leave her *alone* for one second, just leave her in peace so she could *think*. Honestly, she'd given her word. She was old enough to be left on her own for a *second*.

Maybe it was nothing. Maybe she was just getting weird, thinking too much, watching too hard, letting small irritations build on one another until they blurred into a loop, playing over and over like a late-night movie, on and on. Maybe it was just a coincidence that every time she had to go to the bathroom, Ana needed to go, too. But if she wanted to take a walk, well, Jorge wanted to take a walk, too, really needed to stretch his legs, so grateful she'd mentioned it.

She bit her lip and decided to remain in the stall a little longer to see whether Ana would leave without her. Not that she wanted to stay in the smelly bathroom. Honestly, why couldn't they stop at a Mickey D's or a Burger King or any of the other roadside places with decent bathrooms and familiar food? This dead-end café might be cheaper, but the floor hadn't been mopped in weeks. The unmoving fly in the corner wasn't a recent corpse.

She could hear the tap-tap of heels on linoleum. Then a stream of water cascaded into a sink, then silence. The door didn't creak or slam; Ana was waiting. Paolina doubted she was simply standing by the tiny mirror, applying lipstick in the yellow light. Ana didn't wear makeup, not that Paolina could see. She had nice skin, a small, slightly crooked nose, and tiny pearly teeth, like a doll's. She wore her dark hair pulled back and knotted behind her neck. Paolina wondered if Jorge and Ana were sleeping together. She wondered if Jorge thought she was just some little kid, or if he thought she was pretty like Ana.

Ana was defintely older than Jorge; maybe Ana was so strict with her because she thought Jorge might be falling for her. The idea tickled Paolina for a moment, but it wasn't just Ana who was strict. It was Jorge, too, Jorge even more, locking doors, unplugging the phones, almost like she was a prisoner, as trapped as she'd been at home. I mean, she could understand why it had to be a secret and all, but they were treating her like some kid who didn't even understand the swear words on the toilet-stall door.

She was old enough to help nurse her father back to health. Everyone would see what a good nurse she was. There would be soldiers, young, good-looking, her father's troops—

"Paolina, honey, you okay in there?"

She didn't even have a chance to think her own thoughts in peace. That was the problem. It was all happening too fast. They should have put more detail in the letter, let her know there was the possibility of helping her dad, the possibility of leaving town. Not that she regretted anything, but why couldn't she ever do stuff the way *she* wanted to do it? Say good-bye, not to her mother, but to the friends who'd understand and keep their mouths shut.

Ana's heels tapped to the front of the stall.

"Paolina?"

"I have a stomachache."

"That's too bad, honey."

She hated it when Ana called her honey. The woman was always patting her, touching her arms, smoothing her hair. "You don't need to wait in here."

The heels tapped, the door banged, and Paolina felt a surge of relief.

Alone. Time to think. She held a wad of rough toilet paper to her nose to block out the smell. She thought somebody might have thrown up in the stall. The thought almost made her gag so she switched mental gears, but when she did she remembered Julio. She touched the pouch of her sweatshirt thoughtfully as though she expected to find him, even though she knew he wasn't there.

That was the worst. Worse than the stinky bathrooms and fleabag motels, worse than the long bumpy miles shut in the back of the truck and the icky shapeless clothes they made her wear as a disguise. She hadn't brought Julio, hadn't had a clue she'd have to go abruptly or not at all, and they absolutely wouldn't let her go back for him. Nothing she said made a difference, nothing penetrated; it was like they didn't even hear her. Julio, the first gift her father had sent her in her whole life. Julio, the little gold statue who watched over her, who seemed to know when she was sad or happy or when kids were mean to her. He must still be in her locker. He had to be. She couldn't have dropped him.

She expected Ana to rush in while she washed her hands in the stained basin, but the door stayed shut, and she let the warm water drizzle onto her hands in blissful solitude. Her skin was good, too, she decided, even better than Ana's. Oh, she wasn't model-pretty, but who'd want to do something dumb like pose for pictures all day, anyway? If she couldn't make it as a drummer, couldn't find the right band, she was going to be a nurse, or a cop, or even join the army and train to be a pilot. Maybe she'd get married first.

Who knew? Who cared? It was just grown-ups who always wanted you to have a plan, and plan ahead, and go to college. Carlotta was always harping on that, go to college, go to college, like it was some kind of holy obligation. Maybe it would be a good thing, when she was older, when she had her life sorted out and had done more stuff, but what could you do in a classroom for your whole life? What could you really learn there that you couldn't learn better by doing, by living? When she got back, she'd know so much more, she'd be a way better student. She wouldn't be as restless. She'd be able to concentrate better. She'd be different, somebody who'd lived through a real adventure. All the kids would want to know where she'd been and what she'd done; they'd crowd around to listen.

If she came back.

That was it. That was the problem. What if she really liked it there and decided not to come back. She needed to have Julio with her. She could almost feel his solid warmth in her palm.

There was a pay phone outside. She'd noticed the sign when they'd walked in from the van, one of those public phone signs, like the one in Central Square, on the next building over, near an alley. The sign was near a drugstore and on the other side of the alley was a small liquor store. It would depend on whether Ana was waiting smack outside the door or whether she'd given up and gone back to the van. If she was in the van, Paolina could make a quick right instead of a left and get to the alley unobserved.

If she couldn't have Julio with her, at least she'd know he was safe.

She searched her pockets and found a quarter, another quarter, and two dimes. She wasn't sure what the phone would take. She wished she had a cell. Using a pay phone was definitely uncool, but a phone was a phone, really. She thought you put the money in first, but maybe if you were dialing collect, it didn't matter. Maybe she had to dial an operator to dial collect. She knew what to do with a cell phone. You just called, duh.

Paolina considered the phone. She'd given her word she wouldn't tell anyone where she was. And she'd keep her word. But that didn't mean she couldn't ask Aurelia to check

her locker and find Julio and take care of him. That would
be okay. Later, she'd write and tell Aurelia where to send
him, and that would be okay, too.

She half expected to find Ana lurking outside the restroom, but the area was deserted. A smile broke out on
Paolina's face, an upside-down rainbow of happiness. They
trusted her now. They'd decided to treat her more like a
grown-up, and that was cool. Maybe Jorge was secretly in
love with her. Guys liked younger girls. Jorge wasn't that
old. Ana was probably ten years older than he was.

She turned speedily to the right, hoping the phone would
be in working order. The phones on the streets of Cambridge
were usually broken and Marta thought the phone company
was vandalizing their own phones, or refusing to repair
them, so people would have to buy cells. Paolina thought it
was just kids messing with the phones, and as for why, well,
it was because it was something to do, that was all, just
something to do that wasn't boring for a change.

It wasn't boring because you might get caught. Making
the phone call was exciting, too, just because she wasn't supposed to do it. She quickened her pace.

By the time she made the right turn into the alley, the two
quarters and the two dimes were already moist in her palm.
Without reading the instructions, because in spite of her
bravado she was really worried Ana would show up, she
shoved them into the slot and dialed. She knew Aurelia's
number by heart. She hardly knew the phone numbers of
any of the friends she'd made this year. She didn't care
about her new friends, but the thought that she might never
see Aurelia again made something funny happen inside her
throat. She hoped she'd be able to say hello without choking.
She wondered whether she ought to disguise her voice in
case somebody else answered the phone.

The phone rang once, twice, then a hand snaked around
the corner, grabbed the receiver out of her hand, and
slammed it back in the cradle.

Jorge had a weird look on his face and a hand clamped
like a vise around Ana's thin arm.

"Yeah, you leave her for a minute, right, this happens. I told you—"

"Let go of me."

"Yeah, let go of her," Paolina said.

She could hardly believe it when he slapped her, slapped her hard, across the mouth. The pain made her eyes water and sting. She raised her hand to her cheek.

"You'll be sorry," she said. "When my dad finds out—"

"Yeah, sure I will," Jorge said. "Get in the fucking van."

CHAPTER 8

MUGGY. **MY GRAY** silk jacket and wool slacks, too light for the Boston freeze, clung damply to my body as I wrestled my duffel bag into the cab line at the Miami–Dade airport. I shaded my eyes against sunshine so bright it seemed phony, like a late-night-TV ad for some lurid tropical paradise. Ahead of me, a man's floral-print shirt gaped over his belly; he carried a stuffed alligator in one hand and a box of pecan fudge in the other. I folded my jacket over my arm and fumbled in my backpack for sunglasses. By the time I found them, a cab beckoned.

I gave the driver the address and settled into the back seat. The cab was faintly air conditioned, the hum like a lullaby, but I was too wound up to doze.

If I was wrong, I'd waste time and money, but I wouldn't jeopardize Paolina's recovery. Mooney would handle the cop routine, finesse the FBI. Roz had promised to monitor the phones. Gloria would ride herd on Moon and Roz both.

Clients who paid me to retrieve runaways said they felt better once they'd hired me. Once they'd signed responsibility for finding their missing child over to me, they felt somehow released, freed to go on with some skeletal semblance of their lives. No way could I sign this case over to someone else. I had to go with my gut, and my gut said Miami. It said Thurman W. Vandenburg.

Years ago, when I'd gotten a mysterious package of cash

in the mail—special delivery from Paolina's real father to my little sister—Thurman W. Vandenburg, Esquire, had served as go-between. I'd refused to accept it at first, on the grounds that it was drug money, dirty money. But the more I pondered, the more it seemed that money was money, that the cocaine had been paid for and consumed, that Roldán's money, dirty or not, could buy Paolina and her family out of the projects.

I stared out the window at streets lined with low shops and stucco houses, the signs in Spanish as often as English, the colors—bright reds, hot pinks, shades of orange—hothouse and exotic. I cranked the window and the cabbie glared. I was spoiling the AC, but I didn't care. I wanted to smell a breeze that floated in over a blue ocean instead of an icy gray-green sea. After this is cleared up, after it's over, I promised myself, Paolina and I will come here and soak up the sun on a sandy beach. I'll buy her the best strawberry ice cream cone in town.

When the cab pulled up in front of a three-story cement-and tinted-glass structure, I hauled my duffel out onto hot pavement, tipped the driver, and checked my watch. Twenty minutes to spare.

The landscaping was elegant; the palms and colorful broad-leafed plants meticulously pruned and groomed. Entering the lobby felt like entering a cold-storage locker. Inside the frosted-glass doors, the parquet flooring and wide stairway were guarded by a grandfatherly rent-a-cop. I threw him a smile and asked to use a bathroom. He grinned back like I'd made his day and ushered me toward a corner door.

I splashed cold water on my face and made an attempt to tame my hair. The humidity had done its work, making it wilder than usual. I found a clip in my backpack, wound my hair into a curly mass, and plunked it on top of my head. As I held a damp paper towel to the back of my neck, the eyes of a woman who hadn't slept in days stared at me from the mirror.

I signed "Janice Ford" in the logbook at the desk. Grandpa beamed and asked whether I'd like to leave my duffel with him. When I declined he said fine and nodded me toward the stairs without bothering to search my belongings. He didn't check my name against any list of appointments or phone to see whether a Ms. Ford was expected.

Haley, Briggs, and Associates, on the second floor, was the formal name of Vandenburg's firm. As I climbed the steps, I wondered how many associates worked there and what the nature of that work might be. If they all labored for drug cartels, I'd have expected more than Gramps in the way of security.

The waiting room smelled like money—spacious, with fresh flowers and plush gray carpet. I gave my phony name to the tanned receptionist. When I use an alias I often pick a last name suggestive of family wealth.

"He'll be with you as soon as he's available," she said automatically. She was a little too young, a bit too flashily dressed for the surroundings.

The oil paintings on the walls didn't look like reproductions, misty sea scenes with romantic sails in the distance, hints of tropical lushness echoed by gleaming plants and polished mahogany. *Architectural Digest* and *Travel & Leisure* sat on the coffee table like invitations to a nevernever land of the idle rich.

There were two squishy blue sofas and three print chairs, but I was the only one waiting. Five minutes passed. Ten. A famous actor I'd never heard of owned a massive house in Malibu constucted of sheet metal, old rubber tires, and blue glass. Twenty. I was contemplating breaking in on Vandenburg and ousting his client or tossing his lunch out the window when the receptionist approached, apologizing for the delay. I followed her through a paneled doorway and down a long cool corridor. She knocked at a door on the right, waited for a low, "Come in," before turning the brass knob.

The receptionist gave my phony name, nodded, and closed the door.

I'd never met Vandenburg, but we'd spoken on the phone and I recalled his unctuous voice. A smooth operator, a genial shark, that's how I'd envisioned him. Now he rose from behind his imposing desk, a man who'd probably played a little college ball, a good-old-boy, go-along, get-along guy with the easy smile that would get him into the right fraternity, the polish to impress the right people. A fall of blond hair drooped boyishly across his forehead. His suit was charcoal, his smile dazzling, his handclasp firm. The airy office was filled with sleek furniture, healthy plants, and photos of blond children so perfect they might have been issued along with the silver frames. No wife in evidence.

He indicated a plush armchair and waited for me to sit before resuming his throne. His desk was the size of a substantial dining table.

"What can I do for you, Miss Ford?" I wondered whether he'd been in a meeting or on the phone; no client had been ushered out through the waiting room, but his office had a second door that could be used as an escape hatch. I let my eyes wander slowly over his diplomas and awards. There was a collection of framed non-family photographs, men in suits shaking each other by the hand. The place looked like a respectable lawyer's office. No bulletproof vests, no metal detector.

"I thought you might recognize my voice," I said.

He smiled his brilliant smile, not flirtatious, but well on the way. "I'm sorry. I'm sure if we'd met before I'd remember."

"We have a mutual friend. Carlos Roldán Gonzales."

Underneath the golfer's tan, he might have turned a shade paler. He'd never used his client's name when we'd spoken on the phone, always said "the man" or "our friend."

"My name isn't Ford. It's Carlyle."

"Boston," he said. "No, I'm lying. Cambridge."

"Good for you; good memory. What the hell does Roldán think he's doing?"

Vandenburg flashed his shark smile. "No idea what you're talking about."

"You've been at it again, forwarding letters, sending packages. Directly to the daughter this time."

"I'm sorry," he said, "but I don't do that sort of thing anymore. I mean, I never—" He stopped himself and grinned to cover his lapse. "What I'm saying is, I never involve myself in such matters."

I'd brooded about the best way to approach Vandenburg through two airline baggies of salty peanuts, a Pepsi, and a Bloody Mary. Asking for the information was definitely my first choice. I glanced around, but unless someone had an ear to one of the doors, no one was listening. Vandenburg didn't point at a painting or a potted plant to indicate that his office might be bugged. He hadn't lowered his voice.

Neither did I. "I need to talk to Roldán. If you don't help me find him, you may have a long time to regret it."

"Excuse me? Are you threatening me?"

"I'm assuming that before you got in touch with me about that first package, you checked me out. You know I used to be a cop. You know I'm still in the cop business."

"I know you were."

"I try to stay in touch. For example, DEA's Group 26 works out of Miami, right? Jerry Hillier still in charge?"

"No. Uh, no, he's not." His right hand touched the knot of his pink-flecked tie.

The man kept up to date on who ran 26. Why bother if he no longer had any drug connections?

"Doesn't matter," I said. "It's not about individuals once you get those guys involved. They love getting their hands on Americans who stooge for the cartel players. Lawyers are their favorite snack food."

"I am no longer in communication with that man. I never knew what his business was."

"Tell it to Hillier's replacement," I said, "or tell me how to reach him."

"You working for DEA?"

I explained about Paolina because I thought it might work; he had pictures of his kids on his desk. While I spoke, Vandenburg's eyes settled on the door as though he'd like to use it.

I said, "You've built a nice practice here. Shame to bring it tumbling down."

"I heard he was dead."

"We both know that's not true."

"I don't know where he is."

"Too bad."

"It's the truth."

When lawyers insist they're telling the truth, watch out.

I said, "I'll bet you know somebody who knows."

"You don't know what you're getting involved in," he replied.

"I need a way to get to Roldán, and I will mess up your life if I don't get it."

He chewed his lip for a while. I waited. He stared at his diplomas, the pictures of his kids. I glanced at my watch.

He lowered his voice. "I might know someone who might be able to get a message to the man. I might be willing to give you that name, as a goodwill gesture."

"Terrific," I said. "But don't send me on a wild goose chase. I'm an impatient woman and I might find myself wandering over to 26 if I don't get quick results."

He stared longingly at the door again, finally decided that no one was going to come to his rescue. "Drew Naylor."

"Who is he? How do I find him?"

"He makes promotional films for business clients. Works half the year here and half in L.A. Very swanky, very exclusive. Thinks he ought to get nominated for an Oscar."

He sounded resentful; I hoped he wasn't siccing me on a deadbeat client.

"Where do I find him?"

The lawyer flashed his shirt cuff and consulted a gold Rolex. "You don't find him."

"I'm not sitting around waiting for a call. Where does he live?"

"I wouldn't want him to know—"

"I'm not here to make trouble for you; I'm here to find a way to get to Roldán."

Vandenburg rubbed his hands like he was warming them over a hot stove. "Look, Naylor's throwing one of his parties tonight. I'll try to talk to him. He might give me a phone number, a conduit, but—"

"Where's the party?"

"Naylor wouldn't want me to—"

I said, "You have a date for this party?"

His face relaxed into a smile. "Naylor's parties—you go there to meet women, you don't bring them."

"But tonight's an exception," I said. "I'd love to go."

He stared at me with his mouth open, ready for rebuttal. I could see him considering his options.

He nodded at my duffel. "You have something in there to wear to a Coral Gables fling?"

"Underdressed is always elegant. What time? Where does he live?"

"Where are you staying?" he countered. "I'll pick you up."

I gave him my cell number and requested his.

When he handed me his card, he couldn't resist adding some advice. "I wouldn't bother threatening Naylor with DEA if I were you."

"And why is that?"

"I wouldn't threaten him in any way." His voice stayed as level as the low Florida ground, but he stood to emphasize that the interview was at an end.

I stood as well; I didn't like him staring down at me. "Wouldn't it be easier to give me an address? I won't use your name."

"Ms. Carlyle, we do this my way or not at all."

I wanted to grab him by his tailored lapels and shake him, make him understand that Paolina, my Paolina, my golden girl in the photo frame, was slipping away with every delay, with every wasted hour. His eyes were cold; the good-old-boy smile long gone.

"If I find him first," I said, "the deal's off."

"I'll pick you up at eight."

In other words, there was a greater chance of a sudden Miami blizzard than of me locating Naylor under my own steam. Vandenburg marched across the carpet and held the door to his escape hatch wide. He looked like he'd go on standing there, stern and mute as a guard at Buckingham Palace, till I gave up and departed.

He shut the door on my heels; I didn't even get the chance to slam it.

CHAPTER 9

A DISCREET STAIRCASE led from Vandenburg's escape hatch to the lobby where Gramps, happy to take a break from guarding the parquet, called for a cab. When a dirty white Ford with HANK'S TAXI SERVICE boldly lettered in red on the side door pulled up, I checked the driver's ID on the visor while ducking into the backseat. The driver's name wasn't Hank, but his face matched the photo, so I told him to drop me at a motel, requesting cheap but not sleazy, mentioning that I piloted a Boston cab in the hope that he'd select wisely for a fellow member of the community. His bloodshot eyes met mine in the rearview mirror and he hung a sudden left.

"Got a daughter your age," he said gruffly. "Whatcha wanna drive a hack for?"

I shrugged and he accepted it as a reply, which was a good thing because I wasn't in the mood for a discussion. Vandenburg hadn't shut me down completely; it was a relief, but hardly a comfort. Naylor's party might prove a dead end. And worse, it wasn't till evening, long hours away. I watched the traffic, resisting the temptation to order the cabbie to take me to the airport so I could keep an eye on every departure lounge with a scheduled flight to Colombia.

I couldn't watch the flights from New York, I told myself. Or the Delta departures from Atlanta.

The driver abandoned me in front of a low-slung L-shaped building with instructions to tell the guy on the desk that Frankie G. had sent me. The clerk turned pleasant when I mentioned the name, and told me I was lucky they had a vacancy the way the weather sucked up north. The place had a kidney-shaped deco pool and a room worth the price: the carpet soft, the bed firm, the sheets fresh. There was a scratched wooden desk for my laptop and a phone directory tucked away on the top shelf of a cramped closet.

No listing for Drew Naylor; didn't surprise me. I wondered whether the lawyer had tossed me the first name that came to mind, a scrap of meat to a hungry hound. He'd seemed scared enough to cooperate, but threats lead to plenty of phony confessions.

The bathroom had a storage shelf above a small white sink. I unpacked toothbrush, toothpaste, and deodorant, but they didn't make the place feel any homier. Floral air freshener didn't block the harsh ammonia smell of cleaning fluid. I'd forgotten to pack dental floss. My cosmetics kit rustled, reminding me to remove the magazine article I'd stashed in the side pocket.

The same article was probably on my laptop by now; I'd instructed Roz to run a LexisNexis search on Roldán, and she'd have yanked it from the *Newsweek* archives. I hadn't needed to search; I'd found it where I'd left it years ago, in the top drawer of my bedside table.

I once knew a burglar who said the closer a woman kept an item to her bed, the more she valued it. Swore he found more diamond rings in bedside tables than jewelry boxes, and he was a legendary thief while he lasted on the streets. I wondered what he'd make of my storing that particular page near the bed instead of filing it in my office.

The five men in the photograph looked cheerful and unposed, as though they'd been surprised by a friend taking a candid shot. The caption underneath gave their names. Carlos Roldán Gonzales stood farthest to the right, slightly apart; his was the last name given. The story was headlined: ANDEAN DRUG LORDS MEET AT SUMMIT. No photo credit, which made sense; whoever'd taken the shot wouldn't be eager to have the men know he'd sold their likenesses.

The first man, Juan Lopez Everardo, identified in the article below the caption as the heir to José Rodriguez Gacha, the "Mexican," wore a Panama hat with a snakehead on the band, the same style Rodriguez Gacha flaunted before his untimely death. Lopez was reputed to be as violent as his mentor, a man who routinely tortured associates who might be cheating him by holding back cash. The second man, heavyset with a shock of dark wavy hair, was the eldest of the Muñoz brothers, three up-and-comers who'd acquired a chunk of the business run by the late Pablo Escobar of the Medellin Cartel. Lopez and Muñoz were both dead now, shot "while escaping" by the Colombian armed forces. The third man, Jaime Orejuela, currently jailed for life in the U.S., was one of the few cartel bosses ever successfully extradited to stand trial in Miami, convicted in spite of the suspicious deaths of three witnesses. The features of the fourth, Enrique "Angel" Navas, were blurred, as though he'd shaken his head in disagreement with the others the instant the shutter snapped. He had a wide grin and the broad-chested build of an athlete. An unlit cigarette dangled from his mouth. He was rumored to be dead, along with his ex-partner, Roldán.

The article speculated on possible reasons for the unusual get-together. Price-fixing among cartels? An indicator that things were looking bad for the drug lords, that the War on Drugs, with its increasing use of high-tech surveillance, was capturing more product on the way to the U.S. market? Were they discussing new smuggling routes? Few answers were suggested, but the single fact in the piece, that cocaine prices were dropping on the streets of New York, Boston, and Miami, backed up one conclusion the writers hadn't offered. With too much coke hitting the streets, the meeting might concern controlling production in an effort to keep prices high. There was a sidebar about the history of cocaine use, tracing it back from its '80s glamorization via TV and movies to its roots as the "divine plant" of the ancient Incas in Peru. I learned that before the Pure Food and Drug Act banned its use in medicines and soft drinks such as Coca-

Cola, as much coca leaf was shipped to the U.S. in 1906 as was shipped in 1976. Another sidebar addressed the sky-rocketing Colombian use of *basuco,* a cocaine derivative similar to crack.

I returned to the photo and stared at the small image on the right, wishing for the magnifying glass on my desk at home. Roldán was taller than his partner, his build slighter. His thin face was deeply shadowed, almost gaunt, like the face of a saint in an old painting. I searched for a resemblance to Paolina, found it in the wide-set eyes, the generous mouth.

The story, widely reported, was that they'd quarreled, over money or politics or both, that the man nicknamed the Angel had been responsible for several attempts on Roldán's life. Then there'd been the even more widely circulated tale, that a Cessna carrying Roldán to Panama had disappeared, blown out of the sky, some said by the government, some by his old friend, the Angel.

The reports were wrong; Roldán was alive. And whatever else he might be, he was a wealthy man. He could have sent Paolina money, plane tickets, a guide. He'd sent her the little statue, a golden gift, maybe many gifts. To a girl as eager for an older man's approval as my little sister, wouldn't that have been invitation enough? *Come be my daughter. Your mother loves her boys better. Your big sister is involved with a man who takes up all her time.*

Bullshit. I didn't believe it; if my sister was in control, on her own, she'd have told someone, called someone, maybe not me, but her best friend, Aurelia. Roldán had arranged for the girl to be snatched off the street; that's what I believed.

I refolded the worn article and replaced it in the kit. The lamps in the main room were dim. I opened the curtains; the skimpy window looked out on a parking lot. The air conditioner hummed sleepily; it was well past lunchtime, but I wasn't hungry. I wanted to get to Naylor now.

My cell rang and I snatched it, recognizing Mooney's voice as soon as he spoke my name.

"Hi," I said. "Great. I wanted to talk to you. Did you get somebody working on those airline lists?"

"Carlotta, where the hell are you?" I pictured him, tapping a pencil impatiently on his desktop.

"What difference does it make?" I said.

"You went to Logan."

"I'm in Miami. How did you know I—?"

"Picture this: I'm talking to this guy at the feds about how we need to meet today, so we can fill him in on the Paolina thing, and he tells me you're not even in town. How do you think that makes me look?"

"Mooney—"

"Yeah. The feds have a tail on your boyfriend. That surprise you?"

I wondered whether the feds had filled Mooney in on the supposed Miami hit squad. The idea that the feds had told Mooney, a local, that they were watching Sam was as surprising, maybe more surprising, than the fact of the surveillance.

I bit my lip. "Mooney, let's fight about Sam later, after you tell me what's new on Paolina."

"What the hell are you doing in Florida?"

I swallowed. "Following a lead."

"What lead?"

"Moon, I told you. I think Roldán snatched her."

"Yeah, right. He sent her some stuff, and then Marta pulled that shit with the photo. I know. I tried to talk to her, but she's stonewalling me. You think she was in on it from the get-go?"

"She sold the photo, but I don't think she thought it through. When she phoned me, she really was looking for Paolina, thinking she'd be home to babysit."

"Okay, so what's with Florida? If you've got a lead, why not give it to the feds?"

"I give it to them, I've got no pressure."

"You're threatening some drug lord with the feds?"

"Not a drug lord. A lawyer. Moon, listen, there's nothing I can do in Boston that Roz can't do. Or Gloria. That you can't do. I trust you to handle the feds."

"Right."

"I have to follow my gut on this, try every angle. It would help if I knew about the passenger lists."

"Nada," he said. "No similar names."

"All flights?"

"All flights out of Boston, all flights to Bogotá."

"You'll work with the feds? Even if I'm not there?" I took his continued silence for consent. "See if you can get them to put her on the no-fly list. The one for suspected terrorists."

"I'll try."

"What do you think they'll do?"

"Either give me the horselaugh or tell me they have to li-aise with the DEA."

"Yeah." Only the feds "liaise." Once Roldán's name was mentioned, they'd inform DEA. But how long before the right hand told the left hand what was going on?

I said, "Ask the feds if there's a possibility Roldán could be here, in the U.S."

"I'll ask."

"Mooney, why are the feds watching Sam?"

"To see which way he runs, Carlotta. Seems he's in a bind."

"What kind of bind?" Sam had hummed Billie Holiday tunes while he shaved this morning. He hadn't looked like a man in trouble, but I'd been preoccupied with Paolina. I'm not sure I'd have noticed anything softer than an outright cry for help.

Mooney said, "I can't tell you. You know I can't tell you. If the feds think I'm talking to you, they stop talking to me."

Impasse.

He said, "So, is Gianelli down there with you?"

"I can't tell you where he is, Moon."

"Tit for tat? Well, I'll help with Paolina anyway. Any-thing I can do, just ask."

"I've got two names you can run." I gave him the lawyer, Vandenburg, and Drew Naylor. Roz is a whiz when it comes to computer manipulation, but Mooney has access to re-sources Roz doesn't, including NCIC. He might have pals on the Miami force.

"Vandenburg's tied to Roldán?"

"Used to be. Let me know if there are any priors, any drug-related offenses. I'm trying to find links to Roldán."

"Carlotta, the U.S. government, the Colombian government, both of them have been trying to find links to Roldán for years. What makes you think you can do better?"

"For one thing, I'm not going through any government."

"Tell me you're not going to Colombia."

"If I get a lead that Roldán's there, that Paolina's there, yeah, I am."

"Well, don't check in with the local PD. You don't want to go near the cops in Colombia, what I hear."

"Calm down, Moon."

"Jesus." I could hear the pencil point smack his desk, a rhythmic tat-tat-tat.

"Have you got any leads that would bring me back to Boston?"

He didn't. He'd come up empty on Marta's boyfriend, Gregor Maltic. No priors, he told me, and Immigration had no beef with the man. Plus Paolina's disappearance didn't fit any local pattern; there was no rash of disappearing teens.

"Thanks, Moon," I said. "And Moon, if you can't reach me, talk to Roz, okay?" It was a lot to ask. Roz and Mooney tend to clash. Mooney, tall, tough, with seen-it-all cop eyes, tends to scare people. Roz, tattooed, voluptuous, and brazen, in my humble opinion, scares *him*.

"I'll talk to Gloria," he said. "She can pass it on. Miami, huh?" He gave a low whistle.

"Yeah, you know anybody on the force here, somebody might help me with the airport?"

"What hotel are you at?" His voice sounded odd, tense, edged with some kind of suppressed emotion.

I gave him the information.

"Keep your cell charged," he said. "I might have something. I'll get back to you."

"What, Mooney?"

The next thing I heard was the phone clicking into the cradle. It was totally unlike Mooney to end a conversation so abruptly. I stared at the phone in my hand, waiting, thinking he'd ring back.

When he did, should I tell him Sam had flown to Las Vegas? If Sam did have a contract out on him, would he be safer with the feds in the know? What if Sam, realizing the feds were tracking him, intended to lead them astray? Could he have told me about Vegas hoping I'd pass on the information? He knew I'd be in touch with Mooney.

When the phone didn't ring, I called Roz.

CHAPTER 10

SHE'D MADE NO progress placing Paolina after the Friday night party. She'd hung flyers all over Cambridge, Boston, and Somerville, gotten some calls on them, but mostly from PIs trying to drum up business, investigators too lame to run the phone number and discover they were calling one of their own. She had nothing new to report on Roldán's probable whereabouts. He'd disappeared from the press after the plane crash stories. She'd already e-mailed every article she'd been able to unearth.

I gave her Drew Naylor's name. "Mooney's checking him out, but I thought you might have alternative sources. He produces films for businesses."

"Commercials?"

"Possibly. More likely the puff pieces they show at the annual shareholders' meeting. Find out what you can. Find out if he's involved in drugs."

"Film business? You kidding?"

"Ask around."

"I thought Gloria was gonna be phone queen."

"Usually. But right now I need fashion tips." I explained about the upcoming party.

"Wish I could go," she said. "I have so got the perfect outfit."

Roz is apt to show up for a date, a quaint term for her encounters with males, wearing anything from fishnet tights and a mini the length of a book jacket to a fifties shirtwaist, buttons undone, over lace underwear. Still, her advice was preferable to Gloria's.

She said, "You wanna blend in or stand out?"

"Blend."

"And you're his date, huh? What have you got?"

I enumerated items as I hauled them from my duffel. "Black slacks, jeans, white T-shirt, blue T-shirt, black tee, gray silk jacket." I felt like a pre-ball Cinderella, dirt under my fingernails, itemizing rags.

"Boring, boring. Keep going."

"Um. Underwear." If I had to rely on Roz for a fairy godmother, things were bleak.

"What color?"

"Beige." I scrabbled at the bottom of the duffel. "Um, a silk scarf."

"Ooh, the print thing? Black and green?"

"Yeah." I usually pack a scarf or two; they weigh nothing, take up little space.

"Jungle print, right? White background? Got the silver necklace with you, the collar-hoop thing?"

"Yeah."

"You bring a sewing kit or something? Safety pins? The little gold ones, like you use to fix a bra strap."

"I might have a couple. Hold on." In the bathroom, I checked the cosmetic kit's side compartments. It seemed to me I'd tossed a few pins in it a long time ago. One had worked its way open; it stabbed my index finger. I sucked the wound while walking phone and pins back into the bedroom.

Roz said, "Okay, lay the scarf down flat, on the bed, the floor, whatever. It's a square, right? So fold one end up, and you've got a triangle. Okay, now put the necklace at Point A."

"The apex?"

"Whatever. Fold the point of the scarf over the necklace and pin it, so there's like a channel thingy, with the necklace inside."

"I need more pins."

"Go to a store and spring for a needle and thread. It'll look better."

Three safety pins semi-secured the necklace. "Okay," I said, "I got a triangle with a necklace on top."

"What you got is a halter. It ties in back. Try it."

I slipped off my T-shirt. The necklace, a Cape Cod flea market acquisition, didn't have a clasp, just a gap in the metal. It was rigid and silver, about a quarter-inch thick. I fumbled the ends of the scarf behind my back.

"Speaking of bra straps," I said.

"Duh. Take it off."

I did. The scarf clung to my breasts.

"I feel naked," I said.

"Your nipples show? Good."

"Roz, I don't know about this."

"C'mon," she said. "Trust me. You got great shoulders. Your back's got muscles I'd kill for. Ooh, yeah, when you buy the thread, get baby oil. Oil your back. Baby oil's great for that, plus if you score at the party, you're way ahead of the game. Guys love what you can do with a little baby oil in the right place."

"Let's stick to clothes."

"Hey, sorry. I know you and Gianelli are an item again, but I figure he's here, you're there, it's a party, models and shit, South Beach, lifeguards—"

When I didn't respond enthusiastically, she sighed and got back to business. "Okay, the black pants you brought, they the drawstring ones?"

"Yeah."

"Great. Okay, you wear them really low. You want your stomach on display. And turn up the cuffs so they're just below the knee. What you really need is a tat."

Not in this life, I thought.

"They might have one of those rub-ons. On the small of your back, low, it would look so cool. Or on your shoulder. And get some eyeliner. You didn't bring any?"

"Guess."

"Shit, what do you have for shoes? You got heels?"

I had 2½-inch business pumps. Stuart Weitzman, on sale, Filene's Basement, but somehow I didn't think Roz would be impressed.

"Shoes, you can't fake," she said sternly.

"Where am I going to find a store that sells elevens?" Women's shoes effectively cease at size 10. I know tons of women who'd spring for stylish shoes in big sizes; most of us believe it's a conspiracy.

"Ask around," Roz advised. "Lotta cross-dressers in South Beach."

"I'm not in South Beach, Roz."

"Then get size 10 sandals, open toe, open heel. Spikes."

I shrugged and the cool silk rippled across my breasts. The top actually looked pretty good. I imagined it paired with low-slung slacks and precarious heels. I could always kick them off if I needed to run.

Roz said, "Call back when you get the stuff and I'll walk you through it, okay? Thread, a packet of needles, shoes, a temp tat, if you can find one, makeup."

"Get me something on Naylor by then."

"If it's there, I'll get it. 'Bye."

There was no message on my cell saying I'd missed a call, so Mooney hadn't rung back while I was talking. Damn. It was too close in my small room, too quiet. The pulsing tick of the bedside clock only emphasized the blaring silence. I felt restless, worried, in need of exercise. After five minutes of floor pacing, even Roz's shopping trip seemed preferable to waiting for the phone to ring.

CHAPTER 11

THE DESK CLERK advised against walking to a mall barely half a mile away. Too hot out there. Maybe I should have listened, but the idea of a walk appealed to me. Before the heat enveloped me like a fog, I'd considered jogging.

There was no sidewalk, just dusty gravel by the side of the road. People gawked at me in passing from behind the tinted windows of air-conditioned cars. *Look, Ma, a tourist attraction, a woman using her legs for transportation.* Heat and auto exhaust steamed off the gravel and tried to choke me. The air felt too thick to breathe and I was sweating like I'd played a tough volleyball game by the time I hit my destination.

The mall was anchored by a Burdine's so cold it made my damp T-shirt stiffen. I wondered whether all the stores cranked the AC as high, and whether they did it to make the outdoor temperatures seem even worse. Shopping's not my strong suit, but dime stores and shoe stores, while not up there with hardware stores and gun shops, suit me better than most. I hurried through Burdine's, goosebumps prickling my arms, and checked a mall directory.

I found a pair of open-toed Barbie-sandals with clear plastic spikes in a shop that catered to the beach trade. Swimsuits and heels are not a usual pairing in Boston, but that's what this place carried, I swear, bikinis and heels, like they went together, like hot dogs and beer. The shoes were 10s, but I could walk in them, and they were on sale. I could have tried three other stores, but as much as I'd wanted to leave my hotel room, that's how much I suddenly wanted to be back. I checked my cell to make sure the battery was charged, soothed myself with the thought that Vandenburg could reach me here. Mooney could reach me. Paolina could reach me.

I bought the other required items, minus the tattoo, at a Walgreen's, remembering at the last minute to add a disposable razor, a necessity for legs and underarms in wintertime Boston mode. As I left the store, a sign caught my eye.

Jaira Jewels was a small shopfront with more security than a little costume jeweler in a mall might require. I checked my watch, then my cell: no messages. The lawyer hadn't called yet. The party would probably start late. I studied the discreet display in the window. A sign requested customers to please ring the bell, so I did, waiting thirty seconds till a buzzer sounded. The door made a clicking noise, and I walked inside aware that I'd been scrutinized by a video system and found unthreatening. Maybe it was the shopping bag with the shoes.

Inside, it was dark and a little musty. There was a faint smell of oranges, like someone had just peeled one in a back room. A waist-high glass case divided the long narrow space, leaving enough room for a thin salesman to squeeze behind the counter. The wall opposite the counter had glass-fronted display cases, too, but these were attached to the wall at eye level. The back wall featured two large framed mirrors; one or the other or possibly both were one-way glass. Behind them, probably a workroom, and watchful eyes. I studied the contents of the cases on the wall. Wristwatches, Breguets and Rolexes, a couple of high-end, diamond-studded Baume & Merciers, a few nice art-deco pieces Roz would have liked. I'd just turned my attention to the long display case when a man came silently out of the back room, pushing aside a beaded curtain.

A smile brought out deep creases beside his dark eyes and emphasized the lines running from the corner of his mouth to his beaky nose. The smile was welcoming and gentle, hopeful, as though he'd been waiting for me all day. I wondered how many casual customers wandered in and impulsively dropped five thousand bucks on a watch.

"If I can help you, show you something, answer any questions, please, you have only to ask." His English was smooth, but accented.

"Thank you," I said. "You have some lovely pieces."

He nodded solemnly. It was a courtly gesture, almost a bow.

"Do you buy gold?" I asked impulsively.

He shrugged. "Sometimes, on occasion."

My eyes swept the velvet backing of the low case. Pearl cluster pins and amethyst pendants, a group of glinting blue sapphires. Nothing remotely like the little man.

I took the small felt bag from my backpack. The dark man watched as I shook the birdman onto the counter. Without a word, he opened a slim leather folder and placed it flat on the counter. The inside of the folder was black velvet. When he lifted the little figure onto the fabric, it caught the light.

"Ha," he said, after studying it for a minute, "this is very nice."

"What can you tell me about it?"

"You mean, how much?"

"That, yes, but what is it, where did it come from?"

"It's not yours?"

"I inherited it."

He pressed his lips together, and I got the feeling that if I'd been a black male, he'd have slipped into the back room, checked a stolen-property list, and possibly called the cops. The fact that I was a Caucasian female made him think I might be telling the truth.

"Well," he said, lifting it, "for a start, pre-Columbian."

Roz had told me that; I knew that.

"From one of the cultures wiped out when the *conquistadores* showed up. The old cultures. Indian, if you take Indian to mean tribal. I got a guy works for me would know it like this." He snapped his fingers. "He'd say, 'That's early Calima' or 'That's late Quimbaya,' but I don't know exactly where this came from. I've never seen a piece quite like it.

You inherited it? You have more?" He had a habit of running his tongue over his teeth.

"Just the one."

"Well, I can tell you the gold is not pure. Too red in color. One of the tribes, I forget which, had a dozen words for gold, from bright yellow all the way to copper. A lot of tribes used a gold and copper alloy. *Tumbago,* I think, or *tumbaga.* In the modern reproductions, you don't see it too often."

"This is a modern reproduction?"

"A good one, too, possibly Cano stuff, but it isn't quite— I don't know."

"Cano?"

"Galleria Cano. Latin American outfit, but they've got a branch in New York. The Cano family has been involved with gold for generations. They sold the Gold Museum in Bogotá most of their permanent collection." The man ran a finger over the narrow band that edged the wings of the tiny figure and nodded approvingly. "This is very detailed, very nice. Cano uses the lost-wax method, like the ancient tribes."

"What's that?"

"I don't want to bore you."

"Please."

He gave his little courtly bow again. "They use a dental paste, very rubbery, to make a mold of an original. Once you have the mold, one for each side of the figure, then you join the two halves of the mold so they swing open." He made a shape with his hands, the sort of thing a child might make to show how an alligator bites. "Like the two sides of a shell, you see?"

"Yes."

"Into the mold, you pour black wax, molten wax, and you let it cool. You check the mold to make sure it corresponds exactly to the original. The artisan fixes it, then positions it on a special stand with five hollow rods. The rods are the supports."

I nodded.

"Then the artisan puts thin coats of plaster on the mold. With a brush, many layers until he has a solid mold. Then he heats it, so the wax inside melts and drains out through the supports. You see? Lost wax."

"So the mold is hollow."

"Yes, and into the hollow, the artisan pours molten gold." His eyes gleamed when he said the words 'molten gold.' "Today they spin the mold on a centrifuge so the gold penetrates to even the smallest part of the interior, but the Indians, they probably didn't do that. When it cools and hardens, you break the plaster." He held up the figure. "And there it is. Beautiful, no?" The little figure looked smug, as though he was enjoying his stint as center of attention.

"The Spanish," the man added with disdain, "melted down the gold. They sent it away in ships, in plain flat bars or pieces of eight. People still go hunting for those galleons, off the coast, all over the Caribbean."

I wondered if he was a treasure hunter, if that accounted for the gleam in his eye, if working with gold provoked a lust for it. I touched the little birdman. The black velvet backing and the overhead light combined to ignite the golden shape.

"Is it a bird or a man?" I asked.

"Both, I guess. I wish the guy works for me was here. He'd tell you. Animals stand for different things in different tribal cultures. Some of the Indians thought they could transform themselves into animals, become jaguars or tree frogs. Some of these little statues are familiars, some fetishes, some fertility things, but the birdman, I think, is sort of a religious figure. The tribal leaders, not the war leaders, but the spiritual leaders, the shamans, they had visions, you know?" He glanced at me to see if I was following.

I smiled. "Hallucinogenic visions?"

"Some did it through deprivation. Starved themselves till they saw visions, or refused to sleep. But drugs played a part. They used things we don't even know about, mushrooms, leaves, all kinds of plants. They used snake venom and the glands of certain frogs. The shaman would go off into the mountains or the jungle and come back in a month or two, and talk about his journey, about how his soul took flight. Pretty soon, he had everybody believing he'd been somewhere else, on another plane of existence, with the gods, with the holy spirits. The birdman was a representation of the shaman, of the symbolic flight, so this little guy here, he's probably some kind of spirit guide. If you want, I could call the man works for me, ask him."

I had sewing to do and makeup, not to mention leg-shaving. Roz hadn't mentioned my hair, but I'd need to do something about that, too.

"That's okay," I said. "Thank you."

"Eight hundred," he said.

"Huh?" I'd gotten so wrapped up in his story, I'd forgotten my initial query, and his offer took me by surprise.

"I'd go eight hundred for this. The gold isn't worth anywhere near that much, but I know somebody who'd really go for it."

"People collect this kind of thing?"

"People collect anything. Soap dishes, tea trays, cigar bands. Art deco is the biggest down here. You move to Miami, and you've got a few bucks, you collect deco." A smile crinkled the edges of his mouth and eyes. "I talk too much."

"Not at all. But I think I might not want to sell this now that I know so much about it."

"See? I talk too much. Where did you say you got this?" His hand caressed the figure.

"I didn't."

"Hey, no offense. With collectors, the more you know about a piece, the better they like it. Eight hundred's a good offer. Especially if you don't have papers to go with it."

It was more money than I'd imagined. "I'll think about it."

"Maybe I could go another hundred. It's a very nice piece. Do you have a card? A phone number? I could give you a call later this afternoon, or tomorrow. I don't think you'll get a better offer."

"I know where you are. If I decide to sell, I'll come back."

He pressed a store business card on me, scribbling his name on the back before unlocking the door so I could leave.

I was halfway to the motel, walking in the fierce sun, before I realized I still held the birdman in my right hand. His felt pouch, released from my backpack, exuded the perfumy odor of Paolina's locker. The mix of scents blended with the heat, and suddenly it seemed as though she stood there, in front of me, wide-eyed and smiling, a mirage shimmering in the heat.

Where is she? The question was so firmly in my mind I almost spoke to the blank-eyed statue aloud. Dammit, if you're supposed to be her spirit guide, *where the hell is she*?

CHAPTER 12

VANDENBURG WORE HIS blue silk shirt open at the neck and tucked into softly pleated gray slacks. His heavy gold chain matched the glint of his cufflinks. In the backseat of the chocolate-colored Jaguar, a navy blazer on a wooden hanger blocked the tinted window. The lawyer gave me a studied look, then shoved the car into gear with more than a little ostentation, not that the Jag needed more than it already had.

"I underestimated your duffel bag," he said.

I settled into the leather-upholstered cave, inhaling the scent of new car as I fastened the seat belt, my scarf-top securely attached to my necklace with tiny unnoticeable stitches. My late aunt Bea, who'd once imagined she'd teach me to embroider, would have been proud.

Roz had walked me through the do's and don'ts of slutty tropical evening wear, starting with how to properly tie my top so I didn't pop out. I'd been planning to wear my hair up, but she'd vetoed that, voting for wild and curly, which was easier anyway. Bend at the waist, hands through the hair, then makeup, the light base that blurs rather than hides my few freckles, exaggerated eyeliner, shadow, and mascara. Rose-colored lip gloss.

Vandenburg seemed to approve.

He did tourist chitchat as we drove eastward toward the ocean, trying to sound like this was some kind of old-fashioned date while I tried to quell the rising sense of urgency in the pit of my stomach. What if Naylor proved as devastating a dead end as Diego?

The air conditioning felt cool on my bare arms as we drove past low tile-roofed office parks and self-serve gas stations. Vandenburg handled the car well, but didn't push the speed limit. If I'd been driving, I'd have let the Jaguar rip on the freeway, but he held it to a careful sixty-five. When we turned off the freeway onto a narrow two-lane road bordered by a drainage ditch on one side and skinny palms on the other, the tourist patter ended as abruptly as it had begun.

"I'm taking a risk, bringing you here," he said.

"Drop me a block away and I'll wander in without you."

He braked and we coasted to a stop at the side of the road. The Oldsmobile behind us honked and swerved as the lawyer swiveled to face me.

"I have to know; did someone send you?"

"I told you. I'm working for myself, looking for Roldán's daughter."

"Are you wired?" In spite of the AC, beads of sweat stood out on his forehead.

"In this?" I held up my arms. "Are you kidding?" I'd considered the possibility of concealing a weapon and given it up, figuring that if worse came to worse, I could use the thin spike of a high heel. They're not called stilettos for nothing.

"They have small recorders," he said.

"You're too suspicious. Probably comes with being a lawyer."

He pressed his lips together and stared at the steering wheel.

"What else can you tell me about Naylor?" I asked.

"Like I said, produces movie shorts for big companies."

According to Roz, Naylor didn't belong to any of the professional motion picture organizations. She'd come up with a big fat zero on Drew or Andrew Naylor.

"But he makes his money from drugs," I ventured.

"You didn't hear that from me."

"Are you his lawyer?"

"I've represented him in several matters dealing with divorce and, um, matters of paternity. I can tell you this: He doesn't deal well with women like you."

What the hell did that mean, women like me? Tall women? Uppity insubordinate women? I didn't ask because Vandenburg was on a roll.

"Look, it'll work better if you keep to the background, play the girlfriend role, let me do business with Naylor."

"What are you planning to tell him?"

"Nothing fancy. I need the man's number. Old business." He pulled back onto the road without so much as a glance in the rearview mirror. He must have considered the conversation finished. I didn't.

The streets got wider, the palms statelier, the lawns more expansive. The houses grew larger, too, like well-tended hot-house plants. The Jaguar turned down a narrow lane, passed through high iron gates, and came to a halt at the rear of a parade of high-rent vehicles. Instead of waiting his turn in the parking queue, Vandenburg left his keys in the ignition, shrugged into his jacket, and abandoned his ride. I followed suit, accompanying him up a winding shell-paved path. One of the red-vested car parkers chased us down and handed him a ticket stub.

The distant shoreline curved to the left, midnight ocean melting into pale sand. To the right, white fairy lights hung over the portico and pillars of a pseudo-Southern plantation-style Colonial. Urns of red and orange bougainvillea framed the rose-colored double doors, and window boxes under-scored enough windows for a small hotel. On a shaded patio, waitresses in micro-skirts plied guests with drinks in frosted glasses.

Vandenburg stopped halfway up the walk and I was glad to take a moment to steady myself on my heels. Chatter and music drowned out the sounds of the ocean.

"Maybe this isn't such a great idea," he said.

"I'll handle Naylor myself. You don't need to be part of it." For a moment, he seemed to weigh his options. Then he glanced at the drinkers on the patio and shrugged regretfully.

"They've already seen us together."

Dozens of full-blown roses crowded a teak sideboard in the entryway. The house was airy, the paintings abstract, the furnishings modern. We made our way past a pair of leather sofas in the living room, through a mirror-lined hallway into a dining room with a high, vaulted ceiling, but it was the guests that grabbed the eye, especially the women, glossy, poised, and clad like women in a European fashion magazine. With shoulders bare and inches of midriff on display, I was modestly covered, my outfit a burka compared to party standards. Roz was right: I could have worn underwear if I'd had the foresight to pack sexier gear. I wasn't the tallest woman in the gathering and that was unusual enough, but some of these women made me feel large, a middleweight among sylphs, and believe me, I'm thin enough that people use the word skinny.

Models, I thought. Or actresses for commercial films.

"Where's our host?" I murmured as we moved through the dining area into a crowded room beyond. I had to slide close to Vandenburg's ear to whisper because this new room featured a movie-screen-sized TV loudly tuned to basketball. I could smell his musky cologne. In addition to the TV blare, a rhythmic bass came from the back of the house, loud enough to be live. Vandenburg shook hands with one man, slapped backs with a couple others. He didn't introduce me; none of the men mentioned the women clinging to their arms. I was starting to think my nose, broken three times in the line of duty, was too big. None of the other women had noses to speak of.

Vandenburg was checking out the guests, his eyes roving quickly across the crowd, but whether he was looking for Naylor or searching for more agreeable female companionship, I couldn't tell. I repeated my query.

"I don't see him. We ought to mingle for a while, have a drink or two. It'll look funny if I race over and beg for information."

He was right. He might fare better if Naylor were slightly soused by question-and-answer time, but I was impatient. This didn't look like my kind of gathering. Too many capped teeth and dazzling white smiles. Too much lacquered hair, like a Hollywood movie where nobody looks like a real person you might see on the street.

I bit my lip. Vandenburg could see his answer didn't please me.

"Okay, okay," he said irritably. "Let me grab a martini first. Why don't you wait by the pool?"

"Tell Naylor whatever you want. But if he won't talk to you, I'm taking a shot."

"I thought we agreed—"

"You agreed."

We stared bullets at each other till he dropped his eyes.

"Yeah, sure, whatever." He gave me a leer. "Right. Well, come to think of it, dressed the way you are, he might tell you a lot of things he wouldn't tell me."

Some compliment, I thought.

"But no threats," he said.

Within ten seconds of Vandenburg's departure, a waiter stuck a champagne flute in my hand. A man to my left spoke melodious Portuguese. An Asian woman wore an ice-blue sarong. Cigarette smoke hung like fog over the room. As I moved through an adjacent corridor, it joined and blended with the pungent fug of marijuana. If Naylor owned this house, he was minting money. Hell, even if he rented, he was paying big bucks.

A tray of hors d'oeuvres sailed by just out of reach and I realized I was starving. The champagne was fine, icy and dry, but it needed a food foundation. I followed the tray toward French doors, hoping they opened out onto the pool.

In spite of the crush in the house, the pool was clearly the hub of the party. I made my way through a field of round tables lit by flaring torches, skirting a group of men speaking fluent Colombian Spanish, wishing I still smoked, so I could hesitate and light up, the perfect excuse for eavesdropping. I overheard the word "extradition." Further along, a man's bored voice, in English: "You do the math; no way he'll refuse."

The smell of barbecue made my mouth water. I found the source and piled a plate with skewers of grilled shrimp. The tables were full, so I perched on top of a cement wall separating the pool area from a stretch of sandy beach, settled my plate on my lap, and ate hungrily. A passing waiter replaced my champagne flute with an icy margarita rimmed in salt.

The pool, a kidney-shaped turquoise basin with a diving board, was backed by a low cabana. The men wore European-cut Speedos to show off tanned, fit bodies; several of the bodies hardly meshed with seamed fiftyish faces. The women, much younger, wore postage-stamp bikinis or Brazilian thongs. Not the sort of thing you see on Massachusetts beaches, where folks jump into a fifty-degree ocean wearing bike shorts over tank suits.

"Do you swim?"

I nodded through a mouthful of shrimp. The man to my left was young and deeply tanned, with a lifeguard build.

"Plenty of suits in the cabana. Bet you could find one that fits."

"Maybe later."

"I'm Jerry." He gave me a dentist's-dream smile. "You need a refill on that margarita?"

I didn't, but Jerry brought one anyway. He didn't know Naylor, was a friend of a friend who'd worked on a film.

"What kind of film?"

"You been to a car show? You know how they use those models to sell the cars? That's what he does on film, uses pretty girls to promote whatever the company sells. Nice line of work, I'm telling you."

Jerry was low maintenance, the kind of guy who talks and talks and only expects you to nod occasionally. It was easy to do that and watch the crowd.

Everywhere, evidence of wealth, on the men more than the women. Pinkie rings and gold chains, diamond stud earrings. Stuff that could be readily sold. The men at the tables weren't dressed as skimpily as the women. Quite a few wore jackets and with the temperature in the eighties, several of those jackets probably hid shoulder holsters. I'd been to parties like this when I'd first started going with Sam Gianelli. Mob deals, a lot of guests carry.

Sam would fit right in. He'd appreciate the way the men

talked in sentences that were almost incomprehensible because they assumed a certain knowledge. *This thing, that stuff, this business*—terms that could be recorded and played back without the cops learning a thing. I wished he were here, standing where the vacuous Jerry stood, holding a glass, grinning at me with his eyes over the tilted rim.

He hadn't called. I didn't know where he was staying in Las Vegas. I was worried about him, the worry a dull tattoo underneath the more pressing anxiety about Paolina.

The band, a Caribbean group with a heavy-handed approach to percussion, took a break to scattered applause. A knot of men strolled by, discussing the future of the Miami Dolphins. I felt a hand close on my bare shoulder. Vandenburg.

Jerry made tracks. Margaritas and high heels made standing a minor challenge.

"He didn't bite," Vandenburg said. "Wouldn't give me the man's number. But he'll talk to you."

I drained my margarita; the connection between rubbery legs and drink hadn't quite clicked in my head. "What did you say about me?"

"Nothing. When he wouldn't cooperate, I admitted I was acting as an intermediary. He said he'd prefer to deal with the principal."

Damn. I'd had more to drink than I'd realized. Should have poured the rest of the margarita in the pool. "Where is he?"

"I'll show you."

As we glided through the TV room, a man who'd had more than a few drinks himself lurched into my path. "You one of Drew's girls?" he asked loudly. I kept walking. We passed a room where couples shook their bodies to a different band than the Caribbean group on the patio. A couple slid discreetly up a curving staircase, possibly headed for bedroom frolics. *Drew's girls.* Maybe Naylor had a sideline in pimping. Maybe this shindig was some sort of businessman's special, a free-for-all escort service.

I followed Vandenburg through a vast kitchen teeming with white-aproned caterers and bustling waiters, then through a low doorway into a quieter section of the vast house.

"No threats," the lawyer reminded me outside a paneled door. "Knock. You want me to come with you?"

I shook my head.

"Come to the pool afterward."

I waited till Vandenburg disappeared, gave a perfunctory cop knock, turned the knob, and walked in. Cops are always hoping to catch somebody doing something they shouldn't.

My quick entry was wasted. Naylor, if the man on the chaise was Naylor, was doing nothing except reclining with closed eyes in a room that looked more gilded than decorated. The heavy drapes were gold, the walls covered in a gold Chinese paper that added touches of scarlet. The carpet was beige, flecked with gold. A walking stick with a carved head leaned against a desk made of pale wood with gilded scrollwork. The color made me feel lucky; maybe the little golden birdman, the spirit guide, was signaling that I'd come to the right place. More likely I was really starting to feel the alcohol.

"Shut the door." The man opened his eyes, but other than that, he didn't move.

He was heavy at first glance, but it was more a heaviness of shoulders, arms, and chest, like a wrestler. His face seemed long, and while he wasn't old, maybe forty, he had jowls that pulled the corners of his mouth down. I couldn't estimate his height very well because he was lying down. He wore a baseball cap pulled low over his eyes. Even after he opened them, I couldn't distinguish their color.

"You're missing the party," I said lightly, not wanting to start with demands before I got a sense of the man. He didn't look drop-dead attractive to women, yet women heavily outnumbered men at the party. Even a commercial film producer was a man with casting power. He probably had a lot of pop in Miami.

"So you're making Vandenburg jump though hoops, eh?" he said, a smile tickling the corners of his droopy mouth.

"I do what I can."

"You wish to find the notorious Roldán."

"I do."

"Are you perhaps a 'journalist' looking to make some money?" His voice had a hint of generic accent. He wasn't American-born. Possibly South American, but that's about all I could tell.

I shook my head.

"Then what?"

What indeed? I was feeling more than a little queasy. A light sweat glistened on my forehead. Too much alcohol too fast.

Naylor gave me the eye, staring like he could see through my halter, like he knew all about girls like me. But if Vandenburg had told me the truth, all Naylor actually knew was that I was searching for Roldán. The reclining man's assumption that I was looking to make money was his own.

When you work undercover you learn a few helpful rules. One of the best is this: Use what the perp brings to the table. Another good one: Be who the perp supposes you to be. What Naylor brought to the table was lechery. What he assumed I brought was greed.

With hardly a moment's hesitation, I placed a hand lightly on my stomach and said, "It's like this: I need to talk to my baby's father."

"Ah."

I could read in his satisfied expression that I'd blurted an explanation he could easily believe, and for a moment I believed it, too. It had the advantage of truth; Roldán was my baby's father, Paolina's father. Plus it seemed to me a reason that Naylor, plagued with paternity problems of his own, would understand, a strong and urgent reason to find Roldán.

He looked like he'd enjoyed the revelation. I wondered about his relationship to Roldán. If he held any sort of grudge against him, maybe I could spin that in my favor.

"I see." He blinked, something he didn't do often. I wasn't sure, but it seemed to me that one of his eyes was slightly different than the other, a narrower slit in the long face. "May I offer my congratulations?"

"You could offer me a seat."

His mouth twitched, and he nodded toward a brocade-covered chair. For a while we were both silent, but I didn't mind. I like silence. The room was soundproofed, the loud party no more than a distant repetitive bass.

He said, "And where did you meet El Martillo?"

"Panama." One of the packages of long-ago cash had arrived with a Panamanian coin stuck underneath a layer of bubble wrap.

"What took you there?"

"Sometimes I crew on boats."

"Yes," he said. "I see. I knew you weren't a model. A model looks like a model. She can't help it. She cants her hips just so when she stands. The training becomes automatic. An athlete, also she stands a certain way. You play tennis, yes?"

I nodded to make him feel smart. I play volleyball and the arm motion for a spiker is pretty much the same as that of a server. If he was really smart he'd have questioned my lack of a tan.

"Sometimes the people I crew for invite me to parties," I said.

"I would certainly invite you." His stillness was creepy, lizard-like. His mouth opened and shut, but the rest of his face was a mask. His ears were small and close to his head.

"Thank you," I said, "but I don't need party invitations. What I need is the man's phone number so I can find out how he treats women after he sleeps with them."

"He didn't feel it necessary to advise you how to get in touch when you parted?"

"Things have changed."

"You learned he was a wealthy man?"

"I learned I was pregnant," I said flatly.

"You're after money, I suppose."

"You giving it away?"

His head lolled to one side and he laughed, a harsh, grating sound, like the caw of a large crow. "Yes, yes, I see. Well, you have an interesting problem. You like older men?"

"Not older men in general. I like Carlos."

He squirmed to one side of the wide chaise and made a

low noise like an insect humming. His arm moved abruptly and he patted the cushion.

"Then you wouldn't care to join me here?"

"No."

"Not even if I might then give you a number where you could reach our mutual friend?" He rubbed his crotch suggestively. I kept the smile on my face, thinking that if he yanked his zipper he was going to be one sorry SOB.

"I'm not a hooker, mister, just a girl who got knocked up. I don't go for older men. I like Carlos. And he likes me. He told me I could get to him through that lawyer."

"Perhaps he deliberately misdirected you. Have you considered that? Send Thurman back in, please. When you leave."

I stayed seated. "Then you won't help me?"

"What's your name, young lady?"

"Carlotta."

"Carlotta and Carlos. How very sweet."

"After we're married, maybe we'll name our kid after you, Drew."

"You wouldn't mind raising a child in Colombia?"

"Where in Colombia?" I tried to soften the question with a smile but I'd pounced too quickly.

His mouth narrowed. "I'll speak with Thurman now."

"Please, if you change your mind—let me give you my number." I scribbled my cell on a pad on his desk, begged him to give the number to Roldán if he didn't trust me, but I knew it was no go. My intensity had scared him and I was dismissed. I didn't bang the door on the way out but it took effort to restrain the impulse.

I was furious at myself. A glass of champagne, two birdbath-sized margaritas. My head was muddled and I'd blown what might be my only chance to find Paolina. I found myself in the busy kitchen uncertain of the way to the pool. I felt lousy, as helpless and dumb as the pregnant, abandoned woman I'd pretended to be. My mouth tasted sour and I made my way to a sink, intent on water. A man washing dishes glared at me, but nodded to a stack of plastic glasses when I asked.

I drank a full glass, ran the icy stream over my hand, and patted the back of my neck. A woman in a flowered apron yanked a tray of cheese puffs from the oven and clucked at me to get out of her way.

I wanted access to that desk in Naylor's office, that fat pale desk with the golden curves. I wanted the man's Rolodex, his files, his little black books, his memory. To be so close, to come away with nothing . . .

Kitchens, big modern kitchens, have desks. Desks have drawers and drawers have files, and files contain all sorts of domestic goodies, like phone bills. I didn't go back to Vandenburg like a good little girl. I snooped instead, sitting at the desk, pressing the phone to my ear as though I were making a call while my hands riffled through piles of papers. If Naylor was in touch with Roldán, the phone number might be as close as my fingertips. It might never get closer than it was now.

"Can I help you?"

The woman wasn't wearing an apron, but there was a smear of flour on her cheek.

"Jeez, you have any aspirin?" I said. "Drew said there was aspirin in here, but I didn't know it would be a fucking treasure hunt." I let myself sound drunker than I was. It was easy.

She exchanged glances with one of the caterers at the same moment I saw the SBC logo on an envelope. SBC. Southern Bell Company. The day's mail was stacked on a corner of the desk for sorting.

"You know where the closest bathroom—" I made my mouth work like I might be getting ready to vomit, and the woman hastily pointed me east. I made a shambles of my effort to stand, knocked the mail to the floor, and knelt to restore it. I grabbed the SBC envelope and held it to my stomach, clasping both hands over it as I groaned and ran.

In the bathroom, I took a long breath and held a hand to my pounding temple. For a moment I thought I might actually be sick. Then I rinsed my mouth with cold water, tucked the phone bill into my pants, and went to find Vandenburg.

CHAPTER 13

WHEN THE PHONE jangled me from sleep, I swung my legs out of bed, my head split open, my stomach flopped through a bizarre series of acrobatic maneuvers, and I thought: *Paolina, sweetheart, I'm not mad at you. I'm so glad you called. Wheverever you are, stay put; I'm on my way.*

Fumbling for the receiver, a second possibility rushed into my head: *Sam, why didn't you call last night?* I grabbed my cell, flipped it open, and pressed the button only to be greeted by Mooney's growl.

"What?" The word was out of my mouth before I could contemplate substituting a civil hello.

"Carlotta? I wake you?"

The clock on the bedside table said nine. Impossible. I must have turned off the alarm.

"You okay?"

His voice hammered my eardrums. My tongue felt as fuzzy as the hotel blanket, my throat raw. *What the hell was in those margaritas?* I sucked a deep breath and scrunched my eyes shut. It felt like the middle of the night but a steady stream of sunlight poured through the thin curtains.

"Paolina," I said. "Is she—? Did you—?"

"No bad news. No great news, either, but no disasters."

I opened my eyes slightly, flinching at the skull-piercing sunshine. "You said you might have something, that you'd—"

"I'm still working it."

"Oh." I ran my dry tongue over dry lips. "How did the thing with the feds go?"

"If Paolina hijacks a plane, they'll get interested. Seriously, it's all terrorists, all the time down the Bureau. Not in so many words, but I got the message between the lines. If I were on the street, I tell ya, now's the time I'd pull a bank job."

"The Roldán angle didn't grab them?"

"I'm going to DEA direct. One of our narcs is setting it up for me."

"When?"

"You flying back today?"

"I don't know," I said slowly. "I doubt it."

"What?" he said. "You getting somewhere?"

The SBC envelope was lying on the bedside table underneath the clock. "I've got a couple of Colombian phone numbers."

I listened to his silence, but it was my own doubt I heard. Two of the numbers on the stolen phone bill bore the 571 prefix that meant Bogotá. One of them might or might not lead to Roldán. One of them might or might not lead to my little sister's whereabouts.

"It's something," I said defensively.

"Enough to justify a plane ticket?"

"Somebody told me Roldán was in Colombia."

"A guy I talked to yesterday told me he saw Elvis in Cleveland."

"My guy seemed to be running on all cylinders. How about yours?"

"Who did you talk to?"

"I gave you the name yesterday. Drew Naylor."

"No record, no warrants. Who is he?"

I shrugged, then realized he couldn't see the movement over the phone. "A businessman," I said. "A creep."

"But you believe him. Because you want to believe him, right?"

My head throbbed. Without coffee I wasn't prepared to do battle with Mooney. He was right; I wanted to believe

Roldán was in Colombia. I wanted to believe Paolina was with him, safe or relatively safe. Physically unharmed.

"Look," he said, "Triola and I spent last night hitting shelters. Church basements, the Pit, the flops. I called a couple Worcester cops, a few guys in New York. Called in a few favors."

"Moon, thank you." I knew what kind of days he put in. If he spent nights searching for Paolina, he was getting no sleep at all.

"Gloria's got cabbies looking for Paolina from Maine to New York."

"See? You and Gloria and Roz can handle anything that comes up in the States."

"Carlotta, just because we can't find her locally doesn't mean she's in Colombia."

"Doesn't mean she isn't."

I couldn't explain my conviction that she was with Roldán to Mooney because I couldn't fully explain it to myself. It was there in my gut, but I wasn't sure it amounted to much more than taking the path less traveled. If there was nothing I could do to find her in Boston, nothing that wasn't a feeble echo of an effort already undertaken by others, then I wanted the fresh trail, the one no one else would follow.

Jesus, maybe I was still drunk. Maybe the golden spirit guide was prompting me. I didn't try to sell that one to Mooney. He used to needle me plenty about my "intuition" when I was a cop.

He said, "You talk to Sam lately?"

Sam's proposal weighed like a stone in my gut. Dammit, aren't marriage proposals supposed to be sweetness and light, unfreighted with the baggage of police involvement, promising blissful stretches of blue-sky happily-ever-after?

"Why?" I responded cautiously.

"Honestly, Carlotta, for a smart woman you can be—" His voice died.

"You want to finish that thought?"

"I just want to know how much you know about what your beau's been up to the past two years."

Sam and I hadn't been together the past two years; we'd rekindled the flame a scant three months ago. Mooney knew that as well as I did. We'd discussed our mutual lack of significant others over two lingering Chinese restaurant meals. After the second, I'd expected him to invite me back to his apartment. But he'd gotten called out on a case and the opportunity had never materialized again.

He said, "The feds are keeping me updated, so if Gianelli gets a ransom note, I'll know."

"Moon, come on, this isn't about Sam. Marta sold Paolina's photo to one of Roldán's—"

"The lady *said* she was from Roldán. But that could have been a diversion. What's to stop her from being Mob?"

"You want it that way, Moon. You want me scared off of Sam."

As soon as I said it, I wished I could take it back, delete the words like suspect e-mail. My forehead gave another throb and I considered the possibility of pretending I'd lost the connection, hanging up. The silence grew.

He said, "You're right. Guilty as charged. I want you and the kid to have a future."

"Mooney—"

"Hey, I'll call you right back. I got somebody on the other line."

Sure, I thought. *Sure you do.*

The phone went dead and I thought: *Coffee.*

The room didn't run to a lot of extras; no mini-bar, no bathroom phone extension, but a coffeemaker perched on a closet shelf with a small foil bag of pre-measured grounds nestled beside it. I hauled it down, plugged the cord into a socket, and added water. Small pink packets of sugar filled an ashtray. No milk, but I wasn't feeling fussy.

I retreated to the edge of the bed and waited for the coffee to brew, feeling battered and too sick to get dressed. I knew Sam was up to his neck in the Mob, more involved than ever. I'd known it when we'd gotten back together, but I'd avoided thinking about it, overwhelmed by physical sensation, lulled and blinded by chemistry, by lust. Dammit, why did Mooney keep hitting me over the head with Sam? Why now? I couldn't think about Sam now. I had to think about Paolina. Face it: The phone numbers were all I had and they were slender threads, threads that might unspool forever without leading to my sister.

For the first time since she'd disappeared I let myself consider the possibility that I might never find her. Never celebrate her sixteenth birthday. Never argue over whether or not she could borrow the car. Never see her walk across a stage to claim her high school diploma.

I've always considered myself lucky, a happy blend of parental heritage with my father's easy laughter and my mother's supple strength. Lucky to have a mother who never stopped loving me, even after I'd driven her to distraction by refusing to name the man who'd fathered my child. The image flickered and I shut my mind against it; I didn't go there.

I'd been young enough, dumb enough, to deny what was happening to my body till most of my options were gone, not that my Catholic father would have abided any solution that meant, to him, terminating a life. I'd felt lucky to be loved through that stormy time, even by parents who hadn't managed to love each other enough to stay together.

When I was sixteen, my mother's sudden death had stunned me, but my aunt Bea had taken me in without a second thought and given me all the fierce love her frail body could hold. My father, dying, had given me away in marriage. Sometimes I thought I'd married Cal at nineteen just so my dad would feel better about dying, knowing he hadn't left me alone.

I made up for lack of family with friends. When I drove for Gloria and Sam, my fellow cabbies became an unlikely band of brothers and sisters. When I swore my oath as a cop, I joined another kind of family. Sometimes it seemed that no one who came to my door ever really went away. I'd mothered Roz, who'd turned up as a tenant. I'd mothered Paolina, making up for that baby I hadn't mothered, the one I'd given away, the one I'd lost.

I worked alone now. I'd grown used to solitude. I played

guitar late at night. I sang other people's blues and solved other people's problems. Not my own. I kept putting off my own choices, telling myself I had plenty of time, plenty of options. I couldn't decide whether or not to accept Sam's proposal. I couldn't decide whether or not I wanted children of my own, and yet last night, I'd faked a pregnancy without a second thought.

Maybe I hadn't made choices about my own life because I still didn't trust the choice I'd made: to give that baby up for adoption. Sometimes, in Harvard Square, I'd freeze, glued to the sidewalk by the sight of a redheaded child.

I had to find Paolina.

The coffee tasted awful. I drank it like medicine, visualizing the caffeine surging through my veins, nudging the sluggish red and white corpuscles awake. I waited for the caffeine to subdue the headache, for the phone to ring, for the answer to the overwhelming question: Should I follow the thread to Colombia? Or give up and go home, defeated? Go home to wait. I studied Naylor's phone bill till I'd practically memorized it. Account number. Billing date. The billing address was the same as the vast Coral Gables house where I'd downed too many margaritas, but the customer was listed as MB Realty Trust. I'd get Roz to check them out.

When he finally called back, Mooney didn't bring up our previous conversation. He didn't even say hello, just started speaking as though Gianelli's name had never come between us. "You've got a photo of Paolina with you, right? A good one?"

"Yes."

"What do you know about facial imaging?" His voice was charged with suppressed excitement.

"Is this the break you were waiting on, Mooney?"

"Right. I've been trying to get in touch with a guy I know who does facial imaging. You know what that is?"

"Yeah." It was one of a handful of promising identification technologies. Not new. Some company had tried it at the Super Bowl in New Orleans and gotten in trouble with every civil liberties group in the country.

"Okay. I don't think they're gonna let you look at every warm body flew Miami–Bogotá in the past week, but if you get them a photo of Paolina, they'll run a scan."

"What about New York–Bogotá? Atlanta?"

"I don't know. You can try."

I plunked the coffee cup on the bed and started a search for paper and pen. "Who's they, Moon? Where? When?"

He said, "I tried to fax the photo I had, but my guy couldn't get good resolution from a fax, and our scanning equipment is on the fritz—"

"Is your guy in Miami?"

"Close. Del Mar."

"I'm on my way."

"You'll have to wait while he runs it."

"Moon, I owe you."

He gave me an address, told me to ask for Greg Hanson. Then he said, "Word is Gianelli flew out of Las Vegas late last night on a charter. You know he got his pilot's license last year?"

I didn't say anything. I hadn't known. He'd never said a single word about learning to fly.

"Hey," Mooney said, "the thing is, I only want what's best for you, Carlotta."

I didn't respond. I was thinking that if I didn't know about the pilot's license, there were probably ten thousand other things I didn't know as well.

"I care about you," he said. "Remember that."

CHAPTER 14

A COLD SHOWER popped my eyes open. Breakfasted and dressed, with three cups of coffee racing three Bufferin through my veins, I waited for a cab under a sun that felt so far removed from the January Boston variety that I might have been standing on land heated by a different star. I shifted into the sparse shade cast by a skinny palm and thanked God for dark sunglasses.

Last night all the parking slots in the motel's handkerchief parking lot had been filled with white lookalike rent-a-cars. Most had peeled off for a day at the beach. A deep blue Saturn sat in a shaded slot. A man in the front seat adjusted his baseball cap as he read a tabloid newspaper. He flipped the page and the cab arrived.

It sped through an area that looked like the outskirts of a business district. Fast food with drive-through lines, multicolored signs for distant orange groves and nearby car washes. The building corresponding to Mooney's address was long, low, and nondescript, neither shabby nor particularly well kept. No sign out front. No name on the front door. Inside: security. The deskman had the brisk air of someone in the military, trim, muscular, and crew cut. Biodyne was the third of four names on a wall display. The other names were of the Acme school, giving no hint as to the nature of the business. There was an underlying smell of chemical processing, a hint of something to do with old-fashioned photography, the same smell that ruled Roz's darkroom.

"Greg Hanson," I said. If the army man asked for a company name, I'd go for Biodyne over Hemisphere or Rectilinear. The buzzword for facial imaging, fingerprint recognition, iris scanning, and such is biometric security.

"Sign here," he said.

I scribbled an illegible signature. He took the phone off the hook, pressed four buttons.

"Hanson," he said, and waited. "Lady visitor, for you." He squinted at my signature.

"Carlyle," I said.

"Miss Carlyle."

"From Boston," I added.

I was instructed to wait. There was a ratty couch against a wall, a small table littered with technical journals. I paced until a voice called my name.

He was mid-twenties, thin and nervous as a cat. His skin was paper white, pale even for Boston in winter. His hair and eyes were dark; he wasn't an albino, just the unhealthy shade of an office slave. His eyes blinked rapidly as he shook my hand with a damp grip.

"Jeez," he said, "you made good time. Practically just got off the phone with the lieutenant." He spoke softly with a meaningful glance at the man behind the desk.

"He's a captain now." I kept my voice low, too.

"Jeez, yeah, he should be. Man, time goes by, you know? Speaking of, this might not be the best time, you know? The boss is here. Some days, most days, he doesn't show, but you know, just now—"

"I don't want you to get in trouble, but Mooney said you might be able to help."

"Missing kid, right?" He pressed his thin lips together, chewed the bottom one, and screwed up his features like he was trying to make up his mind.

I wondered whether to offer him money or flat out beg. I'd gotten my hopes up. If I knew for certain that Paolina had flown to Bogotá, I'd follow and pick up her trail there.

"Please," I said, so softly I could barely hear myself.

He sighed. "So fuck it, I'll get fired. You know how I know the captain?"

I shook my head no.

He chewed his lips some more. "Okay, look, you mind pretending we're going out or something? If the guy asks, you're my girlfriend. I mean he won't believe it, probably, 'cause I mean, look at you, look at me, but—"

I took his hand and squeezed it. "Greg," I said, "I had the best time last night."

His face cracked into a smile. "Cool. Give 'em something to talk about."

We ducked through a hallway hand in hand, then walked into a large icy room. He didn't introduce me around, but our progress attracted glances. I got the feeling Hanson was a loner without friends at Biodyne. Kind of guy who lived for his work. He talked as we walked. The gawkers might have thought it was personal, but it wasn't.

"We were working bio-recognition before 9/11, but man, the bucks have really rolled since. Used to be DARPA and DOD, but now Uncle outsources, pro–private enterprise and all, so we got both the high-end government research and the profit motive. You could say this is your tax dollar at work, but my boss is gonna be a billionaire."

He ushered me into a gray-sided cubicle. Within its low walls was a metal desk overloaded with PCs, two small- and one large-screen. He sank into a chair and started typing, suddenly oblivious to my presence, as though the keyboard had called him and he had to respond.

"Billionaire?" I said, mostly to remind him I was still present.

"Hey, sit down somewhere."

I moved a pile of manuals off a dusty chair and obeyed, edging the chair over so I could eyeball the screens.

He kept typing. "Yeah, this is the stuff gonna change the game. You know they're gonna have biometric feeds in your passport by '05; it's the law."

"HDTV by 2003, wasn't it?"

"Who cares about TV when you've got terrorists to catch? Homeland Security bucks to spend? We've already bypassed the guys who wanted to replace passwords and PINs with fingerprint readers. That shit's okay for Disney, but not for security. You know about the Gummi Bears?"

"Gummi Bears?" I thought my hangover headache might be causing hearing trouble.

"Yeah, yeah, some Japanese guy proved you could diddle the best fingerprint readers with the same kind of gel in Gummi Bears, made a big stink. And the iris scan can be really hard to read. You need a whole mess of professional readers, and what kind of airport's gonna hire people have to have as much education as the guys who read the X-rays at a hospital? Too expensive, but what's turning out to be the goods is what we got, which is 3-D imaging."

"That's better than just a photo?"

"You kidding?" He was off and running, getting faster and louder as he waxed enthusiastic. I got an earful of sub-pixel calibrations and XYZ distances between facial landmarks at sub-mm precision. Patent-pending algorithms were used to triangulate each tiny visual feature—up to a million points on a face. Hanson was in no danger of getting fired even if the boss wandered over. He knew his stuff.

"This system's good to go?" I said. "Now?"

"That's the thing. We got a setup at Miami–Dade on the known drug runs, but we're not exactly advertising it."

At Miami–Dade. Not Atlanta. Not New York. If Paolina had left the country, I prayed she'd passed through Miami.

I said, "What if you spot somebody, like somebody on the most-wanted list? Whitey Bulger coming to visit?"

"Who?"

In Boston everybody knows who Whitey is. "A mobster," I said. "A crook."

"I dunno. It's not up to me. I just do the work."

I was glad Hanson wasn't developing advanced nuclear weaponry.

He said, "So lemme have the kid's picture and I'll see what we've got."

I reached into my backpack, removed one of Paolina's photos from a padded envelope.

"Hey, hey," he said admiringly.

"She's fifteen."

He muttered something under his breath, "Jailbait," I think. He didn't quite have the tact to keep it to himself, but at least he tried to mute it. He cut his eyes at me to see whether I'd overheard.

"Okay," he said, "I'm gonna scan her in, run for similar facial characteristics. We might get a few pops, 'cause you can see she's Hispanic and it's a plane loaded with Hispanics, and we haven't got the stuff fine-tuned yet."

"Don't the people see the cameras and ask what's going on?"

"Even if they saw 'em, I don't think they'd ask. Most of 'em want more security. Who wants to wind up part of a human bomb? But they don't notice, because the cameras are simple boxes that can be hidden almost anywhere, the 3-D stuff's all software. It's damned near fail-safe without a lot of false positives, which is what gets your airlines really riled. And your ACLU, too."

"What about makeup?" I said.

"Makeup?" He acted like he'd never heard of the stuff.

"Yeah. If I know you're looking for me, I'm gonna reshape my eyebrows, dye my hair."

"Yeah, but you can't change your face."

"Actors do a pretty good job."

"Beards and shit."

"I'm not talking beards. I'm talking changing the shape of your face. Cheek pads."

"I see where you're heading, but we got you nailed. I mean, faces change as people age, the lower jaw sags and shit, but the area around the eye, the setting of the eye, that's what we value most, and you can't change that without major facial surgery. Look, there's nothing I can build that somebody can't gimmick, okay? Any safety field I build, you can tear down, but what I do is I make it hard, as hard as I can, and I have lots of people review what I do because I can't think of everything. You're a PI, right? Maybe we could hire you to do some challenges. You could hang around. We could get to know each other better." He seemed to have taken our boyfriend-girlfriend charade to heart.

I handed him the photo. "Can you find her for me?"

"Sure, right." He rejoined real life and got the twitchy look on his face again, the look that said he'd never have time to code all the programs he needed to code.

He placed the photo in a machine that looked pretty much like any scanner. I tried to follow his fingers as they raced across the keyboard but he typed with blinding speed, and when I checked the screen he wasn't typing anything recognizable as words.

The larger screen came up with a possible, but it wasn't Paolina, didn't even look much like her. He tapped the keys some more and then up came another wrong one. An older girl, much older.

Then bingo, there she was.

In her school photo, she'd tried to look eighteen, using way too much makeup, choosing a low-cut stretchy top that emphasized her womanly shape. In this shot, she was a child, her hair tumbled around her shoulders, her face wiped clean of lipstick and eyeliner, the neckline of her blouse high and frilly. She could have passed for twelve or thirteen. She didn't smile. Her eyes seemed lifeless. Her mouth was drawn into a thin line.

"Which flight was she on?"

"That's the same girl?" Hanson eyed the screen incredulously. "See? This stuff is good!"

"Which flight?"

"Gimme a sec."

Was Paolina cooperating with Roldán? Had he tricked her in some way? Lied to her? I searched her eyes and found nothing to guide me.

"Flight 48, Avianca. Miami–Bogotá, two nights ago."

Two nights. I'd missed her by a day.

"I'm confused," I said. "What is it you do with these images? Which databases do you compare them with? CIA? DEA?"

"That's not my job," he said. "I'm part of the capture team. Capturing the images, I mean. I'm sorry if this isn't what you want."

I said, "This is terrific, Greg, really," while my mind raced with possible follow-up questions. "Now can you pull up the people with her? The people who walked with her, who sat in the seats next to her?" If she was traveling as a twelve-year-old, it stood to reason she'd have parents with her, adults, guardians.

"No. The system's not programmed that way. Not at all."

"But you can get her passport data, right?" She had to be traveling under an assumed name; if I knew that name I'd be ahead of the game.

He shook his head like a wet dog. "We're not allowed right now. We're just doing the one thing: ID. Sorry."

"Greg, you've been a big help." I smiled and squeezed his shoulder.

He ducked his head. "Not big enough, I guess. Hey, I hope it works out for you."

"Tell me, exactly where is the camera located?"

"Huh?"

"The one that shot her picture."

"There are three cameras, to get the 3-D image."

"Yeah, but are they in the security line, on the jetway? Where?"

"Security," he mumbled, glancing over his shoulder to make sure no one else was near enough to hear.

"And it's video, right," I said, "so it must be sequential."

"Yeah."

"So theoretically, if you had the raw tape, you could see who stood in front of her and who stood behind her in line."

"Well, yeah."

"How big a deal would it be to get ahold of that tape, run the people near her through the databases, see if you can get IDs on them? Even if I could just get photos of them, it would be terrific. I'd be willing to pay for the pictures, pay for your time."

He swiveled his chair and faced me for the first time since

we'd entered the warren of cubicles. His jaw was tight. "You know how I know your Captain Mooney?"

I shook my head cautiously. It didn't hurt as much as I thought it would.

"I'm almost twenty-five now, but when I was eighteen, my brother—twelve years old, always twelve, never gonna be anything else—he was killed in the Old Colony Projects. Man, Boston. I left, and I don't think I could ever go back. I don't think about it, you know? I just flat-out don't think about it. And then, out of the damned blue, the lieutenant calls me."

I wanted to say I was sorry, but my tongue was stuck in my mouth.

"I'll try and find what I can, but don't you try to give me any money for it. The lieutenant, he caught the bastard did it and any time he wants my right arm, you tell him, he can have it clear up to the shoulder. Any time. And if this helps you find your sister, would you—I dunno, gimme a call, let me know?"

I got his business card and his home phone. While he was walking me to the lobby, I wanted to ask about his brother, about what happened, to comfort him in some way, but with the guard staring and the walls closing in, I suddenly felt like I couldn't breathe. I'd been planning to ask the guard to call me a cab, but I blundered out into the killing heat instead, walking as fast as I could till I turned the corner.

There are few photos of my little sister in which she does not smile. It's a joke between us, that she can't spot a camera without a joyful grin lighting her dark eyes. The somber image captured by the security camera haunted me.

I caught the flash of a taxi's roof light out of the corner of my eye, raised my hand in the universal salute. The pavement seemed to shimmer in the heat. Running through honking traffic to open the door, I was already making plans. Back to the hotel, airline reservations, pack. I could be on my way in half an hour. I didn't know where she was, but I knew which flight she'd taken. I might not have clicked with Naylor, but I'd gotten my lead. My hunch was solid, backed by fact; my little sister had boarded a flight to Bogotá.

Colombia. My passport was in order. The U.S. government advised against traveling there, but didn't forbid it. I considered Mooney's dismay at the prospect of my jetting off to Bogotá. I thought about Sam.

I hadn't told Mooney, but I'd spoken to Sam, in the small hours.

He'd sounded tired, but he understood my need to follow Paolina wherever she might go. What he didn't understand was my lack of a weapon. When I'd played it light, telling him I didn't need a firearm to find a teenaged girl, he'd stopped me with: "You're looking for a drug lord and don't forget it."

He could arrange to get me a gun in Miami, no paperwork, no questions asked. But how long would it take? I bit my lip, wondering if he could work the same magic in Bogotá.

Some of the Mob guys will tell you they're not involved in drugs. Whitey Bulger used to insist he'd never visit that particular catastrophe on his South Boston home turf. He lied; he turned out to be the major heroin distributor for the area. When kids OD'd in Southie it was on Whitey's shit, Mexican Brown, brought in by Irish mobsters to plague their own backyard.

Did Sam have Colombian connections? I could have asked. Dammit, I should have asked. But there it was: I didn't want to know.

He'd ended the call with another atypical "I love you," and hadn't mentioned leaving Las Vegas on a chartered plane. What the hell was he up to? Once, years ago, I'd angrily told him I'd never marry him unless and until he was out of the Mob for good. Was it possible he'd gone to Las Vegas to try to disentangle himself from the web that had snared his family before he was born? More likely, I thought, he had some new shady moneymaking scheme to share with his western counterparts.

A deep blue Saturn, identical to the one parked in the shade of the motel lot, caught my eye as it changed lanes. It followed, hanging three or four cars behind the cab, shifting lanes frequently. Its windows were so heavily tinted I couldn't identify either of the men inside. One could have been Vandenburg, one Naylor. Both could have been part of a Miami hit squad, I supposed, although Moon had given me the idea that the hit squad pursuing Sam was a traveling act, a Boston thing.

Someone watching Gianelli might have seen us split at Logan and tracked me, might have shadowed me from the airport to the motel, decided to keep watch in case Sam joined me. But I didn't think I'd been followed from the airport to Vandenburg's office. And I was damn sure no one had followed me from Vandenburg's to the hotel.

If no one had followed me from the airport . . . ah . . . I knew who'd been watching Sam at Logan. I stopped trying to identify the men in the Saturn. Most likely, I didn't know them, couldn't have recognized them, because I don't know any FBI agents currently working out of Miami.

Mooney knew where I was. If they were FBI, Mooney must have given them the name of the motel.

PAOLINA

WHAT THE HELL did they want from her? She didn't think they even knew her father. One thing she was sure of, her father would never let her be treated like this. Not her own father, who'd written her such cool letters and sent her lucky Julio. Losing Julio was a sign; the golden birdman knew better than to go with these crazy people.

They were putting stuff in her food, but she could never catch them at it. A bowl of canned spaghetti, heated in a motel microwave, tasted bitter, but she couldn't be sure. All she knew was that the nights passed quickly in a kind of foggy haze, a whirling blur. She wasn't sleepy, but she slept long and hard, and woke befuddled, with the coppery taste of metal filings in her mouth. She tried not eating, but still she slept. And she had to drink, didn't she? You couldn't live without water. She lost track of days, and no one ever let her turn on a TV or even a radio. She couldn't trust the food or the water and she couldn't trust Ana, in spite of her small unexpected kindnesses, the secret gift of a candy bar or soft drink. She couldn't trust Jorge.

When Jorge told her to strip to the skin, she'd thought, This is it, here it comes. She wasn't a little kid; she wasn't naïve. She knew what happened to girls dumb enough to get into cars with strangers. Tears welled in her eyes; *she hadn't thought they were strangers*. She'd thought they were her father's friends. She'd never imagined a woman would bait a trap for her.

Then Ana had appeared and practically shoved Jorge out of the room. But her orders were the same: Take off your clothes.

"Why?"

"So you can wash, baby. What do you think?"

So she'd taken a shower in the scummy stall, and Ana hadn't even let her pull the rotting curtain. Not that she was that shy or modest or anything, but it made her angry, made her jaw feel tight and hard, to be so helpless, without any protection except her anger. While she scrubbed her hair, Ana started to talk.

"Pay attention," she said. "We're all going to dress up, for photos. We're gonna be polite and happy, one big, happy family. You're my little girl, and I'm gonna dress like your mama. You'd like it if I was your mama, right? I'd be a good mother to you. Jorge's gonna be your daddy, and that's what you're gonna call him, you understand? And then we're gonna keep on acting real nice, all the way through the airport."

She glanced up hopefully. Jorge had a gun, an ugly gray automatic, but you couldn't bring a gun into an airport.

Ana said, "Oh, baby, I know what you're thinking, but get it out of your mind. If you try anything at the airport, it's not you who's gonna suffer, you know? Oh, yeah, you can say something to a cop, a security guard. Go ahead, it might get you off the hook. But your mother, your brothers, they're dead soon as I press a button."

"You can't do that." Jaime, her youngest brother, barely eight years old, was a pest, always wanting to play stupid card games. But he was so little. He hadn't had any kind of a life yet, and he hadn't done anything wrong. He hadn't trusted the wrong people.

"Don't you watch TV? Don't you know what can happen in the world, baby? Right, I can't do that. Nothing can happen to you, baby. You're home in your little bed, safe and sound, right? None of this ever happened. Here, put these on."

How, Paolina wondered, could this stone-faced bitch be the same woman who smiled when she handed her a Milky Way?

The blouse was ruffled and too big. The loose pants came all the way up to her waist. They wouldn't let her wear any makeup, no lipstick at all. Ana tried to curl her hair, but that, at least, defeated her. It stayed defiantly straight, so Ana tied it in a ribbon, like she was a poodle or something. The shoes they gave her were too big. When she almost fell out of them, Ana took her to the bathroom and wadded up toilet paper to stick in the toes.

The photos were taken in a busy shop, people going in and out, nobody paying attention. If she'd screamed, nobody would have cared. Ana gave her a glass of orange soda before they drove to the airport, and then she was on the plane and she wasn't sure how she'd walked down the jetway much less how she'd gotten belted into her seat. The middle seat, with Ana at the window and Jorge guarding the aisle.

When she whispered, "I'm gonna be sick," Ana rummaged in the seat-back pocket till she found a paper sack. When she had to go to the bathroom, both Ana and Jorge went along. Ana, in front, checked the bathroom before she went in. Jorge used it afterwards to make sure she hadn't left any messages scrawled on the mirror. When they returned to their seats, she got the window, which was better. At least she could rest her head against the metal wall and fall asleep.

She could hear them talking, a flood of quick light Spanish. That was one thing she had over them. Ana had no idea how good her Spanish was, and Jorge thought she was practically a *gringa*, a dummy who knew little more than high-school Spanish, just because she'd never lived in a Spanish-speaking country. Which was funny because her mother's house was a Spanish-speaking country, for sure. She closed her eyes, kept still, and listened.

And that's when she heard Ana tell Jorge how gullible she was, how she'd believed her about the button she'd punch and the threat to Jaime and her mother. Paolina had to relax her face and keep her breathing steady because she wanted to jump out of her seat and scream, tell everybody on the plane she'd been abducted.

The steward's voice said they'd be landing in fifteen minutes. All electronic devices should be shut off.

"Let her sleep," Jorge said. "They'll pick us up as soon as I call."

She could get away. She could escape. The words sang in her head like a song. But who could she trust? Which grown-up on the plane would believe her? Who, on the ground, would listen to her? She looked like a little kid, a baby. What would happen if she told people that these weren't her parents, that they were kidnappers? Kidnappers who seemed so nice, who carried her passport, who had passports themselves with the same last name they'd picked out for her. Who would believe her, one against two, a kid against grown-ups?

The song in her head dropped to a minor key. She knew no one in Bogotá. The man she'd visited when she was ten, the man Marta had told her to call "Grandfather," was dead. She'd never known his full name or address. To claim kinship with a drug lord would be asking for trouble, but to remain a captive was accepting disaster.

She stayed docile and dumb during the landing and the long wait to deplane. It wasn't an act, the stolid stupidity, not really, because she didn't know what to do. While they waited for their luggage in the terminal, she watched everything. The clock overhead, the sets of double doors that opened into darkness, the cars that passed, with their headlights gleaming. She read the signs: BAÑO, CAMBIO, AUTOBÚS, TAXI. In Boston she knew so many cabdrivers, drivers who worked with Carlotta, who worked for Gloria. Sometimes, when she was walking home from school, a familiar cabbie would toot his horn and offer her a free ride.

She couldn't hail a cab, that was for sure. By the time she got the door open, Jorge would grab her. She let her head nod as though she were sleepy, answered in dull monosyllables when there was no choice other than response, but her eyes were watching and her mind whirring so quickly she felt like she might burst apart in a shower of sparks. She concentrated on breathing, in and out, deep and strong. She flexed her toes in her shoes. If only they'd stay on when the time came to run.

When the moment arrived, she moved without thinking. They were waiting outside. The night air felt crisp, almost like the first days of fall, but it smelled different. Her show of sleepiness and docility must have been convincing, because Jorge barely had his hand on her shoulder and Ana was busy with the luggage. When the bus stopped and the doors yawned, she kept her head down, her eyes half-closed. She seemed to pay no attention, but at the very last second, when the back doors were already closing, folding into each other, she wrenched her whole body, squirming out from under Jorge's grip, and dove through the narrow opening, scraping her arm.

She could see Ana pointing, her mouth opening and closing. Jorge hammered on the door, yelling, and she was terrified, *terrified* the driver would open the door. She knew what it meant now, when someone said their heart was beating so hard it felt like it would crash through the wall of their chest.

Time seemed frozen. Then, like a man with a schedule to keep, the bus driver pressed his foot to the floor.

CHAPTER 15

BREATHLESS. **I POUNDED** down the jetway as the crew prepared to shut the door. A stewardess gave me the look as I edged on board. A woman snarled when I attempted to stick my backpack in the same bin as her carefully folded fur coat. I tried a second bin, this one stuffed with a boxed microwave oven and multiple shopping bags. A third; no dice. The middle-aged man who'd prematurely snatched my aisle seat retreated grudgingly to the center. With the plane fully loaded and the overhead luggage bins crammed, I shoved my backpack under the seat in front of me, muttering a grumpy farewell to legroom. At least I'd made the flight.

Strange, I thought. *Irritating. Weird.*

I'd arrived at the airport early. The blue Saturn hadn't followed me; I'd made sure by demanding a circuitous route that drove the cabbie nuts. I'd drunk a cup of coffee and visited an ATM, drawing out a thousand in fifties on the theory that dollars might be more effective bribes than the pesos paid out by the *cajeros automáticos* in Bogotá.

I hadn't counted on getting yanked out of the security line, placed in a windowless cell, and told to wait.

I replayed the scene in my head while the plane pushed back from the gate. A miracle, really, that I'd made it on board. I'd sat in the cell, minus ticket and passport, tapping my toes and fidgeting, watching the minute hand on my watch creep around the dial. I'm not the sort who has to be first to dash onto the aircraft, but I'd been inspecting my watch at decreasing intervals when a man finally entered the cell and asked me to follow him, please.

He'd ushered me into a slightly larger room occupied by a man and a woman, neither wearing airport security garb. The man, dark-haired and thirtyish, wore a gray suit with shiny patches at the knees, and was busily inspecting my travel documents. The woman, younger, in severe black, took my backpack to a table along the right-hand wall, unzipped the compartments, and started laying out the contents. Gray Suit grabbed a chair from in front of a mirrored wall, straddled it, and beamed me a megawatt smile.

"Have a seat," he'd said cheerfully.

"My flight leaves in twenty minutes."

"All the more reason to cooperate as quickly as possible."

"Who are you?"

"That's the sort of thing that'll slow us right down. If you really want to make your flight—" His teeth were white and even.

"Go ahead."

"Why are you traveling to Bogotá, Miss Carlyle?"

"Vacation."

"Visiting friends?"

"Tourist."

He'd tapped my passport thoughtfully. "You haven't done much traveling outside the country lately."

It seemed like he was trying to start me talking, urging me to babble on to fill the silence. I'd used the same technique too often to fall for it.

Gamely, he'd displayed his teeth again. "Will you be staying in Bogotá? Or traveling to other cities?" While he was speaking, the woman was shuffling my belongings around the table, wanding them, but I hadn't been able to focus on her actions and his questions at the same time.

I'd told him I expected to remain in Bogotá.

"At a hotel?"

"Yes."

"You have a reservation?"

"No."

"You know that Colombia is not on the U.S. government's list of approved destinations."

"Which branch of the government are you with?"

He'd ignored my question so completely, I might never have opened my mouth. Then he'd shot a glance at the mirrored wall, holding it long enough to confirm my suspicion that the mirror was one-way glass. I'd kept the awareness off my face.

"Are you taking any cash out of the country?" I'd gotten the feeling he wasn't all that interested in my response, so I'd twisted around to watch the woman replacing items in my backpack.

"Why?"

"It's a routine question," he'd replied blandly.

"If I were taking more than ten thousand bucks, I'd be sure to mention it." Ten thousand is the magic figure; you take more than that, you'd better declare it.

He'd glanced at the mirror again; he seemed to be waiting for something.

I'd said, "Is that all?"

He'd glanced at the woman, then the mirror. "Yes. If you have any trouble while you're visiting Colombia, don't delay. Go directly to the U.S. Embassy."

"I'm not expecting any trouble," I'd said, "other than making my flight."

They'd returned passport, ticket, and backpack, solemnly thanking me for my cooperation. Then they'd rushed me down a hallway, skirting security, escorting me through the hidden backstreets of the airport, and releasing me into the gate area unscreened by the regular examiners. They'd assured me that my flight would be held till my arrival.

The engines revved and the plane taxied down the runway. Twelve minutes late. I'd never had a plane held at the gate for me before.

The questions had been routine, but the episode hadn't felt like a standard one-in-ten security check. The lack of proffered ID bothered me. Who the hell were they? Homeland Security? FBI? None of their questions had been targeted at my relationship with Sam Gianelli. DEA? No questions about Roldán. And since when was DEA interested in people *leaving* the country? Why the office with the one-way glass?

As the plane lifted off, I popped a lemon drop into my mouth and tried to stifle my regret for the window seat. I haven't flown enough to be jaded; I like to see the ground recede, the water lap the land. But in a window seat, the stewardesses would be too far away to notice the photo of Paolina I intended to prop on my tray table; they wouldn't comment on the pretty girl who'd recently taken the same flight. I considered adding the other photos, the man who'd tagged after Paolina in line, the woman who'd preceded her.

Hanson at Biodyne had come through big-time, with head shots I'd picked up on my dash to the airport. When making the reservation, I'd selected the flight closest to the time line on the airport video, hopefully the same Avianca flight Paolina had taken. I didn't know the ways of flight crews, possibly none of these attendants had worked this flight three nights ago, but searching for witnesses at the same time the subject was observed in the area is one of the golden rules of police work.

My seatmates nodded off as soon as the plane reached cruising altitude, the middle-aged man snoring gently. Most of the passengers followed suit, but I resolutely flipped open my laptop. Earlier, Roz had sent me no fewer than twenty-two clips concerning Paolina's father, Carlos Roldán Gonzales, aka El Martillo, the Hammer, and I'd downloaded the e-mails into a file. Now I adjusted my reading light, twisting the tiny knob to control a stream of chilled air, and tried to adjust my mind to the fact that for the next three hours that was essentially all I'd be able to control.

Tell the truth, airplanes give me the willies. I know about aerodynamics and lift and thrust. I *know* I'm safer as a passenger in a commercial jet than as a driver on the Southeast Expressway, but I *feel* totally out of control, a side of beef zooming through space in a soup can. I want to rush the cockpit, demand the pilot's qualifications, make sure his reflexes are as good as mine.

I sucked a deep breath, loosened my hands on the armrests, and immersed myself in background material on Roldán, from *The New York Times, The Washington Post, The Miami Herald, El Tiempo de Bogotá,* and *El Espectador,* working through the pieces doggedly in chronological order. *El Tiempo* and *El Espectador* had the most coverage, which was only to be expected. There were times I devoutly wished for a Spanish/English dictionary, but considering the unfamiliar words in context, I was able to cope.

Carlos Roldán Gonzales, programmed from birth to lead the charmed life of the Colombian upper class, had grown up in north Bogotá near the country club, spending weekends at one of his family's sprawling ranches and vacations in Spain. He'd earned an economics degree from Jorge Tadeo Lozano University in Bogotá and attended law school in the States. In his late twenties, he'd given up the dances and dinner parties, and disappeared into the jungle to join, and eventually lead, a leftist guerrilla group.

I searched my mind for the North American equivalent, but not a lot of parallels sprang to mind. The scions of wealthy New York families who'd joined the Weather Underground in the '60s were a better fit than Patty Hearst and the Symbionese Liberation Army.

The group Roldán headed was called MM-19, dedicated to the martyrs of the M-19 guerrilla group. I read quotes from his university professors, declaring amazement that a young man from his background had chosen the path he'd taken. Most seemed shocked and horrified; one or two sounded tones of grudging admiration.

M-19 was one of the smallest of Colombia's guerrilla organizations; the largest was FARC, *Fuerzas Armadas Revolucionarias de Colombia,* also called the People's Army. Next came the ELN, also an acronym of its official Spanish name. The larger groups were strongest in the countryside. M-19 had been a mainly urban force until 1985, when they'd stormed the Palace of Justice in Bogotá. Over a hundred

died in the ensuing battle with the military. The Supreme
Court Justices got caught in the middle; eleven of them died.

MM-19 was excoriated as a drug business, with Roldán
mentioned in the same sentences as Pedro Escobar and the
Ochoa brothers. A "war without quarter" against the cartels
included the guerrilla groups in its scope. The cartels cor-
rupted public officials with huge payoffs. They employed
sicarios to assassinate judges and politicians.

A few of the more recent stories mentioned ties between
the traffickers and the AUC, a network of right-wing "paramilitary" groups suspected of killing leftist politicians and
their supporters. I reread two articles, but they didn't make
sense juxtaposed one against the other. If MM-19 had
morphed from a revolutionary cell into a drug cartel, were
they allied with the right-wing paramilitaries or the left-
wing guerrillas?

I closed my eyes, and smoothed my forehead with my
fingertips. There were too many competing groups, too
many agendas. Too much violence. I couldn't expect to understand the complexities of Colombia, and mainly I didn't
give a damn. I was there to find Paolina, to find her and bring
her back.

A dark-haired steward asked what I'd like to drink. I requested a Pepsi, accepted a Coke, and inquired about the
photos. He shrugged and shook his head. Was the girl famous, he wanted to know. Maybe that Puerto Rican singer?

I scrolled on. Roldán and MM-19 had aided a village rav-
aged by disease and paramilitary executions. They'd kidnapped two doctors and held them for ransom. They were
implicated in the bombing of a famous nightclub. As I read,
I noted the names of the Colombian journalists. *El Tiempo*'s
Luisa Cabrera had more direct quotes from members of
MM-19, greater detail, a markedly sympathetic tone. I wondered whether she might know a way to get in touch with
Roldán in case the Bogotá phone numbers on Naylor's bill
didn't pan out. I scribbled her name in my notebook, then
skimmed the articles concerning Roldán's disappearance.
The Cessna had set out from a town called Convención in

Norte de Santander province. Either three men or five men
had been aboard, depending on the article I read. Several citizens of Magdalena province had reported a fireball. I wondered if Roldán had been expected to board the plane, but
missed the flight. Possibly the report of his death had been
made up by the press or planted by friends. I'd need to send
Roz an e-mail after I landed. I wanted more information on
Angel Navas, the man who'd reportedly inherited Roldán's
drug empire. When the passenger in front of me decided to
lean his seat into my lap, I decided to ignore the FASTEN
SEAT BELTS sign and take a walk before my legs atrophied.

There's a game I play on airplanes: Spot the sky marshall.
I have a good batting average because the rules for what to
wear on airplane flights have relaxed over the years while
the rules for proper Justice Department attire have not. Spot
a guy in a suit and tie on other than a Washington–New York
flight, and chances are he's got a shoulder holster to match.

I wondered whether the man and woman who'd delayed
me at the airport worked for Justice. They'd been dressed
well enough.

If the silver-haired man in 32F hadn't dropped his eyes
and looked away, I might not have noticed him. The sudden
motion, the tilt as he shifted his weight to gaze blankly out
the window, drew my eye like a magnet and I thought:
Where have I seen him before? Not in the security line. Not
in the boarding lounge; I hadn't spent any time in the boarding lounge.

I edged into the tiny restroom. My breathing was shallow
and my palms felt damp. Maybe it was simply lack of sleep.
No sleep, Paolina's disappearance, the stubbornly clinging
blue Saturn, the anonymous airport agents—the combination had me reacting like a rookie cop in a bad neighborhood, imagining a machine gun in every violin case. I
needed to steel myself, get a grip. The plane dipped its
wings and gave a sudden lurch. The PLEASE RETURN TO
YOUR SEAT sign flashed accusingly as I splashed water on
my face.

Emerging from the toilet, I stood near the rear of the

plane expecting, hoping, to recover my perspective and re-classify the man as a harmless stranger. I ran my eyes over his muscular back, protruding ears, thick neck. Paranoia crept between my shoulder blades. Dammit, I was right. I distinctly remembered the laughing brunette on his arm, the tall frosted glass in his right hand, the tops of his sunburned ears. I couldn't be mistaken. I'd noticed him near the pool, crossing the patio by the crystalline water.

At Drew Naylor's party.

CHAPTER 16

I FEIGNED SLEEP when the plane landed, but the ploy would have worked better in the window seat. When the passenger next to me prodded me mercilessly awake, I had little choice but to precede the man in 32F off the aircraft. I dawdled in the arrival lounge until he deplaned, then made a minor show of realizing I'd forgotten something, and reentered the plane. Mr. 32F hadn't left anything in his seat compartment, but then neither had I.

He wasn't visible when I exited the jetway, already in line at customs when I collected my duffel. I showed the photo of Paolina to each of the customs agents in the busy room, disrupting the orderly lines and earning scowls from my fellow travelers. My little sister, I explained, had forgotten to tell me where she was staying in Bogotá. Possibly you'd remember her; she was traveling with her aunt and uncle.

No one recalled her. I was urged to get back in the proper line. The line crawled. I caught a glimpse of Silver Hair lingering near a coffee vendor. As soon as I got past customs, I made a beeline for the El Dorado airport ladies' room.

There was no toilet paper in the stall. Oh well, I thought, that's okay; Kleenex in my backpack. No toilet seat on the toilet, either; I retreated into the common area of the restroom to think things over. The next woman in line took my place. She was holding a wad of toilet paper.

Aha. A communal dispenser hung on a nearby wall. I

grabbed a handful and reinserted myself at the end of the line. Plenty of time to kill.

The man in seat 32F couldn't follow me in here, and the terminal was so jammed with travelers there was a good chance he hadn't seen me enter. If I stayed long enough, he might assume I'd rushed outside and grabbed a cab. He might give up and depart.

I considered the coincidence factor. Coincidences happen. Cousins who haven't spoken in years meet abruptly in strange cities. But when I'm working a case, I regard any hint of coincidence with suspicion. I recalled the curious sensation I'd had in the mirrored room at Miami–Dade, the feeling that the man was asking me unimportant questions, holding me temporary prisoner for a purpose, deliberately delaying me. Could 32F have been behind the mirror?

Could he have been the man in the blue Saturn?

Paranoia?

I used the facilities, such as they were, and idled away the minutes washing my hands twice, applying lipstick, combing my tangled hair. None of the women lingered long enough to question my continued presence.

After twenty-two minutes, a bright-eyed cleaning woman brought in a mop and bucket. I dug out Paolina's photo again, and asked if she might have noticed the girl two nights ago, about this time. She was very sorry, but no, she hadn't. There were so many girls and so much work. When I gave her a five-dollar bill, she stared at it speechlessly.

"Keep the photo," I said. "Show it to friends who work at the airport. If anyone saw the girl, tell them to call the phone number on the back of the picture. Call collect. There will be a reward. For both of you."

I'd printed Gloria's number on the back of twelve copies. She doesn't speak much Spanish, but she knows enough to ask a caller to hold on, and there's always a Spanish-speaking driver who'll help her out.

"*Sí. Gracias.*"

I left the restroom. No silver-haired man near the coffee stall; none in the corridor.

I found a money machine that spit pesos and bought a tourist map of the city. At the gift shop, waiting to pay for the map, I hauled out another copy of Paolina's photo. The stony-eyed clerk hadn't seen her. Every time I saw a person in uniform, a security guard, an airport employee, I displayed the photo and got the same response. Twice, guided more by instinct than reason, I gave the photo away, urging the recipient to ask around, to call the phone number on the back if anyone gave a positive response. I emphasized the reward.

A bank of phone booths nestled between the money exchange booth and the entrance to the duty-free shop. I checked my watch. The plane had landed at 10:42. It was well past midnight now, too late to try the numbers from Naylor's bill. In Boston, I'd have grabbed my criss-cross directory, gotten addresses to match the phone numbers, checked them out. A simple public-records search would net the identity of the inhabitants. With cop help, I could quickly learn more, like whether or not a handgun was registered to anyone on the premises.

Mooney's warning echoed in my head: Avoid the local police.

Was it really too late to call? What did I have to lose? If the numbers were office numbers, there might be illuminating recorded messages. If I woke people, I might learn more from their sleepily indignant responses than I'd get in the calm, collected morning.

I studied the directions on the phone, went back to the gift shop, and bought a bag of coffee-flavored candy. A twofer, change and caffeine, both needed.

All the booths were empty when I returned. The number of travelers in the terminal had markedly decreased. No sign of the silver-haired man. I entered the second booth from the right, piled a stack of two-hundred-peso coins on the tiny corner shelf. Each was the size and shape of a quarter.

I tried the number that appeared most frequently on Naylor's bill. It rang and rang. No message machine. I listened, hypnotized by the repetitive sound, hung up and tried again. Same thing.

With a sigh, I punched the less frequently dialed number. Eight rings. Ten. I was about to hang up when the phone clicked.

"Zona Rosa. *¿Aló?*" Loud lively music in the background, laughter. "*¿Aló?*"

I stammered my way through an inquiry about the hours.

Open till three, the gruff voice said, but the line was already out the door. He doubted they'd all get in. Tomorrow night, before midnight, I'd have a better chance.

He hung up before I could respond. Zona Rosa. I scratched the name on the back of my used airline ticket, opened the phone book that lay next to my stack of coins on the shelf.

Zona Rosa; no listing.

I felt suddenly exhausted, drained. Even if the address had been neatly printed, even if the Zona Rosa's greeter had told me they'd be open till dawn and I should rush right over, I'd have hesitated. If the phone booth had been equipped with a seat, I'd have been tempted to spend the night, sleep right there.

In the main lobby, a tape-recorded voice announced that buses were available for transport to the domestic terminal where departures to Cali, Medellin, Pasto, and Monteria were imminent. I went outside and joined the queue. The air, warm and heavy, was scented with the tang of greenery. I watched grandmothers greet children with open arms, fathers slap grown sons on the back with pride. I imagined Paolina, racing across the pavement into my arms. The overhead lights cast strange shadows on the ground. Buses and taxis came and went. I didn't see the silver-haired man.

When the bus came, I showed Paolina's photo to the driver. He shook his head. He looked as tired as I felt. I dragged my duffel through the domestic terminal, asking whether anyone had seen my daughter. Daughter. *Mi hija.* It slipped out instead of sister, and I let it be. A fluorescent light flickered intermittently; it would have brought on a seizure in an epileptic.

After forty-five minutes of denials, I followed the signs

to a cabstand and told the driver I'd appreciate the recommendation of a reasonably priced hotel near the offices of
El Tiempo. Then I opened the compact I keep in my backpack and watched the traffic behind us all the way. I don't
think we were followed, but at night in a strange city, I
couldn't be sure.

CHAPTER 17

I **WOKE TO** sunlight tilting from the wrong angle across a room of the wrong proportions, the wrong pillow beneath my cheek, the wrong smells in my nostrils. I swung my legs out of bed, stilled the alarm, and sat, recalling the rushed journey by taxi, the bright lights glinting from skyscrapers, the softly lit cathedrals.

The little gold birdman stared at me blankly from the bedside table.

"Welcome home," I told him.

The tile floor felt icy under my bare feet as I crossed to the window and pushed the curtain aside. A steady procession of noisy traffic streamed by. Cars of all makes and sizes, boxy sedans, and buses, big and small, red, yellow, and green, commuters waving them down in the streets the way a New Yorker would flag a cab. A mule-drawn cart slowed traffic in the right-hand lane.

Church steeples towered over roofs of Spanish tile. Mountain peaks vanished in the morning mist. When I shifted my attention to the pedestrian traffic, I found the hurrying walkers on the narrow sidewalks well dressed: suits, ties, and slim attaché cases for the men; high heels for the women.

I showered and dressed quickly. My wardrobe didn't allow for much in the way of choice, but after my glance at the impeccable pedestrians, I decided to forego jeans and sneakers in favor of navy pants, a low-cut white tee, and the smoky silk jacket. I did my makeup in the small square of mirror over the sink, draped a scarf around my neck to add some color. After tucking the little birdman into his pouch and placing him in the smallest compartment of my backpack, I took the stairs to the lobby.

The Hotel del Parque, a glass and concrete square, the cabbie's recommendation, fit the bill, cheap and near the newspaper building. Twenty-five thousand pesos hadn't sounded cheap, but once I'd wrapped my mind around the exchange rate, it meant about ten bucks a night, a bargain.

No one in the adjoining diner seemed familiar. The only man with silver hair had a pink seamed face and a flabby build. Not the plane man. When the waitress appeared I ordered *arepas,* the small corncakes Paolina loves. While hungrily forking them down, I studied the morning newspaper. Luisa Cabrera's byline appeared on the third page.

I'd made up my mind last night, after a wee-hours webcrawl through *¡Qué Hubo!,* the Colombian Yellow Pages: Plodding detail work wasn't the key to this quest. I needed to find Roldán, and I needed to find him quickly. The best way to do that was by starting as many hares as I could, by stirring up a hornet's nest. I'd chase down the Zona Rosa and check the other number on Naylor's phone bill, but I'd also talk to Cabrera. Nothing like a journalist for stirring up a hive. I signaled for *la cuenta* and figured the tip.

Walking down the street, I felt conspicuous in ways that don't apply in Boston. There, my Irish coloring, misleading as it is, makes me one of the gang. There, I live surrounded by universities that field women's teams in basketball and volleyball, bringing in an influx of tall women every year to serve as camouflage. Here, even in flats I was tall, and my red hair stood out like a flare. At a busy intersection, two child acrobats tossed juggling pins, then rushed through traffic to collect tips before the light changed.

Entering the *El Tiempo* building was like passing through airport security all over again. I placed my backpack on a conveyer belt for the X-ray machine. An armed guard patted me down, scrutinizing my passport, comparing my face to the photo. When he nodded me through to the front desk, an elderly man used a telephone to ask Señorita Cabrera whether she'd agree to see me. After a moment, he offered me the phone.

"Can you give me some idea of what this is about?" Her voice was low, curt, and businesslike.

"I've come all the way from Boston to speak with you." My Spanish might not flow the way it did when I was a child, but my fluency would improve rapidly once the language surrounded me; I was confident of that. Mexico City Spanish and Bogotá Spanish weren't the same, but Paolina had schooled me in the differences.

"That's a long way to come with no appointment."

I simply agreed with her, assuming that journalistic curiosity would win out over caution. The deskman gave me directions to the third floor and a pass to clip to my jacket. VISITANTE, it said. Guest.

Cabrera was waiting when the elevator doors opened; small, dark, and young. Not beautiful; her features were crowded too closely around a sharp nose for beauty. She was striking, with soft caramel eyes and long hair scraped back from a high forehead. Her figure was slim and her black designer suit gave her some of the gravitas age and stature had denied her.

"Give me a minute. I'm in the middle of something." Without waiting for a response, she moved quickly down a long hallway. A young man emerged from an office and tagged behind her.

Computer screens dominated the twenty-odd desks in the large room. Wall art was confined to news clippings push-pinned to bulletin boards and a few framed Botero prints. Eyes peered at me from behind the screens. If I wanted to blend in better, I was going to need to invest in a bottle of hair dye. I hoped Lady Clairol had a South American distributor.

I turned my back on the curious eyes and focused on a display case containing silver-framed studio photographs. I've visited both the *Herald* and the *Globe*. They have display cases, too, filled with journalism awards, engraved plaques and silver cups. This case was different. There must have been twenty photos inside, each edged in black, each the likeness of a Colombian journalist, killed in the line of duty.

That would account for the security downstairs.

"Sorry." Cabrera was back. "It's a busy morning. What can I do for you?"

"Is there someplace more private?"

"Follow me." Her skin was the color of a good Florida tan. Her heels clicked on the floorboards and I had to walk briskly to keep up in spite of the difference in our heights.

She rated a window office with a mahogany desk and a high-backed black leather chair. She sank into the chair, eyes unfocused, as though she were thinking about whatever story she'd just abandoned.

"I've been reading you," I said. "You're good."

"You must want a favor," she said.

"Maybe I can do you a favor."

"Oh, yes," she said. "People from your country come to do us favors all the time."

"You know many people from my country?"

"Just last week, I spoke to a journalist from a town in Ohio. It was amazing, his ignorance. He didn't know Colombia was a democracy. We have been a democracy since 1830!"

"He was doing an article on Colombian civics?"

"Your newspapers only do articles on Colombia when someone in their town gets killed during a drug deal gone bad. In fact, I would say the average North American knows nothing about my country that can't be summed up in a single word: *drugs*."

Since her hostility was on such open display, I thought I might as well use it.

"Speaking of drugs," I said, "you've written about a man named Carlos Roldán Gonzales."

"You see? Of the many topics you could discuss concerning Roldán, the one you choose is drugs."

"What other topics would you recommend?"

She picked up a gold fountain pen and seemed absorbed in removing the top and studying the nib. "First, we might speak about the history of Colombia."

"Starting when?"

"We have a two-party system, as you do, but there is a tradition of violence between the parties. Eight civil wars were fought here, just in the nineteenth century. *Liberal* and *conservative,* for decades, were fighting words."

The Ohio journalist had probably gotten the same earful. I didn't see what it had to do with Roldán.

"After a brief military dictatorship, the parties reached an agreement to share power. Every four years the presidency shifted from one party to the next."

I supposed that was a form of democracy.

"And when the agreement came to an end, lo and behold, both parties were much the same, parties of the elite. Neither reached out to the rural areas of the country. The only ones who helped the peasants in the countryside were the guerrillas."

"The FARC and the ELN?"

She gave me a look, like a teacher whose slowest student had surprisingly done his homework. "What do you know about them?"

I'd just read a slew of articles about Colombia, but I was no expert. "Marxist guerrilla groups."

"Bolivian Marxists, not Soviet. Some groups stand for agrarian reform, for nationalizing the country's resources, for property redistribution. North Americans come here, they think the old Soviet army is roaming the Colombian countryside. They think all guerrillas are the same, the FARC, the ELN, the MM-19. But then, what else can one expect from people who live where the only decisions they make are whether to snort cocaine or smoke it, and how much money they should send this country to defoliate the ground?"

I kept quiet. She was on a roll and I didn't want to interrupt.

"I would speak to you about the tradition of the outlaw," she went on. "Roldán, because he existed outside the two-party system, became part of a tradition that I would compare to your Western outlaws. Your Jesse James, perhaps."

A romanticized killer, I thought, but not a drug dealer.

She said, "So, are you from the CIA or the DEA?"

"Neither."

"Perhaps you are from my government."

"No."

She tapped the fountain pen on the red leather blotter. "But you're interested in El Martillo. Are you a journalist?"

"A private detective."

She smiled. "Like on American TV, no?"

"If you don't believe me, you can phone the Boston police. Speak to Joseph Mooney, the Head of Homicide."

"You're here about a murder?"

"No. A kidnapping."

"A kidnapping? Kidnapping is old hat here. Routine. The police aren't even interested in kidnapping, except to tell you it's illegal to pay ransom."

"Look, I have a story for you. A scoop." I used the English word because I didn't know the Colombian equivalent.

"And you expect something in return for this scoop?" She understood the word perfectly.

"This much I'm willing to give you for nothing: El Martillo isn't dead."

"You're not a psychic, are you?" The Spanish for "psychic" is *médium*. The way her eyes stayed level, I wondered if she already knew he was alive.

"If I were a psychic, I'd have picked a reporter more interested in my story."

"That's all you've got? That he's alive?" She fiddled with the pen again; she was interested all right.

"Oh, I have more," I said, "but it's a human interest story, not hard news. It has to do with children and families. Maybe there's somebody else at the paper who specializes in that kind of story."

"I write stories about families," she said sharply. "The piece I'm doing now, the one you're keeping me from doing, is about *barrio* kids."

"Possibly a colleague—"

"What do you want?"

"The answer to a question: Why would Roldán snatch his daughter?"

If Cabrera had been a dog, her ears would have flicked at the word *daughter*.

I said, "I specialize in missing persons work. Roldán's daughter is missing, and I have reason to believe he took her."

"This girl lives in the U.S.?"

I nodded. She stayed silent for almost thirty seconds, her lips tight, eying the tip of the fountain pen. Then she stared at her wristwatch. "Would you like some coffee?"

Inside, I relaxed. Maybe I even gloated. The woman was hooked, well and truly fastened to the end of my line, visualizing her headline, mentally writing the first paragraph. When I nodded, she walked briskly to the door instead of summoning an assistant. I took advantage of her absence to examine her office.

The plants on the desk were dark and glossy. On the wall, two plaques held a position of honor, but their dates puzzled me. They were journalism awards from the years 1972 and 1978. In 1972, if she'd even been born, Luisa Cabrera would have been a child. Possibly we were sitting in the office of the managing editor, or an older associate. In the single photograph on the filing cabinet, a man held a stiff formal pose, while the young girl beside him gazed up adoringly. Possibly two people shared the office, one that used the leather blotter and the fountain pen, another who preferred the sleek laptop.

Cabrera's return interrupted my scrutiny. I'd expected two paper cups of institutional liquid, but she carried a tray, china cups, and a plate of cookies. The steaming coffee was strong, the cookies crisp, and she was no longer in such a hurry, avoiding the topic of El Martillo's daughter altogether, inquiring instead about my job. She wanted to know whether many women in the U.S. worked in criminal justice. She was a skillful interviewer. Skillful, too, at evading questions. I couldn't get her to speak of herself, of her career, of how she came to rate her own byline so young.

She slid back to the topic only after we'd finished drinking our coffee. "So you are investigating the case of a missing child?"

"My little sister." I showed her two photos of Paolina, her latest school shot and the copy of the frame from the airport video.

"Excuse me. She's your sister, but she's also Roldán's daughter?"

I explained my relationship with Paolina.

"Why would you think the girl was taken by her father?"

"I have proof she boarded a plane to Bogotá. She had no passport, and I don't know a lot of teenagers with the wherewithal to forge one. I assume Roldán would know people who could handle that."

She nodded thoughtfully.

"And then there's this." From my backpack, I removed the pouch. The gold birdman looked happy to be released.

Cabrera stared at it with no expression on her careful face.

"Roldán sent this to his daughter. Recently. I thought it might help me trace him."

She said nothing.

"I thought you might be able to put me in touch with someone who knows how to reach Roldán."

"Why me?"

"Because of your stories."

She shook her head.

"Have you ever heard of a man named Drew Naylor?"

"Who is he?"

"I was told he might be a conduit to Roldán."

"Never heard of him."

"What is the Zona Rosa?"

She shrugged. "The entertainment district."

"No, this is a club called the Zona Rosa. You know it?"

"I'm not much of a dancer."

"How about this: If you wrote about the girl, put her photo in the paper, someone might come forward with information that would lead to her. If it led to her, it might lead to Roldán as well. If it led to Roldán, it would be an important story."

"I don't know," she said.

"Perhaps it would be dangerous for you to write about Roldán."

The Spanish word for dangerous, *peligroso,* hung in the air. She repeated it slowly.

I said, "I know writing about drug lords can be—"

"How dare you? You make your troubles our troubles, and then you come here and tell me I'm scared to write about a man like Roldán?"

"I'm just saying I'll understand if you don't want to get involved. Maybe it would be better for me to go to the authorities. Once they know Roldán is alive, they might help me locate him."

I watched her eyes, thinking if she couldn't be moved by the implication that inaction was cowardly, she might respond to a threat to Roldán. The way she'd written her stories, she obviously had sympathy for the man, if not for his cause. She'd reacted with a total lack of surprise when I said he was alive, as though she already knew it. If she already knew it, why hadn't she written it?

She frowned and moistened her lips before speaking. "Perhaps the girl ran off on her own. Maybe she has some romantic dream about her father, some Hollywood fantasy. Probably he had nothing to do with it."

"Sorry I bothered you." I stood as if to leave, but her voice stopped me before I took a step.

"The authorities here, the police, the military, they are slow to act, but once you start them moving they are impossible to stop."

"Maybe I'll try them anyway. And I'm planning to try a television journalist. If I get her photo on the TV news, it'll reach a larger audience. It's possible she traveled with two companions—bodyguards, kidnappers, I don't know. But I have photos of them as well."

I waited. Either she'd ask to see them or she wouldn't.

"May I see—?"

I crossed the room and placed the photos I'd gotten from Hanson carefully on the leather blotter. The man's face was thin-lipped and bony, his eyes, possibly distorted by the glasses he wore, seemed too big for his head. His hair was shorn close to a high forehead. The woman was in her thirties. A floppy hat obscured the right side of her face. Her long hair was braided.

As Cabrera studied the faces, her eyes flickered. "Where are you staying?" she asked.

"Nearby."

"If I wished to get in touch?"

"A message at the Hotel del Parque would reach me, but I won't be there long."

"You don't work for the government."

"You seem more worried about the government than the guerrillas."

She smiled with her mouth, but not her eyes. "When they come for me, it will be the *paras,* not the FARC."

"And the *paras* are linked to the government?"

"My father believed they were. He was a journalist, too. Before he was killed." Her eyes shifted to the file cabinet, drawn to the photo that rested on it, and I realized she was the little girl. The fountain pen, the leather blotter must have belonged to her father. His photo was probably in the display case of martyred journalists.

"It's too bad you can't help me out," I said. We seemed to be carrying on a different conversation with our eyes, talking between the lines. I was sure she knew someone who knew how to get in touch with Roldán.

"It's possible I may be able to do something. But right now—"

"I can't wait," I said. "Every minute she's gone is too long."

"Later today, perhaps." She spoke so softly I could barely hear her.

"I can give you three hours," I said, "before I go to the TV stations. Before I go to the authorities."

"And what will you do with your three hours?"

"Any suggestions?"

She stood, pushing back the big leather chair. "One. Why don't you take your little statue to the Gold Museum? You

might learn something there." For a moment, the caramel
eyes gleamed, with amusement, anger, interest; I wasn't sure
which.

"Perhaps I will." I started for the door.

"Wait."

"What?"

"If you need a cab, have the doorman call one for you.
Don't flag a cab cruising the streets."

"Why?"

"It's a good way to get kidnapped. Usually, the cabs that
line up in front of the hotels are okay. I'm just giving you the
same advice I always give tourists. Be careful. Bogotá is a
beautiful city, but it's not a safe city."

I thought of certain Dorchester streets where I'd hesitate
to pick up a fare. "Thanks," I said. "Boston's like that, too."

I sneaked a glance over my shoulder as I left her office.
Her hand was already reaching for the phone.

I could almost hear the hornets buzz.

CHAPTER 18

A BEAUTIFUL CITY. But not a safe city.

I'd made light of the warning, equating Boston and Bogotá, but descending the stairs I tried to imagine a display case of murdered Boston journalists, a New England in which writing about—say, the Gianellis—could get a reporter lowered into the harbor in the trunk of a stolen car. It might happen once, but not regularly, not habitually, not in the kind of numbers that would fill a showcase. The black-edged photos reminded me that I was on alien turf. This wasn't my city or my country. I was alone, with no useful contacts, no knowledge of the streets, no safety net.

Three hours, and Luisa Cabrera might have something for me. Three hours in a normal day was nothing; three hours now was too long.

The public phone in the lobby tugged like a magnet. Paranoia or caution, take your pick, had kept me from using the hotel telephone. I sorted my change, picked up the receiver, and tried the most frequently dialed number on Naylor's bill.

Eight rings. I thought no one would answer, that I'd go back to square one.

"*¿Aló? Base Dieciocho.*" The voice was crisp and businesslike.

"What are your hours, please?"

"*Lo siento*. You have the wrong number."

He hung up before I could respond.

In the Yellow Pages at the hotel, I'd found Zona Rosa under nightclubs. In the phone book on the shelf of the booth, I looked up *Base Dieciocho*. Base Eighteen. No such listing. Base eighteen of what? If it was the name of another nightclub, I might find it in the Yellow Pages at the hotel. It hadn't sounded like a nightclub, no clatter of barware, no buzz of patrons, but it was early. Might not be open for business.

I'd depleted my change with little to show for it. Three hours stretched out like an endless rope. Three whole hours. Back to the airport? The Zona Rosa? The Gold Museum? I'd already tried the airport. Too early for a nightclub.

El Museo del Oro, then. I followed Cabrera's advice and asked the doorman to call a cab. The vehicle, when it arrived, was dark green and cream, and the driver wove an erratic path at high speed through heavy traffic. Oddly enough, his daredevil driving made me feel safer. How could anyone follow unseen in a city where the accepted distance between cars was a coat of paint?

The Gold Museum, a squat square structure on Santander Park, kitty-corner to the Banco de la República, was made of yellowish stone that seemed to shine. The phone booth on the nearby plaza was empty. I'd replenished my change via the cabbie, so I stepped inside.

I had to punch a lot of buttons, but Gloria's musical voice, once I got it, was reassuringly calm. "Give me your number in case we get disconnected."

I did, explaining that I was in a booth, supplying the name and number of the hotel as well. "Anything on the Bogotá phone numbers?"

"Babe, I keep hitting trouble. This guy I know runs cabs in New Orleans, he's Colombian, but the uncle he said could run them is someplace on vacation, some island I never heard of, and my guy doesn't know when he'll be back. I got some other feelers out, and I'll call you as soon as I get some action. You okay? You eating?"

"Call Mooney. Get him to try these places out on some DEA agent who knows his way around Colombia. Zona Rosa, a nightclub. And something called Base Eighteen."

"Also a nightclub?"

"Got me. They go with the phone numbers."

"Okay, that's progress. This is from Sam. He couldn't get your cell."

"It doesn't work here. Wrong kind." *As out of place as I was.*

"He said if you wound up in Bogotá to give you this number. You got a pencil?"

"Yeah."

"He said if you need equipment down there, call and ask for Ignacio." She spelled the name, repeated the number twice. "I didn't ask him what he meant by 'equipment.'"

I didn't either. "Roz get me anything on Angel Navas?"

"Roldán's partner? She's e-mailing you the details. Arrested, extradited, and tried in the States."

I was wondering whether it might be worth it to have someone trace him through the prison system, ask about Roldán's hideouts.

"Died in the clink," Gloria said, putting an end to that plan. "Oh, and Mooney said he got those photos from the guy in Miami, but no progress on IDs yet. He'll keep trying."

"Okay."

Gloria's voice lowered a full note. "He asked if I knew where Sam was."

"What did you tell him?"

"What do you think? I don't exactly believe the man's got Sam's best interests at heart. Know why?"

"He's a cop."

"That, yeah, but mainly I think he's sorry you and Sam hooked up again. I think he's sorry he didn't make his move when you split."

"Lay off the romance magazines," I said.

"I'll read what I like," she said tartly. "You find that girl."

"Gloria, seriously, if Sam calls back, tell him the feds have a tail on him. Tell him to be careful."

"That's exactly what he said to tell you."

She hung up, but I stayed in the booth, biting my lower lip, considering Sam's offer of "equipment." Sam's contact in Colombia might be involved in the drug trade. Ignacio might know how to reach Roldán. I fed more pesos into the machine, punched buttons, and waited. The phone rang six times. Seven.

A woman's voice informed me that Ignacio was not there and advised me to call back later.

"*¿A qué hora?*"

The woman simply repeated that I should call later, then hung up.

Crossing the plaza, I joined the line at the museum, observing those in front of and behind me, wondering whether they were tourists, bored businessmen, or the pickpockets warned against on fliers posted to telephone poles. I used one of the bank notes from the airport ATM to pay the three-thousand-peso entry fee.

Once inside, I was startled by the number of schoolgirls who, from a distance, looked like my little sister, with dark hair and tan skin, a touch of Indian heritage in their cheekbones. The girls were younger, twelve or thirteen, young enough to make me wish I could turn back time, bring the younger Paolina here, hold her hand, and be her guide.

A spirit guide. Did Luisa Cabrera really think I might learn something of value about the little gold man here? Or was she trying to occupy me, fill in the three-hour gap? Keep me busy and out of trouble while she decided what to do?

I skipped over the gift shop and the cafeteria, and headed for the stairs to the second floor. The architecture was modern and severe, the stone steps too narrow for the crowd. Construction was ongoing, a sign declared; the new staircase would probably be broader.

A map of northwestern South America covered one wall of the second-floor stairwell. I skimmed the pre-conquest history of the area: the Sinu, Calima, Tumaco, and San Agustin people had lived in various locales long ago. I wound my way through a maze of galleries. Other names—

Muisca, Tolima, and Tayrona—appeared. Each culture had left behind a certain style of artifact. Good; if I could find Paolina's birdman, he'd be linked to a specific site. I passed displays of carved stone and pottery. There was gold behind glass, a forest of small ornaments, but none resembled the little man.

Armed guards flanked the stairs to the third floor, but the museumgoers seemed to take them in stride. Maybe if Boston's Gardner Museum had posted guards like these, they'd still have their Vermeer, I thought. I imagined proper Brahmin ladies in pearls passing the heavily armed men on their way to lunch at the Gardner café, and the corners of my mouth tilted. I noted the thickness of the doors at the top of the stairs; it felt like I was stepping into a bank vault.

A darkened vault. The heavy doors swung slowly shut. In the momentary blackness, someone giggled. Then gradually, dim lights began to glow, first from the floor, then the ceiling. The walls glimmered, and the glimmer was gold.

The circular room was lined with it, filled with it, a panorama of gold in floor-to-ceiling glass cases, heaps and mounds of glittering gold. With a murmur of voices, viewers surged forward, pushing closer to the glass. Coins, hoops, medallions, bracelets, earrings, crowns, bells, rattles, nose-pieces, pendants, chains, beads—many objects, according to the signs, had religious significance and power. Given the setting, magical properties were easy to accept. There were elongated human figures, birds, animals, and strange, hypnotic masks in gold and reddish-gold *tumbaga*.

The reddish gold was the same metal as Paolina's bird-man. I renewed my search for the original. I saw frogs, caimans, strange birds of prey, fish, snails, and small feline creatures. A gourd-like shape caught my eye and I stopped to read about the golden gourds, called *poporos,* puzzling over unfamiliar words, figuring them out from their context. *Poporos* were receptacles, used for the storage of lime, vital to the *mambeo,* the chewing of coca leaves, a custom and ceremony through which the individual might attain higher levels of consciousness. These treasures, the sign said, had been extracted from the ground by archaeologists but even more often by *guaqueros,* grave robbers, which made authenticating them difficult if not impossible.

I tagged along with a school group and listened to the teacher talk while her charges pressed their noses to the glass, speculating about how much money each object would bring on the market, which item would bring the most. The same questions I found occupying more and more of my mind.

I knew, vaguely, the cost of gold; over four hundred dollars an ounce since the last terrorist attack. When political instability increased, the price of gold inevitably rose. But the gold here, this ancient intricate gold, was valuable not so much for its metal as for its history, for its rarity, for the chance to grasp and hold a time before time. My hand wandered to my backpack and patted the compartment where the birdman nested in his pouch.

Boston's Museum of Fine Arts has a network of underground storage rooms. At no time is all artwork owned by the MFA on display, and there was no reason to believe that every piece of gold owned by the Museo del Oro was here in these cases in this room, but still I hunted for the birdman's twin. I left the school group behind and passed a man explaining an exhibit, a badge on his chest. I waited till he'd finished, then approached and asked whether I might speak to a curator.

"That would be me."

"In private, please."

His eyebrows rose. "I can't leave the exhibit."

"Perhaps another curator, then." I kept talking, trying to imply that the matter would interest someone who knew a great deal about artifacts such as those exhibited in the case he'd been praising to the crowd.

He said, "Maybe I can convince someone to hold my post for a while," and disappeared briefly only to reappear with a young woman in a crisp white shirt and slim black pants. She also wore a badge, and she quickly assumed his position in front of the sparkling glass.

The man was thin, except for a paunch, and middle-aged. His badge identified him as Gustavo Pinzon. He led me to an elevator that climbed a single floor. We didn't speak as it ascended. When he ushered me into a small white-walled office decorated with posters of treasures from the Gold Museum, he left the door slightly ajar. I shut it. He didn't offer me a chair although two were nearby.

"How does the museum acquire objects?" I asked.

"How *did* we acquire? That is what you are asking, no? Because, you see, we no longer acquire."

"Why is that?"

His mouth widened into a smile, displaying dazzling teeth. "Well, I can't say it's because there's nothing out there. There is, but there is also the law. No buying of pre-Columbian antiquities is allowed. They can no longer be exported either. You are not Colombian, no?"

"But copies are made and sold?"

"Certainly. We have our own museum store."

"And there's the Galleria Cano." The store the Florida jeweler had mentioned, the one with a branch in New York.

Pinzon nodded. "They do very nice work."

"How do you tell a copy from an original?"

"Ours are marked on the back. Why?"

I said, "Are you qualified to take a look at a piece I have in my possession, to tell me where it came from?"

"I'm not allowed to buy, by law. I'm not even allowed to give an evaluation."

"I'm simply asking if you're qualified to give an opinion."

"It would depend on what sort of piece."

"From looking at your exhibits, I'd say that what I have is more like Tayrona work than anything else."

"I know Tayrona." I had his attention now, the third floor and the woman with the badge who'd taken his place forgotten.

I took the felt bag from my backpack, removed the little birdman, and set it on a small desk by a window. Pinzon glanced at it, then bent over and scrutinized it from a distance of not more than three inches, so close he seemed to inhale its fragrance. He held up his right hand, glanced at me as if to ask whether he could touch the figure.

I nodded and he flipped it over carefully, handling it with the tips of two fingers. His eyes raked the piece from side to side, head to foot. He opened the top drawer of the desk, extracted a magnifying lens, and peering through it, repeated the examination.

"What can you tell me about it?"

"You have visited the national park? *Las Ciudades de Piedra*?" he said. "*Las Ciudades Perdidas*? When did you go there?"

The Cities of Stone. The Lost Cities. "Where are they?"

"Are you working for someone?" His voice was sharp. "Do you have more like this?"

"I only have this piece. I just want to know what it is."

His brow furrowed. "Perhaps I can refer you to— You know, there's another curator here; it's possible he's available. He could give a much better idea of what you have." I didn't like the phony smile he fixed on his face. "Would you mind waiting?"

"How long?"

"Not long. I'll just show it to him."

"I wouldn't want you to take it with you."

"Oh, no, I wouldn't." As he spoke, he crossed the floor. "I'll bring him here. Really, it won't take long." He opened the door, eased himself out, and shut it firmly behind him.

I didn't like it. Why not telephone the other curator? There was a phone on the desk. Possibly the other curator was wandering the exhibits. Pinzon hadn't phoned the woman who'd replaced him; he'd gone to fetch her. Just like this.

Still, I felt uneasy.

I scooped the birdman into his pouch. Why wait at all? Cities of Stone. Lost Cities. Someone else could tell me where they were. Luisa Cabrera could tell me. Why cool my heels in this office when there might be a message from Cabrera waiting at the hotel?

I tried the door. It swung open easily, mocking my unacknowledged fear that I'd find it locked from the outside. It swung open freely, but I didn't get to breathe a sigh of relief. In the hallway stood one of the machine gun-toting guards.

"Señorita, you are to remain here, please," he said.

Avoid the police, Mooney had urged. What if the item in my bag had been stolen, snatched during a robbery at the Gold Museum? I hadn't heard of any such robbery, but would I? Had the Colombian press covered the robbery at the Gardner? Cabrera was right; almost every article I read about Colombia concerned drugs.

I sucked in a breath. Okay, the guard had a machine gun, but would he blast an unarmed woman in a tourist-crammed building? I smiled sweetly, and asked the way to the rest-room. The guard seemed flustered, and I realized he was barely out of his teens.

"You should stay here," he said. "I have my orders."

"But I need to go to the bathroom. You come too, if you have to."

His cheeks flushed.

"You can stay outside the door and guard it, just like you're guarding this door. But maybe you don't know where the ladies' room is?"

His eyes moved to the right so I started moving that way, too, ignoring his objections.

"This way? Okay. I don't know what that guy told you about me. No way I'm going out with him, even if he sets dogs on me. I mean, I've got a boyfriend, you know?" I kept chattering all the way down the stairs, working to get across the impression that the curator was pressuring me for sex. I got as far as a bathroom located to the right of the main staircase.

The bathroom was packed, with lines for the three stalls and two sinks. I quickly checked the window. It led to a small metal balcony. I'd have to put my faith in the crowd, in the probability that the guard wouldn't risk machine-gunfire. I was counting on his inexperience, too; he wouldn't want to admit to the other guards that he was in trouble. And since I'd hinted that the dispute had sexual overtones, he wouldn't want to get the curator in trouble by being indiscreet. I bit my lip. I didn't like it, but I didn't see a lot of other options. I absolutely didn't want to meet the Bogotá police as an accused thief.

I unfastened my scarf, wrapped it around my hair, and waited till a group of schoolgirls shepherded by two older women started to leave the bathroom, chattering happily about prospects for lunch. Insinuating myself into the center of the pack, I bent my knees and ducked my head. The minute we cleared the door and passed the guard, I charged downstairs. He didn't notice me till I was three-quarters of the way down, well past the rest of the guards.

I heard an inarticulate shout, then hurrying booted feet. Pushing my way through the mob, I plunged down another flight, and flew across the tiled floor. If he'd had the presence of mind to shout "Thief!" someone might have tried to stop me, but he didn't yell "Thief;" he yelled "Stop." I didn't stop, didn't hesitate; the exit was clearly marked. There might be security at the entrance, but no one was manning the exit except a single plump woman in uniform. I was outside before she could react, outdoors and across the plaza, turning the corner, and running hard.

CHAPTER 19

RUNNING FULL TILT down unfamiliar streets would only cause more trouble, invite intervention by some nosy passerby or observant cop. I managed to control my feet, but my heart kept racing. I turned down one street, then another, ignoring vendors who urged me to inspect their leather goods, buy their cowhide rugs, till I'd twisted my way far from the museum and the guards, so far and in such a zigzag path that I was no longer sure of my location. When a man stepped abruptly from a narrow alleyway, startling me, mumbling a single muffled word under his breath, I sidestepped his hulking figure and increased my pace.

If a similar interaction had taken place in Dorchester or Roxbury, the single word would have been "dope," "baggie," or "lid." I'm pretty sure he muttered *"esmeraldas."* Emeralds. Visions of contraband gems sparkled behind my eyes. I turned another corner and stopped to catch my breath.

Cabrera had urged me to visit the museum to ask about the golden statue. Had she intended to get me in trouble? *Had I truly been in trouble?* Or was my impulse to run just another manifestation of the paranoia that had weighted my steps since Miami?

I jaywalked and traveled another block, using the occasional shop window as a mirror. No vehicle tagged behind; none of the pedestrians took an interest in my erratic stops and starts. I sat on a wooden bench in a small green park, disrupting a flock of pigeons. Good old familiar pigeons, city birds, popcorn scavengers, exact replicas of the birds on the Cambridge Common. I felt a swell of longing for familiar places so intense it left me momentarily weak. I told myself to get a grip; told myself it must be the altitude.

Boston is a gray and yellow city; Cambridge is red brick. Bogotá, at least this part of it, was painted dark green, yellow, and orange. Colonial buildings with thick stucco walls lined the streets. Pots of blood-red begonias spilled from second-story balconies.

Get a grip. The prickle-neck feeling had begun with the blue Saturn in Miami, so I started there, working through the mental chain like I was telling beads on a rosary. If the blue Saturn had tailed me, it had come from one of three possible sources. Vandenburg, the lawyer, could have arranged the surveillance, but why would he? Drew Naylor, the suspected drug dealer, likewise. Mooney knew where I was staying; he could have briefed the FBI. They might have posted a watcher, hoping I'd lead them to Sam.

Where was Sam? He'd left Las Vegas, according to Mooney, but when he'd called I hadn't asked. I'd waited for him to mention it, to say something about the private plane, the pilot's license, to tell me he'd flown to Reno or L.A. Maybe, considering the FBI surveillance, it was better if I didn't know his location.

Had the FBI arranged the strange search party at Miami–Dade? Was the man on the plane, the one I'd recognized from Naylor's party, a fed? Was there a link between the feds and Naylor?

Suppose DEA had been watching Naylor's place. Not so far-fetched a notion if the man was a known associate of Roldán's. Possibly they had a man on the inside, which would make the silver fox on the plane DEA.

A pigeon cocked his head at me inquiringly.

But had Luisa Cabrera wanted me detained at the Gold Museum, possibly jailed? As far as paranoia went, I hadn't imagined the armed guard outside the curator's door. And why would a guard be posted unless the little birdman was no copy, but a genuine artifact?

The man in the Miami jewelry store had called it a copy, but maybe he'd just wanted to buy it on the cheap. The curator, Pinzon, had spoken of a mark on the back, but authenticating pre-Columbian gold might be as complex a process as determining the provenance of a reputed Old Master.

The Cities of Stone. The Lost Cities. Where were they? What were they? The sites of archaeological digs? Maybe Pinzon had jumped to the conclusion that I was some kind of *guaquero,* a grave robber who'd stolen artifacts. Which could mean that my little birdman came from the Cities of Stone. Could Roldán be there as well, holed up, hiding?

The Cities of Stone, Luisa Cabrera, the Zona Rosa, Base Eighteen. Plenty of leads to follow, but no answers to the basic questions: Why does Roldán want Paolina here? Why bring her here? Why now?

Fruitless to ask, I told myself. *She was here.* She'd boarded an Avianca flight. I knew that much. I had Mooney's pal, Hanson, to thank for that.

I swallowed and stared at my feet. How foolish I'd been to imagine that she'd stand out like a banner in the crowd. I understood the bafflement of my suburban clients, their disbelief that their child could stay hidden in Boston, as I'd never understood it before.

A teen lost in a big city is like a book lost in a library. I knew that, but I'd forgotten it, ignored it, because to me Paolina was an illuminated manuscript, totally and completely unique, unlike any other manuscript in the world. How amazing that no one else could see the bold colors, the jeweled gold binding. I felt tears start to squeeze beneath my eyelids and I thought: It must be the damned altitude.

I abandoned the bench and the pigeons and walked. As my heartbeat slowed, the blocks of buildings turned into individual shops, the individual shops became places with specific names, and I realized I was looking for a hotel, a cabstand in front of a hotel. A cab, that most familiar and comforting vehicle, smelling of unwashed upholstery and stale cigarette ash. I knew where I was in a cab.

I started piloting a hack part-time in college. Anything to avoid waiting tables, I told myself, but it was the independence, the solitude, the nighttime lure of the city that drew me. And Gloria and Sam, co-owners of the company for which I drove.

The cabs pulled up across the street from El Dorado Hotel alternated between the green-and-cream tourist cabs and the regular yellow cabs. A yellow was first in line, so I grabbed it. No required-by-Boston-law bulletproof-plastic shield divided the rear seat from the front, but the smoky interior welcomed me like an old friend.

"*¿Adónde vamos?*"

Good question, I thought as I gave the driver the name of my hotel. Good question. Follow the leads, I thought. There's no one to help you here, no fellow cops, no team. Follow the leads, one at a time. *Don't panic.*

I watched his hands on the steering wheel because I like seeing a job well done; he steered skillfully through packed streets, whistling silently between his teeth.

"Is the traffic always like this?" I asked.

"Like what?"

"Crowded? *¿Loco?*"

His flowered shirt, worn open over a ribbed white tee, was turquoise and black, and a silver cross dangled from a chain around his neck. He was young, maybe early twenties. Dark curly hair made a halo around his thin face and accented his brooding eyes.

He rested his right arm on the back of the seat. When he smiled any resemblance to saint or poet ended. He had a gap-toothed grin that looked more than a little *loco* to me.

"This is nothing," he said. "Before the restrictions, then there was traffic."

"Restrictions?"

"Rules about when private cars can be on the road. Like if your license plate ends in a five, you can't take your car out Mondays and Wednesdays."

A law like that would go over big in Boston or New York, I thought. The politician who dared to sponsor it would be tossed out of office so fast you'd hear the wind at his back. We passed a bright red articulated giant of a bus, the word TRANSMILENIO written on its side, a cow tethered to a tree on the median strip, and a '59 Chevy, repainted and buffed, with shining chrome. At an intersection, a child of ten solemnly swallowed fire while two younger kids rode unicycles and tossed juggling pins.

At a traffic light, a man rapped on my window, palm extended for alms. Before I could respond, the light changed and the driver pulled away.

"You're not from Bogotá, then?" the driver said.

"The States. Boston."

"Aha," he said. "The Red Sox. Very good team. Red Sox."

His enthusiasm and backseat glances didn't adversely affect his driving. He changed gears smoothly, without a lot of show. He kept up with traffic, didn't press, slid through yellow lights as though he had them timed.

"Your meter doesn't show the fare," I said.

"It's on the card. Meter gives the time, the distance, the waiting time. You add that to the basic fare, unless you hire by the hour." He handed me a card with a grid of prices. His photo in the upper left-hand corner looked stiff and solemn as a choirboy. There was an identity number and a name, Guillermo Santos.

The basic fare was a dollar. To rent the cab by the hour cost eight bucks. The cabbie swerved around a slow truck, the movement as gentle as cradling a baby.

"You ever work the airport?" I asked.

"Sure. Most nights I do at least one run."

"Can I show you a photo? I'm looking for a girl who flew into El Dorado three nights ago."

At a red light I passed both shots of Paolina forward. He didn't ask whether they were the same girl, just studied each one intently.

"She steal something?"

"She's my sister."

"Sorry," he said. "Pretty girl. She run away?"

"Do you know a nightclub called the Zona Rosa?"

He made a quick right, then a left. "Place on the road to Chia?" he said slowly. "That's the only one I know. You ever been to Chia?"

"No. If I reserved your cab for the evening, would you pick me up here, at the hotel, at eight?"

His eyes lit up. "For the whole evening?"

"Four hours, minimum. You'd wait for me, bring me back. Could you do that? Would you have to okay it with your boss?"

"Zona Rosa, they'll barely be open at eight. Let's make it ten."

"Fine," I said. "Ten o'clock. You need a cash advance, to hold the cab?"

"I'll be here."

"Thank you, Señor Santos."

"And you, Señorita . . . ?"

"Carlyle."

I overtipped and watched as he seamlessly reentered the stream of traffic. Must be the altitude, I thought. Look at me, trusting a guy because he knows how to drive a cab.

CHAPTER 20

I OPENED THE door to my room cautiously, wishing I'd pasted a single red hair across the doorjamb, like some old film-noir PI. As if that would work in a hotel. I flicked the light and discovered that the bed had been made and the carpet vacuumed. Dead giveaway: The maid had been and gone.

The message light on the phone flickered. I punched the button and listened to silence followed by the click of a receiver returning to the cradle. Someone had called and waited, then left no word on the tape. Luisa Cabrera? Her three hours were almost up.

I hauled my laptop out from under the bed and plugged it in. Gloria was on target; Roz had sent mail. I skimmed the details of Angel Navas's career. Damn. The rumors that he'd taken over Roldán's drug empire were as false as the tales of Roldán's death. Navas had been extradited to the U.S. around the same time El Martillo's plane had reportedly crashed. There were clips about his Florida trial. Guilty on eight counts of distribution, but it was the racketeering conviction that had gotten him transferred to the federal pen in Colorado where he died. No details on the cause of death. Prison brawl or heart attack, the result had been the same.

I'd asked Roz to check out the outfit named on Naylor's phone bill, MB Realty Trust. I scrolled quickly through her report. MB Realty Trust, titleholder of the house in which

Naylor lived, was a wholly owned subsidiary of Bracken-Corp, with a capital C. BrackenCorp was a Florida-based defense contractor, a billion-dollar outfit owned by one Mark Bracken.

Was Naylor filming a PR masterpiece for BrackenCorp? Was Naylor associated with BrackenCorp, or did the company simply own a lot of properties in the area? I typed the follow-up questions for Roz.

M.B. Mark Bracken. MB Realty Trust. I closed my eyes. I knew something about BrackenCorp, but what? Something to do with the war in Iraq, a no-bid contract scandal? Mark Bracken was definitely a presence, a somebody on the business pages of glossy magazines.

Roz's correspondence continued. Sam had phoned and given her the Ignacio number. Had I called it, she wanted to know? Gotten results?

I stretched and glanced at my watch. Cabrera's three hours were up. I checked her card, got an outside line, and punched the numbers.

"Hello?" She picked up her own line, sounding harried. No secretary.

I identified myself. There was a long silence, the kind a person might use to collect her thoughts.

"Ah, yes, Señora Carlyle. Sorry. I was expecting another call. Where are you?"

An interesting question. I ignored it and asked my own. "What have you decided?"

A pause. "That you were right. It isn't my sort of story."

"Then I'll need to proceed on my own, with the authorities and with—"

"A moment, please." Again, she hesitated a beat too long. "I have done some work on your behalf."

I wondered whether that work might have involved an anonymous alert phoned in to the Gold Museum. She certainly sounded as though she were grasping at straws, as though she hadn't expected to hear from me.

"If you still wish to have this story televised—"

"I do, since you can't help me."

"I have a friend. You have paper, pencil?"

I wrote while she spoke. She'd decided to pass on my story, but if I was determined to go public with Paolina's disappearance, she could recommend a broadcaster named Rivas who worked at Caracol, a local network. Unfortunately, Señor Rivas was away on location and couldn't be reached until tomorrow in the late afternoon. Of course, I could contact someone else, but Rivas would be perfect. She sounded friendly and sincere, not like the sort of woman who'd set me up for a visit to a jail cell.

"So there's nothing else you can do?"

"Just direct you to Caracol. And the Gold Museum. You know, you definitely should go."

"I did," I said. "Very informative. I learned about the Cities of Stone, the Lost Cities."

"Oh. Then you— I hope you enjoyed it. Thank you for your call."

"By the way," I said, "what can you tell me about Base Eighteen? Do you know where to find Base Eighteen?"

A quick indrawn breath, silence.

"I'm so sorry," she said abruptly, her voice almost cracking. "I have to run." The receiver clicked firmly into the cradle.

I'm no human lie detector, but either Base Eighteen meant something to Cabrera or I was no judge of vocal tension. Interesting. . . . In Boston, print journalists and TV reporters squabble. They don't share. They don't trade stories or help each other out. Possibly, what with journalists an endangered species, the game was played differently in Bogotá. I phoned Caracol, the TV station. Yes, Rivas worked there, and no, he wasn't currently available. That much was on the level.

Dammit. I was more certain than ever that Cabrera knew something. Frustrated, I tried Ignacio. The same woman with the same soft voice told me to call later.

"It *is* later," I said. "When will he be back?"

"Soon."

"It's important."

"Soon. Call back later."

Another click. I glared at the silent receiver in my hand. A slow ache throbbed at my temples and I squeezed my eyes shut. Against the velvet blackness, images flashed: the show-case of martyred journalists, an array of rigid golden masks, child street jugglers, museum guards.

I wondered what Santos, the cabbie, would say if I asked him where I could buy a gun.

CHAPTER 21

WHAT DOES A woman wear to a bar?

Lord, what don't women wear to bars? Call me sensitive about issues of appropriate bar dress, but when I was a cop, I got so damned tired of hearing the guys say: "Well, what did she expect?" *Well, what did she expect wearing that miniskirt? I've seen bikini bottoms with more coverage. Well, what did she expect, wearing that low-cut blouse, melons like those?*

Well, truth be told, she probably expected admiration. Expected some guy to belly up to the bar and buy her a margarita. Women, I would say, do not head in droves to bars hoping to get raped. Rape is not fun. It's painful and humiliating, has little to do with sex, and everything to do with anger and control. It's about the perp, not the victim. Normal guys don't rape, and rapists rape for reasons that go way beyond apparel.

Jeez, you broads have no sense of humor.

At a street vendor's cart, I purchased a deep blue ruana, a wool shawl that could have been designed for the express purpose of blurring shape and height. At a drugstore, I debated home hair-dye kits. I didn't want to stand out like a beacon tonight, but I was planning to drop Naylor's name, and if someone called to check my bona fides, he'd remember me as a redhead. The *droguería* had mirrors perched over the aisles to help the employees keep track of shoplifters.

I vetoed the dye, but since I was already in the hair aisle, decided I might as well arm myself. From a shelf of hairspray, I selected a small cylinder, almost as good as Mace or pepper spray, and really, what kind of judge would send a woman to prison for squirting an assailant in the face with hairspray?

What does a woman wear to a bar?

Jeans, the equalizer of fashion. Rich, poor, old, young, you can always get away with a good pair of jeans, and I'd seen enough of them on the local streets to feel comfortable choosing them. Scoop-neck tee; show a little cleavage, make like you belong. Scarf, no jewelry. I didn't want to be the victim of a necklace grab-and-snatch. Thieves *do* pay attention to what you wear.

Shoes. Since I didn't want to be taken for a working girl, the spike-heeled sandals I'd bought in Miami were out, and my business heels were too businesslike. At the last minute I'd tossed a pair of low-heeled sandals into my duffel, figuring they'd double as bedroom slippers. Not perfect by a long shot, but okay. I topped the ensemble off with the ruana.

My backpack was not a great fashion choice, but I didn't have an alternative. I'm the same way at home. I don't know how some women manage to switch purses all the time, coordinating bags with shoes and mood and who knows what else. When I pick a bag, I'm looking for a place to park my keys and Kleenex.

I usually need a place to park a gun, too. As I wedged the small cylinder of hairspray into the pocket of my jeans, I longed for the Smith .40 locked in my Cambridge desk and cursed the elusive Ignacio for his continued unavailability.

Not only was Santos a skillful driver, he was prompt. Arriving under the hotel's awning at 9:58, he got out and held the door to the back seat. You can count the number of cabbies who'll do that in Boston on the index finger of your right hand. Standing, he was skinny, a little under six feet. He wore the same floral shirt and dark slacks, but he'd combed

his hair, slicked it back; I guess, to make himself look older.
It made him look wide-eyed and vulnerable instead.

"Okay if I ride in front?" I asked. "I don't want to get you
in trouble."

He promptly slammed the back door and opened the
front. Flashed a smile.

The streets of Bogotá are laid out in a grid, more like
Manhattan than Boston. *Carreras* run from south to north,
calles from east to west, crossing the *carreras* at ninety-
degree angles. Then there are *diagonales* and *transversales.*
We took a main road out of town to the north. He called it
the *autopista del Norte,* and I remembered it from the map.
We were headed up into the savanna.

"Beautiful country," he murmured.

In the dark, I had to take his word for it. Occasional
streetlights gave piercing views of twinkle-lit valleys, small
towns or settlements so far below we might have been traveling in a low-flying plane. Once we passed a series of green-
houses, the long narrow buildings glistening white.

He talked about the Red Sox and I let the conversation
wash over me, grunting an occasional response while watching the rearview mirror. The incline grew steeper. We passed
bicyclists fighting their way uphill, reflectors glowing red on
the narrow frames of racing bikes.

He talked about himself. He was a student, reading eco-
nomic theory, cabbing part-time. The town further along the
road, Chia, was his birthplace. *Chia,* a word in the native
Chibcha language, meant "moon," so Chia was the town of
the moon. On the way back, perhaps we'd take a different
route. The winding road called the Séptima was more scenic.
He chattered on nervously and I wondered what topic he was
trying to avoid.

"I asked around about this place, the Zona Rosa." He
sounded uncomfortable. I waited for him to continue, but he
stayed silent.

"Is it a place to get girls?" The prospect of escorting me
to a whorehouse might account for his discomfort.

"No, no. It's a bar."

"Is prostitution legal here?"

"It's a gray thing. The police don't stop it, but you can't advertise. The places exist, but they don't have signs."

"Do the cabbies direct the traffic?" It's that way in a lot of cities. When I drive, plenty of men ask if I know where they can "have a good time" in Boston.

"Some," Santos answered. "Not me. If someone asks, I take them to the Zona Rosa, the entertainment area. No brothels there. Drinks, lots of women, but not, you know, whores."

"You ever take people to this place we're going?"

"Not unless they ask." He paused and licked his lips nervously. "There are rumors."

I waited while he pulled around a slow-moving truck, a maneuver requiring full concentration, not to mention nerve.

He said, "At this place, there might be girls, a few rooms upstairs, you know? And drugs, mainly cocaine, but also *basuca,* which means there are fights, too. Not every night or the police would shut it down, but sometimes." He paused. "I don't think it's good for you to go there."

"I won't stay long."

"You think this girl you're looking for went there? The one who ran away?"

"She was taken." I may have said it more emphatically than necessary. It was important, an article of faith by now.

"Taken? Why?"

"Her father's Colombian."

"And the mother American? She wanted to divorce?"

"Look, it doesn't matter. What matters is that her father may have friends there. I want him to know I'm looking for him."

He seemed troubled. "You're paying for the cab for four hours."

"Yes, but it won't take that long."

"I'll come with you, inside. A woman shouldn't go to a bar alone."

I opened my mouth to protest. *A woman should; a woman shouldn't.* Santos might as well have worked at the cop house. Then I thought, Don't be stupid. A woman walking into a bar with a man is more natural. It's better cover.

"Thank you," I said. "That'll be great."

Embarrassed, he muttered, "It's up here on the left."

He turned off onto a curvy road that hugged the side of a mountain, and I asked him about the white crosses by the roadside, thinking they might be some kind of native shrine.

"Just places where people died in car accidents."

Great, I thought. No need to post speed limits.

"Here it is."

Low and long, constructed entirely of wood, with a court-yard and outdoor picnic benches, the place was a cross between a log cabin and an overgrown barn. Bright lights illuminated a vast grassy parking area to the right. Fairy lights and strings of pennants gave the courtyard a festive used-car-lot atmosphere. Music poured through an open door guarded by a turnstyle and flanked by two guys built like upright freezers.

Neither asked for ID, but we got a thorough scanning, al-most a memorization, as we paid the cover charge. The man on the left was armed, the bulge under the left arm unmistakable.

"You play basketball?" It was the cabbie's first comment about my height and I admired both his circumspection and his restraint.

"Volleyball," I said.

"You should play basketball."

The place was even bigger than it seemed, a series of smaller rooms expanding into larger ones, at least two with raised dance floors. The rough-hewn wooden rafters were festooned with star lights, banners, and neon signs for Bavaria beer. Costumed men and women, greeters and dancers, mingled with the paying customers. The costumed women wore tiny skirts that started well below the waist and shirts that ended just under their breasts, leaving a lot of taut bare skin in between. I'd have termed the outfits sexist if the men's garb hadn't been just as revealing. And the dancing, well, it was not what you'd see at the senior prom, unless all the chaperones were dead drunk. The noise pounded my ears, salsa amped to the max.

"Let me buy you a drink," I yelled.

"A *mojito* would be fine."

I got myself a beer. Club Colombia. Bottled.

If I were doing a search for a kid in the States, I'd have exercised my patience, had a few beers, watched the setup, especially after what I'd heard from Santos. I'd work with a partner and we'd check the layout, identify entrances and exits, chart the flow of movement, see what the patterns were. Prostitution has a pattern. Drug deals have a pattern; buyers come, money changes hands, product changes hands.

Instead I watched the dancers, glued to each other from chest to thigh, hips punctuating the beat. I hadn't had much sleep and I had a full day tomorrow with Base Eighteen to find and visit, and a television reporter to convince. I was impatient. Jumpy. You might say reckless.

When the bartender brought the drinks, I dove in. "The manager here tonight?"

"Why? You dance? You want a job?"

Guillermo leaned over and said, "No, she wants to complain about the service."

Both bristled. The bartender might have had an attitude problem, but I was surprised to find Santos acting in such a proprietorial way, like I really *was* his date, and the bartender had insulted me.

I spoke quickly to settle any ruffled macho feathers. "Hey, he didn't mean anything. Just tell me who to talk to. I like to talk to managers. I'm friendly."

"The manager doesn't see people."

"He'll see me because I'm here from Miami with news from a friend. Tell him he *wants* to see me. Matter of fact, he *needs* to see me."

"Just you, or the loudmouth, too?"

"Just me. You'll be doing him a favor."

He stared at me. I returned his gaze till he dropped his eyes and used a phone. Across the dance floor, someone lit a sparkler, two sparklers, a flood of them, to raucous shouts, applause, and laughter, and I thought about the nightclub fire at The Station in Rhode Island with a hundred dead after a brief shower of fireworks. This place was made entirely of wood and the patrons were standing on chairs waving sparklers at pennants that hadn't passed any U.S. fireproofing standards. If Paolina had been there, I'd have ordered her to leave.

Santos said, "I should come with you."

"If I'm not back in fifteen minutes, ask for me. If I'm not back in half an hour, make a fuss."

"Call the police?"

"I hope not."

The manager's office was up a flight of stairs and through another turnstyle. Wood, flimsy decorations, and sparklers, all the makings of a conflagration, plus a subsequent riot when the patrons were unable to flee quickly through the crowd-restricting turnstyles.

He was the fattest man I'd ever seen. He sat on a stool, maybe because he couldn't fit in a chair, and his butt lapped over the edges of the seat and drooped perilously toward the ground. I hadn't seen any heavy people in Colombia thus far, and his appearance, pasty white and ultra-obese, was shocking. He was twice the size of Gloria. The only person I'd ever seen remotely that size was a massive Pacific Islander, and he'd been tan as well as mountainous. The manager wore a white tentlike shirt over shapeless tan trousers. His dark hair was caught in a greasy ponytail and tied with a dangling red cord.

The room that housed the fat man was constructed as a kind of crow's nest; you could see the dance floor below through a series of low smoked windows on two walls. I watched the fat man as he watched the dancers through narrowed eyes. His smile gave me the creeps.

The bartender said, "This is the one. Wants to see you, Gordo."

Gordo being Spanish for "fat," it was possible the manager had a sense of humor, but the cultural differences were such that I wasn't sure.

"Search the backpack."

The bartender obliged, then patted me down as well, a professional job.

"So who are you?" When the manager spoke, his chins rippled. It was the same voice that had answered the phone when I'd called, low and growly.

"Carlotta from Miami," I said. "From Naylor."

He shifted his eyes, a sufficient gesture to usher the bartender out the door.

"Am I supposed to know who Naylor is?"

His reaction when he'd heard the name had already told me.

"I'm looking for someone," I said.

"Someone in particular?"

"Roldán. On personal business."

"Roldán?"

"Carlos Roldán Gonzales."

"Roldán, as in El Martillo?" His chins shook when he laughed, but his dark eyes didn't join in the fun. "If you have personal business with *that* Roldán, you'll need the archangel Gabriel as a go-between. The man is dead these two, three years."

"Listen, pass the word: I want to see him."

"It's true what you say? He's alive?"

"He'll know my name. Tell him Carlotta. Tell him the Hotel del Parque in Bogotá. Tell him quick, unless he wants everyone in South America to know he's alive and well and back in business."

"You talk a lot, Señorita."

"Tell him I talk a lot."

"But I truly have no idea what you're talking about."

"Okay. If you don't know what I'm talking about, who would? The owner?"

"The owner doesn't talk to anyone."

"Does the owner talk to the law? What I hear, you have girls here. You have dope here. Maybe the owner would rather talk to me than talk to the police."

He must have pressed a button concealed under the rug

because two muscled goons appeared at the door and they hadn't been sent by any archangel.

He said, "You're gonna leave now."

"Okay. Fine."

"You don't talk to the police, either."

"Pleasure to meet you," I said.

I'd accounted for the unusual width of the staircase by the fact that El Gordo had to travel up and down, but the dimensions were ideal for hustling a woman downstairs locked between two bodyguards like meat in a sandwich. That's what happened to me, the bum's rush, down the stairs. It got a little tricky at the turnstyles, but the goons had obviously practiced. One preceded me, one followed, and lingering was not encouraged.

Santos, the driver, was already outside, pacing under the watchful eye of the entry guards. They no longer looked like freezers to me; after the mountain man inside, they seemed undersized, underfed.

"Jesus, you're back. I didn't know what to do. Time was running out. They told me to leave."

"Let's go."

"You're acting crazy, making trouble, a place like this."

Valid complaint, I thought, but how do you stir things up without acting crazy? I didn't want to spend the rest of my life chasing the shadow of Roldán. The terrible thing about childhood is the speed at which it passes. I'd missed out on so much of Paolina's childhood; I hadn't been paired with her, Big Sister to Little Sister, till she was seven years old. Seven had been a good year, filled with discovery, ice cream, and field trips. Eight was shorter, nine briefer still. Fourteen had whistled past; fifteen was speeding by like an express train. I didn't want her to be all grown-up, a cool and distant adult, before I saw her again. I couldn't face that; I wanted things to happen quickly.

Just not as quickly as they did.

We hadn't traveled more than two or three miles. Our headlights pierced the darkness, weak cones of light. Santos had taken the alternate road, the scenic route, and traffic was so light that he'd flipped on his brights. His continuing silence may have been prompted by anger, but I found it soothing. I needed rest; I needed sleep.

"There are two motorcycles behind us. A car, too, I think. A big one." The tension in his voice snapped my lolling head up.

"Did they follow us from the bar?"

"I don't know. No headlights a second ago; now, they're on top of us."

I swiveled in the passenger seat, blinking my eyes against the lights. Cycles, yes, they had to be. The engines roared over the cab's steady thrum. The twin lights veered close together, then widened.

Reckless joyriders? The big vehicle behind them followed way too close. Chasing them? We took a curve at speed and the white crosses flashed by.

"Are there any turnoffs?" I asked. "Crossroads?"

"A little farther, half a mile. There's one to—" He gave the place a name, but I couldn't sort the sound into sense.

"You know it?" I asked. "Well enough to evade them, hide there?"

"I can try."

"Don't let them pass us."

"If I bang up the cab—"

"I'll pay. Don't worry about the cab; worry about losing them."

He bit his lip and concentrated. He knew the road and his reflexes were good. When a cyclist moved to pass, he slid over to block it.

"Almost there," he said. "Maybe they're just trying to scare us."

The crossroad appeared so abruptly, with no cautionary sign or light, that I'd have missed it. Santos edged the wheel to the left and we were off the main road, racing downhill. There was a squeal of protesting tires. One of the cyclists, oversteering, must have spun off the road. My hands were clenched. I wished I could clamp them on the wheel, take control of the cab. *Do something.*

I said, "Get the lights off. Find someplace to hide."

Santos's eyes raked the rearview mirror and opened wide. "Oh, no," he said, "we got trouble."

The lights in the rearview mirror had changed. The big vehicle bearing down on us, the one that had ridden so closely on the cycle's fenders, had a light bar on the roof I hadn't noticed before, with blue and red rotating beacons.

"Cops?" The colored lights picked out a single motorcycle preceding the vehicle.

"Not traffic police. Look! Look at the car!"

It was larger than a sedan, larger than an SUV. Not quite a truck.

"Military?"

"DAS. What the hell have you done?"

DAS. My mouth had gone bone dry when we'd merely been outracing a couple of cyclists down the mountainside. Now my tongue was a desert. *DAS. The Colombian Secret Police.*

"They don't want me," I said. *Why would they? They were political; I wasn't political. I was looking for my sister.*

"I have to stop," he said. "I have to."

He braked sharply.

"No," I said. "Don't!"

Too late. Santos's foot stayed on the brake and we rolled to a halt. The remaining cyclist pulled up flush with the cab on the driver's side. The vehicle, big and square like a Jeep, stopped no more than a foot from the rear bumper.

The uniformed men knew my name before they asked to see my passport. The cyclist, slim and young, was clean-shaven. The other man, a passenger in the Jeep-like vehicle, was older, barrel-chested, military in bearing. He opened my door, told me to get out of the cab, and ordered Santos to be on his way. They'd escort me from here.

"Where?" I said. "Why?"

Teeth flashed in his swarthy face. "Señorita, simply because I say so," he returned politely.

"Then I'll stay here," I said, just as politely.

His hand clamped my wrist, turning it as he pulled me off

the seat. Bracing his left foot against the car, he yanked me
out the door. I didn't make it easy, but he outweighed me by
forty pounds; I was afraid my wrist would snap if I resisted
too strongly. I barely had time to grab my backpack with my
left hand before I was out on the grassy verge by the side of
the road.

I yelled, "Go to the U.S. Embassy. Tell them. Give them
my name—"

"You will say nothing," shouted the cyclist. "Do nothing,
unless you wish us to impound your cab. Unless, of course,
you wish to join her. It's a matter of state security."

Santos looked shattered.

"Drive," the cyclist urged him in a fierce whisper. "Say
nothing. Don't even look back."

"I owe him money," I yelled. "Let me pay."

I tossed enough to cover the rental on the seat, then
plunged my hand in my pocket, and came up with the metal
canister. The spray hit the big man full-blast in the eyes. He
grunted, but his hand barely loosened on my wrist. I yanked
and pulled, but I couldn't twist myself free.

Tires squealed as Santos drove off. Even if I did get
loose, where would I run? More hands grabbed me as the
big man's grip weakened, and it must have taken at least
two to carry me to the Jeep. I realized I was screaming, and
I kept on screaming at the top of my lungs, screaming and
cursing even though there didn't seem to be anyone on the
deserted stretch of road to hear.

The Jeep was waiting with doors ajar. They hustled me
into the back seat where a third man grabbed me and twisted
his hand into the hair at the nape of my neck. I felt a sharp
jab on my right thigh before I saw the syringe in his hand.
By the time I connected the jab with the syringe, I felt
woozy and sick. My foot connected with somebody's shin,
but my hands were imprisoned, and I was being shoved to
the floor.

The carpet was fascinating, it was dazzling and wavy. It
had slivers of silver and crawling ants. As I stared up at the
face of the man with the hairspray-reddened eyes, his nose

distorted, spreading and flattening. His right eye slanted and grew, glowing with flickering jack-o'-lantern light. His eyelashes curled like spidery lace. His face was three-dimensional, then two, a human mask bigger and more savage than the golden masks in the museum, with a rough gaping hole for a mouth. I tried to wriggle, to squirm my way up to the seat, but I was drowning in thick air, flailing uselessly against monster tentacles. The windshield turned to fun-house glass, and I saw that my face was spreading and flattening, too, squishing into mud and clay, bones dissolving under fragile flesh.

The mountains disappeared into darkness.

PAOLINA

SHE WOULDN'T, SHE absolutely wouldn't cry. The situation was humiliating enough; the *gallina,* the cheap yellow hen she'd stolen from the corner store snatched from her in turn by two ragged boys. She wouldn't make the disaster worse with tears, wouldn't show weakness. She'd seen what the kids did to the ones who showed weakness, the ones who stank of fear, seen how they made a small boy wade into the filthy river to escape hurled chunks of brick and concrete. She made her eyes as hard as stones and her lips like carved ice, but her mouth betrayed her, watering from the spicy smell of the meat. She licked her fingers greedily and wondered how to find food. And where. And when, most of all, when.

She'd need to widen her territory. And that scared her because the little square was the only space that felt safe. The kids called it the square, but the adults called it Engativa. There was a small fountain in the center of the square at the junction of three stone pathways. Sparse grass surrounded the fountain, blotched with weeds and patches of muddy earth. Three spindly eucalyptus trees grew skyward, but didn't provide much shade.

The square was ringed by a concrete path, and then by cracked concrete roads edged with parked cars and the small *busetas* that chugged in and out at all hours. She liked the little buses. One had brought her here, and another could take her somewhere else, once she figured out where she wanted to go.

She'd been lucky so far. Oh, she'd been smart and quick, but she knew that a lot of it was luck, and she didn't want to press her luck, not here in a strange city. Although this area, this Engativá, didn't look like the same city at all, not like the skyscraper-filled Bogotá she'd visited when she was a little kid. Maybe her memory was wrong. Maybe the city had changed.

Here in Engativá, packs of wild dogs roamed the streets. She'd taken to carrying a tree branch in case she had to fend them off or fend off the other packs, the packs of kids, mostly dirty-faced boys who played endless soccer games in the street. Didn't they go to school, these kids? She'd considered turning up at a school because, at home, teachers were an easy touch, always loaning you money for lunch if you forgot it. If she could find a school, she could get something to eat.

She'd stepped onto the bus as though she were in a dream. The doors had yawned and she'd moved like lightning, the way you had to move when the volleyball flashed over the net and you knew you had to give it every ounce of energy and strength you had, and maybe a little more. She'd thrown herself onto the bus the same way she'd thrown herself across the floor of the gym during the final match of the season, but no one had congratulated her on her winning effort. People on the bus had looked at her like she was crazy.

Maybe she was. Maybe she should have stayed with Jorge and Ana. She'd have food, even if it was drugged.

Once on the bus she'd groped her way through the crowd, stepping to the back, hiding behind the tallest men she could find. What would Ana do? What would Jorge do? They'd grab a cab and follow the bus, follow her when she got off, grab her as soon as she was alone. If they came on board, she'd scream and cry and make a scene as soon as she saw them. She wouldn't wait till one got close enough to stick a gun in her back, no way.

But what if they waited? What if they trailed the bus, and waited till she got off?

She'd started to settle down after the bus made first one stop, then another, and neither Ana nor Jorge appeared. Her heart had stopped trying to beat its way out of her chest. Maybe they couldn't find a cab; maybe they didn't know which bus she'd boarded.

"*¿Está occupado este asiento?*"

She was concentrating so hard on watching the doors she hadn't even noticed the empty seat till the girl asked. Paolina shook her head—no, it was vacant—and the girl sank wearily onto the bench. She wasn't much older than Paolina, still in her teens. She wore a worn blue ruana and her purse was strapped across her chest. Soon the man sitting next to her got off, and the girl tapped Paolina's arm.

"You okay?" she asked.

"Yeah, sure." Paolina was surprised that her voice came out steady.

"Sit here."

Maybe it wasn't as steady as all that. The girl urged her into the window seat, almost as if she could tell Paolina was hiding from someone. She seemed concerned and friendly. After a while, Paolina dropped her eyes and confessed that she wasn't really okay; she was upset because she was running away. She'd decided not to tell the truth. She'd told a story instead, about running away from her stepmother, about a big argument and a slap, and racing out of the house and forgetting to bring money. The girl was really nice, and Paolina wound up trading her jacket for the girl's faded blue ruana and ten thousand pesos, which sounded like a fortune. Paolina's jacket was warmer and newer; she'd had to work hard to convince the girl she'd be doing her a favor by switching. After the girl got off the bus, Paolina felt guilty. What if Jorge and Ana followed her friend, caught her? She tried to see out the small back window, but she couldn't tell if any car was deliberately following the bus. All the headlights looked the same, like bright round cat's eyes.

She'd fallen asleep then, her head lolling against the side of the bus, and the next thing she remembered was the driver, huge and hairy, yelling at her that it was the end of the line, and she'd have to get off. The end of the line was the square called Engativa. Getting off the bus had been scary, but Ana and Jorge were nowhere in sight.

It was seriously weird, she thought, the stuff you could get used to. If kids at home ever told her she'd be willing to sleep outdoors and pick through trash bins for old clothes and half-eaten fruit, she'd have laughed, or maybe gotten angry. But there was something about this place, the colors, the Mexican-style music that blared from the corner café, something about fitting in. She felt strangely safe, like a book hiding on a bookshelf or a stamp hiding in a stamp collection. The weather was beautiful, the breeze as soft as puffs of cotton. Plus there was something about being on her own, living by her wits, that attracted her.

She wasn't the same person. Nobody knew her story, so she could make it up as she went along. Lies sprang easily to her lips: She was an orphan; she'd grown up in Argentina. For a while it had been scary, and now it might be okay, because she had a skill, a valuable skill. She was a drummer.

She'd been too tired to think at first, too tired and scared even to sleep. She'd hung out in the square, but whenever she saw anyone—and the square was a lively place—she'd slip into the alley between the church and the bicycle repair shop. It turned out the church had a small bathroom, and the discovery filled her with delight because the church was almost always open. The bathroom wasn't even filthy, just really old with yellowy tile and a warped board floor. The single tiny window was set too high for any pervert to peer through, the toilet flushed reassuringly, and the sink filled with rusty water if you waited long enough. There was no lock on the door, so she'd shoved a heavy bench in front of it, moving it back when she was done. She was careful.

She'd slept most of the first night in the bathroom of the church. The next morning, she'd gone outside to look around, and it had been like what that stupid teacher was always saying: Today is the first day of the rest of your life. Today was nothing like yesterday, or any other day.

She'd sat on benches and stoops, listening to people talk,

watching the buses dump their human cargo in the square, refill, and leave, pleased by the sheer number of people who traveled anonymously through the square. She was a speck of sand on a beach, unremarkable, unnoticed. A cow wandered the streets, tying up traffic. Too hungry to resist, she'd spent over a tenth of her fortune on *gallina criolla,* a small roasted hen, the specialty of one of the small shops that ringed the square, sort of like a Store 24, and sort of like a butcher shop. It reminded her of stores in Boston's Chinatown, because the chickens and ducks dangled by their necks from a kind of awning in front.

She'd joined a soccer game. The kids didn't ask questions as long as you made a real effort to score. She'd slept behind a cantina, wrapped in her blue ruana, hidden behind stacks of concrete blocks.

The second morning, she'd heard the band rehearsing in the square, a kids' band. They traveled other places, and begged and passed the hat, but the square was their home base. The way they played they couldn't earn much. Right off, she'd known that the trumpet was good, the guitar was bad, and the drummer was terrible. The guy on the accordion was amazing, good enough to front any band, but really ugly.

She'd started by hanging out, listening, not dancing like almost everybody else. The dances were amazing, with intricate footsteps. The music wasn't salsa, that was for sure. She thought people called it *cumbia.* The melodies were different than the stuff she usually played, but the basic rhythm was a simple four/four beat. There were waltz beats, too, but those were called *pasillo.* After a while, she'd offered to pass the hat, which required both selflessness and courage; selflessness because she had to give the money to the band, courage because she had to keep other kids from stealing the pesos that made it into the hat. Then she'd found the top of a garbage can, round like a cymbal, and she'd started tapping, just tapping with her fingers. The accordion had noticed right away, and why wouldn't he? They really needed somebody to keep the guitar steady, and their drummer wasn't up to it.

The drummer and his pals were doing their best to drive her off. Last night, they'd waited for her in the dark, threatening her and laughing, telling her about the bad things that happened to girls on the streets. She hadn't even joined the raggedy band yet, but the drummer could tell which way the wind was blowing. When the kid who played accordion tossed her some pesos from the hat last night, it was a declaration of war. The gift hadn't even been enough to buy the *gallina.* She'd had to steal it. And now the drummer's friends were eating it.

Those few carelessly thrown coins had practically burned the palm of her hand. The two-hundred-peso coin was the same size as a quarter. Quarters could be slotted into a pay phone and used to call home. Even if she didn't have enough change, there had to be some kind of system, like collect calls in the States. But she hadn't seen a pay phone. Ana and Jorge could be watching the pay phones. More than that, if she called home, someone would come, right away, right now. Carlotta would come, for sure, and that made her feel happy at first, safe and warm, but it also meant she wouldn't be able to stay in Colombia. She wouldn't be able to find her father.

Ana and Jorge had told her so many lies, but what if that part were true? What if her father really had been wounded? What if he were dying, waiting for her to come to him, to meet him before he slipped away? If she called home, she'd never get the chance to find him.

In one direction was the *humedal,* the marshland near the river. No shops there. She'd heard there was a military base in another direction. One of the nasty boys had advised her to go there and earn money like girls were supposed to earn it, pulling down her pants for the soldiers. She'd steal the money to phone home before she had to do stuff like that. She'd go to the American Embassy. She knew there was an American Embassy in Bogotá. But Engativa didn't look like Bogotá. Maybe the bus had traveled farther than she thought. She'd been asleep. It was possible.

As soon as she entered the shop three blocks northwest of

the square, the clerk started following her. When she didn't immediately choose something to buy, he told her to get lost. It was like he could smell her hunger, see inside her empty pockets.

She'd thought ten thousand pesos would last, but it wasn't very much money at all. The *gallina* cost more than a thousand pesos all by itself. How long could you go without eating? She trudged back to the square, heading for her place of refuge, the tiny bathroom in the rear alcove of the church. She didn't need the toilet so much as she needed the privacy. She needed to count her small cache of pesos, decide whether she could pay for food or whether she'd have to go farther afield. She was feeling lightheaded and woozy, like she might be getting sick. Maybe it was hunger, but maybe it was the water from the fountain, or the strawberries she'd picked early in the morning, real strawberries growing wild on the other side of the river.

One thing about her foray into the shop, she was getting some idea of what stuff cost, of what was available. There wasn't any packaged mac and cheese. Rice came in big sacks, not boxes. There were fruits she'd never seen before. Dammit, her mouth was watering again, and really she shouldn't spend a single peso on food. She needed an instrument, some kind of drum. No way would they let her join the band if all she had to offer was a garbage can cover. What she wouldn't give for her trap-set now, for the high-hat cymbal, and the deep bass drum.

Once she'd blocked the bathroom door with the bench, she found she needed the toilet after all. She had some kind of wicked diarrhea, a sudden, urgent need to void, and her stomach hurt really, really bad. She counted her pesos, only a thousand left. A thousand was nothing; if Engativa had a McDonald's it wouldn't buy a single Big Mac. She'd have to try the church. Maybe there were nuns. Nuns wouldn't molest you or anything. Maybe they had a bed where she could sleep, with a warm, soft blanket. Maybe there were musical instruments for the congregation, a tambourine, like in a Salvation Army band.

She ran water into the sink, dipped her hand into the rusty stream, patted water on her face and neck. There was no mirror in the bathroom and she was glad. She must look like hell.

The knock on the door was sharp and staccato, a drumbeat. "I'll be out in a minute." She'd gotten so used to this being her own place that the knock startled her, but there had to be other kids who used this place. The cafés sure didn't want the kids using the bathrooms. The boys just peed in the river; no way would she drink from the river.

Maybe it was one of the priests, and he'd yell at her. But maybe it was a nun, a motherly smiling nun who'd ask her to share dinner with the sisters, give her some soup to settle her stomach. When she shoved the bench out of the way, the door burst open and the boys who'd stolen her dinner were inside in a flash.

"No," she yelled. She threw the tin bucket in the corner at the biggest one, and she kept screaming. Always make noise. Keep screaming. It was like she could hear Carlotta's voice in her ear. Scream and scream until someone comes. Never stop screaming.

"Fifty thousand pesos," one of them shouted.

The sum confused her.

"Here! We got her," the other yelled. "We got her over here!"

Ana smiled tremulously as she walked in the door.

"Sweetheart," she said, "your father and I have been so worried."

The funny thing was, Paolina thought, even as she kept on screaming, Ana said it as though she really meant it. The woman's face was haggard, her eyes red. No way anyone would buy Ana as a kidnapper instead of a genuine mom.

She kept screaming until Jorge twisted her arm so hard that all she could do was gasp in pain.

"Shut up or I'll break it," he murmured lovingly in her ear.

CHAPTER 22

THIRSTY. **THE FIRST** time I woke, or maybe the third, I had a long chat with my pillow. I wanted water, and while the pillow had control of all the spigots, it wasn't giving the stuff away. I didn't need water anyway, I confided; I had roots, long shiny green roots that burrowed deep into the earth. I could wait for rain. The pillow smiled and agreed so I slept some more, dreaming of thunderclouds scudding across ocean skies. When my Mojave-dry mouth woke me again, maybe for the fourth time, maybe the sixth, I licked my parched lips and tried to move my right hand to shove the prickly hair off my forehead. Pain shot like electric current across my shoulders and pried my eyes wide. Instead of the interior of my room at the Hotel del Parque, with its soft companionable pillow and the window that peered at the mountains, there was fluttery uneven light and a blur of lumpy wall. No pillow at all.

I probed the area and myself with tentative feelers, senses on full alert. My hands, bound at the wrist, were secured behind my back; no wonder my shoulders felt stretched and achy. I closed my eyes, reopened them. Not a dream. Definitely, not entirely a dream. And since it was more than a dream, I was bound hand and foot, lying in some sort of hammock suspended from uneven wooden poles. Movement made the hammock swing and my stomach lurch in woozy imitation. I was hungry as well as thirsty. Hungry and thirsty and ill. Drugged and slow and stupid, like a fish flopping on a wooden dock, trying to breathe out of water.

I squeezed my eyes shut and told myself I had to remember. I needed to recall what had come before, or how could I cope with this strange and unprecedented place? I'd been in a hotel room in Bogotá. No, in a bar, the Zona Rosa, with a fat man. In a cab, flying down the side of a dark mountain. Each scene was like a puzzle piece. No narrative line connected one to the other. Then the bright shifting chunks started lining up in order, one image dissolving into the next in a montage of error and regret.

DAS. The Colombian secret police. Why the hell would DAS want to keep me from finding Paolina? I'd been forced into the black Jeep. I recalled the terrified eyes of Santos, the cabbie. Would he defy the secret police and go to the embassy? What were the chances that anyone knew I was here? Wherever here was.

A bird called out, a strange and piteous cry. I wasn't gagged; I could cry out as well. I licked my dry lips and hesitated. They'd left me ungagged, therefore no one would come when I called, or possibly someone would come, but not anyone I wanted to see. I tried to lift my feet. My ankles were loosely tied, a hobble more than a restraint. If I swung the hammock vigorously, would I tumble out? If I tumbled out, how far would I fall?

The rough ceiling seemed to be made of sticks, with a kind of cross at the center surrounded by concentric circles of wooden poles that looked almost like bamboo. The hammock was made of rope and loosely woven cloth. What light there was entered through the roof, filtered through the poles. I was still wearing my jeans and T-shirt, but the blue ruana was gone. My shoulders felt bruised, my mouth tasted like copper, and I badly needed a drink.

With a convulsive jerk, I swung my legs over the side of the hammock and tried to sit up at the same time. I still felt like that fish on the dock, trying to breathe in viscous air, but my muscles obeyed, and I attained an awkward, upright position. My stomach lurched again, and I wondered what time it was, what day it was, as I glanced into the dark corners of what appeared to be a primitive hut. My knuckles were sore. I rubbed them gently against each other behind my back, wondering whether I'd skinned them punching somebody, whether I'd injured any cops in the struggle. Maybe I'd be charged with resisting arrest. Maybe DAS didn't need to declare any charges.

DAS, *Departamento Administrativo de Seguridad,* Colombia's intelligence agency, is often referred to as Colombia's FBI, and frequently linked to human rights violations. There's a DAS agency in every big city, each operating under slightly different rules. DAS is also Colombia's Interpol connection, the go-to people for gunrunning, drug smuggling, art forgery, for any international agency needing a window into Colombia.

The man/woman team who'd gone over me with a fine-tooth comb at the Miami airport could have been DEA. DEA could have sicced DAS onto me. DAS, always interested in drugs, would be interested in Roldán. Maybe we could cooperate; I'd trade the man for Paolina any day.

Shit. It was possible I'd triggered DAS myself. *Base Dieciocho.* What the hell was Base Eighteen? I'd tried the number again from the hotel room. DAS could have a trace on every phone in Colombia for all I knew.

Stop theorizing before the facts, before breakfast, before dinner, I ordered myself sternly. I opened my mouth; I had only to call to get something to drink, but pride kept me from shouting. Stubbornness, too. Instead, I swung the hammock one way, my feet the other, and tumbled onto a dirt floor with a thud. My nose was filled with dust. Was this what the U.S. consulate meant by a substandard prison? What the hell was DAS thinking? No self-respecting FBI station kept prisoners in dirt-floored huts.

I waited, but the slam of my weight hitting the floor must have made less of a ruckus than I imagined. Maybe the agents were all busy torturing other prisoners. No one came.

The room was round as a doughnut. Empty hammocks hung from the rafters like drooping vines. I wasn't sure I'd dignify the overhead sticks with the term "rafters." The structure looked homemade, crafted out of tree branches and daubed mud, like a ramshackle hunting camp. I couldn't picture this building in Bogotá, and it suddenly occurred to me that this was not the first place in which I'd woken. Hadn't there been a previous moment of consciousness, walking supported between two hulking men? Hadn't there been a bumpy airstrip, a small skittery plane? I screwed my eyes shut again and felt nausea rise in my throat. Nothing to come up, I thought, and I seemed to remember that I'd been sick before. Where?

I crouched for a while, reestablishing equilibrium, then stood, hesitantly at first. The rope that bound my ankles had six inches of play, allowing an awkward hobbling gait, like a prisoner shuffling from bus transport to prison yard. My arms, secured behind my back, were useless for balance, but my stomach eventually stopped rolling, and I could move in a limited fashion. I could explore the hut, locate a window, a door, possibly find something to use as a weapon or a tool. I'd stay close to the lumpy walls until my balance adjusted to bound hands and feet. Hell, at least the floor was pretty soft. Volleyball players fall on harder floors every day. If I fell, I'd just get up. Right. I halted the pep talk and started to move in a slow circular pattern.

I'd been lucky. Much of the floor was stone, not dirt. If I'd tumbled onto one of the flat hard stones that covered the area nearer the walls, I could have broken an arm or worse. Thoughtful of my captors to place my hammock over dirt.

The noise was a cross between a cough and a snuffle, human, not animal. All my senses, which I'd thought were operating at maximum alert, ramped up a notch. My heartbeat increased, my hearing sharpened, and I froze against the wall, turning my head cautiously side to side. I couldn't see anyone, and the noise had stopped. It wasn't repeated. Again, I could have called out, but I didn't want the other person, the other thing, to be able to site on my response. A shudder rippled across my aching shoulders.

One of the hammocks hung distinctly lower than the rest.

I should have noticed it before, even in the dim, flickering light. I tried for a silent approach, but the rope between my ankles brushed against stones and earth.

At first I thought he was dead: I've never known anyone to sleep that quietly, breathe that softly, certainly not a full-grown hefty man. He slept like the dead. My thudding exit from the hammock hadn't disturbed him; my shackled approach failed to alert him.

He was in his late twenties, possibly thirty. Hard to tell because his narrow face was filthy, his beard scruffy, his angular features pinched with pain. The area around one eye was bruised and a deep scratch scored the bridge of his nose. His mouth was partially open, and his chest expanded gently as he breathed. He wore the remnants of muddy, bloodstained military fatigues.

His right arm, below the elbow, was bandaged in clean white cloth. His left pant leg was ripped off high at the thigh, the leg roughly splinted and wrapped in strips of the same cloth. The bandages seemed recent. They were clean, for one thing. No blood had seeped through the immaculate cloth. A sharp smell hovered, not antiseptic, but green, leafy, a forest smell. I wondered if it came from the loosely thatched roof.

Eighteen inches on the other side of the wounded man's hammock stood two earthenware vessels. Terra cotta in color, they looked as old as some of the pottery I'd seen at the Gold Museum. I bent to look inside, hoping for water, wondering how I'd drink with my hands behind my back even if the thing were filled to the brim. I backed off immediately. The largest was obviously a chamber pot; it begged no further investigation. The smaller held a colorless liquid. I sniffed cautiously, wondering if I could manipulate it between my chin and my chest. No need. I'd found the reason for the man's deep slumber. The smell was heady, laced with some sort of opiate. Not at all tempting as drinking water.

As I knelt near the hammock, a sudden touch set my heart pounding. The wounded man's fingers had grasped my sleeve, and his soft, "Who're you?" was murmured in English, not Spanish, his low, raspy voice a Southern drawl.

Another American. In DAS custody. What the hell was going on? I wondered how long he'd been playing possum.

"Who are you?" I responded more in a croak than a voice. His hold was weak; I could have shaken him off with no effort.

"Where am I?" His eyes were gray as slate, the whites threaded with red veins.

Shit. I was more than disappointed by his query; I was angry. I'd imagined he'd know exactly where we were. It seemed only right; he'd been here first.

"You American?" he managed, before his hand dropped.

"Yes. And you, what unit are you with?" I waited for his response, but he'd gone out like a light. I spoke into his ear, then held my ear to his mouth. He breathed, but he was far away.

An American, another American, wounded, and wearing combat fatigues. How long had he been here? I took another look at the makeshift splint. The poles on either side of his leg could have come from the same plant as the thin rods that made up the inner structure of the roof. I rested my fingertips on the wounded man's forehead. He was hot to the touch, feverish. He ought to be in a hospital.

The U.S. Army had a presence in Colombia, but it didn't include combat troops as far as I knew. Why would a wounded U.S. soldier be held prisoner by DAS?

The man groaned, and I almost followed suit, the ache in my shoulders adjusting to movement with sharper pain. Having my hands tied behind my back made me feel useless. I twisted them, but the rope held. I hadn't found anything sharp enough to use as a tool. I closed my eyes and considered the predicament. My arms are pretty long. I'm no gymnast, but volleyball keeps me supple. I moved from the stone-tiled section of the floor to the dirt-floored area, bent at the knee, and sat backward through the circle of my arms, jackknifing my body and squirming till my arms were in front of me, twisting the ropes. When I got my hands free, I decided, panting, I'd rub my shoulders for a week. For now, I massaged my ego with the small victory.

Then I spent some time playing with the ropes, trying to untie them with my teeth. The ropes won. Still, my hands were more useful in front of me than behind, and maybe the man in army fatigues would wake soon and help me out with his one good hand. I tried to nudge him into consciousness to no avail. With a leg in that condition, he wasn't going to be able to escape. I'd have to do it for him, file a report, a protest. Somewhere.

By now, my eyes had adjusted to the dim and shadowy light. My head pounded, my tongue tasted vile, and my mouth was dry as dust, but I seemed to have no other nasty side effects from whatever substance had been injected into my leg in the Jeep. The wounded man didn't stir, so I shifted my attention back to the hut. Was anyone else hidden in the gloomy interior?

Returning to the part of the hut I'd been exploring before I heard my fellow prisoner's telltale cough, I resumed the task. Everything seemed easier with my hands in front of me. I could reach down and touch the polished stones. I found what seemed to be an open hearth, an arrangement of stones against a lumpy wall blackened by carbon. I tried to heft one of the stones, but it was no use. Too heavy. Where were the fireplace tools, the tongs, the iron? For that matter, where were the bread and water, the Geneva conventions, the U.S. ambassador? U.S. citizens were being held against their will, fodder for a rabble-rousing article by Luisa Cabrera, if I ever got the hell out of here.

Something glinted between the stones. I got back on my knees and pried at it, a tiny ochre-colored stone inset in the mud between the flat polished stones of the hearth. Just as my fingers were about to give up, it popped loose, followed by another flatter stone, then another roundish one, all linked by thread. When I finished yanking, there were six smallish beads. A child's necklace? A bracelet of some sort? The stones were filthy, but I kept it in my hand, wishing it were a more useful article. A knife, for instance.

The door, when I finally found it, took a moment to register as a door because my imagination had painted a prison door, a cell door, barred and formidable. In fact, it was a disappointment, no more than a simple row of sticks lashed to a frame. As far as I could tell there was no lock at all. A bar of light showed at what would have been the jamb, if there had been a jamb.

I considered the prospect of the door, the likelihood of a guard, the possibility of undetected escape. My backpack was gone, my shoes as well. If I'd found anything useful as a weapon, I might have opted for feigning sleep till someone came, attacking them when they tried to rouse me. But the stones were too heavy, and I couldn't see depriving the wounded man of his splint, or lying in my hammock, ceramic chamber pot at the ready. The door was tempting; the edge of sunlight glittered like a diamond.

I hesitated before it, stock-still, listening. The strange and pitiful bird called again, and I wondered why it was complaining, free as it was, able to fly. I spent another two minutes in a futile attack on the rope that tied my hands, gave up, and hooked my fingers around the edge of the door. Slid it open an inch, two inches, pressed my right eye to the gap.

Green. Never had I seen such a profusion of greenery, such a variety of green, from lime yellow to deep blue-green, never, not on the first glowing day of short eastern seaboard spring, never, never in my life. I was gazing at a clearing, and past the clearing, at a forest of trees that looked as old as time, draped with moss and vines, a forest primeval, but not a northern forest, not a single evergreen. In between the close cathedral of trees, low lush bushes covered the ground. *Jungle,* I thought, coffee bushes, maybe coca. Light dappled the greenery, changing the palette of greens from one moment to the next: apple to malachite, jade to olive, emerald to the tenderest chartreuse. There was a wildness to the light, a strange clarity that made the calls of birds and animals seem suddenly louder. I caught a glimpse of a huge and gaudy bird, just a glimpse as it flashed from tree to tree.

I held the thread of the small stone bracelet between my thumb and index finger, twisted the beads over the first three fingers of my right hand, fashioning them into a poor imitation of brass knuckles. Then I used the fingers of my left hand to scrabble at the door, shoving till the gap widened. Five inches, eight inches, and then hope died.

CHAPTER 23

THE ARMED GUARDS wore the same military fatigues as my fellow prisoner. My first thought was that I'd fallen into some secret U.S. Army encampment, but on second thought—and closer inspection—I voted against it. These guys weren't U.S. Army. Dark-haired and deeply tanned, they were kids, most of them, skinny underfed kids in ragtag uniforms, laughing and holding semiautomatics like they'd been born with rifles in their hands. In the split second before one of them noticed the door move, they'd looked more like people playing at soldiers than soldiers.

I tried to swallow. Eight rifles pointed accusing barrels at my chest. My stone-beaded knuckles didn't seem like an adequate response.

One of the men barked an order, detached himself from the group, and hurried to the door, pushing it open the rest of the way, so we stood face to face. I thought he might shove me inside or hit me with the barrel of his gun. I had my mouth open, ready to demand the American ambassador, right here, right now.

"You wish to speak to El Martillo?" he said in Spanish.

I peered closely at his face. Wearing a gray suit, he'd been one of the "DAS" agents who'd kidnapped me. When he saw recognition dawn in my eyes, he broke into a tentative grin, then a wide smile.

"Water?" My request came out in a frog croak.

The water arrived in a pottery bowl shaped like a gourd, and tasted clean and cold as ice, the best water I'd ever tasted. When I'd drunk my fill, the phony DAS guard motioned to a second guard, and together, they led me past a stand of lush foliage into another clearing.

Invisible insects chirped and hummed. A musical ripple resolved into a rushing stream. A woman kneeling on the bank washed clothes the old-fashioned way, beating them resolutely against a rock. She glanced up with the blankest of expressions, as if a woman bound hand and foot and escorted by armed guards were something so ordinary as to be part of the landscape. I decided there wasn't much point in asking her for help. Instead, I asked the DAS guard whether the soldier in my tent had been examined by a doctor.

"You saw him?" His high-pitched voice grew tense. "You spoke with him?"

"He was asleep."

The man's alarm receded slightly. He shared a meaningful glance with the other guard, who shrugged, but said nothing. The DAS guard urged me along the bumpy path. After a minute or two, he dropped back and started telling his fellow guard a raunchy, meandering tale about a barroom drunk.

Not all the other people I saw toted rifles, but the majority did. As a former cop, I'm familiar with street weapons: Taurus handguns, Cobra pistols, your basic Saturday-night specials. I never served in the military, but an old sergeant pal of mine kept a personal museum of exotic arms discovered on Boston streets, so I knew I was looking at Russian AK-47s, Israeli Tavor 21s, and German-made Rugers. There were women other than the laundress, but they wore fatigues and carried rifles like the men. I saw no sign of children, no sign of Paolina, no sign of civilization, unless you consider advanced weaponry civilized. The rope that bound my legs was a waste of time, hampering my steps for nothing. Where would I run when I had no idea where I was? My bare feet stumbled over roots and stones.

Even if I'd had a cell phone in hand, I got the feeling I wasn't anyplace I could dial 911 to ask for help. The land sloped gently downhill, but above—well, above went on for miles, miles of greenery and craggy rock. I thought I caught a glimpse of a far-off snowcapped peak, insubstantial, shrouded in mist, like a vision in a dream.

We marched through variegated greenery over paths and terraces of stone to a sort of camp, a bivouac, maybe a way station to a larger village. Arching trees spread leafy protective branches overhead. I counted two rectangular structures with thatched roofs, surrounded by nine gumdrop-shaped huts. I sniffed the air for the scent of ether, or any of the other chemicals involved in processing coca leaves, got the tang of greenery, the smell of cooking, and the scent of humans who didn't wash often. I tried to gauge the number of inhabitants, but there was no way to estimate accurately.

Probably the same as the number of banana-clipped assault rifles. Each of my guards cradled one in his arms. I studied the man to my right. His uniform might be ragged, but he carried plenty of killing tools. In addition to the rifle, he had a holstered Beretta and a wicked-looking knife strapped to his leg. He wore the weapons casually, as though he'd stopped feeling their weight years ago.

My shoulders ached, but I squared them and marched on. The air felt good. I was alive. I'd set out to find Roldán, and here I was, being led to the very object of my desire. It might not be exactly how I'd imagined the moment of success, but I was, according to at least one armed man, on my way to see El Martillo. The sound of the stream receded as the path led further into the trees. We passed small areas that had been cleared and planted. Gardening and growing crops and selling coke, all in a day's work.

We hadn't walked far, uphill granted, steeply uphill, but I was practically winded, far wearier than I expected, overheated. I stay in shape. I don't work out at a gym, but I play volleyball and swim at the Y. I sucked in deep breaths and wondered what the altitude was, and how far we were planning to climb up the endless slope. The next clearing was barely visible through the trees when the DAS guard motioned me to halt.

"That man in the hut with you, he was hurt cutting down trees. The doctor will come soon. It doesn't concern you." His voice was far too casual.

I nodded.

"It would perhaps be better if you didn't mention him to El Martillo. He is a busy man, a great man. We don't want his mind troubled by this small matter."

Interesting, I thought. The guard was lying about the wounded man, but why? Did the boss not know about the captured American? The possibility seemed remote.

I was out of breath and thirsty again by the time we neared a large circular hut in the clearing. A bare-chested man wearing jeans tucked into combat boots and carrying the required rifle stood guard at the door. Faint music joined the bird calls and insect chatter. The bare-chested guard nodded curtly to my escorts, ducked his head into the low doorway, and in quick Spanish identified me simply as the prisoner.

"Let her come in."

Carlos Roldán Gonzales's voice had a touch of sandpaper gruffness. An attractive voice, it had made an impression the few times we'd spoken on the phone. Now the smooth baritone flowed on, asking the guard to bring some tea, please, and if there was some fruit juice, that would be excellent. Music played in the background, cheerful and upbeat, a Latin dance tune.

The bare-chested guard motioned me inside. I told him to untie me first; he seemed to find my request amusing. I had to duck my head to walk through the low door.

I'd expected military fatigues, the Che Guevara look, a couple of gold chains, whatever passed for macho chic in a guerrilla encampment, but the hut's sole occupant wore a tunic of pure white cloth and trousers of the same material, the legs rolled almost to the knee. He was barefoot. A single polished stone bead dangled from a cord around his neck. He sat on a folding chair at a desk made of wide planks placed across two packing crates. My approach was far from silent with the rope dragging between my legs, but he didn't look up, immersed in what seemed to be intense scrutiny of his fingertips. I studied his profile, a profile I'd never seen in newspaper or magazine photos. Paolina had his stubborn chin.

He was thinner than he'd been in the photos, older. A scar cut his face from the left corner of his mouth across the cheekbone to the corner of his eye. His eyes were Paolina's eyes, deeper and older, but the same shape and color. He turned to face me and a faint smile tilted his mouth.

Music swelled from a small cassette deck. He fiddled with the knob and lowered the volume. The hut was dim and slightly smoky, light filtering through the thatched roof and glowing from a small fire on a rock hearth. It was much like the hut in which I'd awoken, but better maintained, the stone floor neatly swept. One hammock was tucked away behind the rafters, another swung low, weighted with heavy books.

He said nothing.

I've used silence for my own ends. It's an old interrogation trick. Say nothing. Let the perp fill the silence because even lies tell you something. But this stillness was something else. I thought of a crafty reptile lying on a sunken log, waiting, waiting for his prey to emerge from the woods.

"Where is she?"

My question seemed to summon some genial being who lived far beneath the surface of the craggy face. Roldán shook himself as though waking.

"Welcome," he said, "welcome to the MM-19 Hilton! I hope you have had a comfortable stay. We have no mints on our pillows, it's true, but we have many other amenities." His eyes crinkled and his wide smile took ten years off his age. "We will drink together before we speak. I believe there is *lulo* juice."

"Where is she?" I repeated.

"The *lulo* is something like a pomegranate, but the juice is the nectar of the gods. With *lulo* juice and salsa music alone, one can always have a fiesta. You saw the mountain? The high peak is called Simon Bolivar, after the great liberator. It is 5,775 meters high."

"I don't care how high the mountain is," I said. "I don't plan to complain about being kidnapped or locked up or—"

"We have no locks here."

"Just guards with AK-47s?"

He shrugged. "The show of arms is regrettable. We are a farming community."

"Yeah. You beat your plowshares into assault rifles?"

"The guns are a recent acquisition."

I wished the guy with the juice would make it snappy. I tried to wet my lips. "Roldán, I don't want to discuss guns, either. I've come to take Paolina home."

"I have seen your photograph," he said, as though I hadn't mentioned Paolina's name, as though my words had no effect on him, as though I'd said nothing.

His utter unresponsiveness was starting to tick me off. I said, "I don't know why the hell you decided, after all these years, that you needed her. I don't know why a father with a daughter doing fine in the States would rather have her live on a hillside in a camp filled with armed goons."

"It did not truly catch your eyes, or the color of your hair," he said. "It did not tell me how you chose your words when you spoke."

If my arms had been free, I'd have grabbed him by the throat. "What the hell do you think you can offer her here? You'll never have a normal life. If the government catches you, they'll kill you. If a rival cartel catches you, they'll kill you. The paramilitaries, once they realize you're alive, will get in line, too."

The guard entered with a squat ceramic pitcher on a tray and two mugs. Roldán grunted and the man left it on the corner of a crate.

"I will pour," Roldán said, "since you are my guest."

Since I'm tied up. I thought about all the old tales in which once you accepted food in your captor's house you fell under a spell. Food, I could have refused, but water, juice, was another matter.

"You have found a trinket. May I see?"

Roldán took the string of beads from between my fingers.

Then he handed me the mug, and the *lulo* juice tasted so incredibly wonderful, piquant and slightly tart, that I couldn't imagine why the Colombians didn't export it and make more profit than they did on cocaine.

"Freshly made," Roldán said, as though he could read my mind, "it is what the gods drank on Olympus. Hours old, it is diminished. Day-old juice is not worth drinking."

He refilled my glass and waited while I gulped it down.

"Now," he said, "we will talk. First, thank you for the beads. Perhaps they will bring luck; I will return them to their rightful owners. Now, why do you ask about me in Bogotá? You bring me to the attention of those who should forget my name. And pardon me for going through your things, but how do you come to have this?" The little birdman appeared as though by sleight of hand. "Did the girl give it to you?"

There. At least he'd mentioned her. "No."

"You believe she's with me? Why would she come and leave this behind?"

"I found your gift in her locker. When your goons snatched her off the street, she didn't have a chance to come back for it."

His eyes searched mine. "You are right insofar as it was a gift."

"You told her to keep it a secret."

"Her mother would have sold it for what she could get."

"It's real, then? It's genuine?"

"It is what it is."

"You wrote her letters. You sent other gifts."

"A gift is not a summons."

"I picked up her trail in Miami. She flew to Bogotá. She traveled with a man and a woman. Your people."

"Not mine. If it is true, what you say, it is bad."

"Everything I've told you is true."

He lifted the birdman slowly in his right hand. The statuette's golden wings caught the light. "Then I cannot help you. She's been kidnapped, and she is without her guardian spirit. I cannot see her even in my dreams."

"*Secuestrada,*" the Spanish word for kidnapped, hung in the air like some foul-smelling bird of prey. It didn't matter that I'd been thinking "kidnapped" all along, because I'd assumed a different *kind* of kidnapping, *custodial* kidnapping; kidnapping by a parent. Kidnapped, yes, but stolen by someone who cared, who may have meant well, who was terribly misguided, but generally benevolent. "Custodial" modifies the harshness of kidnapping, gentles and tames it. "Kidnapped," by itself, alone, is a savage word, a brutal word.

The air left my lungs like helium from a punctured balloon. If there had been a nearby wall, I'd have leaned against it, a chair and I'd have sagged into its depths. There was nothing, so I held myself upright, and some part of me stayed rational because it asked a question. Not really a question, not the way it came out: a demand.

"You know who has her."

If he knew who had her, we could get her back. *He had to know.*

If he showed any concern for Paolina, it was only in his eyes. His face was calm as a mask and he was studying his hands again, his long elegant fingers. The golden birdman lay on his desk. "I receive many threats. Often they are nothing but smoke and mirrors. They are nothing but a pretense, a ruse to force action. If a jaguar is motionless in the bush, a gunshot might make him jump and betray his hiding place."

I barely heard him because I was still focused on that one word, *kidnapped.* Kidnappers aren't kidnappers for nothing. Kidnappers want something.

"They want to make you react, to stagger about in the bush. Then you become visible," Roldán said softly. "For years, I have been invisible."

"You've heard from them," I said.

"I didn't believe them."

"You're rich," I said. "You'll pay for her. You'll pay whatever they want." If my hands hadn't been bound they'd have been at his throat again. Those guards knew what they were doing, leaving me tied.

"I'm sorry," he began, "but I—"

"He won't pay," said a second voice. It was clear and level. And familiar.

CHAPTER 24

THE JOURNALIST FROM Bogotá, the small, slim woman with the caramel eyes, walked in the door, dressed so differently that, at first, it was only her voice I recognized. She wore combat fatigues and high polished boots. A sidearm was strapped to her military belt. Her hair, which had hung loose in her Bogotá office, was bound at the nape of her neck.

"I see you finally woke up," she said.

"I prefer the black Armani," I said. No wonder Luisa Cabrera got meaty quotes for her guerrilla stories, in-depth features, cooperative subjects.

"This is more comfortable," she said. "This is who I am."

I didn't really care who she was, so I turned back to Paolina's father and asked how much the kidnappers were demanding.

"He will not negotiate." Unbidden, the journalist turned off the low music, and poured herself some juice, commandeering Roldán's cup. She strolled around the hut like she owned it.

"You give the orders around here," I said. It wasn't a question, it was a way of telling her to shut up, to stop interfering. As far as I was concerned, this was a matter between Paolina's father and me. I'd have preferred to keep the decision entirely my own, but he had the money. The kidnappers wanted payment from him, not me.

"Luisa, untie her, please." If there was irritation in Roldán's eyes, it was mild.

"Why?" she demanded. "Why do you even speak to her?"

"Don't question me!" His soft voice stung like the lash of a whip. He didn't move, didn't take a step or raise a hand, but suddenly he seemed like a dangerous man.

For a brief moment, I thought she'd refuse. Then she knelt to untie my legs, and I considered bringing my bound hands high, smashing her on the back of the neck, making a grab for her pistol. I might get the drop on Roldán, but the risk of alarming the guard at the door was too great.

"Her hands, as well," Roldán prompted.

She used a six-inch hunting knife to slice the heavy rope, glaring as though she'd prefer to use it to cut my throat. In the room: Cabrera's knife and gun. Outside the room: an assault rifle. The most potent weapons Roldán seemed to carry were voice, charm, and charisma. I watched as he put them to work on the journalist.

"Luisa, I'm sorry to speak harshly to you, but I'm troubled." He closed his eyes and his hand reached for the stone around his neck. "You move a rock, a tree dies," he said. "You kill a bird, a snake lives. There are far-flung consequences and I cannot see the end from the beginning."

"You can tell me what the kidnappers want," I said impatiently.

He exhaled slowly, opened his eyes, and turned his spotlight gaze on me. "Miss Carlyle, my friend, Luisa, believes you are a grave danger to me."

"Oh?" Cabrera said with a short laugh. "So it's just my belief? You want her to talk to TV reporters and show your photo to the police? I tried to stall her till I could make contact in the regular way, but she moved too quickly."

"You hoped I'd get arrested at the museum," I said.

"It would have been convenient. No one would have believed anything an accused smuggler said. But it was only a possibility. What I hoped was you'd go there and stay put till I could send someone to follow you." She turned her attention to Roldán. "I had to get her out of Bogotá. The Zona Rosa was one thing; anyone might go there to ask about drugs. But she knew about Eighteen. Next, she'd have asked for you at Base Eighteen. Should I have waited for her to do that?"

Roldán rounded on me. "How do you know about this place?"

"I don't know about it. I found the number on a phone bill."

"Whose phone bill?"

"A man named Naylor. Look, I'm not here to harm anyone," I snapped. "I need to know who's got Paolina. If I don't know, I can't decide what to do next."

"The decision is not yours." Cabrera shot me a hard look.

"It's not yours, either."

Roldán held up his hands, palms outward. "Please," was all he said, but his glance silenced both of us. He turned to me and focused on my eyes as though there were no one else in the hut, no one else in the world. "I will tell you what I can. Five, no six days ago, a message came up the mountain by the usual route and made its way to me."

"May I see it?"

He reached into a bag lying by his side. The bag was made of cloth similar to his white shirt and trousers, but coarser and patterned, and filled with a quantity of small green leaves. A few scattered to the ground as he dug to the bottom and retrieved a folded slip of paper.

"I thought you destroyed it," Cabrera said.

The words were typed. "We have your daughter. We will deal for her. We will call. Three rings. Five o'clock." Each sentence was typed as a separate line. It made the note look strange and solemn, like poetry.

"What did they say when they called?" I asked. "What's the price?"

"He will not deal with them," the journalist said. "Tell her, Roldán. Nothing sways you, certainly not a child you don't even know. If you won't use this to make a difference in the history of your country, a difference you once fought for, a difference your friends died for—"

"Enough, Luisa."

"Wait a fucking minute," I said. "Are we talking about something other than Paolina here, something other than getting her back from whoever the hell took her?"

Cabrera ignored me. "El Martillo," she said, "it isn't too late. Together we can still make it happen. We need you to lead us; we need the magic of your touch. When the story of Colombia is written, yours will be one of the great names."

"I don't care about that," he said quietly.

"And I don't give a damn about it," I said. "Paolina's in danger for no other reason than that she's your daughter. You can save her, and that's the only thing that's important here."

"You have no idea what's important," Cabrera said.

Roldán said, "Luisa, you must cool your temper. She doesn't know what you know. And Luisa, you must not forget that you do not know what I know."

For a second or two, Cabrera looked like she wanted to use the knife on him, but she took a deep breath and gulped back any reproach.

"Perhaps," he said, "I must go to *them*. Perhaps it is time for their counsel."

"It's time to act," Cabrera said. "Make her tell what she knows. Make her—"

Roldán interrupted her. "There was something that arrived with the note," he said, fixing his eyes on mine.

I tried to swallow. I know what Colombian kidnappers send with notes. Sometimes a finger, sometimes an ear.

"No," he said, again reading my mind. "Nothing like that. They sent a Kyocera Iridium phone, a satellite phone. That evening, I heard from them, and they asked for something I could not possibly give them, something I have no right to give, in return for the safety of the girl."

"Your daughter."

"My daughter," he conceded. "I made a counterproposal, an offer I believed they would find acceptable, a fair trade. They asked for time to consider, and I granted it. I recharged the battery. We are not without resources here. I have kept the battery charged."

"Yes?"

"They have not called again. It has been three days, three nights. They haven't called. I fear for the girl." He met my eyes. "My daughter."

"But you know who has her," I said.

Cabrera made a noise in her throat. "Here, many victims have no idea who their captors are. It's not so simple here."

"Truly," Roldán said, "I did not know."

Did not. Past tense. He didn't know then, but *now* he knew.

"Something has happened?" Cabrera picked up on it, too.

Roldán stood motionless, with a thousand-yard stare on his face. I followed his unseeing gaze and wondered what he saw that I was missing.

"You went through my backpack," I said. "You saw the photos, the man and the woman with Paolina. You recognized them."

It took him some time to come back from wherever he'd been in his head. "I am not certain. Not at all certain. There is a familiarity, a similarity."

"It's a start," I said. "Does the sat phone work? Maybe it's broken. Maybe they'll still call. If not, we'll go with the photos. We'll go after them."

"He won't," Cabrera said sharply. "There are more important things for—"

"I think I must show her," he said to the journalist.

"Show me what?" I said.

He'd turned into a statue again. The more distant and still he became, the more it seemed to annoy the fiery Cabrera. There was some power struggle going on between them, and while I didn't relish getting caught in the middle, I thought I might be able to use it to my advantage.

"If you're planning to show me the American soldier you captured, I've already seen him," I said.

Roldán's eyes opened wider and I realized that he hardly ever blinked. It made his gaze both hypnotic and otherworldly. "That was very careless of my men," he said softly, staring intently at Cabrera.

"No," she said. "I told them to put the two together."

"That may not have been wise, Luisa."

"You'll have to kill her," she said. "You'll have to kill her now." There was the unmistakable ring of triumph in her voice.

CHAPTER 25

BACK IN THE prison hut, two feet from the guarded door, I sucked air greedily into my lungs. El Martillo had won the round. Cabrera's demand that I be marched into the jungle and shot by an impromptu firing squad had withered under his stern disapproval, but I was under no illusion that the sentence had been stayed indefinitely. Next time, the journalist might prevail.

I exhaled. Blood pulsed in my veins. I was alive and unbound, but my knees had abruptly turned to rubber, and I found myself huddled on the dirt floor. My head spun like some castoff satellite, rotating out of control, and the air seemed heavy and difficult to breathe. In bustling Cambridge, in urban Boston, in my chosen surroundings, I feel helpless so infrequently it took time to diagnose the condition.

It wasn't simply Cabrera's casual brutality or Roldán's lofty indifference. It was only partially the language. I could understand and speak, but it wasn't my tongue. It took effort, concentration; I had to be missing nuances. The surroundings threw me. I'm a city girl; the urban jungle is where I feel at home. This vast true jungle, the endless green, the heavy vines, disoriented me. Not a single tree was familiar. No oaks, no maples, no aspens or firs. Some of the jungle trees had roots so shallow they poked out of the earth like snakes. Even the ground tilted, and the alien smells keyed no memories.

Since the first moment I'd realized Paolina was gone, I'd

kept a tight rein on my imagination. *She's with her father,* I'd told myself. No matter why, the fact was *he wanted her.* He wouldn't harm her, not intentionally. Now, even when I shut my eyes, I saw her abandoned and alone, or worse, with men who'd harm her irreparably, who'd do brutal collateral damage, irrevocable damage.

I'd kept a tight rein on my emotions, too. Now a hammering pulse thudded in my ears. I could have wept. I could have gnashed my teeth, and rent my garments, but I knew it wouldn't help. All my tears and lamentations wouldn't buy Paolina a second's freedom, so I sucked in more air and straightened my spine and tried to recall every word that had passed between Cabrera and Roldán, each smoldering glance, each change of expression. They hadn't shot me. The decision had been postponed until Roldán could *show me something.* What?

Roldán had been furious that I'd been placed in the same hut as the wounded soldier, but now I'd been returned to the same damned hut. Why? I stood and walked to the center of the circular structure. The wounded man's hammock hung heavy with his weight. His chest rose and fell softly. They hadn't moved him; he hadn't died. He was deeply asleep, probably drugged. I paced quietly. *Why had I been brought back to this hut?*

Roldán's enemies had captured Paolina; they were holding her for some sort of ransom. *Not money.* If Roldán had anything, he had money. What had they demanded that he wouldn't give? And what business was it of Cabrera's? Slow, burning anger began to replace the helplessness and I welcomed it.

What was the relationship between the two of them? He was old enough to be her father, but that didn't rule out sexual attraction. There were undercurrents of strong emotion. She was an attractive woman and the charisma came off Roldán in waves. Was it the courtly manners or the thinly shielded brutality? The distant, penetrating gaze? I'd rarely met a man who seemed so completely alive in the present moment. When his eyes met mine, he *saw* me, not his preconception of me, not an American, not a red-haired woman. Me.

Why the hell had I been brought here to wait for Roldán, here of all places, here with the captured American? How much time did I have before Roldán decided to show me whatever it was I needed to see before I died?

I returned to the wounded man's hammock and listened to his ragged breathing. Asleep? Unconscious? Feigning unconsciousness? Aside from the rude splint on his leg and the spotless bandage on his arm, he didn't seem to have other serious wounds. There were abrasions on his arms and legs, as if he'd fallen into some kind of thornbush. No bullet wounds.

I patted his cheek. "Come on. Wake up."

He snorted, and half-opened his eyes, slate gray and wide, the pupils dilated.

"What's your name?"

No answer.

Rank? Serial number? What the hell else was I supposed to ask? When a teammate knocked herself out on the volleyball court, I knew enough to ask the big four: *What's your name, where are you, what were you doing, what time is it?* I ran through the litany, and got no response.

Were U.S. Army troops involved in spraying coca fields? Coca growth had increased in Colombia in recent years as U.S.-sponsored eradication efforts in Bolivia and Peru paid off. As fields disappeared in neighboring countries, enterprising Colombians, formerly middlemen and merchandisers, concentrated on cultivating their own cash crops.

Aside from Israel, no other country received more U.S. aid than Colombia. "Plan Colombia," developed by the Colombian government, was a multi-billion-dollar strategy to tame the guerrillas and combat the narcotics industry. The U.S. footed a large part of the bill, eager to pay because the policy was both anti-drug and anti-Communist. The U.S. military had sent "advisors." Was this man one of them?

I ran my hands over the soldier's chest and behind his neck, but someone had taken his dog tags. If I escaped, *when*

I escaped, I'd need to describe him accurately without the benefit of a name or serial number, so I studied him closely.

His protuberant eyes, when open, had been gray. Hard to get a height on a man lying down, but he was tall and well muscled. His hawk nose neatly bisected a narrow face. His lips were thick, sensuous; his ears, large with dangling lobes. If shown his photo in a six-pack, I'd be able to point him out. I caught the faint hint of a dark line that vanished into the bandage on his right forearm and shoved the cloth aside.

The line was part of a tattoo, a black arrow piercing a blue triangle. I don't count myself among the tattooed, but I have a window on the world: Roz, my assistant and tenant, is a designer and *afficionada* of tats. I didn't recognize this one, but it seemed more like a brand, an insignia, than a personal hearts-and-flowers, I-love-Mom, homegrown job. I committed the design to memory.

The wounded man's hand gripped my arm with surprising strength.

"Hey, Donna, honey, minute I thought I wasn't gonna see ya at all." His voice was gruff and low, his words slurred like a drunk's. He'd thought he was hallucinating the last time he saw me, now it seemed he'd scripted me into the hallucination.

As I opened my mouth to say, "I'm not Donna," the words died in my throat.

"Kids're okay, right?"

If I stayed Donna, stayed part of his waking dream, maybe he'd tell me something I could use.

"They're fine, honey," I said, matching my accent to his, keeping it to a whisper so the guards wouldn't hear. His voice was so soft I had to bend close to hear him.

"The bastards, man, took off and fucking left me. Shoot me with them poison arrows? Fucking bastards."

Poison arrows? His breathing got more regular, and for a moment, I thought I'd lost him to the world of sleep.

He snorted again. "Donna? Kids're good?"

"They're fine, honey."

"The choppers, they get out okay?"

I made a noncommittal, but encouraging sound.

"Middle of fuckin' nowhere . . . whassis name? Indiana Jones. What're they gonna do with it? Bury it in the fuckin' ground, Gee-mo says. That's what Gee-mo says, bury it. Nobody'll miss it."

"Miss what?" I breathed. *What or who was Gee-mo?*

"Wha' the fuck?"

"Bury what?" I said.

"Who're you?" His eyelids flickered. My stint as Donna appeared to be at an end.

"What's your name?" I said quickly. "Come on, we're in the same boat here. We need to help each other. How did you get here?"

I was listening closely, but only to the sounds that came from his lips, so I didn't hear the DAS guard approach till it was too late to pretend I hadn't been talking to the wounded man. This time he didn't seem to care.

"Come on," he said. "Move it. Time to go."

CHAPTER 26

THE LEAF-FILLED SACK hung by a strap from Roldán's right shoulder. His white trousers were rolled to his calves and his bare, brown feet marched steadily uphill. We'd been trekking for three hours, maybe more; I wasn't sure because I no longer had a watch. Birds chittered and sang overhead. Sunlight dappled the ground through the thick leafy canopy and sweat ran down my forehead.

My feet hurt, but damned if I was going to mention it. Roldán had returned the flat-heeled sandals I'd worn to the Zona Rosa—reasonable footware for city streets, hopeless for a steep climb—with grave courtesy. I was debating whether or not I'd do better barefoot when a thin black snake skittered across the path.

It was just the two of us, no guards, no followers. Roldán wielded a machete the size of a handsaw. The path was overgrown, and he slashed at the hanging vines like he'd been born with the blade in his hands. His body moved with the rhythm of the blade, making the task seem effortless.

Was this what Cabrera saw in him? Broad shoulders and quiet determination? A man who can tame his environment, be it changing the oil or slashing a path through the jungle, is, to many women, dead sexy. Add Roldán's gauntly handsome face and mysterious aloofness, and the age difference might melt away. I imagined Paolina's mother, Marta, fifteen years ago, before bitterness dulled her eyes and sharpened her tongue. I tried to picture Roldán as a well-dressed man about Bogotá.

Had she pursued him relentlessly, seeing the wealthy son of her employer as a perfect long-term meal ticket? Had he been the aggressor, raping a young girl in his family's care? I could easily imagine either scenario. Marta would have been beautful, innocent and ripe. And Roldán—well, Roldán, at that age, must have been a force to be reckoned with, a smoldering volcano.

I'd never met a man who projected such an aura of sincerity. If he'd sworn that tiny Marta had tossed him across a mattress and raped *him,* I'd have been tempted to believe it. That straightforward penetrating gaze, the inner stillness . . . He set off every warning bell in my body. Usually I trust myself; I'm good at telling truth from bullshit, but with Roldán, I couldn't read the signals. The alchemy of attraction was getting in my way. He could be telling the truth. He could be lying.

At the start of the trek, I'd talked nonstop, trying my best to paint Paolina's likeness, to make Roldán see his daughter as I did, value her as I did. I'd praised her volleyball skills, her musical talent. I'd attempted to flatter his vanity by describing how much she resembled him. I'd tried to engage him in more general conversation, thinking, like all captives, that once my captor knew me, he'd find it harder to kill me. He'd been unresponsive to every gambit, and the path had risen steeply through a cloud of mist, a challenging climb that silenced me. Now, the going was easier, but by no means effortless.

We topped a small peak. Below us, a mountain stream carved a deep ravine filled with golden flowers. Not Wordsworth's daffodils; those gentle words and flowers were alien to this savage landscape. The sun ignited the gold, and the stream sparkled so brightly I had to squint. Snowcapped peaks formed the backdrop for an image that beggared any picture postcard. I concentrated on putting one foot ahead of the other, and silence seemed to work where speech had failed.

"They say God made Colombia the most beautiful country on earth. Then, to make up for it, He gave us the cruelest, most violent people." His voice was full and strong, like he'd been lounging in an easy chair instead of climbing.

I nodded, too winded to agree or disagree.

"Centuries of bloodshed, from before the time of the *conquistadores*. Hundreds of thousands killed in *La Violencia*, *campesinos* forced to choose between Liberals and Conservatives, hunted by private armies, by guerrillas, by the regular army for making the wrong choice, whichever choice they made, driven from the countryside into the cities to live in shantytowns and starve."

"And drug dealers, too. Don't forget the *narcos*." A little needling might move him from the historical to the personal.

He sliced through a heavy root with a flick of his machete. "I suppose I was what you would call a 'drug dealer,' but only for a brief time." His scorn put quotation marks around the words.

Right, I thought. Bad press.

"I was a revolutionary, no? I had little love for my government, but I loved my country. I was born rich, to the upper class, but not with the kind of money that could change the way things are done here. Not enough to buy up land and redistribute it to those displaced by war. I couldn't build roads and dams in the countryside, or vaccinate against disease. Cocaine, for a little while, looked like a gift of God. The Arabs had oil. We had cocaine. You see?"

I shook my head. Oil and cocaine weren't the same in my book.

"It was romantic. It was fashionable. Everyone, the best people, used it. This was before crack, before *basuca,* you know, before kids started smoking the raw paste. We saw ourselves as heroes, selling drugs to foreigners who lived only for pleasure, for drinking and eating their lives away. We were transferring the wealth from the north to the south, back where it belonged, taking it from the nation that gave us United Fruit and giving it back to the *campesinos*."

"You stole from the rich and gave to the poor. You're Robin Hood and this is Sherwood Forest." My turn for sarcasm.

Unoffended, he held out his arms like a bishop blessing his flock at Sunday mass. "This is the Sierra Nevada de Santa Marta on the coast of the Caribbean Sea. This is the highest coastal range on the face of the earth."

The Caribbean coast was hundreds of miles from land-locked Bogotá. I visualized a map in my head, pictured the northern edge of Colombia, of the continent, near the Venezuelan border. No one would think to look for me here. Even if the hotel staff realized I was no longer occupying my room, even if they informed the embassy, who would dream I was here, climbing the highest coastal range on earth in flimsy sandals? No wonder I found it hard to breathe.

As much to keep from thinking about my predicament as anything else, I said, "Who knew you had a daughter in the States?"

Instead of answering, he asked a question of his own. "Those photographs, where did you get them?"

During a brief stretch when the incline was almost gentle, I explained about the airport surveillance shots, the stills printed from the video film, the proximity of the man and woman to Paolina in the security line. Then the path rose vertically between boulders. Roldán, barefoot, part mountain goat, never faltered. I avoided a sprained ankle by quick reflexes and sheer luck.

"And the phone number of Base Eighteen, where did you get that?" he asked.

"I told you. From Drew Naylor. What is Base Eighteen?"

"And how did you find this man, Naylor?"

"Through your lawyer, Thurman Vandenburg. In Miami."

"Ah." The machete whistled through the air to cut through low-hanging vines.

"You used him before, as a go-between, when you sent money."

"That was years ago." He used a vine to pull himself up a boulder, then offered the dangling end to me. "Now, there are rumors."

"What rumors?"

"We have ground to cover. Your feet—"

"Are fine," I snapped, unwilling to be grouped with idle foreigners, useless for anything but snorting coke. "What rumors?"

"Save your energy for the climb."

"Who is the American in the hut?"

"Save your breath."

"If you're no longer involved with drugs, why was Paolina kidnapped?"

"You think only drug dealers have enemies?" He indicated the scar on his face. It puckered the corner of his eye and sliced the meat of his cheek. "This is the most visible wound, but I came very close to death." His eyes drifted off into one of his thousand-yard stares, but his feet moved on relentlessly.

I grunted, hoping the noise would remind him to keep talking. The more he spoke, the more I learned. He climbed effortlessly. I sucked in thin air, gritted my teeth, and followed.

"I had already escaped death twice," he said, "but I was unsure who wanted me dead, or more precisely, who was footing the bill for my extinction. I decided to go into hiding. I flew at night, in a small aircraft, with a few trusted associates. Do you need a hand? The climb is steep here."

News flash. "No," I said. My left calf muscle quivered.

"I have little memory of the flight, even now. They say the mind often experiences a kind of amnesia when the body suffers such an assault. The plane crashed here in the mountains, but I survived."

My legs churned, left, right, left. I tried not to think about my blistered feet.

"The smallest thing can make a difference," he said. "The rescue of a butterfly on a mountaintop can save a great whale in the depths of the sea. You understand? They say I died many times. I was badly burned and both my arms were broken. I lay unconscious for nine days. Nine is a holy number for them. The priests, when they are trained, stay in the dark caves for nine long years. For nine months, I was blind.

Blindness is akin to holiness for them. They are— Ah, you grow impatient with my tale?"

They and *them.* Spoken with reverence, the way he'd used the same words in the hut with Cabrera. I think I will have to go to *them.* Perhaps it is time for *them.* The little toe on my left foot throbbed.

"I fell to earth on fire, and they cared for me, not because they knew who I was, not for any reward or favor, but because I was a human being. They treated me with the old medicines, and slowly my burns healed. My arms grew strong. I still have little sight in one eye."

I was mountain climbing with a half-blind man. As far as I could tell, an unarmed man, except for the formidable machete. Occasionally, his hand went to his woven bag, but the sack seemed to hold nothing but leaves.

"It's rare for them to care for a Younger Brother," he said. "Mama Parello told me they divined a purpose; they knew we shared a love for the land. They pitied my suffering and my loss. They made me strong again. They taught me, and now I am their caretaker, as they are the caretakers of us all."

After the sharp uphill climb, there was rock underfoot, cool breezes, light mist. The trees grew lower to the ground; the bushes, exposed to more sunlight, grew thicker.

What was that supposed to mean? I thought. *The caretakers of us all?*

"The Sierra Nevada de Santa Marta is home to the Kogi," he said. "Do you know of *them*?"

I only know Paolina is gone. The path was rock now, dark with slippery moss. The river—I thought it was the same one we'd been following for miles—burbled alongside, plunging headlong down the mountain until it disappeared in the mist.

"The Kogi are the unconquered," Roldán said.

Good for them, I thought.

"You need to rest," he said.

"No."

"Yes. Your feet bleed. Come; sit by the river, on the rocks. There's no shame in it. You climb well, *gringa*."

I made it to the rocks without limping. My legs trembled as I lowered myself to the ground. Roldán knelt by the stream, lowered his head, and drank noisily.

"Can you edge closer," he asked, "or shall I bring the stream to you?"

I crawled along the rock till I could reach the water and cup it in my hands. I clenched my teeth at the icy chill. It numbed my throat; it tasted like champagne.

The next thing I knew he was kneeling in front of me, carefully removing my sandals. "Lower your feet into the water," he said. "It will hurt for only a second; then it will help."

It felt like I'd plunged them into fire, then ice. A soothing numbness rose to my ankles.

"The bottom here is mud," he said. "Dig your feet into the mud."

I did as he said, feeling lightheaded and disoriented in the blazing sun.

"Your hair," he said, "is the color of the angels' hair in a church painting I remember from my childhood. It is a good memory, a gift that you give me."

The icy water was his gift to me.

"Wiggle your toes in the mud," he said. "Count to ten, lift them out, and we will see the damage."

I wanted to leave them there forever.

"Come," he said. "Lift them. They'll be better soon."

They emerged filthy and torn, bright red beneath the slimy mud.

"Lean back."

"I'm fine," I protested.

"Lean back on your elbows. I'll tell you a story, as though you were a child, and when I'm finished, you'll *see*."

See what? I wondered. The holy spirit? A miracle? Maybe all my blood would ooze out through my feet, turning the river red.

"Once," he said, and I was so tired, so tired that for a moment he might have been my father beginning an old tale, *once upon a time,* "there was a great civilization here. When Europeans lived in caves, long before the Spanish left their ports, the Tayrona people created here the Garden of Eden. They had fish and salt from the coast and crops from the lowlands. They had abundance and order. *They had gold.*"

The Tayrona were in the Gold Museum, people from an ancient time.

His voice was hypnotic, almost a chant. "Gold was valued here, *valued,* but not for what it could buy. It was holy gold, reflecting the glory of the sun. Shamans danced with the holy gold, and it was shaped into gifts for the Great Mother. Gold was the language she understood, because gold was her very bones."

I thought it might be my Spanish, and then I thought his words might be gibberish in any language, this talk about gold being the bones of the earth. His voice and the sunlight and the touch of his hands on my feet combined to make my eyelids so heavy I could hardly keep them open.

"They made the shape of the maize and they buried it for the god of the maize. They made a jaguar figure to speak to the god of the jaguar and they buried it in the good earth and the priests gave it food."

They buried it. His words echoed the words of the wounded American in the hut. *They would just bury it,* that's what he'd said.

"The Tayrona were wiped out by the *conquistadores,*" I said. "Exterminated." I'd read the text in the Gold Museum twice; Tayrona chieftains had been drawn and quartered, tied to horses and pulled apart.

"There are still Tayrona," Roldán said firmly. "They are Kogi. They have lost much knowledge, but they have kept the secrets of tree bark and plant pulp, things we don't know. They brought me back to life. They made me understand it was my fate to survive."

His words seemed to come from far away, shimmering in the distance, a mirage of sound.

"Who knows?" he said. "Perhaps that will be your fate as well. You must climb a little farther."

God, I didn't think I could move yet. I certainly didn't want to move, not with Roldán on a talking jag.

Quickly I said, "The others on your plane, did they survive?"

"No. I cut my ties with my old life. I work with the *campesinos* here, the peasant farmers, not the *colonos*, the ones who come to carve the land into plots and plant the wrong crops."

"You didn't cut all ties. Cabrera knew."

"For over a year, I was dead. Now, a small number know I'm alive. I have known Luisa's family, her father, her uncle, for years. She has a good heart, but she is impatient for change. She thinks she can mold me to her will, make me do her bidding. Still, she brings money from my bankers. That I must have, to protect the Kogi, because when this land dies we will all die. You understand? Every climate, every—what do you say?—ecosystem on earth is represented here. The coastal beaches, the jungle, the savanna, the *páramo*, the mountaintop. *The Kogi are the keepers of the heart of the world.*"

The heart of the world. I examined the craggy landscape, the piercing sky, the snowy peaks. This place might be the heart of the Kogi world. It might be the heart of Roldán's world, but it was trees and rocks and blistered feet to me.

Paolina was the heart of my world. My sister. A girl who pedaled down traffic-choked streets and chattered to friends on the phone, who couldn't decide which cologne to wear Saturday night. Tough and smart, with the resilience that comes from learning to cope in a broken home. Old beyond her years. I admired that; I regretted it. I couldn't imagine the course of my life without her.

"You must walk," Roldán said.

"Your daughter," I said. "She's the survivor."

He lifted his head and looked straight into my eyes. "You said she is musical, no?"

"A drummer. The best. You should hear her play."

"Drums are good," he said. "Drums are an old skill."

"You should meet her."

"It's too late."

"It doesn't have to be."

"She was a beautiful baby, so tiny, with eyes as bright as stars." His eyes gleamed and I thought, A trick of the mountain light; the sun so close.

"What happened? With you and Marta?"

"Marta, too, was beautiful. My father would have disinherited me if we'd wed, but I didn't care; I wanted nothing of his money then. I wanted only to go to the hills to join the revolution."

"And Marta didn't."

His eyes went cold. "There you have it. One wants something; the other doesn't. Each makes a choice. Each lives with that choice." As he spoke he wrapped my feet in leaves and carefully replaced my sandals.

"Come," he said. "Now you must truly climb."

CHAPTER 27

I WAS AFRAID my legs would buckle when I stood, but I steeled myself and they held. I concentrated on breathing, on filtering the cool mist through my nostrils. I couldn't seem to inhale enough of the thin air to expand my lungs.

"Here. These will help." I must have closed my eyes, because when I opened them, his brown hand was cupped near my face. It contained a quantity of leaves from the woven bag.

"What?"

"Coca leaves."

I shook my head. "I can make it."

He grunted, half amused, half exasperated. "It's an honor I do you, to offer you leaves, *gringa*. Here, they are only for men."

"No, thanks."

"Very well, then. Your feet will hurt less when you walk on sacred ground."

Sure.

"Come."

Not *my* sacred ground, I thought. I'm not a religious Jew, just half and half, uneducated in my mother's faith, but as we climbed, as we kept climbing, as the terrain grew wilder and rougher, I kept imagining Abraham and Isaac, walking up the mountain. Surely it couldn't have been this steep. Little Isaac would have died from the climb.

"You'll see," Roldán said. "You'll see what *they* have done."

This time his voice held no reverence for "they," only revulsion. Two different groups, I thought, a holy *they,* a profane *they.*

The rocks were craggy boulders now. Roldán had to show me where to place my hands and feet. He moved confidently, upright in places I had to crawl. It felt like I'd been climbing forever, like I'd be climbing forever. I made myself into a machine, right arm, left arm, right leg, left leg. I didn't look down. Roldán scanned the terrain with hooded eyes like an eagle watching for prey.

We came to the edge of a deep ravine. I closed my eyes and wondered whether this was it, whether *this was what they'd done,* whether this end-of-the-world cleft was what I'd crawled so far to admire. Retreat seemed the only option, but Roldán knelt at the side of the narrow path, his hands busy in the underbrush, tugging and shoving at a stand of seemingly rooted trees until they moved aside, all of a piece, as though they'd been mounted on a swing gate. Then we were on a primitive suspension bridge, a narrow span of knotted ropes over jagged rocks and empty air. A single length of rope served as a guardrail, and the structure shook with every step. It seemed impossible that it could handle my weight, let alone our combined weight, but Roldán showed no hesitation. I tried not to look down. I counted steps, ten, fifteen, twenty, thirty, and then we were on solid ground. He led me across a jagged ridge, past tangles of shrubbery, and the vista opened like a page in a storybook.

Las Ciudades de Piedra. The Cities of Stone. *Las Ciudades Perdidas.* The Lost Cities.

If the hut in which I'd woken was part of a village, this was its capital, a ceremonial city of stunning grandeur. No birds called out, no insects buzzed, sound itself seemed hushed by the majesty of the site. I understood why Roldán had used the word "sacred." There was nothing savage about the place, none of the aura of human sacrifice that permeates even photographs of ancient Aztec sites. The holy shrines of the Navajo are natural formations, mountain peaks and high mesas, but this was shaped by humans with care and love and artistry. It was a ruin, yes, a shadow of what it had once been. The vines had taken command, and the moss and the shrubs, but the structure remained, the architecture, the steps, the circles, the areas for crowds to congregate. There were retaining walls, to stop erosion. The circles of ground were covered with emerald moss as perfect as putting greens. The river split before diving into a series of swift waterfalls on either side of the stone steps. The towering mountain peak was iced with immaculate snow.

I turned to Roldán with questions on my lips. How did they do this, make this without machinery? The questions died. He was holding Paolina's gold birdman in both hands like an offering. His eyes were closed and he spoke in a language that was neither Spanish nor English. It wasn't the Latin I'd heard when my father dragged me to mass over my mother's protests, but it had the gravity of words spoken in church.

Behind him and to his right, *What the hell was that*? I closed my eyes and squeezed them shut, opened them again, thinking this must be what Roldán wants me to see, this is what he meant when he told me to "*see what they have done.*" Not a hundred yards away, a blackened hunk of twisted metal scarred the mountainside. It was more than an eyesore; it was a violation, an open wound.

I didn't feel my feet as I made my way toward the intrusive mound. At first it was simply metal, misplaced modern sculpture, but slowly, it took shape: the shattered cabin, the twisted rotor blades, the partially melted windscreen. At first I thought drug dealers, crashing in the fog, then I remembered the wounded man in the prison hut. I covered my nose and mouth with my hands, and hoped I wouldn't vomit on Roldán's holy soil. The closer I got, the worse it smelled, a mixture of gasoline and roasted meat and rotting flesh.

How long had it been here? Not a day, not a week. The underlying smell of putrefaction reminded me of corpses discovered in rented rooms by lax building managers, by neighbors returning after lengthy vacations.

A bird called, and I looked up.

Out of the corner of my eye, out of the mist, as though they had taken shape within the clouds, figures materialized, four or five indistinct shrouded shapes. I blinked, and then the shapes were moving steadily toward the wreckage, growing more distinct, larger, becoming figures of little men. Less than five feet tall, each wore a white tunic and long baggy pants. Like Roldán. Pointed white caps covered their heads, and woven sacks hung from their shoulders.

"You see?" Roldán's voice made me start like a deer. "You see. *They have come.*"

CHAPTER 28

FOUR OF THE tiny figures halted at a distance of thirty feet, then turned away and melted out of sight into the fog, their footsteps eerily silent on the rocky ground. One alone continued to approach, moving stiffly as a walking statue. In his right hand, he held a gourd-like object that he carried with the majesty of a scepter.

Roldán bowed and spoke to the little man, using the same tongue in which he'd addressed the gold statuette, musical and gruff at the same time. I couldn't decipher a single word. The language was like nothing I'd ever heard. It had strange clicking noises and odd gutturals. Since my ears were ineffective, I used my eyes.

The top of the little man's head reached no higher than my upper arm. Thick salt-and-pepper hair flowed from beneath his peaked hat to his shoulders. The backs of his hands were as wrinkled as tree bark, the skin on his face deeply lined mahogany, his feet bare. He could have been fifty or sixty, or twice that old. I'd never seen anyone like him. I couldn't help but stare.

Roldán turned to me and said, "You must understand this: They came for the gold." His voice seemed to resonate oddly, almost to echo. Maybe it was the effect of the altitude, some hollow by-product of the mist.

"Who came? Why? Who are you—"

"I will translate for you what Mama Parello wishes you to know."

The little man had a name. "Mama?" I repeated.

Roldán smiled. "It is a Kogi word, a Kogi concept. He is a priest, a shaman, a *mama* of the Kogi people."

"He lives here?" I motioned to encompass the stone city.

Roldán shook his head no.

"But you expected him to meet you here." With no clocks, no phones, the little men might have waited for hours, days, in this timeless place.

"Yes, because I spoke to him in the spirit, in *Aluna*. It doesn't matter that you don't understand, *gringa*. He is here; we are here. *You have seen, but now, you must understand.*"

"Understand what?"

"Why I cannot help my daughter."

Before I could protest, the small man held up his hands and spoke. The words sounded like birdsong as much as they sounded like speech.

Roldán smiled again. "He wishes to know if you are my woman."

"Tell him no."

The little man chirped and clacked, his lined face animated. Roldán answered in the strange clicking language, then translated the little man's response.

"Your reply makes him sad; he says I need a woman. He does not understand how a woman with red hair comes to walk the mountain, but he wishes you to know that this place, the heart of the world, is protected. He asks for your promise that you will never return."

"Consider it given."

"No," Roldán said. "Do not take this lightly. You must truly promise. If I am to tell you, if *we* are to tell you, we must have your word of honor that you will say nothing to endanger these people. If you cannot give your word, I must do what Luisa says I must do."

Kill me.

"If I can save Paolina without endangering these people, I will," I said.

Roldán spoke, perhaps translating what I'd said. Then he held up the stringed beads I'd found in the hut, and gave them to the little man, who beamed and nodded.

I will return them to their owners, Roldán had told me when he'd appropriated them. So the small men had once lived in the gumdrop huts.

Roldán said, "He does not understand the color of your hair, although it is not strange to him because he has seen it in the spirit world."

As he spoke, the little man dipped a stick into the gourd and sucked the end of it. The gourd looked like a relic from the Gold Museum, what was it called? A *poporo*. One of his cheeks was taut and rounded, as though it held a plug of chewing tobacco. The woven bag dangling at his side was stuffed with coca leaves, like Roldán's.

Spirit world, partially explained.

I said, "What happened here?"

"What do you see?"

"A helicopter crash. When did it happen?" I found his reticence infuriating. What did a crashed copter on a remote mountaintop have to do with Paolina's kidnapping?

"Weeks ago, I cannot give you a date. Time is not measured here the way it is measured in cities. Here we have planting and sowing—"

"Just tell me. What happened?"

"You know your country has a military presence here."

"They train Colombian soldiers to wipe out coca fields and arrest drug dealers. They've done it for years. Big deal."

"There are secret troops," he said, "U.S. Special Forces, stealing the last gold from the last tribe that protects the earth. Acting with the knowledge of my government."

"Is this Cabrera talking?" I bit my lip. The helicopter crash must be the journalist's big story, her history-making revelation.

"Your soldiers may say they come only to spray the coca bushes. Look around you. There are no fields of coca here."

The fuselage, burned as well as twisted, had once been

painted black. The cockpit was so badly damaged that most of the equipment had melted into a lumpy mass.

"Luisa wishes to document this travesty, to make a public outcry. She wants me to break my silence, to tell the people what my government, in connivance with yours, tried to do here."

Cabrera was right: The story was made for the news. Roldán, already a folk hero, returning from the dead to level charges against the government. A secret deal with the U.S. involving the theft of archaeological treasures. The heritage of a country betrayed. The U.S. caught doing what it used to do best, interfering in Latin America. If it was true, it was headline news. If it was true, it could topple the Colombian government.

I gazed at the wreckage. I thought the twin-rotor aircraft was a Chinook, a smaller version of the gunship the army was currently flying in the mountains of Afghanistan. I could see no insignia on the downed copter.

I said, "Why are you so sure your government is involved?"

"Do you understand anything of history? That this country is still a democracy is nothing less than a miracle. For fifty years, our candidates have been shot down like dogs, yet someone always rises to grab the standard and lead the charge. And now, betrayal again! There's nothing the government will not sell the *gringos,* our oil, our gold, our heritage."

"When did you learn about this?"

Roldán said, "Learn about it? *I saw it.* My people and I heard the helicopter. At first we thought it was hunting us, but then it disappeared behind the peak and reappeared too close to the ground. I thought the pilot was out of fuel and would crash. I took a party to search. It took us too long to get here."

Mama Parello bowed his head; it sounded like he was praying.

"By the time we arrived, they'd found the gold. They seemed to know exactly where to dig, as though they had a map."

"Is that out of the question?"

"Many of the *guaqueros,* the tomb robbers, have a spot

they research, but never dig. They call it their 'bank account.' But I know of no one who's come this far up the mountain."

"Go on."

"When we got here, the soldiers were loading bags into the copter. They gave us no time to ask questions. They began firing automatic weapons. We returned fire with the few rifles we had. They tried to lift off, but the downdrafts are tricky in these mountains. And gold is heavy."

I imagined the desperation of the hurried departure, the crash.

"Yes," Roldán said. "It went up, up, but only a few hundred meters. The front rotor hesitated, the chopper tilted. There was a moment when I thought they would simply land again, but they had no wish to continue the battle. They tried to rise. The copter crashed on its side. The fuel tank ruptured and ignited."

The *mama* spoke; his face solemn.

"They killed a *moro,*" Roldán translated. "He is irreplaceable."

"What's a *moro*?"

"When a Kogi child is born, the *mamas* come, and if the Great Mother tells them, they take that special child for the priesthood, to be a *mama* someday. These children, the *moros,* are the greatest treasure of the tribe. To make a *moro* is an incalculable cost. The family loses the child's labor forever. The *moro,* to be trained, lives in a cave for nine years without daylight. He must learn the secrets of *Aluna,* of the Great Mother, and for that he needs silence and introspection. He needs to learn to see beyond this world."

"How did the *moro* die?"

"Before the soldiers tried to take off, they shot him like a dog. The *mamas* say his death caused the crash."

I shook my head. What did people like the mahogany man know about the mechanics of helicopters?

Roldán said, "There is everything in *Aluna*. Before a thing can be, the Great Mother must think of it in *Aluna*. Everything is part of the Kogi World, even helicopters."

His way of answering my unspoken questions was getting on my nerves.

"With the death of the *moro,* we thought this terrible thing had come to an end." His eyes seemed to focus on something far beyond the misty mountain peak.

It hadn't come to an end. That's what he'd brought me here to understand: This terrible thing was linked to Paolina's kidnapping.

I said, "Let me get this straight. It was two or three weeks after the crash that the kidnappers got in touch?"

"Yes. Demanding the gold in exchange for my child. Gold they'd failed to steal here. Gold that is not mine to give."

"*But how did they know?* How did they know about Paolina? How did they know about you? Did Cabrera tell them?" The journalist might be trying to manipulate him, trying to grab a big story by the throat to make her name, nationally and internationally.

The Kogi spoke in his strange language.

"What did he say?" I demanded.

"There were two helicopters."

Two. "Then one got away."

"Yes, but that one did not carry gold."

"Someone on the second helicopter must have recognized you."

"Or they could have seen me on the film."

"Film?"

"Mama Parello says they used the 'black boxes' as they looted. I saw cameras pointing at us from the helicopter as it flew away."

"Who would recognize you, know you, wearing what you're wearing? Here in the mountains?"

"I cannot say."

"Can't say or won't say?"

"It makes no difference. The kidnappers have not called back."

"You offered them the wounded American."

"In exchange for the girl. It seemed reasonable, a life for a life."

"What will you do with him if they don't call? Kill him?"

"I pray that, in this life, I am done with killing."

He might be an outlaw, he might have been a drug dealer, but when he spoke about killing, I found myself believing him. Still, the wounded soldier might die in the hut, of infection or disease. The Kogi might have saved Roldán with the bark of trees, but the American could have undiagnosed internal injuries. My faith in ancient remedies was limited.

Thoughts of the wounded man made me remember. "Who is Gee-mo?" I said.

Mama Parello raised both arms, hands outspread. His words sounded like the chatter of birds, but I caught the repeated sound: Gee-mo.

"Where did you hear this name?" Roldán said.

"You stuck me back in the hut with the wounded soldier. You must have hoped I'd learn something."

"He mentioned Gee-mo?"

"Who is he?"

Roldán glanced at the wizened man for guidance. The *mama* slowly nodded his head, and Roldán said, "If his name passed the lips of the *gringo,* possibly a traitor."

"One of the *mamas?*"

"Not a priest, but a Kogi. A few have intermarried with people from the coast. It's difficult for the children. Usually they stay with the tribe, but some learn Spanish as well as the Kogi language, and they help the tribe by bartering with the outside world. Gee-mo is one of these half-and-half Kogi. He will be found and questioned."

"When? How?"

"I can tell you only what Mama Parello wishes you to know."

"Come on; he won't be able to tell one way or another."

Roldán shot me a glance. "He knows."

Whether he knew or not, the picture was starting to make sense, the fragments of the mosaic coming together. Gee-mo, the traitor, reveals the location of the gold. Two copters come for it. One crashes; one gets away. Someone recognizes Roldán, either in person or on film, and sees another way to get the gold. Paolina's kidnapping and the ransom demand follow: Paolina, in exchange for the holy gold.

I said, "Cabrera wants to make this front-page news. She wants governments to fall. What do you want?"

"For myself, nothing."

I stared into his eyes and waited. I thought: A woman could get lost in those eyes.

He said, "I wish only to make it as it was before this evil thing happened. The *mamas* are unsure whether the desecrated gold can be resanctified. The pots in which it was buried are broken, and they no longer know the words to bless the Mothers. They hope, by divination, to ask the Mother for guidance."

Divination. I stared at him blankly.

"The beads you recovered are divining beads. It is a good omen that you found them."

I'm no mystic. I'm a cop to my gut; I collect facts.

I said, "Did they bury the *moro*?"

"They took his body away."

"The others? The soldiers?"

"We covered them with rocks. The scavengers would have taken them if we hadn't."

"Let me look at them. Let me look at the helicopter."

"My men have been over the ground."

"Let me look."

Roldán's eyebrows arched. "You know about helicopters?"

"I know about crime scenes. I know how to search. Let me look."

CHAPTER 29

THE INITIAL SEARCH *team never finds everything.* It's one of Mooney's tenets. The initial searchers can get wrapped up in the crime. Cool heads are needed for a search.

What might I find? What was I looking for? Another of Mooney's rules: *Don't look for anything; look for everything.* If you search for the specific, you'll have eyes only for those car keys, that shell casing.

I blanked my mind while Roldán and Mama Parello discussed my request with clicks and gutturals and waving hands. When Roldán nodded permission, I scurried down the incline, scrabbling over rocks and boulders, grateful for work I knew how to do.

Divination, my ass.

I'd flown in helicopters during police exercises, gotten a quick lift in an FBI copter once, smaller than this one and in pristine condition. I tried to remember where things had been stored, where compartments had been located. Possibly there were places in the copter that hadn't been searched, papers that might tell me who *they* were.

The holy *they* were the Kogi. Who were the evil *they*?

Because of the angle of the crashed copter, I had to clamber onto the fuselage, clinging to a metal bar, to reach a sliding door that was immobilized in the open position. Dropping down into the cabin would have been no treat considering the condition of my feet, so I let my eyes do the initial walk-through. There were no bodies inside, but there were helmets and goggles, charred remnants of scarred machinery. I saw another light source, slid to the ground, and squirmed inside a more convenient opening, a narrow crack in the fuselage.

It was a Boeing craft, model CH-4, something, something. The panel had cracked on impact and the last two letters or numbers were illegible. I wondered whether the radio might be miraculously intact. It wasn't. There had once been labels on the helmets, but they were charred. Same with the goggles.

I squirmed back into daylight. Roldán and the priest sat cross-legged on the ground. The little man was holding Paolina's birdman up to catch the rays of the sun.

"How many men were there?" I yelled.

"Dead?" Roldán said. "Six."

"Dog tags?"

He shook his head no.

No dog tags on the injured American; no dog tags on the dead. Odd.

The signs of hastily abandoned digging were plain, shovels stuck in the earth, picks propped against skinny trees, shrubbery uprooted. A moonscape of holes pocked the earth. Half a huge pottery urn leaned against a rock. Bits of hard red clay littered the ground. Some holes were completely empty; some littered with shards indicating the breakage of an urn. There were bones scattered in the remnants of the urns, human bones, I thought, ancient bones. If I'd been an archaeologist, I'd have been fascinated, but I wasn't looking for bones, pots, or gold. I divided the area into a mental grid. In the first few minutes, I found a package of cigarettes and two partially smoked cigars. After ten minutes, a lump of chewing gum. I worked at a slow, deliberate pace, lulling the men into inattention. I noticed a khaki cap caught on a bush, but it bore no insignia. Why were there no dog tags? Roldán's eyes were glued to the priest; the shaman focused on the birdman.

The pistol was shoved into a mound of dirt, concealed under brush and leaves. If the sunlight hadn't caught the dull metal, I wouldn't have noticed it. I didn't react; I kept walking and stooping, pretending to examine a patch of discolored earth. I glanced downhill. The little man clicked and chattered.

If I grabbed the gun and threatened to shoot the old man called Mama Parello unless Roldán cooperated in getting Paolina back, where would I be? I had the feeling that the two men would simply tell me to do what I needed to do, that the *mama* would be pleased to join the spirit world sooner rather than later.

A Mac-10 might have been more persuasive, but a small pistol like this one could be concealed. It looked like a Beretta, a new one, a .38 with twelve rounds, and I didn't intend to leave the mountaintop without it. Roldán and the priest were peering at something in the Kogi's cupped palms, possibly the divination beads. Where were the others who'd melted into the mist? I did a quick scan of the area, waited till a bird called. Roldán and the little man looked up, and the gun nestled in the back of my waistband like an old friend.

Mooney was right, I thought. The initial searchers had missed a gun. If they'd missed a gun, they could have missed anything. I squeezed my eyes shut, then opened them wide, determined to overlook nothing even if it meant crawling over every inch of the mountain.

I worked for another fifteen minutes, another half hour, forty-five minutes. Roldán was right; time had no meaning in this place. When I saw the scorched leather folder, I almost walked right past it. Someone had trodden it into the earth. It looked like it belonged, like a line of rock under the soil. I sank to the ground and scrabbled at it with what was left of my fingernails. It had started out tan; it was brown now. It peeled away from the ground, slightly damp.

I pried it gently open, afraid I'd find the tattered remnants of a dollar bill, a worthless itemized receipt, other meaningless debris. Half of a photograph of a dark-haired child; that wasn't going to help. Two thin cards were stuck to one another. I tried to wedge my nails into the crack between them. There: The corner of one chipped off, but they separated into a Florida driver's license and a plasticized badge with a corporate logo. I studied the badge, shielding it from the fierce sun.

A black arrow pierced a blue triangle, the same design I'd last seen tattooed on the arm of the wounded American. The tiny photograph on the badge meant nothing to me, a man's face, nothing more, a name: Sean McIntryre. It was the corporate name that hit me like a sudden slap. BrackenCorp. My lips shaped the name. Drew Naylor rented his huge house from MB Realty Trust, a subsidiary of BrackenCorp. BrackenCorp, the big defense contractor.

BrackenCorp in Miami. BrackenCorp here on the mountain. Pieces of the mosaic shifted in my head.

"Roldán!" My voice carried in the clear thin air. I moved downhill as I spoke, rushing as though I'd never known a blister.

"What is it?"

"The lawyer, Vandenburg. Why didn't you send Paolina's gifts through Vandenburg this time? What were the rumors?"

"What troubles you so?"

"Tell me."

"Five years ago, Vandenburg was picked up by the DEA."

"And?"

"That's all. They let him go, but after that, others were detained. You know what I mean?"

He was telling me that Vandenburg was a DEA informant. But if the lawyer was linked to DEA . . .

The small Kogi priest lifted his arms and rattled off a barrage of incomprehensible sounds. I glanced at Roldán, waiting for translation.

"He says you've had a vision. What does it tell you?"

BrackenCorp in Miami, BrackenCorp on the mountaintop, BrackenCorp in the camp. The soldier in the hut had to be weaned off opiates and made to talk, made to talk *now*. I wasn't sure why, but my heart was pounding in my chest, and each beat was sending the same message: *Hurry.*

I said, "To get down the mountain, back to the camp. As quickly as possible."

CHAPTER 30

GOING DOWN WAS faster than going up, but not much. The stone steps were slippery with moss, and the sloping ground too steep for real speed. I tried to match pace with Roldán but whenever I started to establish a rhythm, the terrain would change, from savanna to woods to heavy jungle undergrowth. My feet felt flayed in spite of their leaf padding and I was afraid I'd twist an ankle, break it if I got unlucky.

I had the sequence of events in Colombia: the crash on the mountaintop, the long delay before the ransom demand. I considered the order of events in the States, starting with Paolina's disappearance.

I'd gone to Vandenburg, assuming he must be involved. Now it seemed possible he was involved not with Roldán, but with DEA. But he hadn't sent me to Group 26, the DEA branch in Miami; he'd reacted badly when I'd mentioned them. Instead he'd brought me to see Naylor. Naylor, who rented his huge house from BrackenCorp. Naylor, whose stolen phone bill yielded two Bogotá numbers, one for the Zona Rosa, a bar from which drugs were dealt, one for the mysterious Base Eighteen. A breeze stirred the foliage, a thin whistle of wind mixed with exotic bird calls and forest chatter.

"Roldán," I called. "Wait up!

"What is it?"

"Is Base Eighteen DAS?" Maybe Base Eighteen was the Colombian version of Group 26, the anti-drug force.

"It's a division of the regular army, one that is known to cooperate with the private armies, the *autodefensas,* the right-wing paramilitaries. It has a bad reputation. People who are questioned there do not return. Luisa was right about that: I wouldn't want *Dieciocho* to know I'm still alive."

"Are they involved with drugs?"

"With protecting drug runners, yes. That is the rumor. Luisa would know more."

"She told me she knew nothing."

"You're a stranger. She is cautious. With every right to be cautious. Her father investigated Base Eighteen."

Sweat ran down my back as the air grew warmer. *Her dead father.*

We were maybe three-quarters of the way back when the helicopter buzzed. A flyby, I told myself, an unrelated weather flight, a medical evacuation. Still, I started moving more quickly than the terrain warranted.

"The helicopter, you thought it would come?" Roldán's tone was accusatory.

I shook my head no.

Roldán frowned. "You believe there is urgency? You feel it?"

"I found an ID badge by the dig site. From an outfit called BrackenCorp."

"So?"

"The same name came up in Florida, when I was trying to get a line on you. It connects to the soldier in the hut." I gasped out the words, one by one, as we scurried down the path.

His left hand closed on my shoulder. "Here. You must take this. Chew it. It will make the pain less, the going easier." A ball of leaves from his woven bag nestled in his right palm.

"No."

"Take it or I'll leave you to follow at your own speed." He offered the wad of leaves again. "It will not make you crazy. It will not addict you. It's not refined. It is what the Kogi have used forever, to ease hunger, exhaustion, and pain. Keep it in your cheek. Add a little of the lime. It may make your mouth numb, but that will pass."

If he abandoned me, my chances of finding the encampment were remote. If I didn't find the encampment, I'd never question the soldier, never find Paolina. I took the ball of leaves and stuck it in the left side of my mouth, between cheek and gum.

"Now take my hand," he said.

It was a matter of stones across a brook. If I hadn't been exhausted and in pain, I could have managed them easily. His hand was brown and wiry, and I released it the moment I had solid ground beneath my feet, dropped it like it was too hot to touch. Mooney's right about another thing: I'm attracted to outlaws—good-looking, wolf-grinned outlaws—and this was not just an outlaw, but Paolina's father.

The drug was starting to have an effect. I felt calmer, more aware, and my feet no longer troubled me with each step. It was easier to keep my balance. Roldán seemed to be going more slowly, but I knew he wasn't. The change was in me. I was moving more surely, more quickly.

"Tell me of your vision," Roldán said.

"It was not a *vision*."

"Then why do you feel such urgency? Helicopters have tried to find us before. The canopy of the jungle protects us. We make no fires; we show no signs."

"After you offered the American in exchange for Paolina, the kidnappers didn't call back. Why?"

He shrugged and kept moving. "At first, I thought because the girl was no longer alive. Therefore they could not bargain."

I swallowed. The leaves tasted odd, not bitter, not sweet. "I don't believe it."

"Nor do I. Not any longer. She's frightened, but alive. Mama Parello has seen her in the dream world."

What a goddamn comfort, I thought. A gnome in a pointed hat has seen her in the dream world.

Roldán said, "If you are worried they might attack to retrieve the wounded American, that is why my people go armed. That is why we moved from one small village to another."

I was worried. I said, "Do you hear the copter now?"

"Perhaps they have given up."

"No," I said.

"Why do you say this?"

"Because I don't believe in Luisa's theory. I don't believe this is a conspiracy of governments. I don't know about your government, but mine doesn't steal Indian artifacts."

"You saw what you saw."

"The American in the hut doesn't wear dog tags. The men you buried under the rocks had no dog tags. The helicopter had no insignia. What if this is a private thing, a private raid? For the gold."

"The helicopter is part of the coca eradication plan. That's government."

"I went to the lawyer, Vandenburg. Vandenburg took me to a man named Naylor. After that I always felt followed, shadowed, by a car, by a presence." The blue Saturn, the man on the plane.

"No one could have followed you here," he said.

"There are other ways to track a person."

"There's a famous story here," he said, "of Tranquilandia."

I shook my head; I didn't know it.

"When Colombian government troops discovered the first huge coca processing plant, at Tranquilandia in the southern jungle, it was because the DEA fixed a live transmitter on a barrel of ether."

A transmitter. The sort of thing that would have been detected during an airport screening . . . if I'd gone through security.

"My God, who searched my backpack?" I told Roldán about the airport. The woman who'd unpacked and scanned my backpack could have hidden a transmitter. I'd been marched through the airport, bypassing security.

"Only the government could do that," he said.

Not everyone who works for the government works only for the government, I thought.

"My men would have found it," Roldán said.

Right. The same team that had left the Beretta on the mountaintop.

I increased my pace and Roldán did too. The path kept crossing the river. More stones, mossy this time. I didn't need Roldán's hand, but his grip was comforting.

He said, "When you spoke to Vandenburg, did he mention a man named Navas?"

My feet felt like they were floating inches off the path. I was no longer tired. I could walk like this forever.

"Did he mention Navas? Or the Angel?"

I shook my head. Angel Navas was Roldán's former partner, jailed for life, dead in prison.

"Naylor," Roldán said. "What does he look like?"

I described him, reclining on the chaise in the golden room. Roldán shook his head at the vagueness of my description. "What is the color of his eyes?"

"His hat shaded them, but they were pale. The hair I could see was medium brown. He was heavyset, kind of pudgy. A narrow face, though." The weight gain could have been recent, I thought.

"Did he walk with a limp?"

"He didn't walk at all, but there was a walking stick, a cane, in the room. Does he seem familiar? Do you know him? He lives in a house owned by BrackenCorp."

"What is this BrackenCorp?" Roldán asked.

"A defense contractor."

I no longer concentrated on finding a footfall; my feet seemed to take care of themselves, leaving my mind to speculate. Were the people at the airport DEA? Was the U.S. government using me to find Roldán? It didn't make sense. DEA might bend the rules, but they didn't kidnap children. DEA had no interest in pre-Columbian gold.

Fifteen minutes later, the helicopter buzz sounded again. I couldn't tell if it was the same copter or a second one. It was louder and closer, but the canopy of trees enveloped us. I couldn't see anything above the interlocking branches except a scrap of blue sky. I knew I was walking fast, but it seemed that I was barely moving. I was hurrying, racing, but I had all the time in the world.

Roldán said, "If it's not the government, if it's a private

company, they would not wish their activities to be made public. They should have made the deal. Paolina for the wounded man."

"Yes."

"But they did not."

"Maybe the phone is broken." The ground moved beneath my feet; I didn't feel it.

"The helicopters don't fly here," he said. "No, they're closing in on the camp, triangulating the signal. There must be a transmitter."

He redoubled his pace. We followed a different, steeper course than the one we'd ascended, tracing the path of a plunging stream. It took all my balance, fine-tuned by the coca leaves, to keep from toppling into the rapids. The stream disappeared to the right and soon the trail was nothing but a thin line of footprints through the jungle with an occasional stone for a guidepost.

"I can't wait for you," Roldán said after fifteen minutes at a furious pace. "And I can't give you my gun. If you meet fighters, hide, and later, someone will come for you."

Yeah. Right. Friend or foe? Where the hell did he carry a gun?

"Can you throw a knife?" Maybe he saw the question in my eyes.

"It's better than nothing."

"If I had another weapon, I would give it to you."

I believed him. But I didn't tell him I had a gun.

"Roldán, if you get killed, Paolina will—"

"I'll do my best not to get killed. If it is my day to die, then I will die."

He forged ahead, disappearing into a thicket of high bushes. I tried to keep up with him. I tried, but he faded into the trackless jungle. For a little while I could hear his footsteps. Then nothing.

CHAPTER 31

MY LEGS FELT like overcooked spaghetti. My feet told me to sit, to lie down in the lush greenery and sleep, but coca leaves and adrenaline pumped through my veins, and I moved more quickly than I believed possible, stumbling over roots, slipping on mossy outcroppings, falling over stones.

If it is my day to die, then I will die.

What a useful sentiment. What goddamn wonderful heroics. What a totally useless, stupid thing to say. What machismo, what arrogance. No wonder the man reminded me of Sam Gianelli. Go ahead, I thought angrily. Charge in solo, against all odds. Get yourself killed, dammit. Heroism is easy. What's *goddamn hard* is survival, figuring out how to survive, how to take care of the children so they don't wind up in an orphanage after the disaster. Death is quick and final. Survival is long and hard.

Anger drove me downhill. If Roldán died, filled with his mysterious silences, carrying the answers to my unanswered questions to the grave, how would I find my little girl? Where the hell would I look?

Roldán, as he disappeared, had veered slightly to the left. I glanced at the sun overhead, calibrating the direction the man had taken. I kept to the left, chose the route that led most steeply downhill. Vines grabbed at my face and shoulders. Branches seemed to glower overhead. Roots tripped me. It felt like I was caught in someone else's nightmare.

I only realized I'd been hearing the steady noise of the chopper's motor when it abruptly ceased. The next sound I heard over my own ragged breathing was unmistakable: bursts of automatic gunfire.

"No," I said out loud. *No*.

I drove my legs like pistons into the ground, consumed by the need to catch Roldán and hold him back. If he got there before me, he'd be killed. If he got killed, I'd be lost, with no bargaining chips, in a hostile country.

There was no trail. The scenery closed in. I tried to get a wider glance at the landscape and almost fell over the edge of a ravine. I caught myself on a tree limb, balancing precariously, hanging from a vine and cursing. The gunfire grew louder, sporadic bursts. A loud, high noise, a scream, not a siren.

BrackenCorp. BrackenCorp. What else did I know about BrackenCorp? Where else had I heard the name?

I shoved Roldán's knife into my belt, grabbed the automatic from my waistband. I crashed through bushes, not trying to follow any path, traveling toward the sound. Yelling joined the bullet hail. There was more screaming, more bullets, more yelling, a high-pitched noise I thought might be a woman wailing. The Beretta felt like a toy gun in my hand.

I didn't want to die in this place. The thought surprised me even as I had it; I've always been indifferent to the idea of death. Once I was dead, I'd figured, I wouldn't care how it happened, so I was surprised at my reluctance to die surrounded by strange sights and smells. I didn't want to die in a foreign land where I didn't know the names of the trees.

The firing hit a crescendo; it seemed that I had to be about to burst onto the battlefield, if I wasn't on it already. Suddenly, with a whoosh, a helicopter took to the air not a football field away, and I flung myself flat on the ground.

Dammit, I thought, where was an Uzi, an AK-47, something more suitable than this puny Beretta? To waltz into the clearing the helicopter had just left armed with nothing but the small Beretta and a lousy knife was suicide. But if anything happened to Roldán . . .

Silence. It took a while to realize there was simply silence. It was disorienting, the silence. A void instead of a quiet. The birds had stopped singing; the insects ceased chattering. I lay on my stomach in the tall grass. There was no noise at all.

I lifted my head, got to my knees. Abruptly, I recognized the terrain. There was the stream where the woman had washed her clothes. There was the rock she'd beaten them on. The rock was stained red. I crawled toward it, my eyes scanning the area for movement. There were lifeless bodies on the ground. One of the circular huts blazed, its roof on fire. I knelt, then stood frozen, the Beretta useless in my hand. I walked to a body, noted automatically that it was not an enemy soldier, but one of the guards who'd brought me to Roldán's hut.

I bent and snatched the rifle from his motionless hands. I stuck the small Beretta back in my waistband. AK-47, I thought. Cartridge clip. Bolt. Breech. My fingers found the pistol grip, the trigger.

Had they taken Roldán away in the helicopter? Had they killed him? Where was everyone? Some of the *campesinos* surely must have run into the jungle when the helicopter came. Someone must be alive. Bodies littered the ground, lifeless as rag dolls, uniforms bleeding into the earth. The woman who'd been beating clothing against the rock was half-submerged in the stream, her head bloodied, motionless. Insects hummed inside my brain; I wondered whether the chopper was returning.

No. I yanked myself out of the nightmare, counted the visible corpses. Most wore some version of camouflage gear. I wondered how they could tell each other apart, the attackers and the attacked.

I thought they were all dead. Nothing moved, nothing.

I saw him as I came out onto what must have been the town green, the center, the meeting place. Chickens pecked at the ground, unmoved by the disaster.

Roldán. Roldán alive. He was bending over a body, and by the sweep of dark hair I knew it was Luisa Cabrera, and by the loose-limbed wrongness of her posture, I knew she was dead. He knelt; he seemed to be keening, swaying. His lips moved. He stroked her hair. Almost, it looked as if they were dancing.

Behind him, movement. A corpse moved; a man in a grayish uniform stood, wavered, and straightened his arms, taking aim at Roldán's unprotected back.

I didn't think. I fitted the rifle to my shoulder faster than thought, and pulled the trigger. The recoil almost drove me to the ground.

The man went down. Roldán spun toward me, lifting his own weapon.

I think I screamed, but I may have been screaming from the minute the soldier stood and took aim.

Roldán must have recognized me; he didn't shoot.

CHAPTER 32

WHEN I WAS a cop we held emergency drills, playing out the aftermath of explosions, civil riots, chemical spills, and nuclear attacks. The exercises were meant to be taken seriously, but a mutilated "corpse" would occasionally giggle or sneeze; the practice sessions took no emotional toll. I've been among the first at gang shootings, fires, and fatal car crashes. Horrible as they were, they were always, to some extent, routine, because I was there in my capacity as a sworn officer. I had a job to do, a scene to secure, witnesses to locate or interview.

The guerrilla camp in the aftermath of the chopper attack was an uncensored TV-news image of lopsided battle. It was worse than a train wreck. Roldán and I made the rounds together, counting the dead, closing their eyes. I stopped counting at seventeen. *Why at seventeen?* I remember wondering, but I don't know why. It was as though some part of me shut down after that, decided that the disaster could not be quantified or understood. Other than Cabrera and the guards, I recognized no one. Roldán knew them all; he seemed to age before my eyes. His shoulders slumped. His eyes darkened.

We did what we could for the wounded with emergency medical supplies buried under the corner of one of the huts. Roldán, a competent and merciful medic, used drugs from the supply chest as long as they held out. Then he rolled balls of coca leaves between his fingers and dispensed them to sufferers. Several times he shut his eyes and stayed motionless, his lips moving in prayer.

"This one will need to go to the *mamas*," he murmured as if talking to himself.

The wounded American was gone, hammock and all, the heavy ropes that had supported his weight sliced cleanly, every trace of his existence obliterated. We found my backpack behind another hut, the lining slashed, and I assumed they'd retrieved their homing device.

Every time I glimpsed a female body, I was afraid it was Paolina's. There was no reason for my fear, but I'd passed beyond reason. Any cruelty seemed to be possible in this country; I was walking through a killing field.

Stragglers returned from the jungle, twenty of them, thirty; I didn't realize how many until I noticed that the fires were dying. A bucket brigade had formed, a raggedy line starting at the river where the dead woman had washed her clothes this morning. This morning, I decided, had been a month ago, a year ago. Someone handed me a sloshing bucket and I passed it robotically on, wondering how I'd gotten into the bucket brigade line in the first place. Grab and pass, grab and pass. There was comfort in the rhythm for a while.

When the fires were out, the debris steaming, I glanced around for Roldán. He'd been beside me, but I wasn't sure if it had been minutes ago or hours ago. I spat the soggy ball of leaves onto the ground, and asked the man beside me where El Martillo had gone. I rubbed my palms where the heavy buckets had chafed, but the incipient calluses didn't matter any more than the pain in my feet did. The man pointed. Roldán was fifty yards away, at the center of a circle of gesticulating men. I joined the group, listening for some sort of explanation, as if there could have been any reasonable justification for the things I'd seen.

More would have gone into hiding, a man insisted, but Luisa Cabrera said the invaders had come to negotiate. The chopper was landing, she'd told them. If they'd come to kill, they'd have done it from the air. Troops ran from the chopper, shooting; they wasted no effort in speech. If the invaders had fired before landing, more would have run, more would have believed the man who was now talking, the man Roldán called Flaco.

I slipped between two older men, shoved closer to Roldán. He noticed me and made room.

"Luisa still believed in words," he said. "Even after what they did to her father."

"They came for the American," I said. That much made sense: The American was living proof of foreign involvement.

Flaco had dark skin and braided hair, a scratched and bloody arm. He glared at me before continuing, then glanced at Roldán, as though inquiring whether he could speak freely in my presence. Roldán nodded.

"They took the American, yes," he said, "but they wanted the gold, and they wanted you." His nod indicated El Martillo. "I heard them yelling at Luisa. She said you'd gone away, that she didn't know where you'd gone. They demanded the gold. She said it wasn't here."

"Did they mention the girl?" I asked. "Was there a girl on the chopper?"

"No."

Cabrera was dead, and the chopper that had zoomed into the sky was a twin of the one downed high on the mountain. I wondered whether they'd bomb the remains of the copter on the mountain into smithereens, how far they'd go to wipe out evidence of their incursion, how far they'd go to reclaim the gold. I noticed I was thinking of the enemy as *they*. I felt like I was turning into some conspiracy freak describing the New World Order, black helicopters and all.

"What language did they speak?" I said. "Were they Colombians or *gringos*?"

Flaco shrugged.

"Are any attackers here? Any of the dead?"

He nodded curtly and pointed to a body clad in fatigues newer than those worn by Roldán's men.

"He's a child." I kneeled at the side of the corpse.

"The boy is all of seventeen," Flaco said earnestly. "If he'd lived to be thirty he'd have thought himself an old man."

The dead boy wore a religious medallion on a chain, a knife strapped to his thigh. He'd caught seven or eight bullets; his torso was riddled with wounds, the back of his shirt all-over blood.

"What are you doing?" Roldán, at my side, spoke softly.

I was digging inside the boy's pants pockets. "Who is he?" I said. *"Who are they?"*

He had money in his pocket. Pesos, but also U.S. quarters, dimes, and pennies. One dollar and fifty-seven cents. Flaco and Roldán scrutinized the uniform, the medallion, and the knife before pronouncing him a *para,* a member of the *Autodefensas Unidas de Colombia,* the AUC.

"They call themselves anti-Communist. They work for the army, for rich landowners, drug dealers, for whoever pays them," Flaco said.

They worked with an American who carried ID from an outfit named BrackenCorp. They crashed the copter on the mountain. They snatched the man in the hut.

Flaco said, "There's another one, here."

He, too, was a young Colombian *para*. It made sense; they wouldn't want to risk American dead. For this raid, they'd risked only Colombians. I bit my lip and paced, recalling the man in the hut, his long hair, his beard, his tattoo.

"Roldán," I said, "the helicopter on the mountaintop, you said it was part of a defoliation flight. Don't they use crop-spraying planes?"

"The U.S. defoliation flights use planes, but they're often escorted by helicopters, especially in the south, because guerrilla groups have attacked the planes."

I said, "I don't think this involves the regular army."

"Special Forces, then."

I shook my head. Even Special Forces wore dog tags; the American military is particular about identifying their dead. Then there was the tattoo, the black arrow piercing the blue triangle, the same design I'd seen on the mountaintop, the corporate logo on the BrackenCorp ID. And I knew what I'd read in the news: The U.S. Army had gotten lean and mean. Troops were tied down in Afghanistan, in Iraq, recruitment was down.

Corporate names were coming to the fore, supplying so-called "logistical support": Halliburton and KBR, Blackwater, independent contractors who worked for the pared-down army, corporate giants with rules all their own. *Possibly with agendas of their own.*

"BrackenCorp," I said. "Roldán, that's our lead. If we find BrackenCorp, we can find Paolina."

"There's no guarantee she's alive."

"Your man on the mountaintop saw her in the dream world."

"You're grabbing at straws."

They were all I had left.

I said, "The Kogi on the mountaintop, they saved your life. So you owed them, right? You became the caretaker?"

He shut his eyes.

"I saved your life, too, Roldán."

His face looked gray and his hair wild. I wondered what he was seeing on the backs of his eyelids. The bodies of the dead? Mama Parello framed against the snowcapped peak? Luisa Cabrera? I imagined her photograph in the showcase of dead journalists. Maybe they'd place it next to the one of her father.

"What do you want from me?" He sounded as exhausted as I felt.

"Find them. Find her. Give me a chance to get her back."

"How?"

"Question Gee-mo. Help me trace BrackenCorp."

"We would need many things. Telephones. Access."

"You had the personnel to bring me here, the contacts. You can bring me somewhere else."

"They may have already killed her."

"They may not." There seemed to be no reason in this country, nothing but death and dying. "Will they come back?" I asked.

"Not today. The light is dying."

I was surprised to find that he was right. The endless day had faded abruptly. More stragglers came in, men and women, some weeping and lamenting, more with faces fixed as stone. They got on with the task of helping the wounded and burying the dead. I wondered about the stone-faced ones, wondered who they were to take this so calmly, with so little outward show of emotion. I decided they were people who'd done this before, witnessed destruction, buried their families, and kept on going.

I kept going, too, trying to convince Roldán that Paolina was still alive, trying to convince myself of the same thing.

I hadn't quite succeeded when Flaco came running, yelling at Roldán to hurry. The satellite phone had rung in the big hut. Flaco had answered; he thought it might be important. Come; there was a girl on the line claiming to be El Martillo's daughter.

Roldán grabbed my hand and squeezed it as we ran. "If they demand the gold—it's not mine. I can't give it to them."

"You can lie," I said quickly. "Tell them anything. Arrange to meet them, to hand it over. *Lie.*"

PAOLINA

SHE OPENED HER eyes and discovered she was blind. A scream built at the back of her throat and her lips parted to shriek her terror. *Don't scream,* a voice shouted silently in her head; *don't scream until you know who might hear.* The blackness was a deep muddy hole, a starless void, endless, relentless nothing. Let me be blindfolded, she prayed, but she knew there was no blindfold. There was no obstruction, no feel of cloth or tape. Her eyes were wide and staring, but she could not see. Panic caught at her chest and she thought, I can't breathe either. There's no air here.

Where was here?

Where was she?

She was lying on her back, mostly on her back, her legs, bent at the knee, twisted uncomfortably to one side, her ankles tied. She tried to quell the rising panic, jerked to lift her right arm, but it was bound to her left, fastened at the wrist. *Captive.* Captive again.

A kaleidoscope of fragmented scenes skittered through her brain. Bits and pieces. The bathroom of the church; no refuge. A maroon car, a tiny closet-like room, a shed that smelled of horses. Ana and Jorge, yes, but Jorge more in control now, surer of himself, less under Ana's influence. He'd hit her, punched her, a sharp jab to the chin. He'd put a mug between her bound hands and ordered her to drink. When she'd refused, repelled by the steely stink of it, he'd explained, told her she had a simple choice: Drink now or die now.

The look on his face had been calm and certain, the knife in his hand lethal. If she didn't drink, he would kill her. She'd believed him. She remembered choking the liquid down her throat, remembered thinking it was a trick, that the foul-tasting stuff was poison, that she would drink *and* die.

She wasn't dead; she was blind. When she tried to bring her hands to her face, they obeyed. It was such an odd sensation, knowing her hands were right there in front of her face, feeling them brush her nose, and yet not seeing them. She checked for a blindfold, just in case, although she knew. Then cautiously she extended her hands into the blackness.

Above her, not a foot away, a hard blackness in the scary soft blackness, a cover, a lid. A coffin. Terror seized her with a shudder and she thought, I'm going to be sick; I'm going to throw up.

She forced herself to suck in a breath, to swallow the bitter taste. It's a small dark place, she told herself. So utterly dark she couldn't see. She wasn't really blind. Her pulse was beating in her ears so loudly she missed the noise at first. But underneath the thud of her heartbeat came another thud, and then another, a regular beat. *Ka-thump, whoosh. Ka-thump, whoosh.* It was familiar, almost soothing. She deliberately closed her eyes and made the endless blackness go away. *Ka-thump, whoosh,* like the seams in concrete pavement. Yes. There was movement in addition to sound, and slowly the image of a car trunk emerged. A car trunk, an ordinary car trunk. Two weeks ago, she would have been horrified at being tied in a car trunk, but now the realization that it wasn't a coffin, that she hadn't been buried alive and left for dead; well, there are worse things than a car trunk, trussed like a chicken. Worse things.

She closed her mind against them. She wasn't lying in her coffin. She wasn't blind. What was the point of letting imagination loose, realizing that it could have been, that it might yet be? She took inventory. She was achy and hungry and thirsty. Her mouth tasted foul. Jorge's angry face swam into her spotty memory. Her chin hurt where he'd punched her. A car, a car trunk. How? She didn't remember. She couldn't remember. Trying to remember, uncomfortable as she was, she must have slept.

When she woke again, it was just as black, but the panic receded quickly when she remembered the car trunk. *Kathump, whoosh.* She thought that some trunks had emergency releases, in case a little kid got stuck inside or something. But how would a little kid know? How would you find an escape button if you were blind? How would you manage to open the trunk with bound hands, and what would you do if you managed to open it? Fling yourself onto the highway to get flattened by a following truck?

Shut up, Paolina told the voice in her head, *shut up if you can't say something useful.* Useful. What would be useful? What do people keep in car trunks? A spare tire. Tools to change a flat tire. Maybe there was some kind of tool, something she could find and keep and use as a weapon. How could she explore the trunk with her hands and feet tied? She was small; she was limber; she had nothing else to do. She extended her hands over her head and stretched her legs till her feet hit something solid. She could feel the top and the bottom of her confines with her knees still bent. Top and bottom, or side and side? She wondered if she was lying crosswise in the trunk. She wondered what kind of car it was. There was a smell of rubber and motor oil.

She made her body move crablike in the darkness, rotating and lurching. It was painful tedious work, balancing on bound hands and feet, throwing her hips in the direction she hoped to move, worse than any dumb exercise a sadistic gym teacher could devise. She shuddered, suddenly afraid of what her hands might find, what her feet might touch.

Softness under her hands, a rag of some sort. She held it to her face and smelled oil. Someone had changed the oil, wiped their hands. She scrabbled with her hands and feet into the darkness. Where was a screwdriver, a tire iron? The road was bumpier now, and sometimes, just as she was inching forward, the car cornered sharply and she collapsed and rolled into an area she'd already painstakingly searched. There was nothing, nothing in the trunk but a scared girl and an oily rag. No tools. No food, certainly. No water. Maybe they would leave her here to starve. Her heart started pounding again. She had counted on finding something, but more than that, having a task, having something she could do, had distracted her. Now, in total darkness, with nothing left to touch, the abyss of panic beckoned.

Listen, the voice told her. *Listen.* As if it were music.

The whoosh of the road, the seamed thump calmed her heartbeat. *Ka-thump, whoosh.* She thought of the squalid square of Engativa, the sparse trees and stone fountain, with regret. She never got to play with the band. And now, she'd never have the chance. The sad rhythm of never, she thought, and her bound hands tapped the rhythm of the words into the rubber mat. The sad, sad rhythm of never. She slept again.

When she woke, the whoosh had changed to a grumble of gravel; the thump of the seams had disappeared. She tried to wedge her body against the side of the trunk because the road was so bumpy, because she was tired of sliding. She eased into a corner and tried to find a new rhythm in the crunch of the tires. When she heard a voice instead, she flinched. Then she thought: Wait a minute, the car's still moving. The trunk is still dark.

She could hear a voice though, voices. She didn't think she was hallucinating. She must have crawled deep into the trunk, up against the rear seat of the car. She settled in and tried to ease the pounding of her heart so she could listen.

It seemed like an hour before she could distinguish a single word and then it was only because the curse was loud, a forceful exhalation steeped in anger. Not Jorge's voice, she thought. A second male voice, angry and crude, joking with Jorge while she collected bruises in the trunk. This new man, this ally, must be the one who gave Jorge his newfound confidence. If Ana were still in charge, Paolina knew she'd be inside the car, not abandoned in the trunk, trussed and blind. What if Ana wasn't even in the car? Paolina's stomach clenched at the thought. Whoever the new man was, she hated him.

She tried to make sense of what she could hear, but there were only occasional words, disjointed words that made no sense. "Helicopter" was one of them. They couldn't be in a helicopter. Once she thought she heard Ana's voice, and Paolina's pulse slowed in relief.

When the movement stopped, she thought it might be a traffic light. But there was no noise of traffic, there hadn't been the noise of any other car for a long time. No horns beeping, none of the stop-and-go of city traffic.

The car door slammed like a clap of thunder. Silence, footsteps, then the click of a key in a lock. The trunk creaked and yawned. The slice of gray light widened. Even the dim light made her squint and look away. Twilight? Or gray dawn?

"*Chica,* are you awake?" Ana's voice.

The smell of the air was wonderful; the rush of a breeze intoxicating. She struggled to sit upright, but she was dizzy and disoriented. Ana's arms helped her. She was so thirsty.

"You must shut your eyes," Ana said.

"What? Where—?"

"Shut your eyes. Now."

The instant she obeyed, a sash, a strip of cloth, something, was pressed across her face, across her eyelids. Hands fumbled to tie it at the back of her head, even though she'd seen no more than a clump of distant trees, a rock, a road. A hot tear ran from the corner of her eye at the thought that she would see no more than that. She wished her tongue could reach up and lick the tear off her face.

"I'm sorry, *chica,*" Ana whispered. "Are you listening? You must do exactly as he says. He will kill you if you give him the least excuse."

"Who is—?" Ana's soft apology was more terrifying than Jorge's loudest shout.

"Don't ask questions. Listen and obey. You're going to talk to your father."

"My father's here?

"Don't you listen? I said don't—"

"Is he here?"

"You'll talk over a kind of telephone. I'm closing the trunk now. Stay quiet."

"Please. Don't close it." Don't shut out the breeze, don't shut out the air, don't put me back in darkness—

Hands pushed her down into the depths of the trunk. She struggled to sit, but the trunk closed with a snick. She was blindfolded in a velvet hole. Waiting to speak to her father.

To Roldán.

She'd thought about them for so long, the first words she'd say to her father. She'd play-acted the scene in a rosy haze, pretending he might show up at her *quinceañera,* her fifteenth birthday party, so handsome her friends would swoon. He'd be contrite, so sorry he'd inadvertently abandoned her. Because in her fairy tale, it wasn't the way Marta said at all. Marta had lied. Marta did lie; she often lied. Her father hadn't known Marta was pregnant when he went off to the jungle to fight. He hadn't known about her birth. If he had known—

If.

In her heart, she knew it was nothing but a game, a pastel-tinted fantasy. He wasn't the sort of father to attend birthday parties. He didn't know when her birthday was. He didn't care. Until he'd sent her Julio, the golden birdman, he'd been a total stranger, closed off in his own distant world. And now, what could she say to him? Would he realize who she was?

Dad. Father. *Papi.* What to say? Dad-I-don't-even-know, I've been locked in the trunk of a car. I'm filthy and hungry and thirsty, and I don't know what these people want from me.

Except you. And I never had you.

The trunk opened. Rough hands seized her and hauled her upright. She couldn't see, but she knew it wasn't Ana. Ana smelled like soap. Her touch was gentler. Jorge smelled like stale cigarettes. This new man smelled sharp and bitter, like medicine. He had clamps for hands; they'd leave bruises on her arms.

What would she say?

She heard noises. Footsteps. Ana and Jorge, she thought. Was Jorge bringing his sharp knife? Would she never get to speak to her father? Whispers and murmurs. Clicks, like machinery.

Then something was shoved against the side of her face. It was bigger than a cell phone, but it had to be a phone, because there was a Voice in her ear, telling her what to say. She shuddered as she listened. Because the sound in her ear wasn't human. The Voice was metallic and cruel, a robot-machine-noise, grinding like gears, explaining what would happen if she failed.

She tried to breathe normally, tried to picture the plastic Darth Vader mask her little brother sometimes wore, the gadget that made his voice so laughably like the movie voice, but the Voice wasn't like that at all. The Voice made shivers run up and down her spine. The Voice was terrifying.

"Talk," commanded the Voice. Then there was a click of machinery, like a tape recorder turning on or off.

"Daddy?"

"Who is this?"

Was that her father's voice, so deep and sad, so melodic?

"I'm Marta's daughter, your daughter. Dad, don't do what they—" A hand closed on her arm, above her elbow.

"Where are you, child?"

The pressure on her arm increased. *"I ran away. I ran. I tried. They caught me."*

"You are very brave, *chica.*"

The hand grasping her arm dug in like pincers. She could feel short blunt fingernails. Pain.

Click. "Tell him," the Voice ordered. Then another click.

"Daddy, they say they'll kill me if you don't do exactly what they say."

The phone at her ear was snatched away, and now it was soap-smelling Ana who was holding her, murmuring *hush, hush,* finally clamping a hand across her mouth while the tape-recorder-sound clicked again.

With the phone no longer at her ear, she heard the Voice with no mechanical alteration.

"We have both the American and the girl," it said. "We won't risk another helicopter."

A pause. Her father must be speaking. What would he say?

The Voice again: "Now you will bring us the gold."

Gold? she thought. *Gold? Like Julio?*

"Cartagena," the Voice said.

Cartagena was a city on the Caribbean coast; she knew that. Was she in Cartagena now? There was no smell of the sea, no sound of waves.

"San Felipe," the Voice went on.

She didn't know what that was. Or where. All she knew was that the Voice, with or without mechanical alteration, was one of the spookiest sounds she'd ever heard, a hollow whisper, level and cold.

"No one else. You. You will come alone," the Voice said, "or she dies."

"Let me talk," she yelled. *"Daddy! Daddy! They'll kill—"* But then Ana's arms were shoving her down, holding her while she screamed. The trunk slammed shut and she was alone in the dark again.

CHAPTER 33

HOT. I WAS a huge clay jar, like one of the pottery urns that lay shattered on the mountaintop, stuck in a fiery kiln. My neck burned, my sides baked, my arms blistered. My eyes opened, then squeezed themselves quickly shut. Who the hell had turned off the air conditioning? How had I managed to fall asleep and what dreadful dream had woken me with such urgency? I swung my legs over the edge of a hard bed and rested my head in my hands, fists against eye sockets to block the glare from the tiny window. Nothing blocked the sticky heat. I kicked the sheet away from my damp body. I was sweating, seated on a narrow daybed in a stuffy room, wearing what seemed to be a man's bathrobe. Disoriented and woozy, as though I'd unexpectedly fallen asleep in a movie theater.

How much of the wooziness was the residue of coca leaves? I was thirsty, but not hungry. I was not an urn, not on fire; it wasn't the threat of flames that had woken me. It was a voice within the fire, a machinelike voice similar to the one Roldán had described, the voice on the sat phone. There'd been a mechanical voice in my dream, trying to tell me . . . what? It was important, but gone, and I couldn't tease it back.

Other, more recent, snippets of conversation tickled my memory: Roldán's voice explaining that siesta was the custom of the country people, that he wished to keep to the custom to discourage gossip, that we were safe here. This place, this farmhouse near Baranquilla, was part of a lowland plantation belonging to the Cabrera family, to Luisa's uncle Gilberto, a former member of the Colombian senate, a man Roldán seemed to trust. Cabrera's family would shelter us, temporarily at least, to repay Roldán for bringing her body home.

A quick light knock on the door was followed swiftly by the creak of hinges, and a small woman of fifty, wearing a white blouse, a dark skirt, and carrying a tray with a pitcher of orangey-pink liquid and two crystal-clear glasses. She set the tray on a small table, wished me a pleasant afternoon, and informed me that my clothes were now dry. Would I like them brought in?

I thanked her and told her I would. She was so obviously a servant that I hesitated to ask for further information although I craved facts even more than I craved the sparkling glass of juice she poured and offered. I wanted to know how I'd wound up in this tiny room, who'd undressed me and swiped my clothes, why she'd brought two glasses instead of one; but as soon as my hand closed around the glass, before I could frame a single query, she pivoted and disappeared, closing the door soundlessly behind her.

The glass was beaded with icy drops. I wiped the condensation across the back of my neck, sipped the drink, then pressed the cool glass to my forehead. The juice wasn't *lulo;* it was a blend of several flavors, including mango.

The last time I'd flown across Colombia, from Bogotá to the mountains of the Sierra Nevada de Santa Marta, I'd been drugged into unconsciousness. I'd been awake this time, but the morning had passed like a dream, the rushed journey down the mountainside, the takeoff, the flight, the landing on the bumpy strip that passed for a runway. I'd been grateful for the intense heat as I jumped from the door of the plane to the ground, grateful for any sensation whatsoever, because the tiny plane had been rusty and wobbly, the pilot either drunk or a show-off, and I'd spent the past hour hanging onto the handgrips, praying the damned thing would stay airborne. Roldán, mid-flight, had mentioned that the Cessna reminded him of the one that had crashed years ago in the mountains. We'd flown so low, avoiding radar, that it seemed we'd be landing any minute, diving unscheduled into blue Caribbean waters.

The maid entered with a stack of freshly laundered clothes. When I asked her name, she flushed.

"Amalia, Señorita."

She set the pile on the daybed, placed a small jar of cream on the table, and explained that the Señor recommended it for my feet. Also, the Señor wished me to know I could feel free to use the telephone. When I thanked her, she scooted out the door.

Telephone. Was there an unseen phone in this closet? Hiding places were limited. I found it in the only possible location, a wooden built-in cupboard. As I lifted the receiver, I thought: Would the Señor be listening in on my call? Then I thought: What the hell did it matter? I dialed Gloria.

"Damn, this better be good. You better have one fine excuse for not calling. You find her? You okay? Sam and Mooney been driving me nuts, calling all the time, Where is she? Where is she? This better be damned good."

I filled her in, making a bare-bones job of it, letting her know my phone silence hadn't been a matter of choice. She thawed and responded with an update on Drew Naylor.

"Mooney can't trace him back more than two, three years. Might have changed his name. Lotta movie-type guys do that."

It seemed like I'd asked about Naylor years ago rather than days. I closed my eyes and shifted mental gears, made myself remember. Naylor produced commercial films. Actors changed their names, yes. Not producers of commercial shorts. "Keep digging," I said. "Has the man ever been injured? Does he limp?"

"I don't know. Don't have it here."

"Get it. Did Roz give you more stuff on BrackenCorp?"

She made a noncommittal noise before coming up with the goods. "Okay, first of all, they were recently taken over by this huge company called GSC, initials standing for nothing, far as she can tell. GSC: founded in '59; it's got eighty-nine thousand employees, FY04 revenue: 16.8 billion, Fortune 500." She rattled off more numbers, but I didn't find them enlightening.

"What do they do?"

"Risk analysis, knowledge management, security services. BrackenCorp was big, too; forty thousand employees before they swallowed it. Word is GSC wanted their government biz. BrackenCorp did over six billion in federal contracts, but they had a pile of debt. Good write-off for GSC. Solid acquisition."

"What did BrackenCorp do for the government?"

"Aviation services, base operations, logistics support services, something called range tech services."

"Go back to logistics support. What's that cover?"

"Okay," she said, "Once upon a time, the U.S. Army did its own thing. Fed its own people, handled its own communications, built its own barracks, did its own laundry, but then the government decided to privatize. Now there's what they call a 'partnership' between the armed forces and a select group of private companies."

"Who selected them?"

"That's a story in itself. Quite a few of the CEOs used to be in the government, cabinet positions, undersecretaries of this and that. Like Mark Bracken. But it doesn't work out that badly costwise, government spending being what it is."

Yeah, I thought, and what about accountability?

"It's like outsourcing," she went on. "You know? You hire somebody from the outside, you streamline your operation."

"The army outsources logistical support."

She made a clicking noise with her tongue. "They go farther than that."

Bingo. "Does BrackenCorp happen to fly defoliation missions in Colombia?"

Her "Humph" was eloquent. It said, "Why'd you get Roz to research this shit if you already know it?" I thought, if BrackenCorp was already flying security for government-sanctioned defoliation missions, they could have ordered one or two of their copters to take a "wrong turn" in the fog, get lost for a few hours, carry out a clandestine mission.

I said, "Do they provide actual troops?"

"They call them 'security specialists.' Lots of ex–special ops guys."

"Security specialist" sounded one hell of a lot better than "mercenary." It sounded like a term devised to keep legislators calm and happy.

"What if these civilians get themselves killed in a firefight? Does the body count get reported to Congress?" I asked.

"Got me," Gloria said. "But this privatization ain't new, babe. World War One, the French army took cabs to the front."

Trust Gloria to know something like that. She was probably hoping for a contract to handle future foreign entanglements.

"Bracken," I said. "What about him?" Click. *Will Mark Bracken be fired?* That was where I'd heard the name BrackenCorp, on a radio news broadcast, something about corporate takeovers.

"Mark Nathaniel Bracken. Yale, '67. Skull and Bones. Department of Agriculture, a little time in Justice, Undersecretary of Defense, more administrations than you can count, Republican and Democratic both. Went private in the early nineties, made a mint."

"Is he interested in gold?"

"Christ, Carlotta, I'm interested in gold. Who the hell isn't interested in gold?"

"He's in danger of being fired, right? Because of this GSC thing?"

"Guys like that don't get fired. They get bumped up, moved over, maybe eased out with a golden parachute."

"Who owns GSC?" I asked.

Papers rustled. "Don't have it."

"Find it. Get Roz on it, and if she can't make a connection to gold at GSC, have her start looking at the other end. Find gold collectors, antique gold, pre-Columbian gold, and see who's got a BrackenCorp or GSC connection."

"Okay. Now talk to me some more. You said you heard from Paolina?"

I hesitated. "Roldán did. She's alive." *According to him.* I was upset that he hadn't let me speak to her; I knew her voice better than I knew my own.

"You bring her home soon, hear?"

"I'll bring her home." As soon as the words left my mouth, I regretted them. It was the same expression Roldán had used about Cabrera, about her body, bringing her home.

"You be careful," Gloria said. "Don't you mess up my big chance to be a bridesmaid."

I felt my face grow warm. "Gloria, dammit, Sam shouldn't have told you. I haven't decided."

"Are you up?" Roldán's voice preceded a knock at the door.

"Tell him yes, girl. Man cares about you. Think you'd get that through your thick skull."

"How is Sam? Where is he?" The questions came in a rush, in a single breath I hadn't realized I'd been holding. I was worried about the man, dammit. Maybe the metallic voice in my dream had been trying to tell me something about Sam.

"He's worried about you. I don't know where he is, but last time he called he said if I heard from you, tell you to call Ignacio right away. Call him now."

"Carlotta?" Roldán again, insistent.

"I'm hanging up now, Gloria. Good-bye."

I ought to do it, I thought. Marry Sam. Just for the vision of Gloria rolling down the aisle in one of those frou-frou bridesmaid gowns designed for girls shaped like toothpicks. The image forced a smile.

When Roldán entered the room, he made it seem smaller. He'd left his white Kogi garb at the camp, along with his mantle of responsibility and his thousand-yard stare. He seemed more human in faded jeans and a white tee under an unbuttoned blue linen shirt. As he glanced around the room, the corners of his wide mouth lifted in amusement.

He said, "Just the basics here: a woman and a bed. We could use a little music."

"I must have gone out like a light," I said. In civilian garb, Roldán made me think of Sam. Maybe it was the faint tang of shaving lotion. Or maybe it was just that Sam was on my mind.

He nodded at the phone. "Your friends know you're safe? Good. How are your feet? You used the cream?"

"Not yet."

"It is mainly from the aloe plant, but there is also coca in it."

Great, I thought, I could get stoned through the soles of my feet.

"I brought you shoes," he continued. "Men's shoes, but they should fit."

"I'd rather have information."

The aftermath of the attack had practically precluded questions. After the terse call from the kidnappers, it seemed as if every living soul in the camp required Roldán's presence and undivided attention. Then the *mamas* had come, a strange and unearthly procession, summoned, it seemed, by pure thought, and ever since Roldán had emerged from his all-night confab with them, looking like a man cast out of Eden, he'd told me next to nothing. As an outsider, I'd been excluded from the meeting with the religious leaders. Afterwards, Roldán had shut himself up briefly with his lieutenants, left Flaco in charge of the camp, and led me on a strenuous march to a camouflaged airstrip where I'd watched as men loaded bags onto the small plane, bags that looked heavy enough to be filled with gold. When I'd asked, Roldán had brushed off the question.

"What do you wish to know?" he said now.

There was no place to sit but the rumpled daybed. I moved to one end. He sat beside me, closer than necessary, and I was abruptly aware of the heat of the room, the color of his shirt, and my nakedness under the robe.

The combination made my voice husky. "What did your precious *mamas* do to that man?"

The night before, several white-clad men with pointed hats, among them, I thought, Mama Parello, had marched a bound man into a central hut.

"That was the traitor, Guillermo, the man they call Gee-mo. Do you wish to know what they did to him? Or what they learned from him?"

"They tortured him." I'd seen him carried from the hut in the morning.

"They prayed for him, to heal him and return him to the tribe."

"Prayer made his legs bleed?"

"It's an ancient ceremony, based on the principle of confession, like in the Catholic Church."

Sure, I thought, the Catholic Church by way of the Inquisition.

"They *knelt* him," Roldán said. "They put him to the shells. But first, he had the opportunity to speak. He resisted the wisdom offered by the *mamas,* so he had to suffer the ordeal."

Forced to kneel on a bed of sharp broken shells, his arms outstretched like the wings of an eagle, his head bowed, Gee-mo had listened to the questions, but refused to admit his guilt. Stones, placed on his back, pressed him deeper into the shells. Not till his blood colored the white shells did he speak.

"It was a case of *plato o plomo,*" Roldán said.

"What?"

"Silver or lead. It's a catchphrase, what the drug dealers say to threaten the police and the judges. Take the bribe or take the bullet. Take the money or stand by while we kill your family."

Six, seven months ago, a man had approached Gee-mo in a tavern. The man knew his links to the Kogi, and wanted to hire him as an expedition guide. At first, Gee-mo thought they were photographers, perhaps archaeologists. They hadn't seemed like thieves.

"Did he name names?"

Roldán paused. "He didn't know any."

I was pretty sure Paolina's father wasn't telling the truth.

"Let me see your feet," he said.

"We're not done talking."

"What else is there to say? I'm prepared to go through with the deal."

"The Kogi gold for Paolina?" I wanted to believe him. "I told you to lie to the kidnappers. Not to me."

"I asked the *mamas* for permission."

"Do the *mamas* expect to get it back?"

"You'll get *her* back." His tone said I should stop asking questions. He was giving me a chance to rescue her; I should snatch it with both hands and be satisfied.

I wanted to. But he'd told me too much, intimated that the gold was everything to the Kogi, the holy gold. It governed the lives of the priests. Every ritual, every offering, was dedicated to the Mother, the golden image, of the crop. Without the gold, there would be no priests. Without the *mamas*, the world would end. And he was the caretaker.

"Let me see your feet," he repeated.

I lifted the right one, bending my knee carefully; the robe was short and revealing.

He examined the sole gravely. "You're stubborn."

"Most people read palms."

"You were in pain, but you climbed quickly. The Kogi value a woman who knows how to walk."

Better to be valued for walking, I thought, than for a lot of other things. I hadn't seen any women included among the *mamas*, and the *mamas* seemed to be the leaders of the tribe. So the question remained: How highly did the Kogi value women?

"For a *gringa*, you're tough," he said. "You never complained. I admit I'm attracted to you."

"I should have complained." Face it; my silence was nothing but stupid pride.

He edged closer, and slid his hand up to my ankle. "You should, perhaps, have children of your own."

"I've got Paolina."

"That's not what I mean."

It was clear what he meant, the two of us too close on the narrow bed in the overheated room after what we'd been through together. When you come close to the doorway of death, life and the physical sensations of life seem especially precious. While he'd worn his Kogi whites, he'd seemed set apart, removed from the sexual arena, some kind of mystical priest. Now I was aware that his build reminded me of Sam Gianelli's. Now his hand moved from my ankle to my calf, and his fingers stopped probing for pain.

Children of my own.

It was close to what Sam had said the night before I left for Miami. I thought about children of my own, and Sam, and then—I don't know why—I was fourteen again, in a narrow white hospital bed, empty and alone. I felt the absence of that baby, the one I gave up for adoption without ever holding in my arms, like a recent and terrible loss. Boy or girl? I guess I always think of her as a girl. I think of her as Paolina, my secret Paolina, my missing child.

I couldn't lose her again. Couldn't lose Paolina, my real Paolina, my living, breathing Paolina. A shiver ran down my spine in spite of the heat, and I put my hand on Roldán's chest, to keep him at a distance.

"I have someone in Boston. My fiancé." And not till the word passed my lips did I realize what I'd said. Fiancé, not lover. Slowly I withdrew my leg.

Roldán said, "He should have come with you."

"He was busy."

"He's a policeman?"

"He's a crook."

"Congratulations. Are you sure you wouldn't care to use the bed to celebrate? One last fling before marriage is an old and honored tradition."

"Just for the men, right?"

"Are you so traditional, then?"

He leaned over and kissed me, lightly at first. He smelled like cigar smoke and tasted like mango juice. When I kissed him back, my stomach gave a lurch of dark longing and my back arched involuntarily. The urgency was almost like a drug. The walls of the room receded, the heat pulsed, the light shimmered. When I closed my eyes, I thought of Sam Gianelli in another woman's bed and came up gasping for air.

"Wait." I wanted to ask for a cigarette even though I gave them up years ago. If I asked for a cigarette, took time to tuck it snugly between my third and index finger, to fire a match to light it, I'd be able to consider what I was doing, what I was about to do. The smallest thing can make a difference, Roldán told me on the mountaintop. Actions have consequences. I didn't know it when I was fourteen, but I sure as hell knew it now. The dark yearning was powerful; it smelled like musky sweat and cigar smoke. It tasted like mango juice.

I smiled and said, "Wait a minute. Hold on. Are you planning to get arrested soon?"

His fingertips burned along my cheekbone. "You're saying I'm coming on to you too quickly?"

I said, "If our host, Señor Cabrera, proved less than accommodating, if he called the cops, if you were about to be arrested and sent to jail, that might explain what's going on here."

I concentrated on inhaling, exhaling, on not smelling the cigar scent of his skin, on not licking another taste of mango juice from his tongue. I'm not saying I didn't want to go to bed with him. I'm not saying there wasn't a time I'd have peeled off my robe in a flash. I'm not even saying I didn't resent Sam poking his shadowy image into what might otherwise have proved a delicious interlude. I felt dumb; there was no reward for chastity, no silver cup for keeping my legs crossed. It was as foolish as not complaining on the mountain.

He said, "You mean if I knew I was on my way to prison, where I'd be spending a long time without a woman, then I'd make a play for you? You're very cynical. You don't believe I find you attractive?"

It was extremely cynical of me to think that sex was a great way to pass the time when you didn't want to answer questions. But I thought it all the same.

He placed a mocking hand over his heart. "I tell you nothing but the truth."

I grasped the opening like a drowning sailor grabbing a life ring. "As long as you're telling the truth, why did you ask me to describe Naylor? Did you ask your *mamas* about the limping man?"

"They say only that the future is clouded." He patted the bed. "So perhaps we should take advantage of the present?"

Perhaps we should, I thought. But even though his eyes were Paolina's eyes, I didn't completely trust him. And then there was Sam.

"I don't think so." My robe had come open. I snugged its rough fabric closely around me and his eyes, so very much like Paolina's, lost their liquid warmth and slowly hardened. In no time, he was the remote man of the mountain again, the aloof and stoic priest.

"You should get dressed, then." He blew out a breath and made an effort to straighten his rumpled clothes. "Señor Cabrera would like to meet you."

As soon as he closed the door, I wanted to call him back, hold him and kiss him, and smell the moist earthy scent of him. Pull his mouth down to my waiting breast.

Jesus, Carlyle, I told myself, take a shower.

When I found it, the small bathroom down the hall had only a sink and a toilet. I splashed water on my overheated face. I was toweling it dry when the dream came back—the urn, the fire, the mechanically altered voice.

In the States, where kidnapping is a federal offense, where the FBI is so successful at catching and prosecuting offenders that the crime is rare, kidnappers use a voice-alterer on the assumption that relevant phones will be quickly tapped by the Bureau. Because if the kidnappers are brought to trial, none of them wants to sit at the defense table listening to his own taped voice played back for the benefit of a jury. But here, where, according to Luisa Cabrera, kidnapping was commonplace, where it was illegal to pay a ransom, where the police didn't get involved, where kidnappers were seldom, if ever, caught, why go to the bother and expense of acquiring and using such a machine?

Could it be, I wondered, hanging the towel on the bar, because Roldán would know, would recognize the kidnapper's voice?

CHAPTER 34

MY JEANS HAD been mended and pressed; my torn, bloodstained T-shirt replaced by a man's *guayabera*, too big through the shoulders, but whole and clean. I dressed, then sat on the bed and inspected the skin on my feet. Blisters had subsided. The skin felt tender, but was far from the ragged mess I'd feared. I used the cream, slipped on soft leather moccasins, and went in search of Roldán and Señor Cabrera, trying to recall the twists and turns that had led me to the small room with the daybed and the phone.

I found myself in an enormous tile-floored dining room dominated by a table that could seat twenty, with half that number of high-backed chairs surrounding it. One long wall was filled with light and windows. Peering out I saw a huge grassy courtyard, and the basic design of the house was revealed: a main building, two long low wings. I headed toward the main building and the distant rumble of voices.

In the big front room the gilded chandelier and the patterned carpet spoke of better days. A grand piano hunkered in an alcove. The furniture was plump and faded, beige with a rose-colored print. Roldán sat on the edge of a worn armchair, deep in conversation with an elderly gentleman in a cane rocker. As he rocked the chair gave the familiar half-sigh, half-squeak I still associate with my late aunt Bea, a woman who endlessly rocked as she knitted. A comforting sound in a strange place.

The old man was as elegant and worn as the room in a beige linen suit, white shirt, and striped tie, with a magnificent mane of ash-colored hair. He stood as soon as he saw me; his head dipped in half a formal bow. His jowls quivered. He held an unlit pipe in his left hand. Roldán made introductions: Señor Gilberto Cabrera Fortas met Señorita Carlotta Carlyle.

"You were a friend of my niece?" The old man's voice was shaky.

"I barely knew her."

"Just as well. It was her friends who got her killed."

I'd had a hand in it, too, but no one was making me kneel on broken shells so I decided against confession.

"I'm sorry for your loss."

He sank into his rocking chair, turning his attention to a leather album on a round piecrust table. Next to the album sat a pile of newspapers, a long thin scissors, and a jar of paste. I inhaled the scent of schoolroom collages.

"She was a fine writer," he said. "When my brother, her father, died, the senior editor himself insisted she have his job. Rivals at the paper were jealous, but she proved herself worthy. You read her work?"

I nodded; if I hadn't, maybe she'd still be alive.

"Luisa and I agreed on nothing." He raised the pipe to his lips, noticed that it was unlit, but made no effort to light it. "I work within the system; I believe in the system. I believe in democracy, not endless, senseless war."

Roldán broke in. "How is it possible to have democracy when the only choice is between two of the same, between peas in a pod?"

Cabrera held up a hand. "I won't argue with you, Roldán. Not today." He turned his sad eyes on me. "I fought with Luisa every time I saw her, which was never often enough, but I saved every single thing she wrote. I underlined the phrases I particularly enjoyed, little things that made me smile, deft jabs of the knife. I cut them out and pasted them in this book. I thought after I died, she would see, and know how proud I was of her. Now—I'm a stupid old man."

His mournful eyes were sharp and clear. He sounded more like an angry man than a stupid one, and I hoped his fury wouldn't target Roldán before we got a chance to rescue Paolina. One phone call from Cabrera, a man Roldán had earlier described as still politically well-connected, and Roldán could disappear forever. The DAS, the Colombian army, the police, any official body would be delighted to haul him off to prison.

I said, "Your niece, had she been in touch recently?"

"We spoke on the phone. She was doing a piece about the native tribes of the northeast. She asked me to find out if there was anything odd going on in the government. She'd heard rumors of some kind of plot—you hear these things—a conspiracy between the U.S. and the Colombian government to harm the aboriginal peoples. I still have friends in positions of power. They talk to me, but I could find no trace of such a thing."

"Did she ask you anything else?"

"We argued less over the phone. Only a few days ago, she wanted to know whether I'd heard anything linking Base Eighteen—the army elite, mind you—to drug dealing." He gave a small laugh. "That I would like to prove. And before that, there was something. Ah, this will interest you, Roldán. She asked if I knew how Angel Navas died."

"Did you find out?" I said.

"I didn't need to; I already knew. He died badly. In the U.S., in prison."

Roldán stood abruptly. "Gilberto, you should rest now. I'll call Amalia." He walked to a curtained window, shifted the fabric, and stared out at the patio. "Let's take a walk, Carlotta."

The old man rocked, puffing his unlit pipe. We excused ourselves, and went out through the French doors. The house had been hot, but outside it was worse, humid and oppressive. Rain hung in the air but didn't fall. Vegetation tried to choke the narrow pathway, cracking the flagstones.

"Is Amalia a relative?" I asked.

"She's worked here since I was a boy."

"What are the chances she's already called the police?"

"Nonexistent. She used to bandage my knees when I came in from roughhousing. When we arrived, Gilberto sent the other servants home."

"They'll be suspicious."

"I doubt it. He's a moody man at best, very busy. Often he shuts the place up on a moment's notice and flies to Bogotá. Government affairs."

"Are we close to Cartagena here?"

"Closer than we were."

Close enough to abandon the decrepit aircraft, I hoped. "And we're going to do exactly what they told you. Follow orders."

He nodded, but his thoughts seemed far away, either back in the farmhouse with the man in the rocking chair or farther, in the primitive village of gumdrop-shaped huts, or on the mountaintop.

"Tell me about this Fort of San Felipe," I said. "The place you're supposed to bring the ransom."

He returned to the present with a flicker of his eyelids. "It was built to keep out pirates, like all the forts in Cartagena."

It was old, then. "Big?"

"Yes. It's open to the public, like a museum."

"So you think it will be safe? We'll walk in, do the swap, walk out?"

"I will walk in. Alone, as they asked. I'll send her out to you."

"Carrying hundreds of pounds of gold?"

"Carrying a sample of the gold, as a guarantee. The rest will be in a locker at the airport. I'll surrender the key. That's how they want it."

"You think it will work? You think you'll walk out?"

His feet scuffed the dirt along the path. "I think it may work for you. They may let Paolina go. As for me—" He shrugged.

"You don't believe they mean to let you go."

"They insisted I bring the gold. Me and no one else. Anyone could bring it. All the gold could be left at the airport; I could have mailed the key. Kidnapping is very common here. There are ways to arrange the ransom." He shrugged again, and a smile played at the corners of his mouth. "You've seen pictures of the fort?"

My turn to shrug.

"It's a true fortress. Each level can be sealed, so that if the pirates took one level, the defenders could hold the rest until reinforcements came. It was the scene of many famous battles. I assume they wouldn't go there unless they had the ability to secure the fort, and the ability to secure the fort could only come from the military."

I pursed my lips and gave a low whistle. "So we assume the fort is a trap."

"Whether I go from there to jail or directly to the hereafter is the only question."

"Not by a long shot."

Roldán raised his eyebrows. I stopped walking, waited till he turned and looked me in the eye.

"There are plenty of other questions. Like, why don't you level with me?"

"I'm not sure of this idiom, *level*."

"It means, tell the truth."

"Which part of my intuition do you doubt?"

"I don't doubt your intuition." I thought it likely someone wanted Roldán dead. "I doubt that you're giving away the gold."

He bent and picked up a pebble, weighed it in his hand. "You saw the men load it on the plane."

"I saw them load heavy bags."

"There is gold," he said. "The *mamas* gave me several items, enough to bargain for Paolina's freedom. They said it was a debt they owed to pay for their mistake."

"What mistake?"

That faint grin again. "Saving my life. They've survived all these years by staying apart. Other Indian tribes take what we give them, alcohol and guns. They covet what we have, television and airplanes, and they lose their souls. Because the Kogi refuse to want what we want, they survive."

"What's in the rest of the bags?"

He held out the pebble. "Rocks, stones."

"So you believe we're being watched, that someone reported the bags being loaded on the plane."

"Someone always talks," Roldán said. "*Plato o plomo.* Someone will talk."

We came to the end of the flagstones and passed through a wrought-iron gate. The path changed to gravel and veered to the right, and then we were strolling through a formal rose garden. I wondered how many gardeners had been dismissed for the day, and with whom they were currently gossiping.

I said, "Señor Cabrera has friends in the government. Would he help?"

"I'm not among his favorite causes. Gilberto's old. He wants to be left alone with his roses."

The bushes were grouped according to color in neat concentric circles separated by manicured gravel paths. The contrast with the wild vegetation of the Sierra Nevada couldn't have been sharper. I missed the green smell of the trees, the chatter of birds.

"The government would shoot me on sight," Roldán said.

I didn't need to lean down to sniff the roses; their perfume was everywhere, overpoweringly sweet. "You know who has her."

"Do you like roses?"

"One of the photos in my bag, you recognized it."

"They always make me think of funerals."

"The woman or the man?"

"It's more of a memory." He tossed the pebble in the air, caught it with quick fingers. "She looks like someone I used to know."

"Who?"

"I had a friend . . ." He paused to discard the pebble, then started speaking again. "She could be Angel Navas's former wife. I'm not a hundred percent sure."

I thought he was.

"If it were Ana," he continued, "she would despise me."

"Why?"

I waited while he gathered his thoughts.

"I should have confessed this long ago. Not to you, but to the *mamas*. There are cleansing rituals, for those who come willingly to confession, rituals that return the soul to harmony."

I bit my lip, convinced interruption would only prolong the process, but every minute seemed stretched to the breaking point, every minute another minute Paolina was alone, needing me.

"Angel." He breathed in the word like the rose-scented air, pronouncing it *ánhel,* with the "g" sounded like the Spanish "j" but more rasping. "We were friends and then we were partners, but more and more he saw himself as the leader, the one who made the decisions. Many of those decisions I disagreed with. He became dangerous."

"What do you mean, dangerous?"

"Like a wild animal. Unpredictable. I used drugs to make money, but he saw drugs as a cause in themselves. He started using the product, snorting cocaine like he had a hole in his head to fill with it. Then he tried *basuco,* the cocaine base. He got crazy. Once, I saw him shoot a man for target practice, to test the sight on a new gun. I should have killed him then, but I waited for my old friend to recover, to find himself again. Then he made plans to sell my people and me, and . . ."

"Yes?"

"I should have looked him in the eye and killed him then, stabbed him with a knife, killed him like a man. He deserved that much from me."

I waited.

"Instead, I set him up," Roldán said. "I gave him to the military as a decoy, a distraction for another strike I'd planned, a raid on an armory. And they took him. In the action, he was wounded. They killed his wife. They killed his baby son. I did not know they would be there with him."

"But his wife is alive."

"Ana was his wife before Melania, the one who died. He left Ana when the other woman was pregnant, because Ana couldn't have children. She understood, or she seemed to. She still loved him, even when he was crazy with *basuco*."

Would she have contacts in the States? Contacts with corporations that owned and flew helicopters in foreign countries?

"Navas was extradited," I said.

"With fanfare. The trial was in Miami. Jailed for life. When I heard that he died there, I hoped they'd send his body home for burial. 'Better a grave in Colombia than a jail cell in the United States.' That was the motto of those who called themselves the Extraditables, Escobar and Rodriguez Gacha, all the dead outlaws."

"Is that what the Kogi saw for you in their vision? A grave? Death?"

"If I had the powers of the *mamas*, perhaps we could find our way out of this mess."

"What powers?"

"The power to open the mountains, the power to communicate through the mind, to levitate."

I imagined the pointy-hatted little men rising in the clear mountain air.

"There's a vast disconnect between their world and ours, between our understanding and theirs," Roldán said.

"I'm not asking for magical powers," I said. "I'd be happy if I knew where they were holding her."

"Ana was of an old family. They had property, a country farm, a city apartment."

"Near Cartagena?"

He stooped, picked up another pebble, and tossed it far into the grass. "There's no use thinking about it. There are only two of us. I no longer lead a cadre of armed revolutionaries."

In my hurry to dress and meet Cabrera, I hadn't yet called Ignacio.

I said, "Let's see what I can do."

CHAPTER 35

"I NEED TO speak to Ignacio. It's important." Someone had opened the tiny window in the closet-like room, but there was no cooling breeze.

"Who is this?"

The voice belonged to the same woman who'd answered the phone days before. This time I wasn't about to let her fob me off with any request that I call back later.

"Look, I have to speak to him *now*, or at least leave a message, so he can call me back immediately. My name is Carlyle, and I need his help. I was given this number by a friend of his—"

There was a noise as if the phone had fallen to the floor.

"Hello?" I said. "Hello?"

"Dammit, where are you? Where have you been?"

"Sam?" I sat on the daybed. If it hadn't been there, I'd probably have hit the floor; that's how weak my knees felt. *"Sam?"*

"Carlotta, I've been looking for you everywhere. Your stuff's still at the hotel— Where the hell are you? Have you found her?"

"What are you doing here?"

"Ignacio got in touch when you didn't call. Then I talked to Gloria and—what the hell does it matter? I'm here in Bogotá. Where are you?"

"I'm—I'm near Baranquilla."

"With Paolina?"

"Oh, Sam, no. Not yet, Sam. Sam, who's Ignacio? What can he do?" Some part of me was aware that I was repeating his name over and over. I couldn't help myself. It tasted like honey on my tongue.

He hesitated. "Ignacio is—an associate."

"How much help can he give me? Not in Bogotá, but on the coast? In Cartagena?"

"Cartagena? You just said Baranquilla."

"*I'm* in Baranquilla, but Paolina's in Cartagena. We've got till Thursday to find her. After that, it'll be too late."

"Okay."

I could hear the reservations in his voice. I shared them; it was late Tuesday afternoon.

"Two things," I said quickly. "Three. First, call Mooney for me, okay? See whether he's got an ID on the woman's photo. We have to have an ID, a family name, as soon as possible. Tell him the one Hanson sent from Florida."

"Hanson, Florida, okay."

"Then, once you get her last name, get Ignacio to find out what property she owns, or what property her family owns, near Cartagena." *Mooney had to have her name by now. Had to.*

"If I don't get her name?"

"I'm working on it at this end, too. I'm going through news clips." *Possibly Luisa had mentioned it in her writing about Navas. Possibly Roldán would remember.*

"Okay. You think Paolina's being held by this woman?"

"The woman's involved."

"What else?"

What else? "God, Sam, it's good to hear your voice." I inhaled, closed my eyes. Concentrated. "People. We'll need people to meet us in Cartagena."

"We?" he said. "Us?"

"I'm with Paolina's father. With Roldán."

"He's alive, then."

"Yes."

"What kind of people are you talking about?"

"Can Ignacio provide men as well as equipment?" Men who can use guns, that's what I meant.

"Soldiers," Sam said smoothly. "It can be arranged."

I thought, *This is his business. This is what he does.*

CHAPTER 36

"SO HE'S A drug dealer," Roldán said. "This fiancé of yours."

"He might be." My concentration, such as it was, wasn't on Roldán's words. It was on finding my way in the dark.

"Can you see?"

"Barely."

It was after ten at night and the city of Cartagena no longer shimmered in the hazy heat. We'd flown in hours earlier, the temperature hovering at a hundred, Roldán stubbornly insisting we continue the journey by plane. The less said about the roller-coaster flight and rocky landing the better.

Old friends of Roldán's from the farm near the landing strip had driven us close to the heart of the city in a rusty Jeep; now we were walking along the old sea wall, six feet high in some places, higher in others. The street lamps were far apart and dim.

"He'll sell me to the highest bidder."

"He won't do anything that would hurt Paolina."

The water was indigo; the beaches perfect bands of white sand. Earlier, in the Jeep, we'd passed houses painted blue with bright yellow shutters and parrot green balconies, the colors pulsing in the heat.

"He'll convince himself it's the right thing to do. That Paolina will be better off without me."

"Are we close?"

"We're here. This is it."

The bar had no sign. Like the other nearby buildings, it was made of the same stone as the sea wall. The shutters were closed, the walls thick to keep out the heat. When Roldán opened the door, a bell tinkled and guitar music swelled.

No one greeted us when we entered. The low-ceilinged eatery seemed to be a place favored by regulars who knew their way to the bar or to one of the tables to the right of it. Then I saw Sam and the shape and particulars of the bar receded.

He fit in; he wore a *guayabera* of pale blue cotton, a shirt he'd never have worn at home, untucked over loose khaki pants. He stood out; he might as well have been the only man in the room. I couldn't take my eyes off him. His familiar face seemed thinner, paler, but maybe that was the light. He needed a shave.

We were seated at the long rectangular table so quickly we might have been absorbed into the picture. Sam was next to me, his hand warm on my thigh, Roldán across from us. There was rough wooden planking under my elbows. Smoke stung my eyes.

There were introductions and glasses of warm beer. Conversation flowed over me, around me, in English and Spanish. Sam's Spanish was primitive, but he spoke Italian like a native, and was evidently able to make himself understood. Next to Roldán was Ignacio himself, arrived with Sam from Bogotá within the hour. Ignacio was shaped like a squat refrigerator, broad through the torso, with legs too short for his girth. He smiled whenever he spoke, a menacing smile. A woman named Felicia, short and dark, with prominent teeth, sat next to him. She and a hook-nosed smoker named Rafael, both Cartagena natives, seemed to be old friends. Likewise Silas, a slightly older man with graying hair, and slender Luis, who'd both flown in from the capital. I glanced around the table: Eight people didn't seem like much of an army.

In the blend of voices, Sam's stood out. I wanted to close my eyes and let it wash over me like water, but his words demanded attention.

He said, "Iragorri. Is that Ana's name? The family name?"

"You reached Mooney."

"Iragorri, of course. Yes." Roldán wore a straw hat he'd been given at the farmhouse after we'd landed. The brim shaded his face.

I was grateful it wasn't Garcia or whatever the Colombian equivalent of Smith or Jones might be.

Sam said, "The captain was in Miami, but he left a phone number with Gloria."

"Miami?"

"Powwowing with DEA. This guy he knows says your lawyer, Vandenburg, doesn't work for them. A grand jury's been convened and he's due for indictment any time."

Vandenburg had sent me to Naylor. So Naylor wasn't DEA, and yet he, or Vandenburg, had the juice to have me followed, to have me processed through the airport via alternate means.

"Did he get anything on the phone numbers?" The e-mail I'd sent Roz about Zona Rosa and Base Eighteen, requesting she ask Moon to run them by DEA, seemed like something I'd done in another lifetime.

"He said you'd need to call him on that. I got the feeling he didn't exactly trust me."

I should have realized that Moon would react badly to a call from Sam, that it would raise all his cop hackles.

Sam said, "But he said to tell you that the guy, Naylor—is that the name?"

"Yes." Across the table, Roldán had grown very still.

"Mooney says it may take a while because there's something with the Witness Protection Program, a prefix in his file that means WP. Does that make sense?"

If Naylor was in the federal Witness Protection Program, he might be working for DEA after all. Undercover from the locals.

Roldán said, "The Iragorris, what properties do they own?"

Sam said, "First, do you think you're being followed?"

Roldán said, "At this point, the only thing that matters is finding out where they're holding the girl."

"You look like her," Sam said. "Excuse me, she looks like you."

I was aware not only of how much Paolina resembled her father, but of how much the two men, Sam and Roldán, were superficially alike, both dark, both tall. Sam's hair was curly, his nose more aquiline, but both had the air of command. They dominated the table.

I wasn't sure whether or not Sam had shared Roldán's identity with the others. In the introductions he'd been simply "Carlos." The woman, Felicia, stared at Roldán openly, but he was a handsome man, worth more than a quick once-over.

The woman said, "There are two properties. The farm on the way to Santa Rosa will be easy to check. Raffi and I will rent a car, drive there, and experience a sudden breakdown."

The man named Rafael wiped his mouth with the back of his hand. "She's such a bitch, yells bloody murder at me for not knowing how to fix the car. Everybody feels so sorry for me, they let me in to telephone a garage. Once a man gave me a whole bottle of rum, so I could get drunk on the way back to town."

"Don't get killed," Roldán said. "These people are serious."

"So am I," Rafael said. "Just because I joke, don't think I'm not serious."

"No problem." Ignacio's smooth baritone oiled the waters. "The other property is in the old section of town, an apartment building."

I was watching Silas and Luís at the other end of the table, sizing them up. Everyone talks, Roldán had told me, everyone's bought and sold. How much could we trust Ignacio's people?

"Which site do you consider more likely?" Ignacio asked. Roldán shrugged.

"The apartment building is not half a kilometer from this place. We walked by it on our way to the bar. Felicia?"

The woman passed several Polaroid photos around the table. I wondered whether she or Rafael was a regular customer at this place. The table was the farthest from both the bar and the door, secluded in an alcove.

"I played tourist," she said. "Discreetly. It's the dark green building with the blue trim. It's narrow. It looks like there's only one apartment to each floor. See, both the second- and third-floor apartments have balconies overlooking the street."

Each balcony was covered with a peacock blue slatted wooden grating.

"We didn't want to draw attention to ourselves by circling the building, checking the access from the rear, but you can see the small sign in the window. The third-floor flat is for rent, possibly empty. I called the number a little while ago. It was busy. I'll try again now, if you like."

She left the table just as the waiter brought food, huge platters of fish and bowls of rice, served family style. Steam rose and mingled with the smoke. The food smelled fine, but I wasn't hungry.

I felt like I was having a vision: Sam here in this place. In spite of his hand on my thigh, his shoulder at my shoulder, the scene seemed unreal, something in a movie or a drug dream summoned by pointy-hatted little men. I felt suddenly weak, dry-throated. It was all I could do to clasp a glass of water in my hand and raise it to my lips. Florida, Bogotá, the Sierra Nevada, and now Cartagena. So much done, so much left undone, so much to do. Paolina, still to rescue.

Between bites, Ignacio said, "And if we don't find the girl at either location?"

Roldán said, "We go through with the original plan. I meet with them at San Felipe."

Ignacio made a face. "The fort? A bad place. Exposed."

Roldán nodded.

Sam said, "The woman, Ana Iragorri, what's she like?"

"I don't know. It's so long ago that I knew her."

"Did she know you? Will she expect you to follow instructions? Or will she expect something tricky?

"Again, I don't know."

"She's not in this alone," I said. "She's working with some nasty professionals."

Ignacio spoke to Roldán. "You have a reputation, no? As a rebel? A man with a certain flair?"

Whether Sam had told him, or whether he'd recognized Roldán from photographs, I didn't know. Roldán seemed unfazed.

"They know you're coming to the city," Ignacio continued. "They might have followed you from the airport."

"We didn't fly commercial," Roldán said.

Ignacio nodded sagely, as if that were only to be expected. Roldán said, "But you're right. Even the landing strip where we landed, to the south, could be watched. This woman, if she's who I think she is, knows many of my old hideouts."

"Old friends make the worst enemies," Ignacio said. "And people talk. Maybe it would soothe this woman and her friends if you seem to be doing what you should be doing, if you act the part of a man who's going to pay the ransom without making any trouble."

"What do you have in mind?"

Before Ignacio could reply, I said, "Wouldn't they expect you to go to San Felipe, to check out the terrain in advance?"

Roldán nodded as he chewed. "It's something I would do."

I cast my eyes at the opposite end of the table. Luis, the slender one, stood to let Felicia pass. He seemed around my height, but the light was dim, the air hazy with smoke and steam. His droopy mustache obscured the shape of his mouth.

Felicia slid into her seat. "Anything left to eat? The landlady is unhappy she can't show me the flat. She says it's being painted."

I said, "You don't believe her."

The woman shook her head. "She hesitated too long. Then she said she'd be happy to show me a flat in the building next door, one that resembles the flat for rent almost exactly. I have an appointment tomorrow morning at nine."

Ignacio said, "You hit it off with her?"

Felicia took a neat bite of fish. "She likes to talk. She said the building used to be part of a small convent, very private and quiet."

"If it was a convent, there'll be public plans, blueprints." Silas, who'd been quiet until now, added, "When we passed, there was no sign of painters, no van, no ladders."

"We'll find Raffi another girlfriend for the ride to the farm," Ignacio said. "Felicia should keep the appointment with the landlady."

Rafael said, "Fine; I know lots of bitchy women to take her place."

I said, "We'll need to know everything about the place they're holding her. Every entrance, every exit. Who lives there, who visits. Who goes in, who goes out."

"Don't worry, *chica*," Ignacio said. "We know this kind of work. Silas and Luis are experts."

I said, "Not Luis. Can you handle the apartment with Silas and Felicia? Or find more people?"

Luis gave me a lazy grin. "You don't like the way I look?"

"How tall are you?"

He told me in meters. I had to do the conversion.

Then I asked Roldán when the fort opened to the public in the morning.

CHAPTER 37

"THE MAN WITH binoculars on the south tower. No, don't look." Roldán came to a halt in the center of the walkway between two of the fort's high stone towers, full in the blaze of the glaring sun.

I wasn't tempted to look; I'd noticed the man five minutes ago. I sipped bottled water, savoring its coolness. The sip was celebratory, almost a toast; so far, so good. If it was logical that we'd check out San Felipe, the site of the ransom-for-prisoner exchange, in advance, it followed that Paolina's kidnappers would post sentries to watch for us.

It was essential they see us.

Roldán had warned that it would be hot, but I'd underestimated the word. The farm near Baranquilla had been hot. The city, at night, had been hot. The bedroom, generously ceded to Sam and me, in the bright yellow house where we'd all spent the night, had been hot. I almost smiled, remembering the lazy ceiling fan turning overhead, the small white bed, too short, too narrow, wonderfully adequate.

The fort steamed in the relentless sun. The concrete and red brick scorched the soles of my feet through my moccasins. With each breath, the air seared my lungs. Under any other circumstances, I'd have shed my rose-colored ruana, yanked open the top buttons of my white shirt.

Roldán moved into a rare patch of shade.

"You are happy?" he said.

"I will be." Once we get Paolina back. "How much longer?"

"There could be others. Let's give all of them a chance to see us."

"Right. What else have we got to do?"

Roldán cracked a smile. He knew how little I wanted to stand there baking like bread in an oven, how many other tasks loomed. But if this didn't work, it was more than possible that nothing else would.

We inspected the exterior of the strong room in the center of the courtyard. I imagined Spanish troops fighting here, battling with heavy swords and muskets, yielding ground reluctantly, step by bloody step. Soldiers must have dropped dead from the heat.

"Here they lined up the pirates for execution. See the bullet holes in this wall." Roldán didn't seem undone by the heat. "You spent an interesting night?"

I nodded.

"Your man, he seems like a good catch. Gianelli, it's Italian, no?"

"Yes."

"Mafia?"

"Like you're a drug dealer."

Roldán nodded. "I see. There is some complexity, and also I should not be one to call names. Ignacio and the others respect him, but do they fear him? Is he ruthless?"

He used the Spanish word *inhumano;* it gave me pause.

"He'll do what has to be done," I said finally.

"The others, too, seem like good people."

"Good" was not the right word; Ignacio's people seemed qualified. They seemed competent. They were hired guns. How much of what they did they did for money, how much for loyalty, how much for pleasure or any of a thousand other motivations, I had no way of knowing.

"Do you trust them?" I asked.

"Many choices have been made for me. I must trust them, it seems."

The pavement baked in the sun, and sweat trickled down

my back. The more I saw of the Fort of San Felipe, the more essential it seemed to find Paolina before the scheduled trade-off of gold for girl. Ignacio was right; it was a bad place. Exposed. There was no area out of sight of the battlements, no shelter from guards who could easily be stationed there. It would be like conducting business in a prison exercise yard, under constant armed watch. Roldán would walk in, but not out. And Paolina—

I remembered Roldán's description of Navas's capture by the army, his wife and baby son killed before his eyes. I had no faith in the supposed compassion of women. It was possible this Ana wanted Roldán to undergo the same torment she imagined her lover had experienced before his capture.

"Where are they more likely to keep her, the farm or the apartment?" I asked.

He shrugged.

"If you had to guess."

"The apartment is closer to the fort. That area, the part of the city called San Diego, is one where people come and go, eating in the restaurants, drinking in the bars."

"Either way, we'll have to move tonight."

"Maybe you should stay out of it. You're not unnoticeable, with that hair and—"

"I'm being deliberately noticeable, Roldán, that's why you're talking about it. Trust me, I've worked undercover before. Wait till you see me as a man."

"I look forward to it." He was fairly flamboyant in appearance as well, his red shirt tucked neatly into black pants, his sombrero made of dyed straw, white with a red and yellow pattern around the brim. "More though," he went on, "I'd like to see you as a woman."

"A woman engaged to be married."

"That is not what I meant. Truly, I expected you to weep when you saw this man, to weaken somehow, to cede authority to him."

"After we rescue Paolina, after she's safe, I'll cry for a week."

He nodded.

"What about you?" I asked.

"Me? I would like very much . . ." His voice slowed and stopped.

"What?"

"I would like to walk the mountain with my child. I would like to show her the lost city, the *nihue* where I study, the snow on the mountaintop, and the mist."

She'd go in a flash, at the faintest hint of an invitation, I thought. To walk with her father, listen to the eerie music of the Kogi pipes. I felt a stab of jealousy.

"But we will see," Roldán said. "This man, Gianelli, he is fond of my daughter?"

"Yes."

"He has been a father to her?"

"Often." And in the future, I thought, he'd be more of one.

Not that Sam and I had spent the night discussing the future. The whole situation, the strange band of hired guns, the unfamiliar accommodations, the high level of stress, were too much for sustained conversation. The comfort of Sam was that we didn't need to talk, that I could rest my head on his shoulder and sleep in his arms.

We were staying in the most unlikely of hideouts, a bright yellow house with green shutters and balconies dripping with flowers. Tucked between a monastery and a school, it bore no resemblance to the kind of stripped-down shelter where Mob families "go to the mattresses" in Hollywood movies. A couple of the rooms had extra cots set up next to sofas, but on the whole, it looked like a normal house, with a stocked kitchen, and framed pictures on the walls. The caretaker was a gray-haired granny who'd once been a skilled smuggler, according to Ignacio. She seemed, at any rate, unfazed by Ignacio's personnel or "equipment," which included revolvers, RPGs, assault rifles, Kevlar vests, cell phones, and walkie-talkies.

I'd spoken to Gloria on one of the cells early this morning. She said Roz had so far been unable to make a connection between Mark Bracken or any high mucky-muck at BrackenCorp, and gold. She was now working on GSC. It was a nagging problem, the gold. Why risk a lucrative government contract for gold, for this particular gold, which couldn't be sold to a museum? If the Colombian government found out and alerted the U.S. government, there'd be hell to pay.

Sam had listened in on the call. He'd asked me not to mention his whereabouts to Gloria.

"The woman with the glasses," I said to Roldán, "reading the guidebook." She was keeping close track of us, using a small mirror tucked into her guidebook. The sun had flashed off the shiner once too often.

"Good," Roldán said. "In three minutes, we head inside."

I hoped our trackers were suffering from the heat as much as I was. Felicia would be chatting with the landlady by now. Rafael and his lady friend would be well on their way to the country farm.

The people at the farm, I thought, should admit illicit lovers whose car had broken down. The landlady should speak freely to a prospective tenant. Whether any of Ignacio's people thought they recognized Roldán, whether anyone decided to share the suspicion, remained a niggling worry on top of other niggling worries, like why Sam hadn't wanted Gloria to know he was in Cartagena.

"Can we go in now?" My water bottle was half empty. My lips were parched, but I couldn't afford to touch another drop.

Roldán nodded.

Luis and Sam had entered the fort an hour before us. The skills of the Kogi, levitation and telepathy, might be closed to us, but deception was available. I sucked in a breath. The lowest level of the fort had once been used to store dynamite. Troops stationed to guard it during battle had strict orders to touch off the fuse if all was lost, to blow the castle to kingdom come rather than let it be taken by the enemy.

We had some dynamite of our own waiting in the easternmost gallery.

Roldán led the way, moving with the sure steps that had made quick work of steep Tayrona staircases. I followed, thinking my lungs might burst into flame. I'd cherished the idea that the interior of the fort would be cool. The difference wasn't immediate, but three levels down, it cooled perceptibly. The air was absolutely still.

"This way." Roldán left the main corridor and entered a stone passage marked EMPLOYEES ONLY. We were almost sprinting. We didn't want our upstairs watchers to miss us, to feel it necessary to mount a search.

"Two rights, then a left," Roldán murmured. I'd already stripped off my ruana. I draped it over my left arm. With my right hand, I removed a pre-moistened cloth from my pocket. As we ran, I scrubbed my face clean of makeup.

Sam and Luis were waiting in the appointed place. Luis wasn't quite as tall as I was, but his build would pass, disguised under the ruana. When I'd selected him as my double, he'd taken some ribbing. He'd also grieved the sacrifice of his mustache.

Sam hadn't wanted his role as Roldán's double either, but no one else fit the part half as well.

I traded the ruana for the phony mustache Luis had worn into the fort. I poured the remainder of the bottled water over my head, quickly brushed my wet hair into a knot, securing it with a scrunchy and bobby pins. I topped it with Luis's hat, a shallow straw job in stripes of black and beige. Roldán and Sam traded shirts, hats, and sunglasses.

"Check," Sam said urgently. Each of us regarded our twin, our doppelganger.

"Nice mustache," Sam told me.

I fluffed Luis's wig, the most difficult item to obtain and, I thought, the diciest. I'd styled my hair in close imitation, but the shade wasn't quite true. I wondered whether Luis had done his own makeup.

"Not bad," I said.

"Luis," Roldán said. "Come, let's leave the lovebirds together for a moment, no?" He motioned to the thin man in the rose ruana, and they walked ten, twenty steps, into a low side passage.

"Be careful." I put my arms around Sam and held him close. He kissed me.

"Hey," he murmured in my ear. "I'm always careful. What about you?"

We clung to each other in spite of the heat. I thought I heard a noise behind me.

I turned and called to Roldán. "Now?"

"Take another minute, if you like," he said.

At the time, I thought it was kindness.

CHAPTER 38

WHEN ROLDÁN AND I finally emerged from the steaming fort a full hour after the departure of our doubles, none of the three watchers we'd identified remained in place. Both our departure from San Felipe and our return to the yellow house seemed to go unremarked, and the empty streets of Cartagena, deserted in the afternoon heat, made it easy to tag a follower. Their emptiness made sense; it was too hot to breathe. As soon as we got inside, I ripped off Luis's shirt, peeling down to a tank top, and tried to stick my head under the faucet of the sink in the corner. The phony mustache came off easily.

Hook-nosed Rafael was seated on the couch, drinking a beer. "They took the bait, eh?"

Roldán nodded.

"I'm sure Luis looked fetching," Rafael said.

If the watchers had followed Sam and Luis, we'd succeeded in thinning the opposition troops. I patted my dripping face with a crumpled paper towel, and listened carefully as Rafael continued speaking. It didn't matter whether the substitution at the fort had fooled anyone if Ignacio's troops hadn't found Paolina.

Rafael was telling Roldán that he'd accompanied a woman named Maria Inez to the farm owned by Ana's family. They'd borrowed Maria Inez's brother's battered truck instead of hiring a rental.

He said, "A woman answered the door. Maybe sixty years old, little bitty bun on the top of her head. Señora Octavia, the maid called her. She let me use the phone right away, offered us a cup of coffee, had no problem with me going upstairs to use the bathroom. If she's keeping any kidnapped kids in the house, she's one cool ice queen."

"Outbuildings?" I thought Rafael sounded too jaunty; I wasn't sure he'd done a thorough job.

"A barn, a gardener's shed, a storage shed near a field."

"You checked them all?"

"I didn't ask her to let me inspect the grounds with a microscope."

I glared at him.

"Look, Maria Inez and I had breakdowns at neighboring farms, too. None of the neighbors mentioned any goings and comings, any low-flying planes or trucks or extra cars. It's an isolated district; somebody would have noticed something, said something. If not to me, to Maria Inez; she looks as harmless as a little poodle dog. Ask Ignacio when he gets back. She notices things, Maria Inez."

That left the apartment house. I was all for going out to get a firsthand look at it, but Roldán recommended caution. He recommended waiting for Ignacio, Felicia, and Silas.

Fine for him, I thought, watching him stare off into space. Communing with his *mamas*, no doubt, speaking without words. It would have been a good time to take up smoking again. I didn't want a beer. I was antsy enough that I went into the kitchen and washed dishes. Roz would have fainted if she'd seen me. Sam, too.

I was uneasy about him, and I tried to ignore the feeling. It was hard to do it, but the fact of the matter was I hadn't asked him to come. I needed to treat him the way I wanted him to treat me, as a pro working a job. Still, I was overly conscious of the telephone on the wall, as though it had swelled to three times its size. He or Luis should call soon, give us the all-clear. If everything went according to plan.

A cup slipped out of my sudsy hands and rattled into the sink. It didn't break.

Roldán, it seemed, still had a few trusted confederates at the farm with the bumpy landing strip, the one at which our plane had landed. That was where Luis and Sam were leading the watchers from the fort, to be lured inside, taken, and questioned.

I scrubbed plates and glassware, but the phone stayed silent. Rafael came in and started emptying the refrigerator. We should eat, he said, removing take-out containers of rice and fish, leftovers from last night's meal. He heaped food on the just-washed plates and ferried them out to the low coffee table in the big room.

A key turned loudly in the lock. Voices. The others had returned, and I was in the big room, shaking water off my hands, before they had time to close the door, much less sit down.

"The apartment building? Is she there?"

Ignacio bared his teeth. "It looks promising."

I felt like a spring was tightening in my gut.

"There's a woman there. Fairly young, with long hair. And a young man."

"Did you show the photos around?"

"Didn't want to risk it. A casual inquiry is one thing, a photo another. You show photos, you're a cop."

Roldán said, "Let them eat."

Someone offered me a plate. Rafael punched the button on the CD player, and a Latin beat filled the air. I wondered if chewing coca leaves had killed my appetite forever.

Felicia said, "I saw the man in the photo. He went for a quick walk, bought a pack of cigarettes. He didn't make contact with anyone besides the cigarette vendor. I didn't see the woman or the girl. You can't see inside the apartment. The grating blocks the balcony."

I started shoveling food down because everyone else was eating, because if the man in the photo was nearby, I'd need the energy. As we ate, one plaintive song melded into another over tinny speakers.

Ignacio picked up the thread. "There's definitely a woman. I spoke to a deliveryman. I saw him leaving. I told him I was interested in a job like his and did he make good tips? For instance, the man in the apartment building, what did he give? He corrected me, said the woman was cheap, paid good money for good whiskey, but not much left over for the man who climbed the steps."

I wondered why the man who'd gone for cigarettes didn't buy whiskey as well. Was the woman a secret drinker? "Climbed the steps" meant delivery to someone other than the ground-floor landlady. It meant there was no elevator.

"How often does he deliver?" I asked.

Ignacio shrugged. "I didn't want to question him too closely. You give the impression you're interested, he'll want to know why. Here, everyone is suspicious."

Felicia said, "No one comes to clean. That's unusual."

Not so unusual if you're keeping a prisoner in your apartment, I thought. Was it just Ana, the man in the photo, and Paolina in the apartment? Were there other guards?

"What about food?" I put my barely touched plate down.

Felicia said, "The woman shops occasionally."

"How much does she buy? How often?"

She consulted a small notebook. "Two days ago she bought a kilo of rice, a half kilo of beans, a dozen oranges, some mangoes. If I had more time, I could find a butcher shop, a fish market, get a better idea of how many people she feeds."

The problem was we didn't have more time. With the swap set for San Felipe tomorrow, we had to act tonight.

I stared at my wristwatch. Why didn't Sam phone?

Ignacio poured from an open bottle of Chilean wine. "On the second floor, the window in the back is shut, the curtains drawn. If I were in that room, I'd keep the window open."

"It's a bedroom?"

Felicia said, "In the apartment next door, yes."

She carefully described the layout of the apartment she'd viewed, diagramming the rooms on a napkin: a front room leading into a dining area, a hallway to the side of the small kitchen, two bedrooms, a single bath. "The landlady claims it's identical to the flat next door. The floors are old and wooden, very creaky."

"Are there balconies in back as well as in front?"

"No."

The rear windows on the second and third floors were built out some forty-five or fifty centimeters from the exterior wall and grated on the front and sides, an echo of the balconies, like deep extended window boxes.

Forty-five centimeters; maybe eighteen inches, I thought.

"They're open at the top," she said.

"Three apartments in the target building," Ignacio summarized. "The girl could be in the second-floor flat with the two people in the photos. She could be in the third-floor flat with any number of guards. The ground-floor apartment is the landlady."

Felicia's voice was apologetic. "She likes to talk, but not about her tenants. She said nothing about them even in response to the most innocently leading questions. She's in her forties, maybe fifty. She's lived there over twenty years. Raised four kids there. Her youngest still lives with her, a boy of eighteen who comes home drunk in the middle of the night. She doesn't know what to do with him."

Could be a problem if he wandered in at the wrong moment. On the other hand, the second-floor tenants were probably used to a certain amount of unpredictable noise in the middle of the night. The setup was tempting. I asked Ignacio what he thought about a night raid.

Within seconds the low table was cleared of food, Ignacio rolled out a set of blueprints, and I breathed a sigh of relief; I didn't relish the idea of participating in a raid based on notes doodled on bar napkins.

Ignacio had the plans of the old convent, before its massive square space had been separated into four apartment buildings and its courtyard turned into part of a service alley. Now two of the apartment buildings faced one street, two the next parallel street. Interior access from one building to the other no longer existed, but the buildings were joined in pairs, like row houses in Boston's South End.

Why didn't Sam call? The more I drank, the more I sweated. I switched from wine to water. The ceiling fan turned lazily overhead and Rafael played a second CD.

"Well?" Ignacio said. "What do you think?"

Roldán said, "Anything else, any trivial detail? You didn't, for instance, see a limping man in the neighborhood?"

The limping man again. I shot him a glance, but he stared blankly at the wall.

"No," Felicia said. "But— It's nothing, really."

"Please, what were you going to say?"

"The music made me remember." She nodded at the speakers. "I was standing in what used to be the convent courtyard. Now, it's just garbage bins, a clothesline, weeds. You can see where the trees were cut down, where the patio used to be. There was a noise, not like someone hammering, more like someone beating a drum, except not a drum, maybe— I don't know."

A girl, alone and scared, sketching a beat on the arm of a chair, on the top of a table. I felt a flicker of certainty spread into a flame. *She was there.*

"This is important?" Roldán saw the look on my face.

"She's in a room overlooking the alley." The flame gave off a steady glow, a welcoming hearth on a winter night glimpsed from a snowy street corner. "She can't open the window, but she can move her hands."

While Ignacio beamed and Rafael lifted his glass in a silent toast, I focused on the music, closing my eyes.

"I can tell her we're coming to get her," I said slowly.

"Through telepathy, like my friends on the mountain?" Roldán's voice held no trace of sarcasm.

"No," I said. "Listen." *Music,* I thought; I can speak to her in music. I opened my mouth to explain and the phone rang.

Ignacio was closest, but Roldán grabbed the phone. He listened and grunted and I watched his eyes. When he smiled, I started breathing again.

Things had gone well at the farmhouse. Nothing more than a skirmish, with no shots fired. And one of the watchers had readily turned informer for cash: Paolina was in the second-floor apartment, the back room.

Sam and Luis would return soon.

PAOLINA

DAY WAS DISTINGUISHED from night by the glow behind the heavy window shade. The shade was taped to the inner sash; impossible to see even a slice of scenery on either side. The valance at the top cut off the view and the bottom slit was narrow, less than an eighth of an inch. If she could only approach and glue her eye to the slit, she could see what lay beyond.

She worked her left hand against the rope, circling it, pulling it, stretching it. Sometimes the rope gave the illusion of loosening, but then the tension seemed the same as it had always been. It was all she could do, maneuver her left hand. The right, they untied occasionally so she could eat; when they tied it again, it was always belt tight. Since her left hand stayed bound to the chair, no one bothered to check the rope.

If she could see outside, it wouldn't be so bad, she decided. If she could see stars and trees and sky instead of the cracked white of four walls and the dusty gray of the ceiling. The absence of color had become an ache. Not as bad as the pain at the corners of her mouth where the gag bit her cheeks, but the constant ache of deprivation.

Light and dark were the sole shades and rhythms of her days. Dawn brought bread on a wooden tray, a ceramic jug with thin milk, a hunk of bread, sometimes a piece of pale soft cheese. Ana brought the bread because Jorge was no longer allowed to enter her room alone, and the new man, the Voice, the limping man, was nobody's servant.

She'd been wrong about the pecking order. The new man was the boss, but Jorge, who'd seemed to be next in command, had sunk to the bottom of the heap. Ana had become her protector, her tigress. Paolina smiled at Ana with her eyes. Ana had saved her from Jorge's rough abuse.

She wouldn't have made it on the street. She knew that now. Ana told her what happened to girls on the street, how they were gang-raped and humbled, forced to accept the strongest protector so other boys and men would be scared away. And then that "protector" would put the girl out on the street, turn out to be nothing but a pimp. Her insistence that she was different, that she could play the drums and earn her bread, had provoked only Ana's bitter laughter.

Music won't save you, girl. Nothing saves you from men but age and ugliness, and even then, most men will take what they can get.

Sometimes she thought Ana hated her, and then sometimes she thought Ana loved her. It was hard to figure; it was like there were two women fighting within the same body. The image amused her for a moment as the slow day went by in scorching heat. She wondered whether the limping man was awake.

She'd seen him only once, but she knew him by his cadence. Sam's occasional limp was nothing compared to his. When Sam was tired, if you beat out his stride, he had a slight unevenness to his gait. The limping man dragged his right leg, step drag, step drag. The step was almost a giant step, as though he'd gotten fed up with the slowness of his pace, as though he resented the draggy leg for slowing him down. Sometimes there was a third noise, the sharp beat of a cane. Then his step went step, tap, drag; step, tap, drag.

Ana was afraid of him, afraid of his whistling cane. If Ana was afraid of him, Ana, who'd taken Jorge by the neck, shaken him like a cat, and thrown him across the room, beating him with her fists till he begged for mercy and crawled away, the limping man was someone to fear. He was bald as an egg, and his eyes, when he didn't wear tinted glasses, were gray like old stones. His face was oddly tight, shiny and so pale around the ears that she wondered whether he usually wore a wig.

The devil come back from hell, Ana said when she'd asked who he was. The devil come from hell. The devil was walking in the next room. Step drag, step drag. He paced like an animal trapped in a cage, but she was the one who was trapped, tied to a chair, waiting.

She thought of the place as a house but there was no reason behind the assumption. She'd never viewed it from the outside, never seen another room. She'd been blindfolded when brought here, and often she was blindfolded again, although less now than when Jorge made her touch him.

Maybe she was in hell already. It was hot enough. She couldn't tell if they were drugging her anymore. She felt lightheaded all the time and her stomach felt strange, as though it had shut down like an overheated engine. Maybe she was hibernating, except that was something bears did in winter not something girls did in heat and captivity.

Wriggle the wrist, turn it, bend it. Was the rope a little looser this morning? Maybe the moist hot air made it seem more pliable than it was. Maybe it shrank while she dozed fitfully in the chair. She thought about the movie, the black and white one Carlotta liked, with the guy in prison tossing a tennis ball against the wall. How lucky he was to have a tennis ball. That would be luxury. Sometimes she ran old TV shows in her head and once she found herself doing algebra problems, can you believe it, algebra which she hated, really, and envying friends at school, envying the everyday routines of their lives, the scheduled expectedness. Marta must think she was dead.

The noise in the next room built gradually but she didn't notice until it turned into an argument. Alternating voices: man and woman. Ana, but not Jorge. The other voice was the Voice, unmechanized now, but cold and level, even in anger. It said something about a man, that the other man *had no in-*

tention of showing up. The voice was icy and unfeeling, and she thought: the limping man.

"Bullshit." That was Ana, brave Ana, to defy that chilly voice.

"The honorable bandit. Bullshit is right. How can you buy that, believe it after what he—"

"He was good to me."

Paolina flinched when she heard the sound, skin against skin, a slap not a punch.

"What do I care what you think?" The cold voice again, menacing as a snake poised to strike. "If he brings the gold, fine, we'll swap. But if he tries something, I warn you: Don't cross me."

The voices continued, angry and urgent, but low. She could no longer make out words. She twisted her wrist, wrenching it against the chair. Was the rope any looser?

She'd begged Ana to let her go, begged with her eyes, begged with her mouth when she was ungagged. Sometimes the woman sat with her in the dark and patted her hair. The first time, Paolina was sure Ana would untie her. Once, the woman sang her a Colombian lullaby, and it was so close to a tune Marta used to sing that Paolina thought she might die of sadness and regret. She'd begged Ana to bring her a knife.

"Just leave it near me. You don't have to cut me loose. If he asks, you can say you didn't help me. Ana, please."

When I try again, when I plead for help again, I'll call her mama. That's what she wants. Paolina wasn't sure how she knew it, but the woman's need was as clear as if she'd read it in a book, seen it flashed across a movie screen.

The light was fading. Sometimes with the fading light came faint music, too persistent to come from the radios of passing cars. In her imagination, there were strolling musicians, like the mariachi bands she'd seen in Bogotá. She regretted the lost opportunity to play with the band in the square. Did the accordion boy wonder where she'd gone; did he miss the beat? She thought about the strange songs, the melodies she'd never learned, the beats she could have played, and sometimes it seemed that she heard them, either in the distance or in the depths of herself, in her bones. The blindfold was terrible, the gag disgusting, but if they wanted to torture her, earplugs would have been worse. To never hear music was unthinkable pain.

Her arms were bound to the wooden chair, but her hands were free to tap a beat. She never got too loud for fear they might hear her, but sometimes she got carried away. When she could hear the whole band in her head, it made the time pass, the unbearable time, with what, what at the end of time? What if this was the end of time? What if she would wake, but not wake, every morning in this chair and sleep, but not sleep, every night in this chair? What if this was hell, this hot smelly room? What if the devil had come back from hell?

She tapped the arm of the chair and wondered what they were waiting for, who they were waiting for. Was the "he" who might or might not show up her father? Was she there, tethered like a goat in a folktale, tied to a tree to lure Roldán, the lion, to his death? Would her father come for her? Why should he? What was she to him? What was he to her? How can you be the child of a man you've never met? If she looked in his eyes would she see her own reflection? If he looked in her eyes would he see his future?

The limping man was waiting for gold. The idea of gold made her grieve her little statue. If she'd remembered Julio, maybe everything would have turned out differently. She stopped herself quickly, because "if" was the forbidden game. There were too many ifs. If she'd done this differently, if she'd done that differently. If she hadn't gotten into the white van . . .

Her hand beat on the arm of the chair, drowning the ifs in the beat. Drowning them, drowning them, blocking the thoughts, so she had no idea how long she'd been drumming or how long she'd been conscious of the music.

It was closer than usual. Louder, then louder still. Moving closer? An accordion, a guitar, a thumpety-thump bass. She wove a beat around the strum of the guitar, a secondary syncopated beat, and felt disappointed when they ended the song, then shocked into silence, frozen, as she recognized the whistled fragment.

What was it? Could it—

It sounded again, not a part of the music that had gone before, a whistled phrase, a familiar melody, a key that turned a lock in her memory. Where was it, the little Plexiglas music box Carlotta had given her as a child? Where had she put it? She tried to pucker her lips, to echo the plaintive musical phrase, and she was seven years old, playing hide-and-seek, crouched underneath the stairs. What was that music doing *here,* here in hell?

She wriggled her left wrist frantically. Maybe it was looser, maybe not. She stretched her spine, wriggled and bent, attacking the ropes that bound her left arm to the chair with her teeth, working as though her life depended on it.

CHAPTER 39

EDGY. **TOO ADRENALINE-WRACKED** to stand still, I kicked a pebble across the narrow street. It skittered into the alley while I filled my lungs with humid night air.

Would she hear?

It didn't occur to me that she might not remember. It was whether or not she'd hear that worried me, snatching my breath so the final notes wavered eerily, like a music box winding down. I whistled the phrase again; I couldn't risk more than three repetitions. As far as Roldán knew, Ana had spent little time in the States. The song was obscure; probably most U.S. natives couldn't identify it, but for all I knew one of Paolina's captors was a blues freak. It was a risk I'd decided to take. To have the best chance to escape unharmed, she needed to be prepared, to know rescue was imminent, to stay alert and keep her head down. The song comforted me. If she heard it, she'd know I was near. Hope might give her a jolt of needed energy.

I waited a beat after the third repetition, signaling the strolling band to silence, but there was no audible response. What had I expected? That she'd burst out of the second-floor window like Superman? I sketched a farewell to the accordion player and stepped quickly around the corner. The musicians moved on, laughing and joking. They were part of the scenery here. For a price, they'd return on cue.

I waited eight minutes, then walked briskly through the

service alley to the rear door of the apartment house next door to the target building, and rapped on the door, two loud, two soft. In the tiny vestibule, I handed the waiting Felicia my straw hat. She nodded and gave a thumbs-up. I ascended the steps to the third floor.

The code there was the same, two and two, but softer because we didn't want the tenants of the second-floor flat calling the cops to discuss the strange noises in the vacant apartment above. Rafael opened the door, wearing a paint-splattered jumpsuit and a white painter's hat. Roldán was there, too, also in painter's garb, his eyes glittering like a pirate's.

"Sam and Luis?" I said. "They're here? They're ready?"

"No."

"They called?"

"No."

"How long can we wait?"

"We don't wait."

"What's going on?" Too late, I made the connections: Roldán, more than eager for Sam to impersonate him; Roldán giving Sam and me our moment of privacy in the depths of the fort, while he snatched a few private words with Luis.

"Only the slightest of variations, *chica*. Only what had to be done. This man of yours will not rescue my child. He is not her father. I am her father and the task is mine."

"Where is he? *What did you do?*"

"The play is the same, but the cast of characters will be different. Luis will keep your man occupied for a little while, that is all. He will come to no harm."

"Rafael?" I stared at the hook-nosed man as I spoke his name. He worked for Ignacio and Ignacio supposedly worked for Sam. Luis, as well. But if the watcher at the fort could be so easily bought, why not Luis? Why not Rafael and Luis? Why not anyone?

Rafael shrugged. So much for his allegiance.

"Plato o plomo?" I said.

"Sí." Rafael smiled.

Roldán had been quiet while we'd pored over the blueprints, quiet while we'd made the rescue plans, too quiet when the leading roles had been given to Rafael and me. Rafael and I were both slim and light, climbers by build.

"It's still a two-man job," I said to Roldán. "You and me."

I'd been concerned that Sam wouldn't want me to go. Overprotective Sam would insist that one of Ignacio's hired guns should take the risk, or insist that he, himself, take the risk instead of me. Dammit, I should have been worried about Roldán.

"This time I have made the choice for you. Rafael will accompany me," he said.

"No," I said.

"I will have him tie you up."

"Roldán," I said. "Please."

He raised his eyebrows. "Please? You surprise me again, *gringa*. I thought you would threaten."

"I'll get down on my knees and beg, if that's what you want. Please. This is what I came to Colombia to do. This is what I *can* do. Paolina will have the best chance with the two of us, with those who care for her most. Please. One of us will protect her if anything goes wrong. One to fight. One to protect. *Please*."

He hesitated, compressing his lips before loosening them to speak. "I will be the one to fight."

"Yes." I would have said anything, agreed to anything. "We're wasting time. There isn't time to argue."

"This is a choice you make with your heart?"

"Yes. *Please*."

"I will not have your blood on my hands."

"Same here, Roldán. No blood. We go in, we get her, we leave."

I counted heartbeats till he gave a curt nod.

The pinpoints of light in his eyes made me nervous. He might look like a pirate, but his years on the mountain had made him unpredictable. I was afraid he'd freeze when I needed him most, stop and mutter strange prayers or depend on mystical divination. Rafael and I had practiced together. Rafael was competent.

"Don't worry," Roldán said. "I, too, have practiced. I know what must be done."

We went through the apartment to the back bedroom, the small room facing the alley, the duplicate of the room where Paolina was held captive. I went directly to the window and studied it with the same care I'd given its exterior earlier via binoculars. The glass was old and specked with dirt. When I lifted the iron hook that fastened the casement, both sides of the window swung inward on oiled hinges. Slowly I leaned out into the grated window box. The extension of the window proper jutted out from the wall of the house, eighteen, possibly twenty inches.

"I tested it," Roldán said. "It will hold."

"The balconies might not." Rafael and I had been chosen, among other reasons, because we were lightest.

"Then we will fall," Roldán said.

I hoped he'd spare me the one about how he'd die tonight if tonight was his time to die. I patted the fanny pack I'd borrowed from Felicia. Inside, a knob of putty, a glass cutter, a strip of celluloid, a can of spray lubricant, the Beretta from the mountaintop. If Sam had been there to back me, I'd have pulled the gun on Roldán.

The hook-and-eye was nothing; a simple strip of celluloid would disengage it. It wasn't designed to withstand robbers; the stout wooden grating on the window box supposedly eliminated that hazard. The window box was like a cage, but the cage, while strong, was vulnerable from above.

Roldán stripped off his jumpsuit. Underneath, he wore black; I wore black as well.

"You're wearing the vest?" he said.

I nodded. Earlier I'd voted against the Kevlar; it seemed to me we had surprise or we had nothing. I was tempted to shed the vest here and now. Any weight was a killer in this heat.

"And you?"

"Take this and chew," he said.

The memory of the stamina and clarity the drug had granted me on the mountain defeated any purist scruples. If I'd thought of it earlier, I'd have requested the coca. Even the army provides drugs to keep pilots awake during long flights. Anything for an edge.

I followed Roldán through the apartment to the front of the building where Rafael stood guard near the open door to the balcony. I inspected the lock while Roldán and Rafael synchronized watches and set cell phones to vibrate. The walkie-talkie batteries had already been checked and pronounced good.

Eyes glittering, Roldán placed a hand on my shoulder. "Take this for luck."

I knew it by touch: the gold birdman.

"Whatever happens, return it to her."

He passed through the balcony door as he spoke, effectively ending any conversation since the balcony was so tiny only one of us could fit at a time. The spindly ladder was sharply angled; insufficient room for good footing. The vine-covered grating made the space feel even more claustrophobic. I waited while Roldán's bare feet disappeared up the rungs. It was possible his grim smile was his reaction to tension, possible that this man who considered revolution a fiesta was simply rejoicing in the prospect of danger, but his demeanor made me wary.

A cloud hid the sliver of moon. I waited for its faint light to return before advancing from the first to the second rung. At the top, Roldán extended a hand to help me over the narrow cresting that rimmed the roof. Between us, we hauled the ladder up and carried it across to the roof of the next building. It was an easy journey, even with the ladder; no gap between the two flat roofs. Too easy, I thought.

Dangling the ladder over the cresting and planting its cloth-swaddled feet onto the balcony of the third-floor apartment below made up for it. My hands were damp with sweat. If the ladder slipped, it was over. If we made too much noise, it was over.

"We come from above," Roldán whispered, "like the helicopter."

Descending first, I went to work on the lock. The turncoat at the farmhouse had sworn the third floor was empty, a buffer zone, an armory where no one slept. Soon, I'd find out if he'd lied.

I was having trouble seeing the lock. Ignacio had come up with two pairs of old Nighthawk goggles, but they were heavy, and awkward; I'd voted against them. Roldán aimed the beam of a tiny flashlight at the doorjamb.

The hard thing about locks is time. As I crouched on the third-floor balcony, not quite in full view of the street due to the crosshatched grating, the plants, and the vines, it stood still. I loided one lock. The next one resisted; my fingers ached for the familiar steel of my own picks. Finally, giving up on subtlety, I sliced a circle in the door with the cutter and laid a fold of cloth across it, the same cloth we'd used to swaddle the legs of the ladder. Then I tapped Roldán's shoulder and raised a fist to my mouth. He lifted his cell phone, punched numbers, hung up. We waited three long minutes for the hired musicians to return.

The landlady's first name was Dolores, and I could hear them call to her, laughing and strumming. They began the serenade with a mournful love song, and I gave the circle a sharp light punch. Shards of glass tinkled to the ground like thunder.

Sticking my shielded hand through the hole, I flipped the reluctant lever. I sprayed the track of the sliding door with lubricant. Roldán eased it open. The musicians played.

The memory of the creaky floors in the apartment next door held me momentarily motionless. I raised a hand and pointed at my chest to indicate that I'd go first. I was lighter than Roldán; he was to follow in my footsteps. I edged over to the left-hand wall: creaky floors creak less if you stick closely to the wall.

I'd seen Roldán walk the narrowest of suspension bridges. His balance was as good as mine was, if not better. I moved slowly and as he echoed my steps, I hoped the landlady was hanging out her doorway along with her drunken son, enjoying the serenade. I hoped the inhabitants of the second-floor flat were listening to the music from their front balcony, inhaling the fragrant night air instead of paying attention to sounds overhead.

A song ended with a flourish and another began with a lilting guitar. From the building across the street, a man's voice called out, asking how much he'd need to pay the band to go away and leave him in peace, but it was a good-natured voice, low and cheerful. One song seemed endless; another ended as soon as it began. Time, in the long hallway, expanded and contracted while I carefully positioned my feet. In five minutes or five hours, Roldán and I progressed to the room over the back bedroom, and I muttered a prayer that the rear window boxes would be precisely the same design, that they would hold, that Paolina was awake in the room beneath us, alerted by the notes of "Teddy Bears' Picnic."

Lift the hook from the eye; ease the window open; lean into the still hot air. I edged onto the sill, and the floor held. I backed out and Roldán uncoiled the rope around his waist. He entered the tiny box while I waited in the bedroom. I was the better locksmith, but Rafael knew knots. I could only hope Roldán knew them as well. I felt calm and strong. I didn't know how much of that to attribute to the coca and how much to the relief of finally doing something, taking action after too much planning, too much waiting.

Sam was all right; Roldán wouldn't lie about that. The musicians joked and sang. I listened in vain for the rhythmic tap of a hand against a chair. Roldán backed out, nodded me inside the box.

The vines grew more thickly on this grating; I had to shove them aside in order to plant my feet on the crossbars, clamber out and over the top of the enclosure. There was a moment of panic before Roldán shoved the end of the rope into my hand. The grating felt adequate; the knotted rope strong. I braced my feet against the rough stucco of the exterior wall, but my left hand refused to release the rope.

I knew I had to do it, had to move, but my balance seemed precarious, both feet planted, both arms taut. If I slipped I'd be hanging into darkness like a spider on a silken thread. I wished I'd done more rock climbing, played less volleyball, and then I was scrabbling down the side of the building, aware that underneath, the target was small, the opening narrow. If I fell or somehow missed the second-floor window box . . .

There: the top railing, solid underfoot. I shifted and swung inward. When my weight settled on the foundation of the window box, I gave the rope two strong tugs, the signal for Rafael—for Roldán, to descend.

"Don't let go of the rope," I murmured when he was close enough to hear. He nodded. Whether the window box would hold our combined weights was doubtful.

"You made the calls?" I whispered.

He nodded. That was the setup; the strolling musicians were only the first of the night's distractions. Felicia, on his signal, would call the police; Rafael, the ambulance service; Ignacio, the fire department. I shifted my full concentration to the window, but I couldn't see past the heavy shade. Its dark edges were taped to the window frame.

"Break it," Roldán urged.

I shook my head. We were banking on surprise, surprise and the hope that the girl was alone, her guards lured away by a coerced message from their colleagues who'd followed the wrong duo from San Felipe. I wiped my palms on my pants, and pulled the narrow strip of celluloid from my fanny pack while Roldán's gun materialized in his hand. I felt like I might suffocate, with the vines twining so closely in the hot still air and my heart pounding. I slipped the 'loid through the gap between the casing and lifted the iron hook. It moved easily, but if I shoved the window ajar, the shade would fall with a racket.

Roldán eased a folding knife into my waiting right hand. Carefully I thumbed the catch. The eight-inch blade slid easily through the casing and I sliced the shade, center, top right, top left. Then I handed the closed knife to Paolina's father and sucked in a deep breath.

I pushed hard. The moment the windows parted, I had my foot over the sill. The room was dark as the inside of a mine. I lifted my other leg, stepped inside, felt Roldán surge into the room behind me, a noiseless shadow.

And then I was blinded by light.

CHAPTER 40

THE FLASHBEAM WAS blinding as a beacon. I squinted against the glare, fighting the urge to close my eyes, knowing if I did I might never reopen them.

"Bravo." The slow clapping seemed to issue from a single pair of hands. "You did well with the ladder. I could barely hear you. And such splendid music for diversion, too. The whole effect, very nicely done."

Paolina, five feet away, bound to a chair, stared at me in disbelief, as though I were a ghost likely to vanish. Her hair was disheveled, tangled and dirty, yanked back by the cloth that gagged her. Her face was pale and her eyes enormous. Deep scratches running from her right shoulder down the length of her arm made me catch my lip between my teeth to keep from crying out, and I thought, *I'll kill the scum who did that*.

So focused was my gaze she might have been alone in the room. Then the lens widened to include the body of a woman. She lay on the floor near Paolina's chair, her long braid bloody, her ear clotted with blood. A youngish man, the original of the photo Greg Hanson had given me in Miami, blocked the doorway to the hall. He cradled a leveled rifle. The barrel swung restlessly to cover both Roldán and me.

The source of the sardonic applause sat in a throne-like rattan armchair, Miami tan intact, skull shaved. I'd seen him only once before in the flesh, lying on a chaise in a gold wallpapered study. If invisible lightning connected my eyes with Paolina's, a bolt of equal intensity ran from Roldán to the man I knew as Drew Naylor.

Roldán didn't call him Naylor. He called him Angel, with the hissing *g* of the Spanish pronunciation, and if Roldán was taken aback by his "dead" friend's presence, he didn't show it. Maybe he'd seen Angel Navas, alive, in the Kogi dreamworld, in *Aluna*.

As for me, I'd examined the photos accompanying Luisa Cabrera's articles, the ones her devoted uncle had pasted in his scrapbook, searching for an image of the first Señora Navas, the woman, Ana, captioned photos that identified her by name. I'd come across several photos of Navas instead; I'd studied them, recalling Hanson's words about the shape of eye sockets, the distance between eyes, the things that don't change despite plastic surgery.

Why? Because Roldán kept mentioning *the limping man*. Because Roldán had been presumed dead, but was still alive.

I thought: Firefighters on the way, police cars, ambulances. I thought: *Stall*. Had Ignacio's time estimates been realistic?

"I can't say I like your face better this way, Angel." Roldán, utterly calm, leveled his automatic as though it were an extension of his hand. A slender wooden cane leaned against the chair near Naylor's left hand. His right held a Sig-Sauer "American," a nine-shot cannon.

"Do I have to say what will occur if you don't drop the weapon immediately?" Angel's voice was even and cool, and I wondered how I could have mistaken his accent for anything other than Colombian. At his curt nod, the young man's rifle swiveled and Paolina closed her eyes, anticipating the shot.

"Roldán!" I said urgently.

His gun clattered to the floor.

"You, too." Angel nodded at me. "Slowly!"

The Beretta hit the floor like a stone.

"Kick it here. The other one as well. Thank you."

Could we keep Angel talking till the street and the apartment exploded with sirens and ladders and firemen? I glanced at Roldán, and the set mask of his face frightened me.

"You knew he'd be here?" I said.

"You told me."

"How?"

"With his name. Drew Naylor. Drew is Andrew, no? A.N. The same initials as my old friend. And more, the name Naylor."

I shook my head.

"El Martillo, the name they call me, it means the Hammer."

The nail, I thought.

"The limping man," I said.

Roldán's smile made Ignacio's savage grin seem tame. "I never thought my old friend died in jail."

"And I returned the compliment." Angel's chin dipped in a nod. "I never thought you died in the crash."

"He was jailed for life. He died in prison." I kept my eyes on Roldán, hoping he'd communicate, hoping he had some plan beyond determining whether or not it was our night to die.

Roldán said, "That's the story your government gave, the one they leaked to mine. But think about it: Angel knew where the coca fields were. He knew which of your government officials were crooked. He had access to more money than you can count."

Paolina sat frozen in her chair, eyes alert. My ears yearned for sirens.

"You think your country's so incorruptible?" Roldán said. "It's just us banana republics that reek of evil? The profit is so vast; why should it surprise you that millions could corrupt anyone? This futile war on drugs has killed more people, put more people in prison. It's killing justice itself."

"Bravo, again," Angel said. "Such passion. Roldán thinks buying cocaine should be as easy as buying soda pop."

"I think it should all be legal: alcohol, cocaine, even heroin. That doesn't mean I want it for myself, or think it's good for others. Legalize and regulate. Why not? Look at history. Look at Prohibition, the lawlessness that only re-

ceded after the law was changed. The only difference now is
it affects the whole world, Afghanistan to Peru."

Where were the goddamn firemen?

Angel said, "Any time's a good time for politics, no? We
had famous arguments, Roldán, before you turned into a son
of a bitch."

"Is Ana dead?" Roldán asked abruptly.

"What do you care? Another bitch."

Paolina's pupils shifted from Ana's body to me, there and
back again, as though she was trying to speak with her
frightened eyes.

Angel said, "You could never trust her with children. She
tried to help the girl and forgot her loyalty. You two shared
the same kind of loyalty. When it came to the heart, you
went your own ways. You deserted your friends."

Paolina could use her legs, upend her chair. If shots were
fired, I needed her on the floor. I was trying so hard to communicate that message, and listening so hard for approaching sirens, it took me a while to realize the band had stopped
playing.

I spoke to blunt the silence. "You're saying Naylor—
Angel—made a deal with DEA?" What was it Vandenburg
had said the first time I'd questioned him? *Don't bother
threatening Naylor with DEA.*

Angel said, "Why deal with institutions when you can
deal with individuals?"

A single corrupt senior DEA operative, someone with
money and access, could have convinced a prison warden
that the government wanted to make the secret deal. Could
have placed the man in the federal Witness Protection Program. It could have been a ring of corrupt officials, eager to
make quick, dirty money.

"He'd cooperate with the devil himself if it would get me
killed," Roldán said.

"Or jailed for life." Naylor smiled. "ADX Florence, you
know it? The super-max prison in Colorado, where the
Unabomber lives? You two can have long political chats."

Angel Navas hadn't disappeared into small-town Idaho.

He'd lived high in L.A. and Miami. Had he come into contact with Mark Bracken while pinpointing the location of coca fields slated for destruction? Was he a legitimate DEA asset as well as a rogue?

"Now that you've got Roldán," I said into silence, "you can let the girl go."

"Ask the mystic whether they let my wife and son go free."

I didn't need to ask; his wife and son had died.

"We have the gold," I said. "We can deal." The woman was lying on her side, her spine to me, her face to Paolina. Paolina's index finger moved in a yank-the-trigger motion. Could the woman be alive in spite of the pooling blood?

Angel said, "I don't give a shit for the gold."

"The gold was Bracken's idea?"

I studied the blood on the woman's scalp. Possibly her weapon was visible, accessible, closer than the guns I'd kicked to the man I'd known as Naylor.

"I spoke of it casually at first. I led him to it with tales of hidden cities and exotic treasure. I used BrackenCorp to collect what I wanted: my friend, Roldán, and those he cares for. What is gold compared to vengeance?"

Roldán spoke. "How did you know I was alive?"

"I sat in the Yankee prison, bastard, and I dreamed of you. I sat there long enough to break the habit of the drug, and I thought only of you. News of you, bastard, alive or dead, was worth good money. I had time and I spent money. The government, the army, the DAS has nothing like my dossier, because the secret police never knew you the way I did. They never cared about finding you the way I did. After I made my deal and came out, I focused on you. I heard tales of the mystic on the mountain."

"You used the gold as bait," I said.

Angel nodded. "My friends would break the law for treasure, not to hunt down my old friend."

"You didn't know for certain till you saw the film from the second helicopter, the one that got away," Roldán said.

"El Martillo to the rescue. And it wasn't till my DEA friends scared your lawyer, Vandenburg, into cooperating, that I got the best news: Your child was living in the States."

"Bracken will still want the gold." I tried edging an inch forward as I spoke.

"You're so eager to have Jorge shoot you? The gold is nothing to me. I've decided not to go back to the U.S., so what do I care? This plastic surgery is a good thing, but even more, being in Colombia is a good thing. They need me here, Roldán."

The fire department could have driven here from Bogotá by now. The cops could have scaled the building twice. Roldán hadn't given the signal; I was sure of it. I longed for Sam, but I was grateful he was safe, glad he wasn't part of this. My mouth was so dry, I could hardly keep talking.

I said, "You were working with Vandenburg, so you knew about me all along."

"Yes, I enjoyed our little game. Roldán, you know, she blushed when she confessed she was the mother of your unborn child? She was so determined to find you, I thought I might as well let her help. You were lucky; you were absent from the camp. Then I got lucky; when the little one escaped, we recovered her."

"Luisa's dead," Roldán said.

Angel shrugged. "Almost everyone I knew from that time is dead."

"You remember her uncle, Gilberto?"

"Is he dead, too?"

"When we brought Luisa's body home, he asked me to turn myself in, but I told him the army would shoot me on sight."

Angel smiled. "At San Felipe tomorrow, a captain would have been allowed to shoot you while you were escaping. I told him not to count on it; I had faith you'd come here to Ana, especially when someone tried to lure my troops away. The captain will be disappointed."

"Did you know Señor Cabrera is now Minister of Justice?" Roldán's tone was conversational. "He assured me he has an independent group, a highly trained cadre untainted by paramilitaries, unswayed by politics, left or right."

"This we have both heard before," Angel Navas said.

"I didn't find the tracking device in the backpack, but I did find something else. A phone bill from the States, a phone bill with the number of Base Eighteen, a number that proves what many suspect, that the army connects to the AUC and the AUC connects to drugs. I traded that phone bill to the Minister. His cadre flew to Cartagena yesterday. I've been in touch with them all evening. They're here, Angel, all around us. The lure of catching both of us, you know?"

Roldán had spent time alone with Cabrera. I hadn't seen him dress; he could be wearing a wire. I didn't know whether or not he was bluffing.

"You'd never give yourself up," Angel said.

"Things exist on different planes, Angel, so the *mamas* taught me. You enjoyed one level of diversion—the music, the noises overhead. But you didn't see the other level. *We* are the diversion, Angel. In exchange for us, Cabrera will return the gold to the Kogi." Roldán looked straight at Paolina for the first time, and his eyes glittered. "Don't worry, *chica*. No matter what, the heart of the world will be preserved."

He threw himself at Angel as amplified voices, like the thunder of God, reverberated across the room. Before the first word registered, a burst of rifle fire erupted as Jorge shot out the window. Glass shattered. Angel raised his pistol as I dove for Paolina's chair in a flat-out horizontal volleyball desperation dive that knocked her to the ground.

On the floor, I swiveled, using Ana's body to shield me as I shielded Paolina. The woman's motionless right hand partially concealed the blue steel of a gun. I grabbed for it as Angel's pistol sounded and blood bloomed on the back of Roldán's shirt. I thought: No, that can't be, the Kevlar vest.

The rifleman turned and shot Roldán again as I raised Ana's pistol and emptied the clip. He screamed. The barrel of the rifle swung toward me just as the ceiling gave way and troops poured into the room, shaking the walls, boots pounding the floorboards like jungle rain.

It was thunder; it was chaos. All the lights went out. I lay on top of Paolina, expecting to die, and all the time I kept murmuring, "It's all right, baby, it's all right," over and over, even though I knew it wasn't.

A soldier stepped on my leg, on my hip; I didn't move. *It's all right.* My fingers fumbled with unwieldy knots in the rope that bound my sister to the chair. *It's all right.* My hands felt slippery; waves of panic washed over me as I envisioned them covered with Paolina's blood. I called out her name, shouted it, screamed it, but I couldn't hear myself and part of my brain said *stun grenade.* Deaf, almost blind, I willed my hands to move, to find her nose, her mouth, explore her neck. The pulse raced in her throat and I breathed. Troops had a bloody, cursing Naylor in custody. They were hauling him from the room, but no one seemed to believe me when I said his name was really Angel Navas. Maybe they were all deaf, all blind. How long before someone, bought with his millions, let him go?

It's all right. How could it be right when Roldán was bleeding on the floor, asking whether his daughter was alive, begging for coca leaves, blood welling out of his mouth, hands clasped over the terrible wound in his chest?

Instead of Kevlar, beneath his black shirt, he wore the snow-white tunic of the Kogi, his choice, his pain. The smallest thing can make a difference. I opened my mouth to yell for a medic, closed it, clamping it shut, remembering the code of the outlaw. *Better a grave in Colombia than a jail cell in the U.S.* His lips moved in a silent chant as I watched the light die in his glittering eyes. When I ripped the gag from Paolina's mouth, his name was on her lips and she was sobbing. I buried my face in her tangled hair and cradled her like a baby.

CHAPTER 41

THE DEAL WAS multifaceted. Roldán had given Gilberto Cabrera the connection between Miami and the army's Base Eighteen. He'd detailed BrackenCorp's attempt on the Kogi gold. He'd promised him Angel Navas, living proof that extradition to the U.S. was no guarantee of punishment for drug offenses. He'd tossed in Ignacio's gang as a bonus.

He'd protected Sam Gianelli.

In exchange, the sacred gold would return to the Kogi rather than go to any local museum or foreign collector. The Kogi would be left alone, the heart of the world remain a no-fly zone. And Paolina and I would be handed over to the U.S. Embassy, cleaned up, and put on the first available flight to Miami.

In spite of the agreement, if it hadn't been for Sam we might still be in Colombia, shuttled between diplomats forever, questioned and requestioned, separately and together. Once Sam turned up, barriers fell. I don't know if he bribed the members of Cabrera's cadre wholesale or paid off the U.S. Ambassador, but we were at Rafael Nuñez Airport within an hour of his arrival, moving so quickly I never got the chance to ask Señor Cabrera what he intended to do with the information Roldán had provided.

Who knows what story will appear in the newspapers? Or whether any mention will surface at all, with no Luisa Cabrera to relate the facts. "Nothing," as Gabriel Garcia Marquez famously wrote, "ever happens in Colombia."

Aquí, no pasa nada.

It was a tiny airport: two runways baking in the tropical sun, a single dimly lit terminal. Passengers disembarked down metal stairways directly onto the steaming tarmac, stepping off the pavement into an oasis of palm trees and butterflies. The heat was overwhelming, heavy and damp.

Paolina wouldn't look at me. She'd hardly spoken to me. Whenever I tried to break through her glazed silence, she took refuge in the bathroom, or feigned sleep. I read survivor's guilt in her unresponsive eyes, guilt and the glum knowledge of fault. As a seven-year-old, she'd taken full responsibility for the bruises splayed across her cheek, assuring the police that Marta's current boyfriend had hit her only because she'd been bad.

As soon as she saw him, she took shelter in Sam's arms, and I told myself, Don't push. Don't push. She'll talk when she's ready. There's time. There's time. I closed my eyes. They felt heavy with unshed tears. First, I thought, I'll sleep for a week; then, I'll find the energy to cry.

"I'm sorry," Sam said.

We were seated in a small alcove. The plastic chairs felt sticky. A group of vendors clustered just inside the terminal doors. One sold bright silk scarves. A woman spun clouds of cotton candy on tiny wand-like sticks.

"It's all right." How many times had I said it? It seemed as though it was all I was capable of saying. The words had lost their meaning. *It's all right.* An empty chant. A chorus to a song that no longer played.

Every now and then Paolina would peer out from the folds of Sam's shirt, watching the cotton candy lady, fascinated by the spun sugar that seemed to materialize in the round bin before adhering to the stick. Probably the only cotton candy she'd seen before was packaged, sold in plastic bags at Fenway Park.

"Do you think they'll send his body back to the Kogi?" I

said. "Roldán would want to be buried on the mountain." It seemed to make sense when I said it, as logical a response to Sam's "I'm sorry" as anything else. And why would Sam be sorry? None of this was his fault. He'd been locked in one of the farmhouse out-buildings, held prisoner by Luis for hours. Nothing he could have done. Roldán had taken his choice away, stacked the deck, manipulated us all.

"I'll see what I can do," he said. Paolina's face was hidden in his shirt again.

"From Miami? I don't know," I said.

"Paolina, sweetheart," he said. "See the vendor over there? The one selling cotton candy? Please, could you buy three of them for me? Do you think you can carry three?"

Her eyes appeared and I thought: Whenever I see her eyes now I'll think of his eyes, his faraway eyes on the mountaintop, his energy and his bravery, her father's dying eyes. I'll remember the golden hillside and the freezing stream, the City of Stone.

I watched Sam watch her and I thought: He's so good with her. I swallowed and remembered how he'd doubled for Roldán in the fort, doubled for the father she'd lost.

"We'll watch you," he said. "We'll be right here. We won't go away."

For a moment I thought she'd speak, but then her hand snaked out and took the money and she moved. I watched her cross the floor, tentatively at first, as though she was learning to walk again. I thought, *It's all right.* She'll be all right.

"Carlotta, I can look into Roldán's burial from here," Sam said.

"Isn't there room on the plane?"

"Carlotta—"

"What?" Paolina was speaking to the vendor. The woman looked at her with laughing eyes.

"I can't go back," he said.

I suppose people kept moving, coming in and out of the glass doors, but for a moment it seemed as though all motion stopped. There was only Sam and me, in sticky plastic chairs.

I think I started to respond, began two or three unformed sentences and left each one hanging.

"Something happened," he said. "In Las Vegas."

The cotton candy maker was whirling the pink stuff onto a stick. At Fenway, it came in different colors, pink, blue, and turquoise. The vendors clipped the plastic bags onto long sticks and carried them through the crowd. Paolina watched solemnly, the way she used to watch me serve a volleyball when she was small.

Sam said, "I didn't know. I found out when I called Mooney. He warned me. He shouldn't have. He could get in trouble if anyone finds out."

"Warned you? About what?"

"A secret indictment. Grand jury. Supposed to be a secret indictment."

"Racketeering," I said.

"Murder," he said.

Murder.

"How? Why?"

"It's complicated, *cara mía*. It's not what it seems. But the thing is, I can't go back."

"You asked me to marry you."

"I'm asking you again. Stay with me. Marry me. I have a place in Italy, property there. We'll see how you like it. I know you'll like it. It's beautiful."

"Paolina," I said.

"She'll come with us."

I couldn't meet his eyes. "She wants to go home."

Those were the only words she'd spoken, besides her father's name. She wanted to go home. It would be all right, once she got home.

"It'll be good for her," he said. "She'll forget about all this."

She'll run away with her new father and her new mother to a new country. Run away and forget, like some make-believe girl in a fairy tale.

"Sam," I said. "I can't. We can't."

"Can't or won't?"

I don't believe in forgetting; I don't believe in avoiding. Paolina didn't need to forget this. She needed to remember it, to face it, to learn to live with it, to make it part of her life. Not to make it *all* of her life, but to fold it into the rest of her life, to accept and understand it. *This is what happened when I was fifteen.*

If she didn't it would fester, become the hardened secret thing my forgotten and never forgotten child had become.

Everything I have, I thought, I have in Boston. My business, my friends. Gloria, Roz, Mooney. I thought about choices. About Josefina Parte choosing her abusive man over Paolina's boyfriend, Diego, her nephew. About Roldán choosing the white shirt over the Kevlar vest, the way of the Kogi over the life he'd been raised to inherit.

"I can't," I said.

"If I go back, I'll be stopped at Immigration," Sam said.

"I can't," I repeated.

Then we were standing, holding each other, but I had no memory of leaving my seat. I clung to him and was crushed in return, and then Paolina was there, and I could tell by her face that she'd heard everything. If not everything, enough. One of the cones of cotton candy fell silently to the floor.

CHAPTER 42

MOONEY MET US in Miami along with a DEA honcho who hustled me into a tiny room for debriefing while Mooney and Paolina went to get something to eat. I was so tired my knees wobbled and my mouth felt dry as sand, but Mr. DEA offered neither chair nor water. Tanned and glib in his three-piece suit, he pinned me with piercing brown eyes and encouraged me to think things over carefully, very carefully indeed, before revealing anything I'd learned concerning BrackenCorp's relationship with the agency. What would be the benefit of talking to the press, giving the country a black eye, when this was the work of a few bad apples? Rogue DEA agents were being identified and disciplined as we spoke. If Mark Bracken hadn't done his deal with GSC—

"What's a damn merger got to do with it?"

He hemmed and hawed, and finally told: Bracken, worried he was losing control of the multi-billion-buck company he'd built from scratch, had been actively searching for a major influx of cash. The man had spent money like he was minting it; if he got booted as CEO, he was afraid he'd get caught short, be forced to sell property and investments at a loss. When the man he knew as Drew Naylor, a wealthy Colombian with DEA ties, assured him he had a billionaire buyer for pre-Columbian gold, that he knew exactly where Bracken could find it, that the profit would be astronomical—

Navas had manipulated him, played him. Just like Roldán played me at the end.

I said, "You're telling me Bracken wasn't involved in smuggling cocaine?"

"That's an ongoing investigation. I can't say he and his people are clean. I can't say they didn't destroy fields that had nothing to do with coca. And I can't say Navas didn't use his coke money to buy his way out of prison and set himself up as the kind of guy who'd have a chance to deal with the likes of Bracken, but why would Bracken go for the gold if he had cocaine money coming out his nose?"

"What will happen to him?"

"Depends how the investigation plays out. I can tell you this: He would have been a shoo-in member of the GSC board. He won't be now. We'll make sure of that."

His voice as relentless as a battering ram, he kept talking. About shaky funding for the Witness Protection Program. About the reputation of the DEA. About the importance of maintaining strategic links between government and the business community.

But the goddamn policy, I said, the lack of oversight.

But your license to work as a PI, he countered.

Aquí, no pasa nada.

"Let's go home," Mooney said, when he and Paolina returned laden with plastic-wrapped sandwiches. "Hey, it'll be all right."

Sure. Nothing happens here. It'll be all right.

On the Delta flight to Boston, Paolina, squashed into the middle seat between Mooney and me, interacted briefly with the stewardess, managing to mutter a request for a Pepsi.

"Hey," I said softly as I passed the plastic cup, rattling the ice cubes, "watch the bubbles."

"They go right up your—" she whispered automatically.

"Nose," I said, finishing a ritual prompted by an early encounter with carbonation. The exchange must have warmed up her vocal chords.

"It's all my fault." Her voice cracked as she spoke. It sounded rusty, a low and painful moan. She didn't face me, but she didn't turn to Mooney. Her eyes were fixed straight ahead as though staring at something only she could see, maybe imagining the crosshatched screen of a confessional. "If I hadn't gotten into the white van. If only I hadn't—"

"Look at me, Paolina." I tilted her chin with my hand, so I could see into her dark, red-rimmed eyes. I spoke slowly and deliberately, as though she was hard of hearing and needed to lip-read to follow the words. "Look at me. Listen to me. This was a professional job. If you hadn't gotten into the van, they would have snatched you off the street. They were going to get you, no matter what. If not that way, another way. If not that night, another night. You did everything you could do and more. You got away once. You escaped. You were strong and brave and none of this, not one bit, was ever your fault."

She started crying before I finished speaking, averting her face and disappearing into Mooney's leather jacket. I hoped she'd heard me. I closed my eyes and thought, I'll keep on telling her, telling her till she's ready to hear. When I opened my eyes, she was asleep, breathing regularly, snuggled under Mooney's left shoulder.

He winked at me and I thought, *He hates to fly. He hates to fly. He works so hard. He hasn't taken a vacation in years.*

I swallowed and tried to make my lips form a smile. If it weren't for him, I wouldn't have learned Ana's name. If it weren't for him, Sam would be in jail.

"Thanks," I said.

"De nada." It's nothing. The polite Spanish reply, diminishing the service rendered. If Paolina hadn't already been asleep on his shoulder, I'd have been tempted to rest my head there, to breathe in his familiar, reliable smell, to let the tension seep from my shoulders, to finally sleep.

The three of us flew into Logan on a night so cold the Cartagena sun might have beaten down on another planet. Paolina clutched the gold birdman in her hand.